Z
WARNING

WARNING

Dan Oran

and

Lonn Hoklin

BALLANTINE BOOKS · NEW YORK

Manufactured in the United States of America

First Edition: April 1979
1 2 3 4 5 6 7 8 9 10

Library of Congress Cataloging in Publication Data

Oran, Dan.
  Z Warning.

  I. Hoklin, Lonn, joint author. II. Title.
PZ4.O67Ze   [PS3565.R3]   813'.5'4   78–11886
ISBN 0–345–28096–2

MONDAY, MAY 10

5:15 A.M.

The '63 Chevrolet pulled onto the wet gravel shoulder of Connecticut 7. A freckle-faced man emerged in a slicker and cap that hid his features in the darkness. He carried a tool case through the drizzle toward a blinking yellow traffic light that wasn't scheduled to begin a full traffic cycle for nearly an hour.

The man opened a control box at the near corner of the deserted intersection and with practiced motions added something from the tool case. Scarcely thirty seconds passed before he relocked the control box and headed back toward the Chevrolet. In the next half hour he added something to control boxes for three more intersections along Route 7 near the interstate.

5:50 A.M.

The yellow school buses of Emerson County School District 1 sat in quiet rows inside a large fenced lot on Cumberland Road. The rusted padlock on the driveway gate offered little resistance to the black man and small Oriental woman who went straight to one of the buses. In wet weather, drivers often made early starts toward outlying routes, so nobody noticed the bus leave the lot and head north on Cumberland. Presently, it turned onto a road that was far too rough and narrow to be a regular school route. Ruts and puddles slowed it to a crawl as it brushed through low, rain-heavy branches toward a distant clearing where another man and woman—both white, but obscured by hooded rain gear —waited in a green Datsun pickup.

Little conversation passed as the four hurriedly transferred a half dozen bulky packages from the cargo bed of the pickup into the bus. The black man climbed into the rear of the pickup and hid under the tarp, which had protected the packages from the rain. The Oriental woman stood by the bus, her features plainly visible in the glow of the Datsun's headlamps, and waved tentatively as her three companions departed over the rutted road. Once inside the bus, she wasted little time changing into army fatigues.

7:55 A.M.

An unmarked Kenworth trailer truck hissed to a halt before a chain-link fence. Its appearance disclosed neither its cargo nor its mission. A trained eye might have noticed the slightly off-color transparency of the bulletproof glass in its cab or the unusual array of radio antennas sprouting from the driver's compartment. In addition to the FM whips like those on police and emergency vehicles, there was a dull black UHF antenna that looked like the tip of an airplane wing mounted on the roof of the cab.

Most people in nearby Timber Rivers Junction, Connecticut, were still eating breakfast as the Kenworth was ushered, diesel wheezing, through the chain-link gate, which a uniformed guard then locked as the truck drove cautiously through the early spring rain past a brick sign flanked by carefully shaped bushes. Raised aluminum lettering on the sign read:

AMERICAN NUCLEAR CORPORATION
Fuel Recovery and Processing Division

The grounds of the ANC complex were lush with well-kept eastern hardwoods and rolling bluegrass, but the border security posts gave the bucolic scene an atmosphere similar to that of an expensive mental hospital. The truck followed a gentle curve in the wet asphalt past a rain-spattered window in the main administrative complex. A man behind the window grabbed a telephone to report to someone, somewhere, that the truck had at last arrived.

8:01 A.M.

The Kenworth heaved to a stop before yet another chain-link gate with a sign that read:

PROTECTED AREA

Smaller lettering warned against unauthorized entry and served notice that every visitor must be accompanied by a guide, that electronic devices would detect intruders, and that armed guards were authorized to employ "deadly force" to prevent intrusion. Visitors must also expect "random and unannounced searches of their persons and vehicles," the sign indicated, "in conformance with regulations pursuant to licensing for manufacture, transport, and storage of special nuclear materials as established by the U.S. Nuclear Regulatory Commission."

Once through the gate, the truck pulled into an asphalt courtyard between two modern circular buildings. More raised aluminum lettering announced that these were Numbers Five and Six of the Oxides Fabrication Section.

A man in a khaki-colored raincoat trotted up the drive, which sloped down into the innards of Number

Six, and used truckers' hand signals to ground-guide the rig toward a heavy, jointed garage door. The truck followed its guide inside and the door heaved down behind.

A half mile away, nestled in the wet foliage of a high hill well outside the complex, a man lowered his binoculars. Strapped to his back was an army PRC-25 radio. He reached over his shoulder and unclamped the telephone handset. He depressed the push-to-talk button five times in rapid succession, waited ten seconds, and repeated. Soon the familiar rushing sound of another radio "breaking squelch" came to his ear through the handset. His wordless signal had been received on a similar hill flanking nearby Tower Road. He replaced the handset and prepared to leave his vantage point.

8:03 A.M.

Ralph Goldman, Safeguards Inspector, Nuclear Regulatory Commission, was not in a good mood. Superimposed on his natural scowl was another, more intense and more acidic, born of too little sleep. He'd been awake since before six.

Goldman glared at the Kenworth's driver. "You were supposed to be here at seven-fifty," he growled. "Now we won't be loaded until eight-thirty."

The driver merely lowered his eyes and walked through the tangle of jumpsuited workers around the truck. Goldman crammed a thick hand into his rumpled sportscoat and mechanically withdrew a pack of Pall Malls before remembering that smoking was prohibited by the federal regulations he'd come to enforce. "Christ," he muttered through heavy jowls. "Let's go, let's go, let's go!" He needed a cigarette badly.

Suddenly a bellow came from behind him: "If it isn't my fine federal friend!" Goldman swung his thick torso around to confront ANC Division Transport Di-

4

rector Alex Kostos, who was young, slight, energetic—everything Goldman wasn't.

"So, you decided to show up after all," said Goldman. "Just where the hell have you been?"

"Aren't we in a vile mood today." Kostos laughed. "Finish your inspection so you and I can get some coffee and doughnuts."

Goldman loosened a little at the mental image of coffee, for coffee also meant a cigarette. Besides, he couldn't help liking Kostos.

"Awright, you win," Goldman said, trying to force the semblance of a smile into his scowl. "Let's get it over with. But this is a hell of a way to start a Monday."

"Check the truck first?" asked Kostos, stepping toward the cargo ramp. Goldman nodded and followed him up into the Kenworth's trailer. Once inside, he flipped through a dozen pages attached to his clipboard to find the right checklist.

Less than a minute passed before Kostos spoke again. "Everything's ship-shape, right, Ralph?"

"Yeah, I guess. Except maybe for you. Must've been a pretty wild weekend."

"If your idea of wild is fighting three kids, then I guess it was," said Kostos. "By the way, I *am* sorry I was late, Ralph."

Goldman studiously marked his checklist while talking. "The regs say that the transport director has to supervise the relocation of any strategic quantity of special nuclear material, Alex. Before you got here, I watched three of your monkeys move eighty kilos of oxide from Number Five to Number Six. You know, I could call that a violation if I wanted to."

Kostos laughed again. "I guess you could at that. But you're not serious, are you?" Goldman stared silently at his clipboard.

Together they checked the padded mount that would soon hold four casks, each containing twenty kilograms of plutonium dioxide. Goldman examined the combination locks on the trailer's inner vault and marked his checklist accordingly. He then tested the small UHF transmitter mounted in the front of the trailer. Once the radioactive cargo was safely stowed, the transmitter would be turned on to put out a steady tracer signal that could be followed if the truck was ever diverted.

8:18 A.M.

Goldman finished a perfunctory examination of the truck's FM and UHF radios—perfunctory because the garage's shielding prevented radio checks with the three security vehicles parked outside—and slammed the armored door of the cab. He could have insisted that the Kenworth be moved outside to allow radio checks with the state and local police. But it was raining, after all, and he'd already chewed out the driver for tardiness and Kostos for allowing unauthorized transport of special nuclear material. Additional thoroughness would interrupt the morning coffee of several dozen people. What the hell.

"Want to take a look at the arsenal?" asked Kostos.

Goldman turned to another officious-looking man standing nearby. "You from Watne Incorporated?" he asked the man, whose uniform and name tag answered the question.

"Yes, sir," answered the man. "I've inspected all the weapons and everything's go."

Goldman narrowed his eyes on the checklist. "The cab will have two individuals, each equipped with a sidearm and a semiautomatic twelve-gauge shotgun. Right?"

"That's right, Mr. Goldman," answered the security man.

"That's good enough for me. Let's look at the crap, Alex."

8:22 A.M.

Goldman and Kostos entered a small anteroom off the garage through a shielded, electrically controlled door. Inside, two Watne agents with shotguns guarded four steel casks, each of which was strapped to a dolly and marked with brilliant sky-blue and white bands—the painted symbols of nuclear material. Each carried printed warnings against various kinds of mishandling and tampering.

Goldman scrutinized the seals over the tops of the casks and checked for radiation leakage with his portable alpha-ray detector. After marking his clipboard, he turned to Kostos. "Okay, they're all yours."

Kostos signaled his men to load the casks onto the Kenworth. "Let's get some of that coffee before I call the cops to tell 'em I'm leaving," he said to Goldman.

"Yeah, sure. We got a few things to talk about."

8:29 A.M.

The Datsun pickup pulled to the side of a wooded lane next to an old Chevrolet. A woman climbed out, entered the Chevy, and started it cleanly. She threw the rusty sedan into gear and followed the Datsun down the road.

The woman sat, suspended in a private universe, and fought off visions of death. There would probably be some deaths within the next few minutes, she thought. Perhaps some strangers', perhaps her friends', perhaps her own. The thoughts were equally frightening—her hands were moist and cold on the wheel, her back stiff against the seat.

She had gone over this day again and again with her companions. And she had run the thoughts of killing and being killed through her mind so many times that the rigidity and clamminess they always evoked no

7

longer interfered with her actions. She followed the Datsun, wishing that the overcast morning were over, but ready for it.

8:31 A.M.

The door of the rolling vault shut on enough special nuclear material—SNM—to annihilate most of the capital city of Hartford. Outside the garage, Watne agents started the engines of the escort vehicles and waited for Kostos, who they assumed was notifying the state police and the county sheriff that a shipment of SNM was about to move. Now that Goldman was seated in the staff lounge of Number Six with a Pall Mall between his lips he was in no hurry, and it was Kostos who kept glancing at his watch.

Goldman gulped some coffee and inhaled deeply from his cigarette. "Alex," he said, "I hate to have to say this, but I can see little things around here that tell me you guys are getting loose. You're going to have to tighten up."

Kostos looked disturbed. "I'm sorry about this morning, Ralph. I'll personally chew out those guys who moved the SNM from Number Five, and I'll guarantee that it won't happen again."

"I hope your guarantee's good, because the Commission doesn't like to hear about ten-grand-a-year grunts throwing plutonium around the premises. Tell that hairy-armed foreman of yours that he's on thin ice if he ever takes it upon himself to move crap again."

"It won't happen again."

Goldman focused his scowl. "But there's more to it than that, Alex. The fact that it happened at all shows me that your chain of command is rusting out. If ANC can't handle the simple regs like who has to give the order to move SNM within a protected area, how can the Commission assume that ANC can handle the hard ones? Suppose we threw a full-scale investigation of the company and saw weaknesses like those I saw today. Publicize those weaknesses and the antifission freaks go nuts, Congress sticks its long nose even deeper into the industry, and heads roll. Do you know *whose* heads? Yours and mine."

Kostos glanced impatiently at his watch. "You're absolutely right, Ralph. We've gotten a little casual around here and I'm going to start tightening things up —starting right now." He reached for his raincoat.

"Just one more thing," said Goldman, poking his cigarette into the air. "The lecture's over, but in return for not issuing a citation, I'd like to know why in the hell this shipment's so big. I almost gagged when I saw your inventory sheets."

Kostos seemed to wince a little. "Well, I'm not supposed to know these things, and I'll be in deep shit for telling you, but we're about six weeks behind on our fabrication contract with Eastern Labs. Our project director here quit two months ago, and it took us a while to shuffle in a new guy. In the meantime, Eastern Labs' outfit in Pennsylvania runs low on oxides and starts looking for other suppliers. Naturally, ANC didn't want to get the reputation for being slow or unreliable, so we accelerated our fabrication schedule. When this shipment rolls into Pennsylvania tonight, we'll be back on schedule, reliable as ever."

Goldman pointed to the ceiling and made little circles with his index finger. "Now tell me why you had to put the entire eighty kilos on one truck."

"No rule against that, Ralph. We don't do it more than maybe once or twice a year."

"Jesus Christ, I *know* the rules. There's enough plutonium in this shipment to build a couple of nice bombs, for God's sake. Or think what would happen if it got into a head-on collision and eighty kilos of plutonium powder ended up all over the freeway. Why couldn't you have moved it, say, at twenty kilos a throw?"

Kostos shook his head and smiled faintly. "Are you going to suggest that it's a hell of a lot better if only twenty kilos is stolen or spilled on the highway? Come off it, Ralph. You know there's less chance of something ugly happening to *one* truck than with four, or three, or two. Besides, do you have any idea of how much these new safeguards cost the company? That Kenworth out there, equipped the way it is, is a two-hundred-thousand dollar rig. Now think about paying all these Watne people, with their 'hazardous duty' compensation. There's a limit to what we can afford without jacking up the price of our product."

8:45 A.M.

The man with the army radio on his back hurried down an old logging trail that roughly paralleled the ANC access road, splashing through puddles and ducking branches. The buzzes he'd received moments before had told him that his colleagues—all four of them— were in place. The school bus, the pickup, and the old Chevrolet were in position, the weapons were armed and ready. Soon he himself would be in place and there would be no turning back.

8:46 A.M.

Goldman stood in the rain, collar up, watching the convoy as it headed toward the gate. Ahead of the truck was a dull yellow Mercury Monarch and behind it were a light blue Dodge van and a beige Ford Torino. The Watne team leader rode in the van with two other agents, monitoring state and local police radio frequencies. Kostos rode at the end of the convoy in the Torino and maintained radio communications with each of the other vehicles.

Goldman hoped the roads wouldn't be slippery. As he walked toward his own car, he remembered the queasiness he'd felt once, a few years before, when he discovered that a major industrial firm had transported a large load of weapons-grade uranium from New England to the Deep South on a flatbed truck with one unarmed driver and no predetermined route. Along the way, the driver had left the cargo unattended in truck stop parking lots and outside motels. He'd driven at breakneck speeds. Like the Congressmen who eventually heard the story, Goldman had shuddered to think of what *could* have happened.

And there were other memories, equally unwelcome at this particular moment. A few years earlier, a steel cask packed with "hot" cesium and cobalt had vibrated loose from a truck bound for a reactor in Massachusetts. After bouncing along the highway, the cask plummeted down a seventy-yard embankment, but by some miracle remained intact.

During the past seven years, Goldman had investigated dozens of attempted thefts of nuclear material. Nearly all the "incidents" involved people who had incredibly naïve notions about stealing the stuff or about using it. This, however, did not comfort him.

8:51 A.M.

Connecticut State Patrolman Ron Geld drove through the tangle of last-minute rush, past an interstate exit marked "American Nuclear Corporation—9 mi/14.5 km." It was a bad morning. Rain slowed the long-range commuter traffic into New York City and mixed it with locals heading toward "nine-to-fivers" in White Plains, Greenwich, and Stamford. Earlier accidents caused by watery road film prolonged the congested rush.

"A bunch of people are going to be late this morning," Geld remarked to his partner, Patrolman Morty Watts.

"Damn right," Watts agreed. "I'll bet the interchanges are a mess farther in."

8:52 A.M.

Three traffic signals went dead. Small explosive devices on the cable joints inside the signal control boxes had been simultaneously detonated by wristwatch timers. The blasts disintegrated the cables and blew the switches apart.

Several miles above one of the now uncontrolled intersections, the ANC convoy crawled toward Tower Road, an artery connecting the Timber Rivers area to Route 7. The traffic on Tower Road had thinned substantially, since most area commuters had already reached the major highways.

In the blue van immediately behind the Kenworth, the Watne team leader listened to the reports of the Connecticut 7 traffic tie-up on the state police frequency. He in turn reported the news to Kostos in the Torino behind.

"Sounds like a real mess, doesn't it?" said Kostos's driver, a tall black man named Hodges.

"Shit," said Kostos. "Just what I need. I don't like the idea of fighting traffic." He gazed silently through the wet windshield at the wooded hills flanking the highway. Occasionally, the taillights of the van ahead blinked, an indication that its driver was straining to maintain the prescribed three car lengths behind the slow-moving Kenworth.

"How far is that traffic jam from here?" asked Kostos.

"Oh, I suppose eighteen or twenty miles."

"Maybe it'll be cleared by the time we get there," said Kostos. Something made him wonder if he should strap on the pistol he'd chucked into the glove box. The regulations, after all, required that he be armed.

8:55 A.M.

The convoy was less than half a mile from the intersection of the ANC access drive and Tower Road. A hundred yards north of the intersection, a green Datsun pickup was parked with its hood raised and its emergency flashers blinking; behind it was an old Chevrolet sedan with its trunk open. Two people dressed in hooded rain gear leaned over the Datsun's engine compartment. Minutes earlier, a Connecticut State Patrol car had sped past, blue lights ablaze, toward the traffic tangle on Connecticut 7.

Three hundred yards south of the intersection, Tower Road curved in a narrow cut between two hills. On the face of the far hill, hidden in foliage, the young man who had witnessed the Kenworth's arrival at the ANC complex waited on his new perch. He no longer had his binoculars or his heavy radio. In his arms, he cradled what U.S. soldiers in Southeast Asia had called an RPG-7 ("rocket-propelled grenade"). This shoulder weapon launches what looks like an oversized cannister of a Fourth of July sky rocket—cylindrical with a pointed head and propellant tube behind. The U.S. Army considers the armor-piercing weapon comparable to its own obsolete bazooka. To the man's left, another RPG-7 rested against a tree trunk, loaded and ready to fire; to his right was an army M-16 rifle, its fire selector set on "semi."

He wore skin-tight surgical gloves and a black ski

13

mask that hid his lean features, his auburn mustache and hair. Draped over his chest were two cloth bandoliers with food for the black M-16 rifle. A bulky canvas bag containing sticks of C-4 plastic explosive lay on the leafy ground between his knees.

A few paces away, the black man crouched, identically armed and dressed. The Oriental woman who had stolen the school bus knelt on the hill across the road, a single RPG-7 within her easy reach and an M-16 rifle slung across her shoulder. Beneath the ski mask, her facial muscles twitched nervously as she reached for the rocket launcher.

8:56 A.M.

In violation of operating regulations, Kostos switched the car radio from the convoy frequency to the state police "push," just in time to hear Patrolman Ron Geld report a chain collision on Route 7. While there were no serious injuries, Geld reported, there was an urgent need for wreckers and additional police units to assist in traffic direction.

Kostos leaned back in the seat and closed his eyes. "Christ," he muttered to Hodges. "They'll never get it straightened out before we get there. Why in the hell do you suppose those traffic lights went out at once? Who ever heard of traffic lights going out all at once?"

"Just the way things happen," said Hodges with a philosophical smile. "Feast or famine."

"They'll need every cop in Connecticut to get things back to normal," said Kostos.

Hodges noticed the two people bending over the Datsun pickup a short distance from the Tower Road intersection. "Hell of a day to have engine trouble," he observed as he followed the convoy into a right turn.

The Mercury Monarch led them southward on Tower Road after slowing to allow the truck to catch up after the turn. Except for an occasional northbound car that met the convoy and was gone, the road was clear.

Hodges eyed his rearview mirror. "They must've fixed whatever was wrong, because they're back on the road. Lucky they didn't have to pay the towing bill to Timber Rivers on a day like this."

Through the rain-streaked rear window, Kostos could see the blurred outline of the Datsun pickup a few car lengths behind. The convoy followed the Mercury into the narrow curve between the hills as an old Chevrolet fell in behind the pickup.

8:57 A.M.

The Oriental woman's mind raced through the instructions drilled into her by the black man over months of training with the RPG-7: *Aim for the windows because that's where the round will do the most good; don't follow the car with the weapon; rest the weapon against the tree and let the car come into the sights—that's it, Yoshi, just squeeze.*

The trigger squeeze followed like an afterthought and a blue flash flowed from the warhead's propellant tube. The mild *whoosh* ended with an ear-piercing clap as the warhead detonated against the driver's vent, exploding into the passenger compartment. The driver died instantly and the car careened madly before coming to rest against the left shoulder. The passenger, knocked out by the concussion, succumbed to the intense heat of the phosphorus-induced inferno. Flames leaped skyward from the car's shattered windows.

8:57:15 A.M.

The air brakes of the Kenworth huffed fiercely and its tires squealed on the wet pavement as the driver fought to avoid hitting the demolished Mercury. The black man leveled his first RPG at the bulletproof side window of the truck, calculating that the round would strike the glass at about a forty-five degree angle. The recruitment phrase, "Army skills stick for life," jumped into his mind, and he smiled as the round detonated against the window, decapitating the passenger. The blast deafened the driver and threw him against his door. Somehow he managed to open the door and leap free of the cab before the phosphorus flames could overpower him. He tumbled onto the wet gravel of the shoulder, his clothes smouldering.

8:57:27 A.M.

Black smoke rolled over the highway from the Kenworth and the Mercury as the men in the van braced for a collision with the truck's cargo door. They slid to a halt a yard from the trailer. They'd seen two flashes of blue light ahead of them, but because of the armor plating on the van, had heard little.

The two men on the hill fired their RPGs almost simultaneously. Blasts moved the van sideways, boring holes the size of quarters in its armor plating. Shrapnel and phosphorus streamed inward, killing two of the three instantly, and knocking the other unconscious.

Hodges hit the Torino's brakes and pumped them furiously, bashing Kostos's head against the windshield and dash. Kostos had neglected to wear his seatbelt. When the car finally came to a stop, he tried to sit up, his head swimming. Blood ran from his nose and his lacerated lips. Hodges, completely unharmed, jumped from the car with his .357 magnum drawn as the world burst into a frenzy of sharp, popping sound. While Kostos lay in wide-eyed bewilderment, Hodges hit the wet asphalt and sprawled on his belly. He'd recognized the sound, the *snap-snap* of small projectiles breaking the sound barrier.

"Get out of the car!" he screamed at Kostos. "Get down! We're taking small-arms fire!" The men on the hill were firing their M-16s with murderous speed, launching a wall of metal at the Torino.

Powdered glass from the windshield stung Kostos's chin and neck as a bullet bore into the upholstery near his shoulder while another splintered the rearview mirror into shreds of metal and glass.

8:58:33 A.M.

The driver of the green Datsun pickup came to a stop about sixty yards behind the Torino, pulled off his plastic raincoat, and grabbed the rifle that lay beside him on the seat. He could see the prone figure of Hodges, pistol in hand, trying to pinpoint the source of the rifle fire. The driver of the pickup opened his door, crouched behind it, and leveled the rifle at Hodges.

8:58:58 A.M.

The Chevrolet stopped several hundred yards behind the pickup and turned to block partially both lanes of traffic. Ski mask and fatigues hid the fact that its driver was a lean young woman who at this moment fought desperately against panic. With trembling fingers she pressed the timer switch mounted on the lid of a metal box. She glanced reflexively back at the two oil drums where the rear seat would normally be, remembering that she had twenty seconds to shelter herself from an explosion that would ignite over a hundred gallons of gasoline. She flung open the door and raced for the pickup.

8:59:18 A.M.

The woman threw herself on the ground behind the pickup seconds before the blast ripped the old Chevrolet into fiery airborne scraps that fell like a curtain over the road and landscape. The shapeless mass of metal that remained was a torch that blocked traffic as surely as a brick wall across the road.

8:59:21 A.M.

Kostos scrambled from the car toward the foliage along the road. Suddenly an M-16 round tore into his right hand and he went into shock, sprawling headlong into the gravel and weeds. A ragged hole in his jacket sleeve marked the bullet's exit.

8:59:23 A.M.

Hodges recoiled from the shock of the explosion to his rear and glanced over the hood of the Torino in time to see Kostos go down, obviously hit. Hodges's right knee exploded as a bullet spun through cartilage and bone. Muscular reflexes jolted him off balance as a spear of pain shot upward, and he fell to the pavement on both elbows. The man by the Datsun pickup fired again, and the round crashed through Hodges's hip, knocking him backward. He was unconscious before his head hit the wet pavement.

8:59:40 A.M.

Four of the attackers stowed their weapons in the rear of the Datsun pickup, which had pulled up to the front of the Kenworth. The army expert attached a small charge of C-4 to the lock on the trailer's cargo door. While he inserted an electrical blasting cap into the charge, the others took cover near the front of the truck. Unrolling a length of coaxial cord attached to the cap, he took cover and produced from his pocket a small electrical detonator known in the Army as a "clacker." After wiring the cord to the clacker, he turned to the others and screamed, *"Ready!"*

Another explosion ripped the quiet Connecticut morning as the locking mechanism of the cargo door disintegrated into tiny metallic bits. The cargo doors swung open.

9:02:59 A.M.

The next explosion shook the ground. Flame and metal spewed through the cargo door and showered the crippled vehicles behind the Kenworth as precisely shaped charges of C-4 opened the trailer's inner vault.

The Datsun pickup was quickly moved directly behind the trailer as the attackers rummaged through smoke and fumes to find the steel casks mounted inside. At length, a cask fell with a loud clank into the bed of the pickup. The great weight of the containers and the unsure footing of metal debris on the floor made the task difficult, but soon all the remaining three casks fell into the pickup's bed. The men followed the last container and lay flat on their chests on the damp metal in the rear of the Datsun, and the woman ripped off her ski mask as she drove away past the burning Mercury.

9:04 A.M.

Motorists, stopped by the catastrophe on Tower Road, notified authorities in Timber Rivers by CB radio, and the ambulances, police, and firefighters naturally took the most direct route to what everyone assumed was a dreadful traffic accident. This meant that they came in from the far side and encountered the wildly burning Chevrolet parked across both lanes of traffic before reaching the Kenworth. The combination of steep, forested hills flanking the road and the inferno in the center slowed knowledge of an attack.

9:05 A.M.

The Datsun pickup turned left onto Cumberland Road, then left again onto an unpaved road once used for logging. This road had no name. Lurching and swerving through puddles of water and mud, the pickup came at last to a junction and turned off the road into a canopy of hardwoods. Its occupants immediately unloaded their cargo.

A bright yellow GMC school bus lumbered out of wooded cover across the road. Its driver was the Oriental woman who had stolen it and who had fired the first RPG at the convoy. She was tired from her scramble over hills thick with wet undergrowth, but she had had time to shed her sopping fatigues for a turtleneck and jeans. She smiled a wordless hello to her four colleagues.

They loaded the casks of plutonium dioxide and their weapons aboard the bus and retraced the path that the Datsun, now hidden and abandoned, had used. Before reaching Cumberland Road, they took off their ski masks and fatigues. The young man who had first signaled from above the ANC complex looked like a graduate student with his longish auburn hair, mustache, and cableknit sweater. The army-trained explosives and weapons expert wore his Afro like a helmet. The man who had placed the charges on traffic signal control boxes sported doubleknit slacks and a tan golf sweater.

The white woman who had driven the old Chevrolet replaced her fatigues with a rust-colored wool pantsuit and a single-strand copper necklace. Her carefully applied makeup and flowing brown hair suggested affluence and a career. No trace of the near panic she'd felt moments earlier remained; her face was composure, control. She helped her comrades set dressed, child-size mannequins in the window seats of the bus.

9:19 A.M.

Patrolman Ron Geld got a call to proceed to a major multivehicle accident on Tower Road just south of Timber Rivers Junction. Sixteen minutes later he maneuvered his cruiser between the state and local police vehicles clustered around the burned-out cab of the Kenworth semi. The sketchy reports he'd monitored had done no justice to the spectacle he now surveyed. A principal rule of highway patrolmen is to maintain the flow of traffic, but this event superseded rules. Police cars of every conceivable jurisdiction arrived on the scene every few seconds to compound the traffic jam already created by ambulances and fire trucks.

Geld sought out a familiar face, that of Sergeant Daniel Gustafson, State Police.

"Jesus, what happened here, Dan?" asked Geld. "This is no ordinary accident—if it is an accident."

Gustafson spat on the ground. "Looks like somebody robbed a truck."

"It looks like a goddam war zone," replied Geld, aghast.

"Whoever did it must've been armed to the teeth, that's all I can say."

An ambulance attendant reported to Gustafson. "We're taking two more in, Sergeant, both with gunshot wounds. One's bad, a black guy, but the other one's going to be okay. Shot in the hand."

The attendant raced breathlessly away.

"How many?" asked Geld.

"Five dead, four wounded."

"What was in the truck?"

"That's the hell of it—we don't know. Right now, I don't even know how to find out."

They soon knew. David K. Glover, director of ANC's Timber Rivers plant, pushed through the police barrier and reached Gustafson after presenting his credentials three times. Painfully, Glover told how he'd been stopped between home and work by what looked like a dreadful traffic accident. The truth dawned upon him as he recognized the specially equipped Kenworth. An ANC convoy with eighty kilograms of plutonium dioxide—perhaps the most hazardous substance known— had been attacked.

The policemen escorted Glover to the Kenworth's trailer and helped him climb inside, where he picked his way over the metal shards strewn over the floor. He knew that if any of the casks had been ruptured in the blasts, he, as well as probably most of the police and even the motorists behind the barriers, were as good as dead. Glover's face paled as he saw that the heavy vault door had been shattered by a terrific explosion that pocked the sides of the trailer with jagged holes. Clearly, the thieves had had little difficulty penetrating the vault after the blast. Inside were the empty padded mounts, which less than forty-five minutes earlier had held four steel casks of atomic bomb material.

Glover turned his ashen face to Gustafson. "You've got to get them, Sergeant," he stammered. "You've got to get them right now. Can I use one of your radios for a special alert . . . and to bring in an alpha counter?"

9:50 A.M.

Camera crews and reporters began live coverage of the events on Tower Road, coverage that was heard by the occupants of a bus marked "Emerson County School District 1" riding southeastward. Someone in the bus turned up the volume of a transistor radio as others turned down the volumes of three more.

"Have you determined what was in the truck?" asked Terry Maslowe of WTTO News.

"We've been asked not to comment on that until more specific . . . uh . . . determinations have been made," answered Sergeant Daniel Gustafson.

"But there's no longer any doubt that what happened here was a robbery of some kind, right, Sergeant? An armed robbery?"

"That's right."

"What's being done to capture the robbers?"

"Everything possible—roadblocks, aerial search, and as you can see, a lot of detective work."

"What are you looking for?"

"Well, for the moment, a green or blue pickup—small, probably a Datsun or Toyota—last seen heading south on Tower Road. Anyone who sees it or anything like it should call the state police immediately."

"How many people do you think were involved in this attack?"

"It's hard to say, Mr. Maslowe, but I'd guess that over a dozen people would be needed to cause this damage."

"Then there must be more than one small truck, right?"

"We just don't know right now."

"One of the other officers said that some cartridge casings have been found farther north on the road, and that they look like they came from an Army rifle, an M—"

"An M-16, that's right. That means they're heavily armed and very dangerous."

"Obviously. But what stopped this truck, Sergeant, or wrecked the other vehicles? I'm no expert, but it seems like they'd need something more than rifles to do this kind of damage."

"Well, it's clear they used something else, but we haven't been able to determine exactly what it was—yet."

"A few moments ago I heard a detective from the state police say that federal authorities will be coming in. Why is that?"

"I'm sorry, but I can't comment on that right now."

"Is it because this convoy was involved in interstate commerce and that the FBI now has jurisdiction?"

"I'm sorry, I really can't comment."

"Could the nearby American Nuclear plant be involved and . . ."

The transistor was quickly muted and attention shifted to the police band as a Connecticut state police car met the bus. The police car continued on to set up a roadblock at Cumberland Road. A helicopter flew low over the bus as the bus riders picked up conversation between the pilot and the police command post at the attack site nearly thirty miles away.

"This is Romeo Six," said the pilot. "All I got is a school bus and a couple of cycles headed for Emersonville. Negative on blue or green pickups."

The Oriental woman's name was Yoshi Nakamura. She labored single-mindedly over the steel casks wedged in the aisle of the school bus. The white man, Duncan Rossiter, assisted Nakamura in removing the plastic seal on one of the casks. Once the seal was off, the two donned blue surgical masks.

"Get the plastic bag ready," said Nakamura. "I'll unscrew the safety cap." While she slowly turned the cap on the cask, Rossiter readied a thick plastic sack, the kind normally used to line garbage pails. The cap came off.

Inside was a clear polyethylene cylinder about eight inches across and thirty inches long.

It was one-quarter full of greenish yellow powder.

"Careful now," cautioned Nakamura. "If we spill any of this, we could be dead from fibrosis within a month."

Rossiter lifted the cylinder carefully out of the cask and rested it upright on a bus seat. Nakamura placed plastic bags over the top and bottom of the cylinder and sealed them tightly with two lengths of elastic surgical tubing. The edges of the bags overlapped to form a double seal.

As the bus lurched along, Nakamura groped through the plastic with padded pliers to loosen the adjustable seal clamp that held the cap of the cylinder in place. Next, she lifted the unsealed cap slowly from the mouth of the cylinder and positioned it out of the way.

Rossiter acknowledged a nod from Nakamura and upended the cylinder, sending the plutonium dioxide powder into the plastic bag. Nakamura sealed the bag of powder with surgical tubing close to the mouth of the cylinder and signaled Rossiter to place the entire setup horizontally on the seat. She then worked the cylinder down into the original plastic bag, tightening the lengths of tubing to ensure that plutonium-contaminated air could not escape the bag.

The empty cylinder and its cap were encased in plastic beside a neatly sealed bag of powder. Perspiration beaded Nakamura's forehead as she scanned both bags with a small alpha-ray detector to check for leakage. The needle on the dial remained flat against the left edge. She traded relieved glances with Rossiter.

They placed the bag of plutonium into yet another bag and then into a compact suitcase. A few pieces of clothing were piled on top to pad the inside of the suitcase and to protect against a perfunctory search.

25

They repeated the ritual three more times, once for each of the casks. When the fourth transfer was completed, Rossiter wearily removed the sweaty surgical mask and looked up at Nakamura's delicate face.

"You can do anything with Baggies," he said.

Nakamura laughed for the first time in many days.

10:16 A.M.

The bus driver, John Bates, swallowed hard at the sight of flashing lights near Maple and Thurgood in the business district of Emersonville. A pair of local police cars were parked on either side of Maple. Cars were backed up in the southbound lane as patrolmen interviewed each driver. A blue Toyota pickup and a green Datsun pickup were parked at the northbound curb, apparently detained.

"Could be trouble, folks," said Bates in his Oklahoma drawl. "Cops 'er gonna talk to us this time."

The other four scrambled for hiding places behind bus seats. M-16 rifles were readied. Jean Murdock, looking totally like a marketing executive, crouched incongruously with a rifle. Though she'd helped plan this day for more than two years, she could not escape a sickening, dreamlike feeling.

Leon T. Jackson, veteran of many an Indochina firefight and an Army-seasoned demolitions expert, was ready. As he took cover, he shouted to Bates, "How many cops and where are they?"

"Four that I can see," answered Bates as he brought the bus to a halt. "Two on the left and two on the right."

"Okay," barked Jackson. "John, if you think we're gonna have to shoot our way out, you holler. Nobody do anything unless John gives the word. If he does, get your weapons out the window and shoot like hell."

Bates nodded. He groped under the driver's seat for the .38 he'd put there earlier. He positioned it in his crotch so he could kill the patrolman coming to the driver's window, if need be.

The cop looked up into the window as Bates slid it open. "How's it goin'?" he asked the officer.

"Could be better" was the reply. "It'll be a few minutes, I'm afraid. We're checking every vehicle—"

"You lookin' for those guys that caused the trouble up by Timber River?" interrupted Bates, wanting to keep the cop's attention away from the stony, expressionless faces in the other windows.

"That's right." The patrolman's sunglasses hid his eyes.

"Anybody know 'zactly what happened up there?" asked Bates, wondering, absurdly, if all cops wore sunglasses on rainy days.

"Nothing much right now." The cop turned to walk the length of the bus, and probably to look into the windows. Bates's blood pressure climbed.

"Ah'd sure hate to be the man who catches those boys," he said. "You reckon they'd shoot it out with you if you caught 'em?"

"I s'pose so," said the cop. Bates's mind raced on.

"Hey, is there any way you guys can let me through?" he asked. "I'm s'posed to have these kids back at Emerson by ten-thirty."

"Afraid not. I'll have to check your bus." The patrolman started to walk around the front to board through the right front door. Bates jammed his pistol between the seat and the side of the bus.

"Jeannie!" whispered Rossiter. "You're the teacher! Meet him at the door. Get us through or it's the Fourth of July."

Murdock's stomach climbed into her throat. She stripped off her surgical gloves and reached the door as the hydraulic system whistled it open.

27

"I'm Clara Lux." She smiled at the cop.

"Hi, I'm Dick Gaither," he said. He hesitated. "Mind if we give your bus the once over?"

"Not at all." She smiled. For a hideous instant her mind went blank. "Dick," she said as the patrolman started to board, "you could sure help me out by getting us through the traffic. The kids have a civics test next hour." She smiled her job-interview smile. "This is the second time this has happened to me," she said, laughing sweetly. "The last time I took the kids on a field trip, the bus had a flat tire. Somehow it was my fault we were late getting back. You should have heard the principal."

The patrolman laughed. "Yeah, I know Bill Crawford. My kid goes to Emerson. Raises some hell now and then and even drinks a little. Twice Crawford has called me about it. Me! I said to him, 'Why call me? Kick the kid's you-know-what,' I said, ''cause that's your job. I'll take care of him at home, you take care of him at school.' "

Bates and "Miss Lux" laughed exuberantly. The cop, thinking he'd entertained everyone pretty well, laughed too. Bates kept his left hand on the pistol.

"You just follow me," said the cop. "And if Crawford gives you trouble, tell him Gaither will be layin' for him and that I'll give him the fattest moving violation he's ever had."

"You're a lifesaver, Dick," said Murdock. "See you at PTA."

"Well, now, that's some reason to go to PTA. Maybe you will," said the cop. He raised his sunglasses and rendered what was apparently a lecherous wink.

Patrolman Dick Gaither stopped the oncoming traffic and led the school bus into the intersection where Bates turned left on Thurgood. "I checked 'em out," Gaither told his superior. "School kids on a field trip. Gotta get back to Emerson by ten-thirty."

Murdock was drained. She fell into a seat near a dummy schoolkid and gulped air.

"You were magnificent!" crowed Rossiter from his hiding place. "Just magnificent."

10:33 A.M.

No one glanced twice at the school bus entering the parking lot of Emerson Junior High. The few people in a position to notice might have thought it slightly peculiar that the bus did not wheel into the circular drive to unload its human cargo at the front doors of the school. It went instead to the very center of the large teachers' parking lot, where it stopped, emergency flashers blinking as though temporarily parked, to unload another kind of cargo. The bus blocked from view the blue Lincoln Continental parked with the teachers' cars.

M-16 rifles bundled into a laundry bag were carried by Jackson. He also toted a bag containing the spent rocket launchers.

Bates carried the radio equipment, including two army PRC-25's.

Rossiter handled the suitcases, one at a time. The two women methodically knocked the mannequins into the aisle so they would not be visible from the outside. They gathered up the remaining paraphernalia—clothing and other personal effects—and stuffed it into bags.

Bates stowed the radio gear in the spacious trunk of the Lincoln. He then used skeleton keys, an ice pick, and a modified nail file to open the trunk of an Aspen sedan parked next to the Lincoln. Army-surplus fatigues, ski masks, and sundry other items were stowed inside to be discovered sooner or later by a surprised teacher. By the time Bates had relocked the trunk, the others were waiting for him in the Lincoln. He reboarded the school bus and moved it to a legitimate parking place, carefully locked it, deposited its keys in the gas tank, and joined his friends in the car.

11:40 A.M.

Less than an hour after leaving Emerson Junior High School, the Lincoln emerged from a wooded country road into a clean, prosperous suburb of not-so-clean or prosperous Bridgeport. The car was not the least out of place with its stolen Connecticut license tags.

The midday sun promised a beautiful afternoon for a ride on the ocean. The smell of salt air and the sight of gulls off the wharf made Murdock wish she were going with Nakamura, Jackson, and Rossiter. The trip to Maine would take two days. Within hours, virtually every enforcement arm of every federal agency would be loosed in an all-out effort to recover the stolen plutonium. They would have extraordinary powers. They would search waterways, roads, airports, cars, and private homes with a vengeance intensified by confusion and lack of experience. Nothing like this had ever happened before.

Meanwhile, she would return to Washington from her "long weekend." The senator would be there, but so would her "colleagues," the self-important functionaries behind the simple-minded stage hounds for whom they drafted legislation, mollified constituents, wrote speeches, and scheduled trips to the bathroom.

Murdock piloted the Lincoln into the parking lot of McPherson's Marina, an old establishment that boasted care of the community's most luxurious yachts. McPherson's Bar and Grill, a rickety hut that should have collapsed two decades earlier, was an exclusive watering hole for pleasure sailors.

Rossiter left the Lincoln to find the proprietor, Randall Craig, a wrinkled yachtsman of seventy who claimed seagoing history with three navies.

"Mistah Godwin, yes, suh!" said the old man as he bounced from the office into sunshine. Craig knew Rossiter as Sam Godwin, Jr., the son of a prosperous sheet-metal contractor from Corpus Christi, Texas.

"Hi, Cap'n," said Rossiter, calling up his native Texan accent. "How's m' *Golden Girl*?"

Golden Girl was a forty-seven-foot Hatteras yacht that Rossiter had entrusted to Craig a week earlier. "My partners and I are fixin' to head northward 'n git after some stripers 'n rockfish."

"She's fit," said Craig. "Changed the oil in the three-fifties, though, an' put in new filters. Cleaned up the inside a mite. It'll cost you an even twenty."

Rossiter traded small talk with the old man and paid him twenty-five plus docking and keeping fees. Bates, Murdock, Nakamura, and Jackson followed him to the deck bearing suitcases full of plutonium, bags containing weapons, and the other gear.

The yacht's registration was phony inasmuch as there was no sheet-metal contractor in Corpus Christi named Godwin. Rossiter had purchased the vessel two years earlier under that name. He'd kept licenses current, had never violated any rules, and had never given anyone reason to check further on registration and title.

When the gear was stowed, Rossiter returned to the deck where Murdock stood. Her face was drawn, her eyes tired. "We haven't gotten a chance to talk much, have we?" she said.

"Nope, guess we haven't," answered Rossiter, pushing a strand of auburn hair away from his eyes. "But we will, you can be sure of that."

Murdock pulled a cigarette from her pocket and lit it with Rossiter's cupped hands shielding the match from the sea breeze.

"It's hard to believe," she said, exhaling smoke, "that we've actually come this far. It all seems so unreal."

31

"We've only started, honey. Only started. When we've jacked the whole goddamn country around enough, you and I are going on a long vacation, maybe out there somewhere." He nodded toward the ocean. "We'll find some little shoreline with a shack and a bed and never worry about getting up until we want to. Then you can help me plan my next move."

"This will be a hard act to follow," said Murdock, forcing a smile.

Rossiter chuckled. "You just leave it to me, honey. I'll do the arranging. You just stick around to help me out and to make sure I get to bed on time."

"I'll miss you," Murdock answered, and added more emphatically than she wished, "and I hope you *will* stay in touch."

"Just like we wrote down in the plan. We'll be in touch through John. Don't you worry."

"And no *other* way."

"I said don't worry."

They kissed each other lightly as Bates joined them.

11:59 A.M.

The *Golden Girl* shoved off with Rossiter, Nakamura, and Jackson aboard. Murdock and Bates watched the yacht chug into the bay with Rossiter at the helm, carefully obeying all rules.

TUESDAY, MAY 11

The day dawned hot and still in Washington. At 7:00 A.M. a hazy morning sky, still full of May 10 auto exhaust, promised an even hotter day.

The stench of elk and gnu drifted over the leafy borders of the National Zoo, across a winding alley called Hawthorne Street, and through the open window of Kelly Gilliam's apartment. He stirred, squirmed, and sneezed. Half awake, he stumbled to his window and slammed it closed, cursing his broken air conditioner and his allergy to hooved beasts.

The clock radio, one of his few perfectly functioning mechanical possessions, snapped on at 7:01. As Gilliam padded across a cluttered floor to the bathroom, a newscaster wrapped up the lead story.

". . . and still no official word from Connecticut authorities or the Nuclear Regulatory Commission on whether the hijacked truck contained nuclear material."

The words did not penetrate Gilliam's morning consciousness until he flushed the toilet. Through a hint of a headache from last night's many beers, he remembered that TV and radio had given conflicting reports on whether the truck had carried nuclear cargo. By now the media should have known. By now someone somewhere should have confirmed that the truck had been empty.

Gilliam pondered the matter as he scraped dark

33

stubble from his long, bony face. While in the shower, he resolved to launch an inquiry through the NRC congressional affairs office in order to satisfy his curiosity.

As he munched burned toast and sipped lukewarm orange juice, he scanned the morning *Post's* front-page account of the mysterious robbery. The story provided a smattering of new information. Connecticut's governor, for example, had activated a troop of National Guard armored cavalry to cordon the attack area on Tower Road. Late on May 10, authorities had discovered the green Datsun pickup hidden off a wooded road less than a mile southeast of the attack site. Last-minute attempts to elicit a statement on the truck's cargo from officials of the American Nuclear Corporation had failed.

He combed his hair one more time before departing for Capitol Hill. At thirty, he looked twenty-five and felt fifty. A year and a half as assistant counsel to the Senate Energy Committee had aged everything but his face. His boss, the grizzled Senator Harold J. Hammer of Pennsylvania, was chairman of the Committee and the nation's most vocal nuclear power advocate. The Committee was viewed by the fission industry as a group of unpredictable dilettantes governed by political self-interest. The industry's opponents thought that the Committee was the willing tool of powerful corporate moguls whose "Christmas bonuses" somehow ended up in congressional campaign coffers. Gilliam himself thought that the nuclear industry believed in what they sold, but that their belief was, at the least, misguided.

Gilliam's previous position in the Bureau of Consumer Protection of the Federal Trade Commission had become an anonymous dead end, but at least it had trained him for being "in the middle." He'd been surrounded by sparkling young careerists whose luster, like his own, had been worn dull against opponents whose resources dwarfed those of the FTC. By the end of his fourth year, Gilliam had been desperate to get out.

Private law firms were not hiring young people with business specialities in his salary class. His skillfully worded resumes elicited skillfully worded thank you's. After months of looking, a friend told him of an opening with the Energy Committee.

Gilliam had been pleasantly surprised to find that the new job meant more money. He had been *unpleasantly* surprised to find that he was totally under the thumb of Senator Harry Hammer.

On paper, his job was to advise the chairman and the Committee on the uranium enrichment industry. Prior to a newly passed law, the federal government had owned and operated the nation's only three plants that "enrich" nuclear fuel by increasing its proportion of highly radioactive uranium-235. Natural uranium contains half of one percent U-235. Three percent is suitable for use in light-water fission reactors to generate electric power. Weapons-grade fuel should contain 90 *percent* or more U-235. New experimental reactors such as the HTGR—high-temperature gas-cooled reactor— need fuel that is over 90 percent U-235.

The uranium-enrichment process is very expensive. Each of the three enrichment plants had cost the federal government more than $2 billion for construction alone. The three complexes occupy a total of 1,500 acres of federal land. Their operation consumes enormous amounts of energy—almost 3 percent of America's electricity. Congress was not about to create competition for such an expensive monopoly without close supervision. Hence the need for Kelly Gilliam—on paper.

Off paper he was scarcely more than a staff lackey for Hammer. He answered constituent mail. He wrote speeches and press releases. He lobbied for Department of Energy contract awards to Kelleher Labs in Hammer's Pennsylvania. He regularly reported to Hammer's administrative assistant, Jean Murdock. His immediate supervisor was Committee staff director Burt Strong, an aged pro who had held together Hammer's organization from its beginning. Gilliam was caught in a cold war between Strong and Murdock.

He had resolved to stay with the Committee for two years before going job hunting again. If need be, he would hang his shingle on a rented frame house in his native Bozeman, Montana, and go happily broke. He would find a simple mountain girl, marry her, and have sturdy mountain kids. By Christmas, he would have rid himself of Hammer, Murdock, Strong, nuclear fission, and Washington. Just thinking about it was exhilarating.

Gilliam left his old brick apartment building and drove the winding Rock Creek Parkway into the heart of Washington, D.C. His dirty red Volvo sedan was a part of a surge bound inward from Cleveland Park, Chevy Chase, and Bethesda. He traded traffic scowls with State Department officials headed for Foggy Bottom, with Health, Education, and Welfare paper wasps headed toward their hive on Independence Avenue, and with White House staffers headed for the Old Executive Office Building on Pennsylvania.

Kelly Gilliam was important enough to have a parking place in the garage under the Dirksen Senate Office Building. The amiable Capitol cop at his entrance, already sweating from the morning heat, stopped oncoming traffic so Gilliam could enter. "Better get that thing washed!" he said good-naturedly.

Gilliam walked along the subterranean railway leading from the Dirksen Building to the Capitol. Skipping the one-minute ride assuaged his guilt for having virtually given up tennis. As he reached the Capitol end of the passageway, he waded through groups of Senate staffers and rushed past soda machines and white plaster reliefs of forgotten faces in American history. Moments later, an elevator deposited him on the fourth floor.

He was scarcely out of the elevator when someone grabbed his arm. Burt Strong's face looked as though he'd already put in a ten-hour day dealing with the senator. His eyes were bleary, his rutted forehead awash with sweat in spite of the air conditioning. "I'm glad I caught you, Kelly," he said. "I just talked with Murdock. The boss wants us in his office."

"What's it about?"

Strong shook his head and glanced around at the horde of staffers, tourists, and hurrying pages. "I'll tell you what I know on the train."

They managed to get a car to themselves. Strong leaned across toward Gilliam's seat as the train moved back toward the Dirksen Building. He explained that the Nuclear Regulatory Commission's Executive Director for Operations, Chester McGafferty, had called Hammer at 6:00 A.M. to request a meeting with the Committee leadership. The meeting concerned a matter of national security. The President had instructed NRC Chairman Lionel Osgood to arrange for an immediate briefing of the House and Senate committees.

Gilliam and Strong were ushered into Hammer's private office, Dirksen 200. Midnight-blue carpeting, sky-blue and white brocaded drapes sweeping to the floor from a fifteen-foot window, elaborate chandelier, diplomas, books, monstrous polished desk—all added up to Importance. As was his custom, Hammer did not receive visitors from behind his desk, but sat in an arm-chair amid a cluster of leather furniture. He felt that he could get closer to his visitors this way, be they fellow power holders or supplicants. Closeness showed friendliness, equality, and trust. Closeness also allowed useful weaknesses to be picked up more easily. Hammer's disheveled white hair stood out against a sunlamp tan.

Locked in his teeth below a frazzled gray mustache was the famous pipe, which emitted a shifting bluish white cloud. Gilliam's allergic nose twitched at the stinking vapors.

Hammer glanced up at his underlings as they entered. His eyes were nearly black and were rendered doubly penetrating by thick bifocals and outrageously bushy brows. "Sit down," he told them unceremoniously. "They'll be here in a minute."

Jean Murdock came into the room from the outer office, ignored Strong and Gilliam, and went to Hammer's chair to whisper something. "Fine. Send them in," he said. She deposited a pair of legal pads on an armchair between Gilliam and the senator and breezed out again.

Gilliam suddenly realized that he'd brought nothing to write on. During an important meeting like this, he should at least give the appearance of taking notes. He glanced at Strong, who was nestled comfortably on a sofa at the far end of the room, armed with only a small spiral notepad. Gilliam's eyes fell on the two legal pads in the chair next to him. Murdock obviously meant to sit there next to the senator. He agonized over whether to take one of the pads. He heard low, intense voices gathering on the other side of the door. It was now or never. He swiped the top pad from the chair and withdrew pen from pocket.

A parade of important-looking people trouped into the office, most of whom Gilliam recognized as congressional biggies. The House members did everything short of genuflecting to Hammer, who rose and clutched their outstretched hands with both of his. Gilliam thought he detected something in Hammer's behavior that wasn't quite normal—an unsteadiness, perhaps, a slight overcompensation for . . . what? He couldn't tell.

He recognized Paul DeSmit and Chester McGafferty of the NRC, peas from the bureaucratic pod—Ivy League, conservative poplin suits, eyeglasses with milky brown frames and almost round lenses. The three men following DeSmit and McGafferty had familiar faces, but Gilliam couldn't place them. Each paid his respects with a forced smile and took a seat. Murdock picked up her legal pad and sat down.

Hammer relit his pipe and introduced everyone in the room. The three men Gilliam had thought familiar were from the Department of Energy—DOE; Theodore Rippling was the Assistant Administrator for Nuclear Energy, Clayton Mercado, the Director of Reactor Research and Development, and Geoffrey Tuttle, the Director of the Division of Safeguards and Security.

Hammer began the meeting by holding aloft a letter on White House stationery presented him by DeSmit. "The President has asked," intoned Hammer, "that this meeting be kept strictly confidential." He narrowed his gaze unflatteringly at Gilliam. "I trust that no one will divulge to anyone else the topic of these consultations." Everyone nodded silently. Hammer then explained how the meeting had been called.

Gilliam thought that Hammer seemed to be holding back, that his words were chosen too carefully. At length, Paul DeSmit was called on.

"You are no doubt aware of yesterday's incident concerning a convoy in Timber Rivers, Connecticut," he said. "That convoy, I regret to say, carried eighty kilograms, some one hundred and seventy-six pounds of plutonium dioxide. It's been confirmed that the cargo is missing, presumably stolen. Up to now all efforts to recover it have been futile."

"What do you mean, up to now?" asked Senator Marble anxiously. "Have you got it back?"

"To my knowledge, sir," responded DeSmit weakly, "the plutonium is still MUF."

"For Christ's sake, what's MUF?" growled Marble.

"Materials unaccounted for," replied DeSmit.

"Eighty kilograms is enough to make a bomb, isn't it, Paul?" asked Congressman Kneeland, his face ashen.

"Yes, sir, it is. Let me explain how things are progressing and then we can elaborate on that. Do you agree, Mr. Chairman?"

Hammer nodded.

DeSmit continued. "At noon yesterday, Commissioner Osgood of the NRC notified Connecticut Governor Bergson that a theft of SNM—special nuclear material—had occurred in the Timber Rivers area. He strongly advised the governor to use National Guard units to cordon the area to prevent contamination or displacement of articles that might be helpful to the investigation. The governor complied. Commissioner Osgood then sent our SERT people—that's special enforcement and recovery team—to the site. I think you'll all recall when formation of the team was authorized last session of Congress. It includes a special FBI unit, a nuclear physicist, a portable crime lab, and people from the intelligence community."

"You mean CIA?" asked Strong.

"Yes, sir," said DeSmit.

"As I recall," said Strong, "SERT's also blessed with power, right? Can't these guys use whatever's available, state and local police, and that kind of thing?"

"The law's somewhat vague there," said DeSmit. "So far we haven't run into difficulty with state and local people."

"What difficulty *are* you having?" pursued Strong.

DeSmit glanced nervously at his NRC colleague, McGafferty. "The FBI," he answered. "The director has taken over the investigation. The CIA is going its own way, independent of SERT. The President, however, has issued directives to clear things up, and we expect to have a top man appointed by noon today."

"What will this 'top man' do?" asked Jean Murdock tautly.

"He will oversee the entire investigation," said DeSmit. "He'll be accountable solely to the President."

"What do we know about the hijackers so far?" asked Murdock.

DeSmit removed his glasses and vigorously cleaned the lenses with an immaculate handkerchief. "They've switched vehicles," he said. "They're now driving some kind of large truck. SERT's gotten plaster casts of the tire treads and some fingerprints from the pickup they used." Murdock sat back, biting her lips. She would let someone else press for more details.

Senator Marble pressed on. "You said a portable crime lab was dispatched. Have they found anything?"

"The SERT ballistics people determined that army M-16 rifles were used and that some sort of self-propelled explosive round was employed to disable the truck and two of the escort vehicles. They've collected every spent cartridge casing they could find and are examining them for fingerprints. The state people are using a sifter on the old car the attackers blew up. So far, nothing."

"Does this investigation have any operational theme or direction?" asked Congressman Kneeland. "Does anyone have any theories that are being explored?"

Geoffrey Tuttle, the DOE safeguards man, took over. "Yes, sir. Admittedly, everything's speculative at this point, but the investigation is proceeding on the assumption that inside collusion occurred. There's no other way to explain the precise timing and methods used by the attackers. They knew the shipment schedule well enough to time the demolition of the traffic lights on the interstate exchange and—"

"What?" exclaimed Kneeland. "What demolition?" Tuttle explained with great precision and then continued the speculative profile of the assailants.

"They knew exactly how to handle each part of the security escort. They even knew how to position their charges on the locks of the vault for best effect. Obviously, people outside the industry could not have known all the particulars of transporting SNM without help from the inside."

"What's being done to test that theory?" asked Kneeland.

"Computer profiles on every employee of ANC are being scanned," responded Tuttle. "The profiles themselves are somewhat inadequate since there's reason to believe that ANC has been less than diligent in constructing and updating them. The employee profile reference system—EPRS—is only an experimental licensing requirement. Right, Paul?" Tuttle looked for confirmation to DeSmit, who nodded. "The NRC thought that such a system might come in handy in a circumstance like this. As I understand it, however, EPRS still isn't a compulsory licensing requirement. DOE provided the funds for ANC's participation in it as an experimental program."

Senator Hammer cleared his throat and spoke up. "You must be doing something besides this . . . this . . . scan. What about good old-fashioned police work? Is any of *that* being done?"

"Yes, oh, yes," answered Tuttle. "Every available federal and state enforcement officer has been pulled in to interrogate witnesses and ANC employees. Their reports are flowing into the FBI, where they're analyzed and acted on. Local police are interviewing anyone they think might have been near the Timber Rivers area yesterday. Roadblocks are out, planes are searching the area, and virtually every truck on Connecticut's highways gets stopped and searched at one or more points. The intelligence community has started digging into everything known about any terrorist, subversive, or criminal group. It's all being done, Mr. Chairman, and we're optimistic that it'll pay off."

"And what if it doesn't?" asked Strong. "What if these people aren't in Connecticut or New York? Say they're in Colorado or maybe another country?"

Theodore Rippling, from DOE, broke the silence

that followed Strong's question. "Burt, there's good reason to believe that the attackers are Americans, or at least foreign nationals living in America. In the first place, there are many places overseas where nuclear material is stored under pitifully loose security. The same goes for shipping. Our new safeguards are far and away the strictest and most difficult to penetrate of any in the world. These attackers, we can assume, wanted ANC's plutonium for something along the eastern seaboard. Otherwise they would have gone somewhere else."

"Which," interjected Kneeland, "brings us back to my earlier question. You said, Paul, that eighty kilograms is enough to make a bomb. How much sleep do I lose over *that* one?"

Clayton Mercado, who ran DOE's Reactor Research branch, responded. "Enough to make a bomb is right, Congressman. *Enough*, in fact to make perhaps three bombs. While I don't intend to minimize this incident in the least, I can nonetheless assure you that we needn't worry about bombs."

"Some people would debate that, Doctor," ventured Gilliam, surprising himself.

"Oh, you're quite right," responded Mercado with a tight smile. "Many people choose debate for its own sake, regardless of the attendant facts. Prior to taking my present position, I served as weapons development consultant to the old Atomic Energy Commission. Subsequent to that, I assisted the Defense Department's weapons materials branch in developing our current generation of nuclear ground-to-air antiaircraft warheads. Unlike some with whom I've debated over the years, I know what I'm talking about when it comes to bombs. Our stolen plutonium may cause us great heartaches, but bombs will not be one of them." The room was silent again.

"Are you going to tell us why?" asked Senator Marble.

Mercado smiled again. "Engineering, Senator. Now,

our bandits may know about atomic bombs. That knowledge—the *principles* of nuclear fission—can be picked up in almost any library. In fact, some rather good unclassified reports have been circulated that describe the various configurations of light, efficient, high-yield bombs. The secret is in the engineering." Mercado looked pleased with himself, too pleased to suit Gilliam.

"What's so special about the engineering, Doctor, that lets us assume so surely that the attackers don't know about it?"

Mercado was prepared. "Our bandits, Mr. Gilliam, stole concentrated $Pu\,O_2$, plutonium dioxide fabricated especially for use in a liquid metal fast breeder reactor experiment. To build any kind of a decent bomb, they must first fabricate metallic plutonium—that is, get rid of the oxygen in the $Pu\,O_2$. Once they've negotiated that very complicated and somewhat dangerous course, they must assemble a device capable of bringing pieces of the metal together very quickly and very precisely. Doing it just any way is of little value.

"I'm told that our missing shipment is 'delta phase' plutonium-239. Plutonium-239 is relatively stable, but has a propensity for capturing a neutron to form plutonium-240, which can't be fissioned by neutrons of just any energy. Amateurish handling increases the likelihood of our bandits' ending up with plutonium-240, which needs very special treatment by bomb builders. The reason is that 240 is likely to pick up yet another neutron to become interesting-but-not-very-violent plutonium-241."

"What does all that mean?" asked Strong.

"Plutonium-240 alone can't be used for the core of an atom bomb, Mr. Strong."

"Does that mean our worries are over?" asked Kneeland.

"Unfortunately, no," said Mercado. "Any form of plutonium is extremely dangerous. While it may take sophisticated engineering to assemble an explosive device, it takes very little intellect to contaminate vast areas with a substance as toxic as plutonium. Breathing even a millionth of a gram can mean death from lung cancer. Increase the dosage to a few thousandths of a gram and we die from fibrosis of the lungs within weeks. The effects of someone emptying plutonium into a city water supply or the ventilation system of a factory would be ghastly. That's why we must recover our plutonium as soon as possible."

The meeting went on. McGafferty of the Nuclear Regulatory Commission explained that a vaguely optimistic statement would be given to the press after the President's meeting with the new head of the investigation. The statement would be made by NRC Chairman Osgood with the hope that public reaction would be minimized by the apparent lack of concern of Cabinet-level officials and the President. McGafferty asked the Congressmen and Senators to convince their colleagues to minimize the inevitable congressional outcry. Senator Hammer, his face pallid through the sunlamp tan, said, "I'm sure we'll do all we can."

The meeting lasted slightly over an hour. Kelly Gilliam was numb. He walked quickly from Hammer's office into the busy corridor, scarcely feeling his stride on the tile. Strong followed. Neither wished to trade clumsy chit-chat with Murdock, who lingered in the senator's office.

"Scabs! I need a cup of coffee," breathed Gilliam as they entered S. 403 in the Capitol.

"You can have your coffee," said Strong, not smiling. "I need an early lunch." He disappeared into the office annex of S. 403. Gilliam wondered how Strong kept his guts intact. He'd never seen the old man drunk, but his sensitive nose told him that Strong consumed scotch through most afternoons.

Gilliam collapsed into his rolling typist's chair behind a cluttered desk. A half dozen yellow message slips were taped to his fluorescent lamp and impaled on his spindle

—messages fielded by his fellow staffers in his absence. He recognized the names of several legislative aides. They'd called, no doubt, to quiz him on what he knew about the mysterious happenings near Timber Rivers. Gilliam dreaded returning the calls.

He glanced absently at the yellow legal pad he'd swiped from Murdock. Clipped to the cardboard backing was a yellow phone note identical to those taped to his lamp.

TELEPHONE MEMORANDUM

TO: _____ Ms. Murdock _____

YOU WERE CALLED BY:_____

_____ Wesley Rice, ANC _____

PLEASE CALL: (214) 555-6601

MESSAGE: _____ Urgent ! _____

TIME: _____ 8:01 _____

DATE: _____ May 11 _____

He didn't see the name "Ms. Murdock." The initials "ANC," however, exploded like skyrockets. Gilliam bit his lip and strained to place the name of the caller. He finally remembered seeing him at the recent Committee hearing on the DOE budget. He recalled a middle-aged man with a fashionable mustache, dark hair streaked with gray, and expensive cowboy boots. Yes, cowboy boots, a common sight in Gilliam's native Montana, but almost nonexistent in Washington. The man was a Texan who had testified on proposed amendments to the DOE authorization bill. Wesley Rice was near the top in the nuclear industry.

Gilliam congratulated himself on his systematic memory method as he punched the buttons of his phone.

The area code was Dallas. As tiny long-distant tones bleeped through the receiver, Gilliam conjured his "important" voice. He was, after all, a principal aide to one of Congress's most powerful men, a "somebody" who talked to corporate moguls daily, almost.

As a telephone in distant Dallas rang, Gilliam tried to imagine why Rice would call him, especially so early. It was now only minutes before 8:00 A.M. in Dallas. Perhaps Rice wished to share some news concerning the robbery. As a woman with a heavy voice answered, Gilliam's eyes widened stupidly. It was Murdock's callback!

"G-good morning, Mr. Rice's office."

Gilliam's "important" voice fluttered away through his nostrils.

"Uh . . . oh, yes. Is Mr. Rice, in please? I'm returning his call."

"Who's this?"

"My name is Kelly Gilliam. I'm counsel for the Joint Committee on Atomic Energy in Washington."

"M-mister Gilliam?" The woman seemed to choke.

"Right. Is Mr. Rice there?"

"M-mister Gilliam, something has happened."

"Yes, we're aware of the robbery. Is Mr. Rice in?"

"I-I don't know if I should tell you this, but Mr. Rice committed suicide this morning in his office."

Jean Murdock pawed through the pockets of her pantsuit, then through her briefcase. She scoured the top of her desk. She retraced her steps into the senator's office and back out to the reception area. The yellow memo slip bearing Wesley Rice's name and number was nowhere.

She was certain that she'd clipped it to the back of her legal pad just before the briefing. Now it was gone.

Not that she really needed it. Rice would be available somewhere in Dallas and she had his telephone numbers in her card file. Though it wasn't critical, she could see no good reason to leave *that* particular memo slip lying around. More important, she was hesitant to return Rice's call with other people around. Maybe later.

Still, Rice had called her. He probably needed calming, which was understandable. Murdock knew that despite Rice's weaknesses, he was far from stupid. From the first news flash on the Timber Rivers theft, he had probably pondered every piece of classified information he'd given her over the last two years. By now he would be desperately trying to convince himself that she'd used the information only for her stated purpose—briefing Hammer privately on matters germane to the Senate Energy Committee. Ultimately, of course, he would fail. Rice's final tidbit had been the most critical: the timing of the Timber Rivers plutonium shipment.

Murdock was willing to wager long odds that he'd do nothing crazy. She'd carefully calculated the risks of dealing with Rice, an emotional and somewhat undisciplined man. She banked on his knowing that he was in this thing up to his receding hairline. She knew that despite his weaknesses, he would remain under control.

Yes, she would call him and say the right things to comfort him, *provided* she could find him. *Damn it, where is that memo?* Would he be at home, at work, at his racquet club? Murdock lit her sixth cigarette of the morning and punched the number of Rice's racquet club.

Two minutes later, Murdock darted through the door connecting her office to Harry Hammer's, leaving a cloud of cigarette smoke in her wake. The senator watched quizzically as she locked the door behind her.

"Harry," she said, "Wes Rice is dead. Killed himself this morning."

"Killed himself?" hissed Hammer, leaning forward suddenly. "Why in hell . . . ? How do you know?"

Murdock answered the latter question first. She'd returned Rice's call to his club, assuming that's where he'd be at this early hour. Though the suicide was but hours old, word travels quickly in high corporate circles. Rice had not shown up for his usual early-morning tennis match, but other moguls who did already knew about his death. Consequently, the secretary who answered the racquet club telephone also knew.

"That goddamned weakling!" roared Hammer. "What made him do it, Jeannie?"

Murdock tamped a fresh cigarette from her leather-bound pack. "If you're finished yelling, I'll give you my theory. But it's only a theory."

Hammer nodded, rose from behind his desk, and crossed to a portable file that had been converted to a hidden liquor cabinet. "I'll listen to your theory, but not before I have a Bloody Mary. Want one?"

"It's too early for a Bloody Mary," replied Murdock. "Besides, around here you're supposed to be reformed. Forget the Bloody Mary and sit down, Harry."

He stared at her for a moment, worrying the bowl of his pipe in his fist. Then he obeyed, selecting a leather chair and resting his head against the cushion. "Before you start, let me guess what your theory is," he said.

Murdock took the sofa across from him. "Be my guest."

"Our friend Rice heard about Timber Rivers, put two and two together, and came down with an acute attack of guilt. He decided that he was a disloyal and unreliable son of a bitch, a real wart on his company's nose. More than that, he decided that he'd been duped, used. Notwithstanding that all of this is true, he suffered an emotional crisis. He had no way out but to do himself in. Am I right?"

Murdock nodded. "Now the question is what *else* he might have done."

"Besides killing himself? You're quite right. That's a *real* question." Hammer added tobacco to his pipe from a pouch in his breast pocket. "Did he, for the sake of discussion, feel guilty enough to tell someone what he'd done?"

"I doubt it," said Murdock. "That would have taken too much courage—more than Wes had. His strong suits were brains and persuasion. But when it came to having balls—" Murdock cut herself off, but not before Hammer's eyes widened slightly.

"Interesting subject, Rice's balls," said Hammer. "Something you know more about than anyone, I'd say."

"Harry, I'd rather not—"

"Well, I'd *rather*! Besides, what the hell difference does it make whether we talk about it or not? What's happened can't be changed, can it?"

Murdock's eyes became hard and threatening. "I don't know what you're leading up to, but if you're suggesting that Wes Rice meant anything . . ."

"Did you like it, Jeannie? Did you like doing it with him? Be honest."

Her gaze dropped to the polished surface of the coffee table. Seconds passed as she studied her own reflection. "I don't lie to you, Harry, you know that. *Yes*, I liked it. But I did it because I had to, because you and I needed information. He meant absolutely nothing to me."

The senator puffed on his pipe and contemplated a brocaded flag of the great state of Pennsylvania in a corner of the office. "So you liked doing it to Rice. How about Rossiter? Was he any better?"

Murdock wrinkled her brow. "Just bigger, not better."

Hammer's mouth dropped open, then his jowls twitched. Suddenly he guffawed. "Just *bigger*!"

Murdock smiled broadly, congratulating herself for swiftly ending an increasingly ugly line of conversation. She winced when the senator stopped belly-laughing and picked the conversation up again.

"So Duncan Rossiter is bigger than Wesley Rice, but

no better," he mused. "I wonder how *I* place in your comparative analysis."

"Harry, this is getting absurd," Murdock replied sharply. "I balled Wes because we needed his inside information. I ball Duncan Rossiter because he's an unstable maniac who won't play our game unless he thinks he's running the show. I ball you because I want to, and for no other reason. End of conversation."

Hammer chuckled and stood up. "I agree. We've talked long enough for a while. Let's go up to the private office. It has a softer sofa."

"I'm afraid not, Harry," said Murdock. "We both have important things to think about."

"But you just said Rice didn't have the guts to tell anyone that he blew the security rules. I happen to agree with you. So what's to think about?"

Murdock stood and planted her fists on her hips. "Like maybe what you'll *do*, once we've pulled this thing off. You're the expert on power. You may want to make some plans on how to use it."

"For God's sake, all we've done for years is plan. I'm sick of planning."

"We've done a hell of a lot more than that, Harry. We've *acted*. Now it's paying off, and after all this time you'll be the leader you deserve to be."

"The leader nobody wanted, you mean," said Hammer, choking momentarily on inhaled pipe smoke. "But you're right, of course. Two unsuccessful shots at the presidency certainly don't relieve me of my present responsibilities. If I'm to lead, I'll need a more detailed plan."

"Make one," said Murdock, grabbing his arm. "Have it ready so you can act quickly and forcefully when the time is right."

"Quickly and forcefully," echoed Hammer, placing a wrinkled hand over hers. "You can be assured that I'll do exactly that."

He turned slowly and strode to the window. Across Constitution Avenue loomed the Capitol. Cars jammed its east plaza. Hordes milled amid trees and shrubbery. A high school band from Salem, Oregon, posed for photographs in full regalia on the rear steps. Senators, congressmen, aides, and lobbyists bustled through the crowds, avoiding flying Frisbees and rubbernecking drivers.

"What are you thinking?" asked Murdock.

"I'm thinking about how beautiful that building is," he replied, "and how more than anything else it symbolizes the life and career of Harold J. Hammer. I'm also thinking of how miserable it's been to stand by all these years, watching gutless bureaucrats and politicians make a mockery of that symbol, distorting the public will." He turned from the window. "I'm leaving now for home, and I won't be coming back here. At least not until it's all over."

Murdock was dumbfounded. "Harry, what are you talking about? You can't just go home. There'll be committee meetings, press conferences . . ."

"This will all be over in a matter of weeks," he soothed. "I can monitor things through you until it's time to go to the bunker. This briefing today has been my last official act as a U.S. senator. That has sort of a ring to it, doesn't it? Sort of historical. Tell the world I'm sick or something, but please don't try to talk me into staying. It would be a totally useless exercise."

"But, Harry . . ."

"I'm having a Bloody Mary before I leave, Jeannie, I don't care what you say."

"Harry, would you please think about reality for one goddamn minute?"

Hammer was already pouring Snappy Tom over ice. "Reality, as my old friend Burt Strong would say, is just a crutch for those who can't take booze."

Joel Kaznik wasted no time after leaving the Oval Office and his briefing with the President. He drove directly to the CIA complex in Langley, Virginia, to establish his command post. By 1:00 P.M., Kaznik was ensconced behind a small gray desk in a two-toned pastel cubicle as bland in appearance as he was. He might have been a low-level bureaucrat or a nameless corporate "bean counter." Kaznik, however, had been transformed by a short meeting with the President into one of the most powerful men in the country.

His power was complemented by the fact that no one, not even himself or the President, understood its limitations. It sprang not from written law but from the lips of one man—the President: "Recover that plutonium, Joel, before someone uses it. Do what you have to. If anyone gives you any shit, pick up your phone and I'll be there."

By 2:00 P.M. telephones were at his fingertips. He had direct lines to the President, the attorney general, the director of the FBI and the Bureau's Washington crime lab, to law-enforcement agencies throughout the eastern coastal states, and to the Pentagon. He had assurances from the President that recent changes in the CIA charter allowed domestic actions when nuclear security was threatened. His first official act was to summon ranking officials of the Department of the Treasury to determine how to use that agency's vast enforcement arm in the investigation. Top Treasury officials would drop their daily chores and report to Langley promptly at 3:45 P.M., ready to brief and be briefed. Power.

He had barely replaced the receiver when Colonel Nathaniel Billingsly, U.S. Army, poked his head through Kaznik's open door. Billingsly was temporarily assigned as armed forces liaison to Kaznik. He was a stumpy black man with facial creases, but no extra weight. A conflagration of ribbons over his left breast informed Kaznik of his extensive experience as a combat officer in Vietnam: Green Beret, Purple Heart, Silver Stars, Cambodian Incursion. Billingsly was "hard core," a self-made success who obviously knew how to function under pressure. He was not a West Pointer. Kaznik had emphatically stipulated that the Pentagon not send him a West Pointer. Billingsly would do just fine, Kaznik knew, even before amenities were exchanged.

Amenities were short and made even shorter by the simultaneous arrivals of special liaisons from the FBI and the Nuclear Regulatory Commission, Curt Quillico and Stanley Perchale. Kaznik distributed styrofoam cups of coffee and situated the three men around his desk in metal folding chairs.

"Are you Nate, Colonel?" asked Kaznik of Billingsly.

"Yes, sir, I am."

"Good. I'm Joel, but not 'sir.' I'll tell you what I need from you, Nate. A complete rundown from CID, that's the Army's Criminal Investigation Division," Kaznik said, nodding to the others, who nodded back, "on any and all missing weapons and ordnance over the past five years, the status of current investigations of thefts, and any leads. Your job will be to relay that information here to Langley, where it will be digested and related to this investigation. That's thing number one."

Billingsly looked disturbed, but he knew better than to say so. In spite of stringent security measures, the Army had never been able to keep a tight rein on its arsenal. A company commander who was missing an M-16 might notify a close friend in a weapons repair division. That friend would falsify records to show that the weapon had been turned in and subsequently judged irreparable. A green trainee may, in fact, have innocently lost the rifle during a long field exercise— nothing to get excited over; certainly no reason for a long, damaging CID investigation.

There was also a sizable black market in military hardware, and the CID had its hands full with backlogged investigations. A civilian sufficiently determined and willing to pay could acquire nearly any army weapon short of a tank and leave virtually no clue.

Kaznik sensed Billingsly's misgivings, but he continued on to "thing" number two: "I want as many military intelligence agents as we can get by twenty-four-hundred hours tonight to report for field assignment on the east coast. Put a premium on those with experience in clandestine counterterror activities. We'll assume the maximum threat, that the East has been infiltrated heavily by a group whose mission is public terror. You'll need an office in the Pentagon to handle the assignments and some experienced officers to run it."

Billingsly took careful note.

"Thing number three," said Kaznik. "I want a complete capability assessment of all military installations from Fort Benning at the southernmost point, up the eastern seaboard to Maine at the northernmost. Go as far inland as the coastal state borders, Nate. Use your judgment on the criteria. I want every installation alerted to supply armed personnel and transportation if we need it." Billingsly looked confident. "Things" two and three would be no problem.

Kaznik directed his next set of orders to Quillico, the FBI man. "On to you, Curt. You'll be a busy man for the next few hours. Thing number one: Consolidate the lists from the Company and the Bureau of all the likely and known terrorists in the country—those with records —and give me the top two hundred. Then I want you to pull out all the stops. Use every available asset and get me a rundown on each individual's whereabouts and activities over the last thirty-six hours. If anything shady turns up, I want full clandestine surveillance. But no arrests yet. I want to avoid a show of force. I'll put you in touch with our computer people to make the job a bit more manageable. Any questions so far?"

"Just one thing," said Quillico. "We'll have to rely

heavily on state and locals for the surveillance since we've got so many agents already committed to Connecticut. That will extend our time factor. How much delay can we handle?"

Kaznik's gray eyes narrowed, but he held the nearly expressionless mask that thoroughly screened his thoughts and emotions. "None at all" was his answer. He paused for an instant while Quillico squirmed. Kaznik did not revel in his ability to cause such discomfort. Unlike many other CIA agents, he felt no competition with the FBI. He'd once worked for the Bureau himself. He understood its weaknesses and limitations but had great respect for its strengths. He admired the Quillicos who tirelessly pursued their mission in spite of politics and entangling bureaucracy. Quillico's question had been ventured sincerely to determine the investigation's priorities. Kaznik, however, had no choice but to demand the impossible.

"Thing number two: You've got to kick that crime lab in the ass, Curt, because I need a make on the explosives used on the truck and I want to know what kind of artillery they used. I want all the witnesses reexamined. Most of all, I want the damn state troopers and county mounties out of our hair but standing by. Next, I want to know where that Datsun pickup came from and a complete follow-through on everybody who's ever had any contact with it. Can you add anything?"

Quillico's brow wrinkled thoughtfully. "Let's get people on the street looking for anyone who might have seen someone tampering with the traffic signals that got blown up. We just might get a description."

"Good thought," said Kaznik. "Do it. One more thing. Put out the word to state and locals in the East to get people in airport terminals and bus and train stations. Have them look for anything suspicious. And I mean *anything*."

Kaznik turned his attention to Perchale, NRC. "How

many employees does American Nuclear Corporation have, Stan?"

"Just over thirteen thousand."

"Good. That means we have a manageable number to work with. I want a list of every employee who could possibly have known about that particular shipment, from the president of ANC on down. I want the same thing for Watne Incorporated. Somebody in one or both of those companies is working for the bad guys and I want to know who. Have the data here by tomorrow noon."

"You'll have it," said Perchale.

"One final note," said Kaznik. "As I mentioned earlier, we must assume the maximum threat. That assumption means that there may be a try for another shipment, and I'm sure we all agree that one theft is enough for us to handle right now. Stan, I want you to instruct the NRC to suspend all scheduled shipments of special nuclear material."

Perchale's mouth dropped open. "I, uh . . ."

"You what?" asked Kaznik evenly.

"I'm not sure, Mr. Kaznik, that the Commission regards that kind of—uh—decision as within your purview."

Kaznik allowed perhaps ten agonizing seconds to pass in silence. As before, his voice and facial expressions did not change. "I'll dispense with asking why, Stan. In fact, I won't *ask* you anything. I'll simply *tell* you. I've been close to the issue of SNM security for a long time. In addition to carrying out Company operations against some people who wanted to steal SNM, I've read everything there is on the subject. I've even read the garbage you people put out on how well the material is guarded. Your fearless Commissioner Osgood told the Committee that the chances of any private citizen ever being harmed by the fission industry are far less than being hit by lightning. I know how you people rack your brains to rationalize away the danger. I'm not John Q. Public sitting here waiting for you to tell me everything will be okay.

"You tell Dr. Osgood that pending shipments of SNM are off. You also tell him that things are out of control, that someone else is calling the shots now. If he doesn't like it, he can come and see me."

Perchale rose, his face white. "I'll do that, Mr. Kaznik." He departed silently with Billingsly and Quillico.

Two and a half hours later, Kaznik's phone jangled just as the Treasury Department officials were departing. He let them get through the door before picking up the receiver. It was Quillico calling from his office in downtown Washington.

"Mr. Kaznik, I don't know what this means, but I knew you'd want to know."

"Go ahead, Curt."

"A top ANC executive, a man named Wesley Rice, blew his brains out this morning in Dallas. One of our Dallas agents just phoned it in."

"Be on the roof of your building in five minutes, Curt. I'm sending a helicopter to get you and we're going to Dallas."

At 5:10 P.M., Central Daylight Time, Kaznik and Quillico stepped off the Air Force plane in Dallas. Walking to the awaiting helicopter was like walking through a sauna. The chopper soon rose and veered toward Dallas's jumbled skyline. Below them, grayish brown ribbons of asphalt teemed with miniscule bits of steel rushing somewhere. They flew over the northern suburbs and turned eastward as another helicopter, this one carrying a traffic reporter, gave them berth.

The architectural gluttony of suburban shopping centers and commercial strips gave way to gentle brown hills spotted with sagebrush. Nestled between the hills were clusters of low homes on vivid green lawns amply garnished with palms and cacti.

At length the helicopter began to orbit what Kaznik

first thought was a small golf course. Closer examination revealed groups of low, contemporary buildings shaded by clumps of manicured trees. Kaznik strained to read a large brick sign with aluminum lettering:

AMERICAN NUCLEAR CORPORATION

The helicopter eased itself earthward onto a grassy clearing near the largest of the buildings. Several police cruisers and a police van were parked in the traffic oval a short distance off. Kaznik and Quillico were met by a tall blond man in his late thirties, Inspector John Vance, FBI, and a balding man with a leathery face and a western tie, Lieutenant George Smiley, Homicide, Texas Rangers.

The air conditioning of the "Executive Center" was at first a relief from the heat of the late afternoon. Soon, however, Kaznik began to feel cold and found that he was keeping his hands in his pockets.

They were led through thickly carpeted halls to an elevator that took them to the second and uppermost story. A few steps from the elevator they passed through Wesley Rice's polished walnut doorway.

The room was spacious. One entire wall was movable glass, which allowed access to a roofed balcony. A group of photographs adorned another wall. There was a shot of Rice, a handsome man, shaking the hand of Texas's governor. There was another of Rice addressing a convention dinner. Yet another showed him smilingly pumping the hand of Senator Harry Hammer.

Vance conducted a short briefing while Smiley obligingly provided colorful details augmenting the bare facts. "Had to have happened before seven A.M.," said Vance, pointing to a dark spot on the thick beige carpet. "The body was lying here. The lieutenant's people say he was sitting behind his desk when he pulled the trigger, but that he recoiled and fell over the side of the desk to here."

"Used a forty-four magnum Luger," added Smiley

needlessly. "Spattered bits of cranial material all over this far wall."

"Thank you, Lieutenant," replied Kaznik. "Did he leave a note?"

"No, sir, he didn't."

"Did he call anyone?"

"Not from the office," said Vance. "We obtained a list of metered calls from the phone company. On Monday he made only six calls, all to business acquaintances. I've checked on three of them, the others we're still checking. Everybody so far says he sounded and acted normal."

Kaznik withdrew a pencil with which he poked and touched various items strewn across Rice's desk. He didn't know what he was looking for, but he looked nevertheless. He avoided that area of the shiny surface covered with small bits of Rice.

"What about his wife?" asked Kaznik.

"She's in the hospital under sedation," responded Smiley. "She did manage to give us a statement though. Said that her husband came home yesterday afternoon very depressed. Guess it was the news of the robbery on the East Coast that did it. She said he couldn't sleep and that he tied one on pretty good late last night. Got up at five this morning and told her he was going out for a drive. Guess we know the rest."

Kaznik was thoughtful. "Did he call anyone before leaving this morning?"

"No, sir, he didn't."

"I want to talk to his boss," said Kaznik.

Kaznik was led through a corridor to an even larger, more luxurious office. Behind the door, sipping a strong bourbon and soda, was Derek Lindstrom, executive vice-president of ANC. Lindstrom was scarcely five feet four. He was also old, possibly seventy, and had thick white hair combed straight back. His bright blue eyes were set in a deeply tanned and wrinkled face. He came to his feet and shook Kaznik's hand with a surprisingly firm grip. "I'm pleased to meet you, Mr. Kaznik," said Lindstrom crisply. "Inspector," to Quillico.

"If you'll excuse us, Lieutenant Smiley, we have federal business with Mr. Lindstrom." Smiley looked stricken but retreated obediently, closing the heavy door behind him.

"May I offer you gentlemen a drink?" asked Lindstrom. His accent was eastern.

"Thank you, no," said Kaznik. "Forgive me for detaining you, Mr. Lindstrom. I'll make it short. Do you know any reason Wes Rice might have had to kill himself?"

"I'll make it shorter," said Lindstrom. "No."

"Did he have a good marriage?"

"No."

"How so?"

"Few top-flight executives have good marriages, Mr. Kaznik. I've had two, neither of them good. Big jobs mean bad marriages."

Kaznik could understand that because he'd had two himself. "You don't think his marriage could have driven him to this?"

"No, I don't."

"Did he confide in you?"

"Yes, he did. We were close. That's odd, really, up on this level. But I suspect Wes knew he had nothing to fear from me. Hell, I'm old. Wes knew I liked him and that I'd always back him up. I was no threat and he knew I'd make way for him when the time was right. That time would have come soon."

"What about the robbery? Would he have killed himself over that?"

"You're joking. He was strong. This company was his life. He'd be here to pick up the pieces from this robbery thing if he were alive. Best goddamn lobbyist this firm has—had."

Suddenly the old man dropped his glass and put both

hands to his face. Then he took a deep breath, raised his head, and fixed his visitors with a dry-eyed stare. "Too old to even produce a tear, I guess. My eyes often feel dry at the end of the day." He withdrew a bottle of Murine and applied the liquid to both eyes without spilling a drop.

Kaznik left Lindstrom to his bourbon and rejoined Vance and a grateful Smiley in the outer office.

"It doesn't make sense," said Kaznik to Quillico. "A big-time executive with impeccable credentials, an outstanding record, the world by the balls, and suddenly he offs himself."

"Maybe Rice took his home life more seriously than he let on to Lindstrom," Quillico said.

"I don't think so. They were *close*. You saw how the old man broke down. If Rice had been ready to kill himself for that, Lindstrom would have known about it."

"What then?" asked Quillico.

Kaznik sat at an empty receptionist's desk, leaned back in the rollered chair, and drummed his fingers on the blotter. "Financial setbacks, maybe? What about it, Lieutenant? Was Rice solvent?"

Smiley thumbed through his scribbled notes. "According to Mrs. Rice's statement, they had $91,000 in preferred ANC stock, $120,000 in savings, and controlling interest in a new racquet club valued at a million and a half. I figured it out and it comes to $1,700,000." Smiley smiled.

"That's $1,711,000, Lieutenant," corrected Kaznik. "And that doesn't count homes, boats, cars, and planes. Okay. He didn't kill himself over money unless he thought he had too much. What about his kids? Any problems there?"

"Nope," said Smiley. "Just the one daughter. Freshman at University of Colorado. Good student."

"We've ruled out love, money, and kid problems,"

thought Kaznik aloud. "We keep coming back to the robbery, where we should be. Curt, there's one other thing that'll make someone kill himself."

"What's that?"

"Guilt. He had something to do with that heist, one way or another. When it finally happened, he had an attack of guilt. It takes something pretty big to make a big-time executive feel guilty enough to put his own lights out. Vance, go over that phone company meter sheet again. Talk to everyone Rice called. Dig deep. Check the background of everyone on that sheet. Lieutenant, get me the stenos who answer Rice's phones."

"But Mr. Kaznik," protested Smiley, "it's after five. Everybody's gone home."

"Get them, Lieutenant." Smiley obeyed.

After consulting an ANC office manager who was working overtime, Smiley presented to Kaznik a complete list of Monday's incoming calls. Kaznik and Quillico went over the list, name by name, with Lindstrom. The old man knew most of the callers and could venture guesses as to the topics of conversation. Nothing emerged, however, that appeared even slightly conspiratorial or out of order. Kaznik nevertheless issued orders that everyone on the list be investigated.

"Looks like we drew a blank on the incoming calls," said Quillico wearily. "More coffee anyone?"

"What about Tuesday?" asked Kaznik. "Let's look at Tuesday's calls."

"Now wait a minute," said Smiley. "He killed himself before eight o'clock this morning. How could he talk to anybody on Tuesday?"

"I'm assuming, Lieutenant, that whoever called didn't know Mr. Rice was dead. The identities and backgrounds of those callers might be helpful. It's also possible that Mr. Rice might have tried to call someone earlier but was unable to get through for some reason.

That someone may have called back, and if so, I'd like to know who that someone is. Now please find me a similar list for Tuesday. That's *today*, Lieutenant."

Smiley responded grumpily. Kaznik settled down to look at the list after a long sip of hot coffee. His gray eyes widened upon reading the first entry.

"Quillico," said Kaznik. "Look at this. Tell me what you see."

"K. Gilliam," Quillico read aloud. "Time eight-eleven. Senate Energy Committee, Washington area code. It says, 'he returned Mr. Rice's call.' "

"That's right. Now, what phone do you suppose Rice used to call this Gilliam?"

"I don't know. He didn't use an office phone on Monday or we'd have seen it on the meter sheet. His home phone, maybe?"

Kaznik signaled to Vance. "Get on the horn to the phone company and find out if Rice's home phone meters a call to this number." He handed the agent a slip of paper bearing the scribbled number. "Next, get the meter sheets to this office for the past week and have them picked up and delivered here immediately."

While Vance used one line, Kaznik used another to call Langley. He ordered a complete profile on K. Gilliam, presumably an employee of the Senate Energy Committee. A surveillance team was to be readied for immediate dispatch in search of Gilliam. Kaznik would call back with instructions for the team.

An hour passed during which Kaznik revisited Rice's personal office. The police had neatly stacked the contents of the desk on the carpet. He sifted through all of it, placing telephone number lists, personal correspondence, and other potentially helpful items in a separate stack. He would have these copied for shipment to Langley. The rest, the vast bulk of material, he judged to be of no value.

He used the remainder of the hour to telephone the FBI, Billingsly, and his own office for updates on the various phases of the fledgling investigation. The crime lab still had nothing concerning the explosives or the artillery used on the convoy vehicles. The Datsun pickup, however, had been traced to a rental firm in Hartford, Connecticut. The rental clerk had issued the truck to a black man, late twenties or early thirties, no distinguishable features. The man, however, had left a handwriting sample in signing an obviously fake name. The rental form could be dusted for fingerprints. Since the clerk was certain that the man had not been wearing gloves when he took delivery, there was the possibility of finding additional prints in the truck.

The phone company confirmed that no calls to the Committee number had been made during the previous week from the Rice's residential telephone. The meter list confirmed the same for the ANC telephones.

Kaznik bit the eraser tip of his pencil. "That means," he said deliberately, "one of two things. Thing number one: Rice called Gilliam sometime before today from a phone other than his office or home phones. Mr. Lindstrom, do you know if this Gilliam was a personal friend of Rice?"

"I doubt it, Mr. Kaznik. I never heard Wes mention that name."

"So it's extremely doubtful that Rice would call someone who is not a personal friend from any phone but his office phone. And we know Rice called Gilliam because the log says 'returned Mr. Rice's call,' after Gilliam's entry. Had it been a business call, Rice would have used his office phone. But he didn't. The meter sheet says so. A busy executive sometimes uses his home phone for business calls, but again, the phone company says no."

"It's possible that Wes called this Gilliam while out on a business visit to some other office," observed Lindstrom.

"That's true," conceded Kaznik. "Except nowhere in Rice's personal effects or desk was Gilliam's number written. I just checked. Which brings us to thing number two: Rice called Gilliam from another phone, possibly a pay phone, this morning before killing himself. Now, why would a busy executive with a full day ahead of him go to the trouble of finding a pay phone to make a long-distance call to someone whose number isn't written anywhere in his office? Could we say that Rice didn't want his associates or his wife to know that he was acquainted with this Gilliam?"

"We may have our first lead," said Quillico.

Lindstrom looked both weary and troubled. Kaznik picked up a telephone to call Langley.

WEDNESDAY, MAY 12

Gilliam and Strong emerged from the midmorning "follow-up briefing" at the NRC's downtown office and joined the stream of pedestrian traffic. Neither noticed the well-dressed man watching them from across the street.

" 'The Commission recognizes that certain exigencies may constrain current operations and policies vis à vis apparent shortcomings in safeguarding SNM during transport and storage,' " mimicked Strong in a contemptuous falsetto that approximated the tone of the NRC staffer who conducted the briefing. "Why in God's name don't they speak English like everybody else?"

"It *was* a worthless meeting," observed Gilliam. "They obviously called it because someone decided it was the thing to do. No one cared that there wasn't anything to discuss."

"What pisses me off," said Strong, "is their low opinion of *us*. They obviously expect us to go back to the Hill and tell our bosses that the NRC has the whole situation well in hand. If I had misgivings about the NRC before, I've got downright stomach cramps now. The situation is not well in hand, Kelly, and it never has been. You'd think those idiots could see that a theft of eighty kilos of atomic bomb material means that something is wrong somewhere and that some policy should change. But no! Business as usual, they say. No reason to get excited, they say. It's incredible."

Gilliam hailed a taxi as the well-dressed man darted across the street to avoid losing sight of the pair. Strong continued to rave about the incompetence of the NRC and career bureaucrats in general as Gilliam opened the rear door of the taxi.

"Dirksen Building?" Gilliam asked the driver.

"Yes, sir."

"May I share your taxi?" asked the well-dressed man. "I'm going to Capitol Hill."

"Be my guest," responded Gilliam. "That's where we're going."

"Thank you so much."

Once in the cab, with others to overhear, Strong's invective against bureaucrats became more general. Gilliam had heard it before and he half listened, nodding in the right places, idly viewing the profile of their fellow passenger.

The man's face was intelligent, middle-aged, and dominated by a rather large hooked nose. His thinning brown hair receded in an unusually straight line from his temple. His suit was a middle-of-the-line doubleknit. Midwest middle class. Undoubtedly a lobbyist. Gilliam coped with his type daily.

As the taxi threaded its way through the traffic toward Capitol Hill, Gilliam allowed his mind to float into an image of the "Lobby Factory," a place that manufactured hundreds of neatly dressed, earnest men like the one sharing their ride. For a brief moment, he forgot the Timber Rivers theft.

Gilliam and Strong checked in at Dirksen 200 on the off-chance that Harry Hammer might have at last shown up at his office. Jean Murdock, prim and businesslike as always, informed them that the senator was still feeling ill and could not be disturbed at his home.

"I hope you've informed him of how important his being here really is," said Strong rather testily.

Murdock leaned back in her leather chair and smiled tightly. "You don't have to worry, Burt, about the senator's grip on the situation. I've been relaying everything important."

"Have you told him not to be surprised if the other members of the Committee start issuing press releases screaming for somebody's head?"

"He'll be in touch with the other members of the Committee at the appropriate time."

Gilliam watched Strong's neck grow crimson the way it nearly always did when he confronted the woman who had displaced him in Hammer's power structure.

"I hope he's getting enough sleep at night," said Strong. "That's important if he's got the flu like you say he does."

Murdock replied with a silent stare that Gilliam was certain could have frozen battery acid. Strong endured it for a moment and then turned on his heel in retreat. Gilliam followed, grateful that the confrontation was over.

Strong offered scotch upon their return to the Committee staff office in the Capitol, an offer Gilliam broke his "too-early-in-the-day" rule to accept. The old man cradled his drink after a healthy pull and gazed thoughtfully through the window at the bucolic scene in the Capitol plaza. "Something's wrong, Kelly," he said at length. "This isn't like Harry. I've seen him work twenty hours a day when he's had Hong Kong flu and should've been flat on his back in bed."

"He's not young any more, Burt," offered Gilliam. "Maybe he just can't do it like he used to."

Strong grimaced in disagreement. "I'm not young either, for Christ's sake. Harry's bigger and stronger than I am. I know because we became alcoholics together. He kicked it and I didn't—couldn't. That's how

69

I know. I just wish I had the guts to go directly to him, even though I know it wouldn't do any good. I'm only here because Harry would feel guilty if he threw me out. I can't compete with *her*."

Gilliam spent the remainder of the day fielding questions from legislative aides and reporters. His jangling telephone became the most dreaded object in his life. The reporters became especially tenacious when they sensed that he was withholding information about the Timber Rivers theft. To make matters worse, Strong assigned him the task of writing a memorandum for use in answering the deluge of constituent calls and telegrams concerning the incident. It was the usual brain-wracking challenge: Answer convincingly without answering.

By the end of the day Gilliam was drained. He shed his suit and tie in favor of corduroy jeans and tennis shoes and strolled from his cluttered apartment up Connecticut Avenue to the small liquor store across from the National Zoo. A knot of customers waiting for a chance to place their orders mingled around the counter trading quips about traffic and humidity. Gilliam loitered on the edge of the knot and stared absently through the plate-glass window at passersby.

Suddenly he froze.

Seated on a bus-stop bench maybe thirty steps away was a man in a frayed gray tweed coat (much too hot for this weather) and badly mismatched seersucker trousers. He wore a battered black hat tilted back to reveal hair that receded in an unusually straight line over the top of his head. His face, in spite of the shadowy stubble, was intelligent, middle-aged, and dominated by a rather large hooked nose. In one hand he clutched a brown paper bag, which he put to his lips as though to sip from a bottle hidden inside. As Gilliam stared in disbelief, the man's lips moved in whispers that seemed to be directed into the sack.

There was no mistaking it. This derelict was the man —the *lobbyist*—he had shared a taxi with earlier in the day. The change, skillfully executed and nearly total, would certainly have fooled Gilliam had he not had a good look at his fellow passenger in the taxi.

As Gilliam left the liquor store with his customary six-pack of Heineken Light, he allowed his eyes to absorb every detail of the bum on the bus stop bench. *Why?* Gilliam wondered. Four-day beards don't grow in eight hours. The guy was obviously made up.

Confusion turned to coldness as Gilliam passed by the bus-stop bench and happened to catch the eyes of the derelict figure. Gilliam knew somehow that this derelict was here because of him. The walk to his apartment building seemed incredibly long.

The following day Gilliam and Strong lunched at the Monocle, a plush Capitol Hill restaurant with lavish trimmings and low, intimate lighting. Yesterday's encounter with the derelict, Gilliam had nearly convinced himsef, amounted to paranoia and delusions of importance on his part. Hardly a spy thriller. The waiter brought dinner salads, a scotch and milk for Strong, and an iced tea for Gilliam.

Though they had vowed to spend one entire lunch hour without "talking shop," they fell naturally into a rehash of the mysteries surrounding the Timber Rivers incident. Strong expressed increasing concern over the strange absence of Harry Hammer and cursed Murdock, whom he believed was deliberately shielding the senator from his responsibilities. Through mouthfuls of salad they discussed possible tactics for extracting from the Nuclear Regulatory Commission an assurance that needed policy changes would be made.

Gilliam nearly gagged on his salad as two men handed their hats to the maitre d'. "If you don't mind, we'll just sit at the bar," said the man with the unusually straight hairline and the hooked nose. This time he was an Army colonel, a common sight on the Hill. His companion was civilian, early thirties, cropped blond hair. Both very common to anyone whose habits did not include scrutinizing strangers. Gilliam noted that even though they were seated with their backs to his table, the mirror behind the bar afforded the men a clear view of himself and Strong.

"You okay, Kelly?" asked Strong.

Gilliam labored to force a wad of lettuce down his suddenly dry throat. "Yeah. I just swallowed wrong. Let's talk about something else, Burt."

Instead of going with Strong back to the Committee staff office, Gilliam headed for the Congressional Reading Room in the Library of Congress. On the way, he picked up two legal pads and a box of pencils from the office supply store in the basement of the Russell Senate Office Building. Ensconced in the quiet, restful grandeur of the library, Gilliam undertook what most others find too time-consuming or emotionally impossible: dispassionate analysis of a personal problem. Long ago he'd found that putting his thoughts on paper was the only way to see things clearly.

Point one: He was being followed, or at least he *suspected* he was being followed, based on his own observations.

Point two: There was a *reason* he was being followed, though he could not imagine what that reason was. He would return to point two later.

Point three: He was being followed by at least one person who took pains to disguise himself. Twice he had heard that person speak, once in the taxi the day before and once in the Monocle. Based on the accent, the person was probably—though not necessarily— American.

This particular observation intrigued Gilliam. What if the follower were *not* American? Could it be that he was a spy? Spies use disguises, and Gilliam had seen the man speak into a paper bag as though there had been a microphone inside; that in itself was very spy-like. His follower could very well be some sort of undercover agent, American or foreign, an idea that gave no comfort whatsoever.

Suppose the agent was American. He could be a federal agent—FBI or CIA or any one of many other agencies—or a local police agent or a private detective. If not a "legitimate" agent, the man could be a criminal, a mafioso perhaps; but intuition told Gilliam that his follower was not a criminal. At length he wrote in capitals on the pad, SPY OR UNDERCOVER AGENT.

Back to point two. The agent was obviously conducting some kind of surveillance to determine his comings and goings, his daily personal contacts and acquaintances. But why? To confirm a suspicion, maybe, that he was involved in something illegal. Now, what possible association could he, Kelly Gilliam, have with illegal doings? He contemplated his connection with the Timber Rivers theft. While his association with the Committee linked him in a loose sort of way to the Timber Rivers episode, he was hard-pressed to discover a connection that would justify his being followed in so dramatic and purposeful a manner.

Perhaps he was being checked out as a possible security leak. His position with the Committee afforded access to classified information on the nuclear fission industry. The authorities, after all, were using computers to scan profiles of American Nuclear Corporation's employees to detect potential terrorists, and a similar operation aimed at federal and congressional employees was not only conceivable but also probable.

He was momentarily heartened by the prospect that other staff members might be under the same kind of surveillance. The good feeling ended, however, when he realized that an investigation should have revealed that he could not possibly have passed information on shipments of nuclear material because he'd never had access to that kind of information. Moreover, his credentials were immaculate; he'd been a lawyer with the Federal Trade Commission, for Christ's sake. Even a casual background check should have revealed that there wasn't a terrorist bone in his body.

For all the resources at the disposal of the federal government, it was inconceivable that so much attention should be devoted to *all* those whose access to information on nuclear matters equalled or surpassed that of Kelly Gilliam. Could it be that literally thousands of agents were employed to stalk *everyone* as remotely associated with the theft as himself? Hardly.

He was convinced that there had to be another factor, a reason for his being singled out for special attention.

He listed the names of the various legislative aides, staff members, and reporters with whom he'd discussed the Timber Rivers matter, starting with Burt Strong and continuing through those who were present during the first briefing in Senator Hammer's office. He wondered if one of those people, thirty-three in all, could have misconstrued something he'd said and have told the authorities that he was somehow connected to the robbery. With great care and deliberation he contemplated each name on the list, meticulously reconstructing in his mind the conversations he'd had with each person. His forehead and neck moistened as he labored through the mental gymnastics toward the unavoidable conclusion: He'd religiously observed Hammer's charge to disclose nothing of substance to anyone who had not participated in the original briefing.

Then it hit him. He'd forgotten to list his mistakenly placed telephone call to Rice in Dallas. That realization, however, raised more questions than it answered. In the first place, he'd spoken only to Rice's secretary. In the second place, Rice had called Murdock, not

Gilliam. *Murdock* should have returned the call. Why would Rice have placed a call to Murdock just before committing suicide? How could Gilliam's mistakenly returned call have mattered in the least? Unless . . .

FRIDAY, MAY 14

Since the on-off switch of his old typewriter was broken, Gilliam stooped to yank its plug from the wall after finishing the long-neglected letter to his parents. He rested his cheek on his fist and gazed wearily at the first page of a letter full of lies.

How do you tell your parents, he wondered, that their only child is *not* fine, but lonely and womanless? Or that your job has become a nightmare of fighting off suspicious reporters and little old ladies from ban-the-bomb groups? That you've been drinking far too much imported beer? Or that you suspect you're being followed?

You don't tell your parents such things. You describe instead how oppressively hot Washington has been (it's not the heat—it's the humidity). You bemoan the outrageous expense of tune-ups, gasoline, and auto insurance. You wish that the perennial tourists would bypass Washington and proceed, like lemmings, directly into the Chesapeake. You carefully imply that all is normal, avoiding any clue that you're starting to wonder about your sanity.

Gilliam rose from his cluttered, second-hand desk and walked to the door of his tiny brick balcony. Struggling to appear perfectly casual, he stepped outside into the traffic noise of Connecticut Avenue, filled his lungs with humid air, and stretched as any tired congressional staffer might do after a grueling day at the office.

The night was cloudless, but the powerful orange glow of "anticrime" street lamps obscured the stars. He'd heard that these arc lamps could kill nearby trees and shrubs by keeping them "awake" at night, and he believed it. The city, he mused, looked like a weird Faustian nightmare in their light.

Gilliam leaned on his hands and studied the immaculate hedges that bordered the lawn one story below. His eyes drifted to his right and settled on the bus-stop bench a quarter of a block up Connecticut. There, in front of the small neighborhood liquor store, was the "derelict" with a rolled *Washington Post* under his arm and a brown paper bag clutched between his hands. The arc lights cast the solitary figure in harsh relief. Gilliam walked back into his living room, locking the balcony door behind him.

It was 10:15. By now there would be no one left in Senator Hammer's office suite. Jean Murdock's office would be open to anyone with a key to the suite and a Senate I.D. to satisfy the Dirksen Building guards. Gilliam had both. He tucked his blue button-down shirt into his tan Levi cords, slipped into a pair of dirty white tennis shoes, and left the apartment.

The elevator deposited him in the basement of the old apartment building. He walked the length of the structure through the dreary underground corridor with its ancient mint-green paint to the short flight of cement steps in the rear. A steel door at the top with a small barred window would admit him to the alley called Hawthorne Street. The door, though carefully locked against entry, could be opened from the inside.

Gilliam ascended the stairs two at a time and peered through the window. Floodlights illuminated tenants' cars, which were crowded against the fence bordering Hawthorne Street and the National Zoo. Though he was certain that the rear of the building must also be under surveillance, he reasoned that inability to see an agent was unimportant. He must behave as though he suspected nothing, at least until he could determine why he was being followed. Seeing no one, he stepped through the door onto Hawthorne.

As he walked toward his Volvo, he became conscious of shadows shifting confusingly in the rustling night breeze. Every movement of tree limbs and branches acquired a threatening significance. Fears loomed from his childhood, fears that defied rational explanation. The scuffle of his sneakers on the grainy asphalt seemed inordinately loud against the distant backdrop of traffic noise on Connecticut Avenue. The millions who lived and moved in metropolitan Washington might as well have been on another planet.

A loud cackle turned his knees to water. Seconds passed as he fought against bolting away in blind panic. His mind sorted through an incredible list of monsters before he realized that a hyena had rendered its night call from somewhere in the zoo.

"Perfect," he muttered to himself while reconnecting his nerve endings.

The Volvo, as always, balked at being started and Gilliam, as always, vowed to get an overdue tune-up. The engine finally coughed to life with a barrage of clicks and clanks that gave way to rough idling. He had trouble rocking the car out of its tight parking place. When he'd at last positioned himself for a final swing around the car in front, he paused to make a final visual check of the area.

Another movement caught his eyes. It was not, he was certain, the shadow of a tree limb disturbed by the breeze. It came from a car parked near a trash dumpster to his rear, from where a driver should have been. He focused on the driver's seat a dozen yards away but saw nothing. The car, a late-model Mercury Cougar with a CB antenna, appeared empty and yet he'd seen something.

Gilliam gunned the engine, perhaps a bit too lustily, and wheeled away toward the T-intersection of Hawthorne and Cathedral avenues. The Volvo thudded over potholes and buckled asphalt while he kept one eye on the mirror. Behind him, Hawthorne Street remained black and still.

His plan called for rounding the block to Connecticut, quickly ditching the Volvo on a dark side street to confuse his followers, and catching a city-bound Metrobus for the thirty-minute ride to Capitol Hill. Cathedral Avenue traffic halted him at the T-intersection just as headlights snapped on behind him. He strained to determine whether the lights belonged to the Cougar, but his dusty rearview mirror obscured the view. He wished fervently for a hole in the traffic so he could turn right and put distance between himself and the headlights.

The lights grew larger in his mirror, and it became clear that he needed a new plan. A red light on Connecticut Avenue would detain him long enough to let his pursuers catch up, and he would never be able to turn off on a side street unobserved. He simply could not take the risk of encountering a red light.

At the first possible opportunity, he popped the clutch and swung into a left turn that would take him along the wooded eastern boundary of the National Zoo to the Rock Creek Parkway. The Volvo's engine promptly died.

"Fuck!" he whispered harshly to himself. The Volvo rolled to a stop diagonally across Cathedral. As Gilliam wound the starter and pumped the accelerator furiously, cars in both lanes braked to avoid hitting him. Horns blared as other drivers steered gingerly around the stalled Volvo.

"Fuckin' son of a bitch! Start!" Headlight beams sprawled across the left side of his face. As the Volvo's engine finally sputtered to life, Gilliam glanced over his left shoulder to see the Cougar resting at the intersection of Hawthorne and Cathedral, its left-turn signal flashing. Giddiness crawled down from his head to his stomach.

He raced the engine and feathered the clutch. With a squeal of rubber, the Volvo lunged ahead, just missing a head-on collision with a taxi. Gilliam fought the wheel to maintain control and hoped that oncoming traffic would delay the Cougar's turn until he was safely out of sight.

It did not. The driver of the Cougar defied the traffic and turned. The maneuver forced an oncoming car into a screaming emergency stop that ended with an outraged blast of its horn.

The Cougar followed him to Georgetown, a quaint jumble of nineteenth-century architecture, fashionable shops, popular bars, and notoriously poor parking. The streets were jammed with Friday nighters in search of entertaining sights, sounds, and each other. Gilliam led the Cougar around block after block in the hope that he could time a traffic signal to leave his follower at a red light, but the chance never materialized. Traffic was so thick that the Cougar always had time to recover whatever distance he was able to put between them.

In desperation, Gilliam grabbed the first parking spot that opened up. He plugged three nickels into the meter before remembering that parking tickets weren't issued after six o'clock. As the Cougar passed by, he recognized the driver—the man with the cropped blond hair who had accompanied the lobbyist/derelict/colonel to lunch at the Monocle. Whatever doubts had lingered over his being followed were now destroyed. The evidence was devastating; either *that*, or he had gone completely off his knob.

Gilliam walked briskly to M Street and paused near the entrance of the Publick House, a place well known for its steaks and atmosphere. He toyed with the idea of going in but decided not to after observing through the picture window that the late dinner crowd had thinned. He needed a crowded bar.

Further up the street was Clyde's, where a queue of sports-coated and pantsuited Friday nighters waited restlessly for other patrons to leave and provide drinking space. A bouncer who looked and smelled like a refugee from a men's cologne commercial stood guard at the door. Since Gilliam's scheme did not include waiting in line, he went straight to the bouncer.

"I'm sorry, sir," said the bouncer. "Clyde's requires a jacket after five. It's a silly rule, but it's still a rule."

Gilliam smiled as broadly as he could under the circumstances. "Tell me about it. I left mine inside earlier tonight. I'd sure appreciate it if you'd let me go get it."

The bouncer looked mildly skeptical. "What's it look like? I can have one of the waiters look for it."

"It's green corduroy," Gilliam lied, knowing that a sports coat would have looked ridiculous with jeans and sneakers. "But God, don't bother the waiters when it's this busy. I think I know where I left it. It'll take a minute."

The bouncer acquiesced and Gilliam slithered through the glut of humanity clustered in the doorway. Toward the rear was the entrance to the main dining room where a boisterous group of drinkers waited for tables. He threaded his way into the group and stood so he could keep an eye on the front door. His major concern was whether the driver of the Cougar—the man with the cropped blond hair—had seen him enter Clyde's. The question was soon answered.

The man appeared through the open door after showing something that looked like an identification packet to the bouncer. Gilliam bolted through the crowd into the dining room, spilling patrons' drinks, uttering breathy excuse-me's, incurring scowls and curses. He collided with a waiter at the swinging doors to the kitchen and just avoided knocking the man's tray of sandwiches to the floor. Chefs and dishwashers stared wide-eyed as Gilliam negotiated the counters and rolling trays that formed a miniobstacle course to the back door.

"Hey!" someone shouted from behind him. "Did you pay your check?"

The darkness of the alley did not prevent Gilliam from breaking into a dead run toward the light and bustling sound of the distant street. As he ran, he was vaguely aware of human figures in the shadows, genuine derelicts maybe, and something slimey on the ground. Once he tripped on an empty can but caught himself in time to avoid a headlong sprawl into the garbage. At last he burst into a crowd of pedestrians headed toward the corner at M Street. Panting and charged with adrenaline, he hailed a taxi and slipped inside.

"Dirksen Senate Office Building," he said breathlessly to the driver.

Friday nights seldom saw much activity on Capitol Hill—even from notorious congressional "workaholics" —and Gilliam was alone. He was grateful that his tennis shoes softened his footfalls on the Dirksen Building's tiled floors.

He decided not to enter Senator Hammer's office suite through its main door, but chose instead a research room at the far end. Before closing the door behind him, he glanced in both directions down the corridor to satisfy himself that no one had followed. Traffic lights from Constitution filtered through the venetian blinds and helped him steer around desks and type-writers as he moved toward the entrance of the next room. He placed his head close to the door and listened for movement on the other side before entering. Cautiously, he progressed through the suite toward the main offices until he came to an office adjacent to that of Jean Murdock.

He stopped. For some reason the venetian blinds in this particular office had been closed, yet his eyes adjusted to a faint glow. He heard something, a muffled clanking of metal on metal. After a silence of seconds, the unrhythmic sound came again, then yet again as though from something alive struggling with something inert. Gilliam recalled having once captured an enormous rat in a woodpile next to his family's vacation cabin in Montana. Much to his mother's displeasure, he'd kept it in a cage in the garage. At night he could hear the animal, its teeth clamped about the wire grating, struggling patiently in the hope that metal would give way before living tissue.

His eyes zeroed in on a thin crack of yellow at the bottom edge of the door to Murdock's office. Whoever was on the other side had chosen to use a table lamp rather than the fluorescent overheads, which would illuminate the reception area as well as the inner room.

Gilliam approached the door as the sound came again and again. The fact that it reminded him of *struggling* led him to believe that it was not Murdock. He couldn't imagine her struggling, ever; she was always in complete control, especially in her own office. Equally unlikely was the chance that someone else on the staff might be working late, or that the senator himself might be in the office. Not at midnight on a Friday.

Gilliam's skin crawled as he contemplated another possibility. Those who had been following him *might* have reason to be here. They might need information in Murdock's file or they might be planting listening devices. The events of the previous several days had convinced him that anything was possible.

He considered the prospect of encountering an armed burglar who would fill him full of bullet holes. His apprehension eased somewhat when he realized that any intruder would know that gunshots would attract the Capitol Hill police.

A prickly sensation spread across his neck and shoulders as his hand tightened on the doorknob. He held back for an instant and considered going to a telephone in the steno office to call the cops. Then he thought of how silly he would look if the "intruder" turned out to be a janitor or one of the senator's staff. On Capitol Hill, being wrong is no sin. Arrogance, vindictiveness, and demagoguery are tolerated. Looking silly, however, is usually unforgiveable.

Gilliam had already launched his muscles against the door when his mind screamed, What if the guy's got a *silencer* on his gun? Too late.

He bounced into the light with a breezy "Hi," certain that no one, regardless of how monstrously ruthless, could kill someone who'd just said Hi.

The intruder shrieked as she whirled away from a filing cabinet, her long blonde hair flying crazily. She tripped backward against the corner of Murdock's desk and sprawled on the carpet, her eyes wide with panic.

Gilliam started clumsily forward but stopped when he recognized the senator's daughter, Elizabeth Hammer. He started to feel sick.

"Jesus," she gasped. "Don't you ever knock?"

"I—I'm sorry," he choked. "I didn't mean to scare you." He steadied her as she rose and settled on the edge of the desk to catch her breath.

"How would you feel if I'd had a coronary because of that little trick?" she asked.

"I'd feel shitty—I mean awful. I *am* sorry, Miss Senator—I mean Miss *Hammer*. I had no idea it was you."

She regarded his long, angular face, calflike eyes, brow wrinkled in total apology under piles of unruly brown hair. Then she saw herself shrieking and out of control at the sound of his "Hi," and visualized how it must have looked to him. She burst out laughing.

Gilliam was confounded. The humor of the situation

took longer to reach him, but he finally managed a tentative giggle. Then he laughed.

The two laughed at each other laughing until their ribs ached. Gilliam hadn't felt like laughing since before Tuesday morning.

"You looked so funny standing there like you'd just filled your pants," she gasped between giggles. "Miss *Senator!*"

"*Me?* You should have seen you with your hair out to here, just like a cartoon."

At length their echoes returning from deserted corridors brought them back to earth.

"I'm Kelly Gilliam," he said. "I work for your father on the Committee staff."

"I know," she responded. "We met at a reception last fall. Remember?"

"I do. Frankly, I didn't think you would."

"I have a good memory for faces. In case you forgot, I told you that people call me Lizzie."

Gilliam groped for the next stage of conversation while noting that Lizzie's face was a softened version of the senator's with its strong jaw and prominent cheekbones. He'd seen her eyes in an old framed photograph on Burt Strong's desk: Senator and Mrs. Hammer happily sipping cocktails with Mr. and Mrs. Strong. Lizzie's eyes, though tired and bloodshot, were those of her dead mother.

"Is your office in this building?" she asked.

"No, I work in the Capitol with Burt."

"Then I'd have nearly as much right to ask you what you're doing here as you'd have asking me," she said, smiling.

"You're absolutely right. But I know what you're doing here so I don't have to ask. I heard you trying to get into that locked filing cabinet."

Lizzie looked uneasy. "I was looking for some briefs I did for Dad."

Gilliam recalled that she was a third-year law student at Georgetown University. "Those must be important briefs," he replied, "since you'd risk breaking into locked filing cabinets at midnight to get them back."

Lizzie tensed again and avoided his eyes. "I shouldn't have expected you to swallow that. On the other hand, do you mind if I ask you what *you're* doing here at midnight?"

"I thought maybe you'd demand to know what right I have to conduct an inquisition," he said with a smile intended to put her back at ease.

"It had occurred to me."

An awkward silence followed, during which Gilliam fought against disbelieving her story of briefs. He failed. While he badly wanted to share his own troubles with someone, he wondered about the time, place, and person. He could see that she was troubled, and was certain that his own state of mind must also be readable in his haggard face. They'd inadvertently caught each other doing . . . something, and like it or not, their troubles were now intertwined.

"We're both here for dark and sinister reasons, aren't we?" said Gilliam.

She answered with silence. He suspected that she was contemplating leaving, for several times she glanced at her large handbag on the floor next to the filing cabinet. Gilliam decided that his own mission in Murdock's office could wait.

"You look like you could use a drink," he ventured. "What do you say we walk over to the Hawk 'n Dove?"

"Maybe I do need a drink," she said.

They left the Dirksen Building and strolled south on First Avenue past the boldly lighted Capitol, the Supreme Court, and the Library of Congress. The night had cooled substantially and Gilliam, now conditioned by the events of the past several days, could not repress the impulse to glance backward over his shoulders, to poke his stare into every shadow, to dissect visually every passerby. If the "derelict" and the man with the cropped blond hair were near, they were invisible.

At Independence Avenue the pair turned left past the newly finished Madison Building, a rectangular marble bunker housing annexes for the Library of Congress and congressional offices. A block east of the Madison Building they bore right on Pennsylvania and strolled past bars still alive with patrons. The Hawk 'n Dove, an English-style pub patronized heavily by congressional staffers, blared Mick Jagger's "Wild Horses" as Gilliam and Lizzie entered. They followed a waiter to a rear room hung with ancient tintypes of Civil War officers. Gilliam ordered beers as the jukebox changed to an instrumental.

Neither had said much during the short walk from Senator Hammer's office. Gilliam had devised a scheme for subtly relieving Lizzie of her motive for burglary and was taken aback when she suddenly told him.

"I suspect that Dad's being blackmailed," she said rather matter-of-factly before taking a sip of beer. Gilliam drained half his glass while searching for a response.

"By whom? Murdock?"

"How did you guess?"

"You were in her office trying to get into her files."

"Brilliant. She locks absolutely *everything*."

"Why do you suspect her?"

Lizzie hesitated. "I really don't know why I should get into this with you."

"Aside from the fact that I caught you doing a very naughty thing, there's always the chance that I can help."

Lizzie took another long draft of beer and closed her eyes for a moment. "And I suppose you are perfectly justified in sneaking around other people's offices at midnight. I have something on you, too."

"So let's trade stories," said Gilliam. "We owe each other an explanation."

"Okay, but when you hear what I have to go on, you'll think I'm crazy." She finished her beer. Gilliam liked women who liked beer.

"The same goes for me. Now, why do you think Murdock's blackmailing your dad?"

"For starters, I know that Jean lies to him," she said. "A few months ago, February to be exact, I went to a convention in Dallas—a Women in Law convention. When I arrived at the airport, I just happened to see Jean waiting to get on a flight to Washington."

"So?"

"She was feverishly kissing a guy."

Gilliam signaled the waiter for two more beers. "People do that all the time in airports," he said.

"Not when . . ." Lizzie hesitated and dropped her eyes to the wooden tabletop.

Gilliam finished the sentence for her. "Not when you're Jean Murdock, administrative aide to Harry Hammer. Right?"

"Among other things," she answered softly. "She saw me but pretended not to. I waved to her, but she just turned away, hanging on the guy's arm."

Gilliam had a rush of intuition but allowed the waiter to deposit two fresh beers and retrieve the empty glasses before speaking. "This guy. Was he tall with graying hair and a mustache—sharp-looking guy?"

Lizzie looked astounded. "How did you know?"

"Do you know him?"

"Yes, of course I do. That's what set me off on this blackmail trip. His name is Wesley Rice and he's a big operator with American Nuclear Corporation. But I didn't realize it until I met him last month at a reception on the Hill."

"This is becoming very interesting," Gilliam said. "Keep going."

Lizzie narrowed her eyes. "I'm still not sure I should. This is a very private thing and I really don't know you."

Gilliam fought down impatience and tried to be calming. "Lizzie, I know from what you've told me so far that our problems have some of the same trappings. Believe me, I'm on your side. I'll tell everything I know if you will. Now, *please* . . ."

"Okay, okay. Before I knew that it was Wesley Rice I saw kissing Jean in the airport, I told Dad that I had seen her in Dallas. Naturally, I didn't mention the circumstances. I'll confess to having a little cat in me and I wanted to see how much he knew about her—specifically, whether Dad knew if Jean had someone else on the side."

"Someone else?"

"What you've probably heard is true, Kelly. It's no secret, not even from me."

"You don't like her much, do you?"

"I won't pretend that I don't resent her. I guess the memory of my mother is still too strong. Even though I would never expect Dad to become a monk, I just wish he'd fallen for someone else."

"Did you feel this way before you saw Murdock with Rice?"

"Yeah, I did. She's as different from my mother as cats and dogs. My mother was totally devoted, just gave and gave and gave. While Dad was busy with politics, my mother not only took care of my brother and me but went on the political circuit with Dad. She shook the hands, ate the crummy catered food at political dinners, threw receptions and parties, the whole bit. She never even asked for a thank-you. She just gave.

"Jean's the total opposite. She's a *taker*, Kelly. Have you ever noticed how some people seem to exude energy that others can pick up on? Well, there's another kind of person—Jean's kind—who saps the energy of those around her. But she can turn it off and on like a switch. When she's around my dad, she *drains* him. It's hard to explain, but I've seen it. How else do you think she was able to take over at the office?"

Gilliam nodded his agreement with her theory, for he, too, had seen Murdock in action, especially with Strong. "You still haven't told me about the lie," he said.

Lizzie took a slow sip of beer before continuing. "Well, when I told Dad about seeing her in Dallas, he very emphatically told me that I was mistaken. When I insisted that what I said was true, he blew up. At me! I haven't seen him like that since I was ten. He said that Jean had been in Milwaukee visiting her parents and that he didn't want to hear another word about it."

"And that proves she lied to him?"

"Of course. That was obviously what she told him and he believed her."

"I'll accept that. Now get into the blackmail part."

Lizzie explained how she had often overheard Murdock convincing her father to support federal measures and policies advocated by the nuclear industry. Quite often, she said, these "lobbying" sessions occurred after hours at the Hammer home in Lake Barcroft, Virginia, where Murdock spent much time. Her father had often been convinced, said Lizzie, to act against his instincts by Murdock.

Lizzie told how it had been Murdock who convinced Hammer to support a bill to create competition for the federal government in the uranium enrichment industry. The senator had always had misgivings about turning enrichment technology over to private enterprise because he'd been concerned that the nuclear industry, once in possession of the technology and federally backed loans and subsidies, would sell the ability to enrich uranium to any nation with the money to buy. Enriched uranium is used not only to fuel reactors, but also to build atomic bombs. Despite the senator's concern over nuclear proliferation, Murdock had convinced him to push passage of an industry bill.

"It's happened time and again, Kelly," said Lizzie. "Dad always knuckles under. I'm convinced that Jean is holding something over him and that the situation has become a crisis, especially since they changed the subject once or twice when they knew I was listening."

"In other words," said Gilliam, "you think she's blackmailing him for his cooperation in getting laws passed to benefit people like Wesley Rice."

"Maybe, but I don't know. It's been bits and pieces over the past few years, and now it seems like Dad has just gone over the edge. Recently, he's stayed hidden away in his den until Jean comes to the house. He won't talk to me or to anyone except *her*. Not even Burt can get through to him."

"Have you said anything about this to Burt?" Gilliam asked.

"No. He's got problems enough of his own, and I don't want to hurt him any more. I guess I feel sorry for him. For all his gruffness, he's a great old guy. He and Betty never had any kids of their own, and they sort of adopted my brother, Scott, and me. When Scott graduated from med school, Burt flew all the way to L.A. just to be there for the celebration. Dad couldn't make it."

"Do you have any idea of what Murdock might have on your father?"

"It could be that she's just using herself, but I think there's something else. I have no idea what it is."

"I hate to bring this up, but why were you in her office?"

Lizzie took a long, weary breath. "Two reasons. I was looking for something, *anything*, that might incriminate her, that I could use to jolt my father out of her grip. Correspondence, maybe, or a secret file with stuff linking her to the nuclear industry."

"That's one. What's the other?"

"The office payroll records. I've been around here long enough to know that staff is reimbursed for business travel expenses. It's a long shot, I realize, but I thought maybe Jean might have gone to Dallas in

February on *business*. If I could find a finance office voucher, I could take it to Dad and show him that she had lied to him, that she had gone to Dallas and not Milwaukee. If he could see for himself what she really is, I'm sure he'd straighten things out and send her on her way. I hate the thought of hurting him, but he can't go on like this, Kelly. He doesn't sleep, he doesn't talk, he doesn't go out, and he's started drinking again. That's a war I thought we'd won years ago."

"Lizzie," Gilliam said softly, "I think this thing is much more serious than throwing Murdock out of the office or getting your father to jilt her."

He began his own story with his mistakenly placed call to Rice in Dallas. News of Rice's suicide shocked Lizzie, since she'd missed the sparse coverage the event received. Like Gilliam, she wondered at the timing of the Timber Rivers theft and Rice's death.

He related how he was being followed, how he'd evaded the man with cropped blond hair, and then sought her opinion on whether he was out of his mind. She agreed that the evidence pointing to his being under surveillance was convincing. Next, he revealed his theory that the authorities somehow knew of his call to Rice. The investigation, he theorized, must have revealed Rice's complicity in the theft. Then someone had wrongly deduced that Gilliam's call meant that he too might be involved. The investigators must be shadowing him to confirm their suspicions or to see what he would do next.

Lizzie observed that his call to Rice seemed like a weak reason for suspicion, but conceded that any other possible reason for total surveillance was at least as unlikely.

"What are you going to do now?" she asked.

"Well, I had planned to search Murdock's office for some record of her having talked to Rice—a memo, maybe—that I could use to shift the focus away from me. Like a fool, I threw away the phone message that she'd clipped to the legal pad right after I returned her call for her. I quizzed the office receptionists about the call from Dallas, but none of them remembers getting it. Things were happening pretty fast that day."

"One thing seems certain," said Lizzie. "If the cops suspected you were guilty before, they're probably convinced of it now. You'll have to admit that you've acted pretty guilty, eluding your tail like that."

"I'm afraid you're right," Gilliam confessed. "I'm also afraid that there's not much we can do about this thing all by ourselves. If Murdock is blackmailing your father, it could be related to the Timber Rivers thing. If that's the case, you and I are way out of our league."

Lizzie looked frightened. "What are you suggesting?"

"I'm suggesting that our problems—yours and mine —have two things in common: Murdock and Rice. You suspect that Murdock was romantically involved with Rice. I suspect that Rice was somehow involved with the Timber Rivers theft. I've got *my* problem because Rice called Murdock just before he put a gun to his head. You've got *your* problem because Murdock may be blackmailing your dad. Ergo, I should talk to the guys who are following me."

Lizzie's eyes opened wide. "Kelly, you can't do that. You'd put Jean right into the spotlight. If the press ever learned that she was being investigated for the Timber Rivers theft, Dad would be finished. You know how these things are."

"Now wait a minute," protested Gilliam. "I work for Harry Hammer and I'm being investigated. Don't you think that reflects on him?"

"You don't even know for certain *why* those people are following you," whispered Lizzie. "Besides, you're not Dad's administrative aide and you haven't been his mistress for the last six years."

"That's true. I am not, nor have I ever been, his

mistress. But doesn't it bother you that Murdock may be involved in the heist up to her ears? It's possible, you know. Where does that put your father?"

"Kelly, we need some time. There's no reason to jump to conclusions or to do anything drastic."

"That's easy for you to say. You don't have to live with those goons watching every move you make."

Lizzie reached across the table for his hand and gripped it with both of hers. "Kelly, give me a week before you do anything. Give me a week to find something that I can give to Dad to prove Jean is a liar. I know he'll throw her out on her ear if I can only prove something. By that time, you may find out that those people who are following you aren't what you think they are. You've got to admit that you're scared and that you might be on the wrong track. Those people—the CIA or the FBI, or whoever they are—might have nothing whatever to do with stolen plutonium. Please, Kelly. You said you were on my side. Give me a week."

Gilliam stared into space and pondered the ugly prospect of another seven days in the company of the "derelict" and the man with the cropped blond hair. Distasteful as the thought was, he did want to help Lizzie. She'd told him her troubles in presumed strict confidence, a major factor in his lawyer's mind. Moreover, she was desperate. On the other hand, waiting a week could have disastrous consequences if Murdock, by some outlandish stretch of the imagination, was the key to solving the Timber Rivers case. He'd come to appreciate well the implications of eighty kilograms of missing plutonium.

Against his better judgment he said, "Okay, one week. That gives you until next Friday. But you've got to promise that you'll stop trying to break into filing cabinets. That's illegal." Lizzie smiled her thanks.

On the walk back to the Dirksen parking garage, Gilliam suddenly realized how exhausted he was. While the beer had numbed his tension, the effects of fitful sleep and strain were taking a toll. Lizzie offered to save him cab fare by taking him to his car in George-town, and he accepted gratefully. His head lolled wea-rily against the headrest of her green Datsun 280-Z as they drove away from Capitol Hill and within minutes, he was snoring noisily.

Lizzie wheeled to a stop in the loading zone fronting the Park West Apartments on Connecticut Avenue next to the National Zoo. Gilliam awakened with a yawn and blinked at the discovery that she'd driven him home.

"I didn't take you to your car because I was afraid you were too tired to drive," she said. "Do you remem-ber waking up to tell me where you live?"

Gilliam smiled. "No, I don't. Thanks, Lizzie. Don't forget to call the minute you learn anything."

"I won't. Bye."

He waved as she sped away. As he walked to the entryway of the old apartment building, someone was leaving his apartment. Gilliam had no way of knowing that just minutes earlier, electronic listening devices had been placed behind light switches in every room of his apartment, and that five hidden pairs of eyes now watched his every step.

Someone wanted to be sure that Gilliam could not again escape surveillance.

SATURDAY, MAY 15

Jagged inlets and fjords reach landward from the North Atlantic into Maine's coast like arthritic fingers. Countless natural harbors shelter the wood-blanketed inner shore from an often-angry ocean while the outer points endure the constant pounding of whitewater surf.

Forty-five miles northeast of Portland, the first major city on a northbound coastal route through Maine, lies the tiny village of Damariscotta, a bayside cluster of rickety docks and lobstermen's shacks fringed by neat houses with brightly painted shutters. A thick forest of northern hardwoods and evergreens ventures to the edge of the stony bayshore. Damariscotta's handful of year-round citizens take lobsters and shellfish from the sea in wooden boats and grow summer gardens for vegetables to sell with their seafood. Others rent out small summer cottages nestled in the forest along the coast. Many of the permanent citizens came from distant cities on holiday excursions and became quietly addicted to the moody sky and sea, the fragrance of conifers and salty air, and the lack of urgency in the rhythmic pounding of tides.

Damariscotta has lobster markets, a seasonal seafood restaurant, a general store-post office, and a Gulf station. Those needing bars, churches, or other signs of civilization continue up the curving asphalt highway to

Newcastle, or better yet, head south to Bath, a moderately busy little city with a moderate sense of urgency.

The elderly owner of a wharfside market plunged his scarred hand into a water tank, withdrew three live lobsters, and crammed the trio unceremoniously into a collapsible cardboard box. After winding string tightly around the box, he clapped it onto the counter.

"That's thirteen-fifty for the lobsters, even three for the clams," he said to the lean young man with auburn hair and mustache. "Sorry I can't sell ya vegetables. End o' July, though, I'll sell ya all ya need. That's sixteen-fifty."

The young man dug through the pockets of his jacket and pants in search of something smaller than a fifty-dollar bill, but found only a few ones and some change. Hesitantly, he held the fifty toward the old Downeaster. "Got change for this?"

The proprietor squinted at the bill and then glanced into his till. "I can handle it."

Duncan Rossiter's next stop was the general store, where he pawed through a sparse selection of lettuce, green beans, cucumbers, and tomatoes, all imported from the south. Having gathered the makings of a garden salad, he loaded his cart with sundry household goods, paid, and left.

He deposited the sacks in the rear of his white Volkswagen "Thing" with the box of lobsters and the plastic bag of clams as the midmorning sun peered briefly from behind great piles of clouds. He wheeled the Thing north onto Highway 1, away from Damariscotta.

He relished the air whipping through the open window across his face. Familiar salt and wood smells brought back youthful memories of weeks spent on this coast, of times when he could be alone—away from his barking father who turned summer-long Maine outings into contrived hells—to climb and laze among the jagged rocks along the shore. He remembered venturing perilously close to the crashing breakers without the slightest fear of losing his footing on the slippery boulders. The possibility of falling into the sea and being dashed to death against the shore had never entered his head.

His father had hated fear more than any other weakness and had forced his son's confrontation with every conceivable childhood dread. To combat his son's fear of the dark, he locked the child for hours in a dark room. Only when the boy was able to assert in a clear and unquivering voice that he was not afraid would he be let out. The fear of dogs was dealt with by forcing the child to stand just out of the reach of a tethered German shepherd that had been trained as a guard dog and cued by its trainer to attack. Only when the boy could stand within inches of the enraged animal and smile unflinchingly at his father would the exercise end. His father dreamed up an unending succession of such jarring exercises.

"It was no jittery pansy that came to Texas to find oil," he'd once thundered to Duncan in reference to his own father. "Making a fortune takes nerves, and *keeping* it takes even more. My daddy showed me early that a man doesn't need to be afraid of *anything*, because no matter how bad things get, there's only so much that can happen to you. Don't you ever forget that, Dunk."

Driving up the familiar coast took him deep into his past, deeper than he cared to go. He sat helplessly at the wheel as memories unfolded in his head like a movie he had no wish to see. The scenes were disjointed and dangling, the characters extinct, but the story held together too well.

The small boy stood in his pajamas at the top of the stairwell, his eyes wide against the dark. Angry shouts came from the room below, the library. His mother's voice, thick with alcohol, rose in a crescendo of obscenity hurled at his father. While the five-year-old child could hardly fathom the vulgarity of her words, he had no trouble catching the hate. The anger seemed to swirl about like an invisible, poisonous cloud that seeped upward and outward, freezing everything it touched. He'd heard it and felt it before, but never as intensely as this.

"You seem to think I'm like a piece of property that you can manage or store like a goddamn oil rig," his mother screamed. "I'm tired of slinking around here like a pet dog. I've *had* it with being carted off to your fuckin' parties. I've had it with getting your permission before I can go to the john. I've had it with *you!*"

The small boy heard the movement of his father's stride across the library.

"So you've had it, eh? You seem to forget, honey, what you *were* before I came along. Do you think maybe I don't know you were screwin' every roughneck in the Panhandle who walked into your daddy's diner? Do you think I don't know you were trying to screw your way out of waiting on tables and washing greasy dishes? Well, I know, honey, and I knew *then*, too. What I don't know is what you're trying to screw your way out of now."

There was more movement below.

"Well, pardon *me*, reverend. I won't offend you any more. I'm getting out of here, and if you try to stop me, so help me I'll kill you!"

"And just where do you think you'll go?"

"It's none of your goddam business, that's where. No more goody-two-shoes wife bullshit for me. If I never see this barn again, it'll be too soon!"

"You take so much as a piece of silverware with you, and I'll have your ass thrown in jail."

"Don't worry. Being broke is worth being rid of you and the little beast upstairs. Maybe you haven't noticed, but you're turning him into another *you*, which suits me just fine because you deserve to go through life with another *you*."

"He's not a little beast! He's our son!"

"He's a *beast!* And he's *yours,* not mine. You've turned him into something that's not normal, but you can't see it. You're too blind. He's a *beast!*"

The child never saw his mother again and often tried, but failed, to rediscover her face in the depths of his memory. Though her face was lost to him, his recollection of her voice was vivid. So was the unquenchable hatred it had conveyed on that final night before she vanished with nothing but the clothes on her back and a bus ticket to somewhere. He could not separate the sound of her voice from the content of her words. She'd called him a *beast.*

Yet the small boy had studied his reflection in a mirror, letting his eyes wander over every detail. At first he had seen nothing that was not in the faces of other children. He had eyes, ears, a nose, hair. If he looked very closely, however, he could see . . . something.

As he grew, his ability to see the difference improved. He imagined that under the flesh of his face was the real Duncan, the creature his own mother had found so ugly that she could not claim it.

The boy began to perceive other children as having been stamped out of a common mold, like robots or ants. To him, their voices all sounded the same. They laughed at the same things. Their crayon drawings were incredibly alike, all sticks for arms and legs and misshapen heads. Their faces varied, but superficially, in color of hair and eyes, only his own, he believed, hid something different—a beast.

Duncan's schooling at Houston's exclusive Danby Academy became a veritable hell. Like his father's house, the school had what seemed a never-ending list of rules: *wait for your turn at the drinking fountain; raise your hand if you want to speak; no running in the halls; keep your desk tidy;* and so on. He discovered very early that fear enforced these rules, which he perceived as having been designed to make everyone behave alike. Since he considered himself the only individual among the multitude of obedient robots, he concluded that the rules were really aimed only at him.

Duncan marched onto the sunny playground with the other children following a man in a white T-shirt and a baseball cap. It was time to try out for the Spring Inter-City Track Meet. Duncan broke off from the group at the apron of the track and sat down in the grass.

"What's with you, Rossiter?" shouted a boy with blond hair and a face spattered with freckles. "Are you too chicken to try out?"

Duncan had no intention of joining the tryouts and ignored the jab.

"He's just a pansy-ass," shouted another boy. "Let him sit by the flowers like a fairy." The group laughed in unison.

"That'll be enough of that!" shouted the man in the baseball cap. "What's your name, son?" Duncan raised his eyes to see that the man was speaking to him.

"Duncan Rossiter."

"Don't you want to try out, son? You know, you just might be the star of the team."

"I'm not going to try out," Duncan replied evenly.

The man squatted beside him in the grass, pushed the baseball cap back on his head, and leaned close to speak in a low tone. "Hey, don't you want to show these other guys that you're no pansy? Heck, you look strong to me. I bet you could run the socks off these other guys. How 'bout it?"

"I'm not going to try out."

The man was taken aback by his utter failure to develop rapport and soundly miffed by this blunt disregard of his authority. "Now, what if everyone was scared of trying out? What if they all just sat down like you? I'd have a mess, wouldn't I? Get up and get in line."

Rage began to boil beneath Duncan's face as a thick

hand grabbed his arm just below the shoulder and hoisted him into the air.

"You're going to be the first to try out for the standing broad jump, young man." The rage bubbled over. The man let go of Duncan and turned back to the other boys. "Okay, we've got our first entry in the standing broad jump," he shouted. Duncan crouched next to the apron lined with painted white stones.

"Coach, look out!" shouted the boy with the freckles. Duncan threw the stone with all his might at the man's skull.

A year passed. The special school tried to teach the boy that harming others would not solve his problems, and he pretended to learn. He even feigned remorse for having injured another human being because he knew that's what the doctors and counselors wanted. He knew that they would eventually let him go, and they did.

The gangling fifteen-year-old stared at the red Jaguar convertible in the driveway. The car was his father's newest toy and taking it would require breaking an arch rule. "When I'm sure you can handle a stick shift, I'll take you out in the Jag," his father had said. "Your learner's permit doesn't mean you're ready for a car like this." Duncan couldn't imagine being more ready.

As he put the car through its gears, he discovered that his reflexes were easily a match for the gearbox and clutch. The stupidity of rules was again exposed and the glory of breaking them was intensified by the rapture of speed and control.

After a half hour of increasing speed, confidence, and exhilaration, he was still within the limits of his reflexes, but driving without past experience or body-learned judgment. His mirror flashed red lights just as he veered into the oncoming lane of a country road to overtake another car. The Jag flew by the slower car and returned to the right side of the road, just missing a large truck that loomed to meet it at the crest of a shallow hill. The truck took the shoulder to avoid the pursuing police car.

The flashing lights grew larger and, for an awful instant, Duncan fastened his eyes on the mirror, as though the hate that streamed from them could be reflected backward to annihilate the pursuers. He missed seeing the road sign that warned of a curve to the right. An experienced driver might have negotiated the turn at ninety miles an hour in the low Jaguar, but such a feat was well beyond Duncan's skill. The car slid into the left lane with a scream of rubber on asphalt. His foot missed the brake pedal entirely as the Jaguar tipped madly to the left and careened into a squealing spin toward the far ditch.

Through some miracle the car didn't roll, but skittered into the ditch, flailing a stream of dirt and weeds into the air behind. The wheel wrenched itself from Duncan's aching fingers as he instinctively threw his weight again and again to the brake pedal. He watched helplessly as fence posts loomed in front. Momentum carried the Jaguar into the depression and up the other side. The car bucked angrily as it sheared through three posts, leaving splintery spikes in the ground, before whirling to a halt in a cluster of tall weeds.

During the beating, Duncan remained silent.

"See what happens when you break the rules, you little bastard!" his father thundered. "You end up in a heap o' trouble that makes trouble for everybody around you." A fist slammed into Duncan's jaw and the world became a dizzy display of sparks and stars. His father's voice sliced through the pain and fire as Duncan thudded to the floor. "If you were a year older, they'd send your fuckin' ass to jail! Get up! You're not hurt. Not like you're going to be."

When it was over, he was hurt. He lay on the carpet of the library, his head swimming with images of cops, fingerprints, and hard jail floors, his ears echoing the low voice of his father's lawyer. All of it was extinct, all part of another age. His father gripped a handful of his auburn hair and jerked his head up off the carpet.

"Let me tell you something, boy. This time you fucked up royally, but I'm gonna get you out of it. It ain't gonna be easy. In the meantime, you're gonna stay in this house, do what I tell you, and be what I say—every goddam minute of every day. You'll see nothing but the inside of classrooms and this house. And that's the way it's gonna be until you're too big for me to handle. Understand?"

He lay quietly as the sound of his father's boots on the carpet vanished. When he'd regained his equilibrium and tested his muscles and bones, he rose painfully and went to his room. It was late, but he had no intention of sleeping.

The house grew dark and quiet. Duncan's rage fed on the tension and eagerness he'd felt in the moments before the accident.

Dewy grass rippled over his ankles and the tops of his deck shoes as he walked past the pool toward the gardener's shed. He had no need of the moon since he knew every inch of this sprawling estate. The pair of guard dogs his father had bought to discourage prowlers escorted him playfully to the shed. He could not feel their tongues on his hands because he wore the mittens his father had bought him on their most recent hunting trip to Idaho. Duncan didn't want to leave fingerprints.

The beam of his flashlight sprawled across neatly hung yard maintenance equipment on the walls of the shed. The pungent smell of gasoline and oil bit his nostrils. In one corner of the shed, amid various kinds of tools, was a large riding mower—a small tractor, really —that was fueled from a gasoline drum equipped with a hand-operated pump. He primed the pump and began to fill a five-gallon can he'd found among the gardener's paraphernalia. As the gasoline flowed, he visualized every detail and movement of his mission, taking great care to leave out nothing.

Duncan congratulated himself on bridging the gap between reacting to emotion and using his brain. Hadn't the doctors said that he was brilliant? Hadn't his teachers consistently noted his intelligence? He would prove exactly how intelligent he was. Rage had been tempered with calculation. The beast waited patiently as he readied the gasoline can and a length of nautical twine that hung in a coil on the wall. The twine, he knew, was strong enough to withstand his father's weight against the bedroom door. . . .

Rossiter snapped back to reality at the sight of gulls floating high above a boulder-strewn cove flanked by wooded hills. Maine—the present—many blurred years after the great killing fire in a rich Houston suburb. The unwanted play came to an end. Rossiter turned off the road toward the ocean and maneuvered along a rutted path that seemed like a tunnel through the forest. Soon he would come to a house overlooking a rocky slope into the sea.

Deputy Sheriff Fritz Steadman unwrapped a Snickers bar he'd just selected from the candy case on Nattie Rosenheim's counter. He wadded the wrapper noisily and arched it over Nattie's head to the wastebasket, where it landed with a clunk.

"Two points," he said through a mouthful of chocolate and peanuts.

"And twenty cents," said Nattie, thrusting her open palm over the counter.

"I remember when Snickers were a nickel," complained Steadman as he dug for two dimes. "Everything just keeps going up and up."

Nattie rang the sale on her ancient cash register and cast a glance at the gouged and broken fishing tackle cabinet on the shop's opposite wall. "And things are going to get higher in this place if we don't stop those damned burglars," she said. "Three hundred dollars worth of rods and reels this time. Second break-in in two months."

Steadman pushed the remaining bit of Snickers into his mouth and sauntered across the shop of Rosenheim's Marina to the empty cabinet. With chubby hands resting on an ample waist, he bent close to the broken lock and squinted.

"We just might get some fingerprints, Nattie. Must've been kids. A pro could've picked this little lock with no trouble. No need to bust it up like this. Yeah, we'll get some prints." He enjoyed sounding professional.

"Fingerprints won't do any good unless you catch the little hoodlums," observed Nattie.

"We'll catch 'em when they try to unload the goods. I doubt they're smart enough to go any further than Bath or Newcastle. They might even try it right here in Chamberlain or Damariscotta." Steadman hoped that his confidence impressed the woman. It didn't.

Steadman got his fingerprint kit from his cruiser in the parking lot and made a great ritual of lifting the "latents" from the cabinet. Nattie's two teen-age sons watched the procedure with mild interest until their mother intervened with a list of chores. Steadman finished jotting notes in his spiral pad and stepped through the dockside door of the shop into the brilliant morning sunshine. He planned to scout around the premises in search of little clues that might help him "get the goods," as he was fond of saying, on the burglars. He'd once found a pocket knife at the scene of a similar crime and had traced it to a tackle shop in nearby Damariscotta. The shopowner happened to remember the youth who had bought the knife and the rest was simple.

This was one of four crimes Steadman had solved in sixteen years as a deputy sheriff. Scores of others had gone unsolved. Fortunately, this little length of coast was seldom the scene of any really serious crimes. When such crimes did occur, the state police most often took charge under the usually correct assumption that out-of-staters were at the root, and the investigations were coordinated at levels far above Deputy Sheriff Fritz Steadman.

Steadman's youthful resentment of his lack of serious work and his subsequent inability to make his mark in the world of law enforcement had long since faded. He'd become content with his cheery wife, their warm little house near Damariscotta, and weekend fishing excursions to Monhegan Island. Occasionally he succumbed to fantasies that saw him shooting it out with armed bank robbers to rescue at least a dozen thankful hostages. At times he'd even toyed with the idea of running for sheriff himself.

Steadman was nearly blinded by the dazzling whiteness of the huge Hatteras yacht moored astern in Rosenheim's largest slip. He donned his sunglasses and focused on the ornately painted name on her stern:

GOLDEN GIRL
Corpus Christi

Nattie emerged from the boat's canvas-covered bridge and descended the gleaming chrome ladder to the deck as Steadman approached wide-eyed. She climbed onto the dock as he came within earshot.

"Doesn't look like they touched any of the boats," she said.

"Who?" said Steadman.

"The burglars, Fritz, the *burglars*. They didn't break into the boats. I was especially concerned about this one."

"Oh, yeah," replied Steadman sheepishly. "Say, that's some boat. Ship would be a better word. Who's she belong to, anyway?"

"Fella by the name of Godwin, from Texas."

They strolled away from the yacht toward the marina shop, past gasoline pumps, moored dinghies, and neatly stacked lobster traps made of wood and chicken wire.

"This guy Godwin must be the first of the big-time tourist crowd, eh?"

"I s'pose so," answered Nattie.

"Vessel that size is big enough for a whole clan, I'd say. Was his family with him?"

"No, just a couple of friends. I know they weren't his family because one of them was a black man. The woman was Japanese, I think. Come to think of it, she might have been his wife though she looked a little old for Mr. Godwin."

"Did you catch the names of his friends?"

"Nope, didn't ask. They just loaded their stuff into their car and took off after paying six weeks of keeping on the *Golden Girl*—in advance."

"When did they get here?"

"Wednesday."

Steadman's memory flickered back to the previous Monday—five days earlier—when Sheriff McIntyre had assembled all the county's deputy sheriffs to read a dispatch issued jointly by the FBI and the state police. Law enforcement officers of all jurisdictions, the dispatch said, must be doubly alert for all unusual activities in the wake of a violent and well-planned theft of radioactive material in Connecticut. Federal authorities warned that the robbers were heavily armed and extremely dangerous, that they had probably crossed a state line, but there was no clue as to which state line they may have crossed. Sheriff McIntyre stressed the urgency of the situation and impressed upon his men the need to explore every unusual incident, no matter how small or seemingly inconsequential, with an eye to the possibility that the robbers might be in this jurisdiction.

Steadman recalled thinking to himself how absurd it was to suggest that the attackers might have fled to this little stretch of coast. Nothing big ever happens here, he mused. He found himself half wishing that they *had* come, that he could have an opportunity to vary his routine of small burglaries, family quarrels, and car accidents. He wondered how he would perform if one of his violent fantasies suddenly became a reality. *All unusual activities . . .*

"Just how big is that boat, Nattie? Fifty feet, maybe?"

"She's a forty-seven-foot Hatteras with two big diesels and lots of range. She's a beauty, isn't she?"

"Yeah, sure is. You get many of these?"

"Some. Not usually this time of year, though. Mr. Godwin and his party are a little early."

"Are they going to take her out fishing this weekend?"

"Doubt it. Mr. Godwin said we probably wouldn't see them again until they're ready to shove off for home."

"Seems a little strange that someone would come all the way from Texas in a boat like that and just leave her at the dock while the fishing's so good, doesn't it?"

"They're probably visiting friends, Fritz. Lots of rich people just leave their yachts in the slips. They don't have to worry about using them to make them pay like we would. I'll tell you what's strange. Mr. Godwin wouldn't leave a number where he could be reached. I'd think anyone with a boat like the *Golden Girl* would want to know if there was an accident or fire or something."

Steadman agreed and ventured several more questions concerning the Godwin party's baggage and car. Nattie remembered nothing unusual about their baggage except that they seemed to have an awful lot—some of it apparently very heavy—and that it had to be tied down all over their car.

"Fella from a rental outfit brought the car over and left the keys for Mr. Godwin with me in the shop. It was a VW open jeep. Said Mr. Godwin had rented it by mail and had already paid by money order—in advance. I'll tell you, Fritz, this Mr. Godwin must not like any loose ends. Cash in advance, all the time. He would have gotten along fine with my dear departed husband."

"Did they say where they were going to stay?"

"Nope. Figured it was none of my business unless they offered to let me know."

Steadman reflected silently for a moment over the previous Monday's dispatch and wondered if what Nattie had just told him qualified as an *unusual* activity. "Well, I guess I'll head out now, Nattie." He turned to leave.

"Don't forget your fingerprint stuff, Fritz."

"Oh, yeah. Thanks." He retrieved the carefully taken latents along with his fingerprint kit from the counter in the shop and departed Rosenheim's Marina, deep in thought.

Veterans of jungle warfare often awake to sounds they've almost heard—distant rustlings of leaves disturbed by a passing foot, movement of clothing against flesh, changes in the air caused by approaching engines or any of a hundred things—to brace for a danger that may or may not come. Leon T. Jackson awoke well before the engine of Rossiter's Volkswagen actually became audible and sat upright on the sofa bed. His four tours in the damp, canopied forests of Vietnam had matured the survival instincts that a childhood in the Bedford-Stuyvesant ghetto had planted, and he knew intuitively that there was no danger.

Jackson glanced at his watch and, seeing that it was nearly noon, grimaced for having slept so long. Of course, a long sleep was probably just what he needed, especially since he'd not slept much since the boat trip from Connecticut. The edge of adrenaline was still too much with him to permit much rest.

He was glad that Rossiter was returning; he was hungry and knew that Rossiter would bring food. It was good to feel hungry again, now that they were safely hidden in an isolated house in the woods, far from the likely hiding places that federal officers, soldiers, and police must now be frantically searching. He half regretted that he would soon leave the rustic little house with its warm, wood-paneled rooms, massive stone fireplace, and spectacular picture-window view of the thundering Atlantic. In the preceding months, while laboring to convert one of its three small bedrooms to a laboratory, he'd become attached to the place. With Rossiter and Bates, he'd worked under Yoshi Nakamura's watchful eye—for she'd designed the lab from the ground up—until the shielding was in place, until Formica-covered tables and special drains were implanted in the floor and sinks were installed. Then came the shelving that soon accommodated the various kinds of radiation detectors and metallurgical equipment that Nakamura had ordered, the dies, grips, and assorted lengths of tubing, the electrical generator and its heavy-duty wiring. A converted closet was insulated and fireproofed to house an array of dangerous chemicals and metals, one of which was in a box padded with styrofoam, held together by steel bands, and marked:

CAUTION!
Toxic Metal
BERYLLIUM

The heaviest work was installing lab plumbing from the outdoor well. Propane gas was piped in from an extremely unwieldy tank that Rossiter had brought in on a rented flatbed truck. The final piece of equipment was something Nakamura called an induction furnace, apparently a critical item in preparing plutonium metal for what Rossiter had in mind.

Jackson gathered up the sheets and blankets, folded the sofa bed into itself, and pulled on a clean pair of jeans and a shirt from his suitcase in the living room. From the laboratory came the sounds of Nakamura puttering around with her atoms, chemicals, and whatever else nuclear physicists putter around with. He vaguely wondered what she might be doing. He knew that she and Rossiter planned to initiate a rigorous training session during which they would go over the metallurgical steps needed to reduce the plutonium to its pure metallic form. He assumed that Nakamura was preparing for the practice sessions or, for all he knew, maybe even *practicing* for the practice sessions. He considered going to the lab and simply asking what she was up to, but soon dropped the idea, since he could hardly expect to understand her inevitably precise explanation of exactly what she was doing.

Yoshi Nakamura sure was strange, he observed to himself for the hundredth time. Of her past, he had only a vague knowledge—that she was orphaned during World War II and had somehow ended up in an American detention camp in California. He'd often heard Rossiter remark about her brilliance and her qualifications for this particular job, but Jackson hadn't the faintest idea of why a brilliant scientist who looked a decade younger than her actual age would entangle herself in a scheme that demanded robbery and murder.

By contrast, he thought he knew the motives of his other colleagues. His own were a promised one million dollars from Rossiter, together with revenge. Jean Murdock was obviously the love slave and willing compatriot of Rossiter, while John Bates was simply a poor, unbalanced soul who knew his way around electrical circuits but whose taste for blood, like Murdock's, had to be skillfully cultivated by Rossiter.

Other than his own, Jackson knew and understood the motives of Duncan Rossiter best of all. The two had met seven years earlier in the federal penitentiary at Fort Leavenworth, a brutally gray place that stank alternately of urine and antiseptic, where colorless food was heaped in moist piles on steel trays. Jackson had been sentenced by the United States Army to three years at hard labor for dereliction of duty, refusal to obey a duly issued order by a superior, and assault with intent to kill a commissioned officer. He'd been stripped of his sergeant stripes and faced a dishonorable discharge after completing his term.

There were no words to describe his anger when the steel doors slammed and locked behind him. As he was later to tell Rossiter, his cellmate, he'd tried to kill the first lieutenant who had repeatedly ordered him to take his section of men into an area notoriously infested with Viet Cong. On the two occasions that he'd obeyed that order, the enemy had attacked with an awesome display of firepower and resolve, killing six Americans and wounding as many others. Both times, Jackson maintained, he'd radioed to have the supporting fire directed at hopelessly inaccurate grid coordinates. Fearing that his men might be wiped out completely, Jackson ordered them to withdraw; the lieutenant monitored the order on his radio and immediately countermanded it, screaming that no nigger was going to screw up his operation because of a little contact with the enemy. The incoming fire from the Viet Cong had by this time become murderous, and Jackson's men eagerly followed him in retreat.

Upon returning to the fire support base, the lieutenant informed Jackson that he would face charges of dereliction and refusal to obey. Jackson responded by trying to blow the lieutenant's head off with his service .45 and, had his trembling rage not made him miss the first shot and given him time to get enough of a grip on himself to throw the gun aside and beat the lieutenant to a dazed pulp, he'd have spent the rest of his life in the stinking grayness of Fort Leavenworth.

The panel of officers sitting in general court martial disbelieved Jackson's claim of innocence to charges of dereliction and refusal to obey in the face of his attempt to kill the lieutenant. They ignored testimony from other soldiers that the lieutenant hated black men, that he was widely regarded as incompetent, or that many within his command were reluctant to follow him to the mess hall, much less into combat. The Army closed its ears to a man with seven years of service and four combat tours under his belt, a professional soldier who'd come from a ghetto to earn bronze and silver stars, to lead and train men, to make the Army his life.

Before coming to know Rossiter, Jackson believed that his own rage must certainly have been the hottest ever to consume a man. The low brutalities and indignities of the penitentiary fanned his hunger to lash out at the system that had turned against its willing supporter. It was not until he'd met Rossiter, however, that his wild hunger was given direction, that the prospect emerged of satiating it.

Their closeness began when Jackson intervened to save Rossiter from rape by three long-termers. Together they broke teeth and jaws, cracked ribs, and were themselves bloodied until the assailants lay battered and senseless on the floor of the cell. Jackson was impressed with Rossiter's ability to handle himself against bad odds. Rossiter had not asked for Jackson's help and had been prepared to fight the attackers alone in spite of his slight build. His only advantage was a hidden but incredible rage.

Rossiter told Jackson how his father's beating had led to that clear, dark night with the pinpoint stars and a hideously screaming man framed in his bedroom window by jagged orange flames. Rossiter stood on the lawn with the housekeeper, who had been awakened by his cries of danger, watching his father being taken by the fire. It was a perfect crime—his blind hate had been tempered with planning and craft.

The next morning, fire inspectors found small, charred threads of twine, miraculously unburned, clinging to the elder Rossiter's doorknob. This led them to notice that Duncan's escape path from his bedroom would have taken him by his father's door. The housekeeper told of the previous day's crash and its ensuing beating. That was enough.

Duncan never admitted his "perfect" crime; not to the police, to his lawyer, to the juvenile judge, or to his fellow adolescents at the psychiatric detention facility to which he was sent.

While the old joke about killing your father and throwing yourself upon the mercy of the court as an orphan did not strictly apply to Duncan's case, he was not hurt by the fact that he was young, white, good looking, articulate, and very rich. The lawyer who was appointed as his trustee and guardian made sure that Duncan was placed in a country "juvenile hall" that allowed some comforts and psychiatric care.

Duncan did his time. Distrusting doctors who were there to "help" him while holding him prisoner, he answered with monosyllables the inevitable questions about his state of mind, his childhood, and his father's death. He attended school and read voraciously. All the while, he knew that the day he became an adult his whole life would turn around.

First, according to his father's will, he would inherit everything. As a juvenile, and a possibly mentally ill one at that, he had never been charged with murdering his father. The money would be his. That same magic day "of majority" would set him free of courts, doctors, and lawyers.

Several months before his birthday, Rossiter mauled an attendant who tried to shake him down for a few dollars of his presumed fortune. It happened out of sight of others in a remote part of the grounds. The incident set him off. He gathered the hundreds of small bills he'd stashed over the years and escaped easily, assuming that he could await his inheritance more comfortably in sunny California. The authorities would forget about him until he resurfaced at his majority. They wouldn't care about him, he assumed, and if they did, good lawyers would be cheap.

He got as far as the airport. Paying for a flight in small bills automatically triggered a search by the guard supervising boarding inspections. Duncan had no identification, and when told he would be held until someone identified him, he broke free and ran. The ensuing chase and capture involved a drawn gun, a bullet accidentally lodged in the thigh of a federal officer, and a trip to Leavenworth, Kansas, for Rossiter. In this one respect, he was no longer a minor.

Over the next few months, Jackson had watched Rossiter's hate evolve from a sullen, almost defeated inner turmoil into a cool, directed, and at times frightening concentration. Rossiter soaked up Jackson's street and jungle fighting stories, pumping him for his know-how.

One day, Rossiter pulled Jackson out of the lunch line, and, in an intense but calm voice, said, "Leon, neither of us is going to flake out again. Ever. We are not going to spend one minute more in this shithole than we have to, and we are going to make them pay for what they did to us."

Jackson nodded mutely and shook Rossiter's outstretched hand, not knowing whether Rossiter meant to try an escape or to enroll in college. They rejoined the line, resuming their prior casual conversation.

Rossiter's inheritance came through. Both he and Jackson started attending religious services and participating in every rehabilitation program open to them. Though neither was an alcoholic, they joined the prison AA. It looked good. They became inseparable, prompting comments from other inmates that they must have had a church wedding. They ignored the hecklers.

Rossiter bought hundreds of books and donated them to the prison library. That also looked good. Some of the books, but not enough to attract attention, contained practical information, which he and Jackson read voraciously.

After a decent interval, Rossiter hired a battery of lawyers and psychiatrists to prepare for his next parole hearing. When informed that outright release was unlikely, his counsel arranged for parole conditioned on Rossiter's commitment to the security wing of a California mental hospital.

Jackson enjoyed Rossiter's tongue-in-cheek letters from the mental hospital in California. To support the line he fed his doctors, Rossiter wrote about how he had conquered his youthful fears and was able to confess his father's murder. He wrote about his remorse, his rehabilitation, and his plans for higher education. He unveiled his desire to donate a large, but not crazy proportion of his inheritance to found a "big brother" program in Texas for juvenile criminals.

Release couldn't be pushed, but in the meantime, Rossiter enjoyed telling his "pen pal" about his new friends, Yoshi and John, and their shared interests. Also, a nice woman in Washington, he said, was taking a strong interest in all their cases.

Once back on the street, Rossiter wasted no time in springing Jackson and the others.

Friends, thought Jackson as he headed out of the door of the Maine cottage to greet Rossiter's return, are wonderful. Especially when they give you a million dollars to do what you wanted to do anyway.

Saturday dawned through dark clouds that threatened rain in time to spoil Washington's weekend plans. Jean Murdock rubbed grains of sleep from her eyes and rose to briefly survey the morning from her window. Six stories below, an elderly woman walked among the trees of DuPont Circle with her slender Irish setter. On weekday mornings, Murdock often met them on their return from their ritual outing.

After a speedy shower, she dressed in cotton pants and shirt. Rain in Washington does not usually mean relief from heat. Skipping breakfast, she called a taxi, giving Sal's Café in Rockville as her destination. The taxi arrived ten minutes later, its windshield speckled with the day's first droplets. Rain fell heavily by the time they turned onto Wisconsin Avenue. Murdock had no reason to suspect that she might be followed and was oblivious to the green Datsun 280-Z behind her.

She was eager for the meeting with John Bates because he would have news from Maine. He would brief her on the progress of the plutonium treatment process and inform her of any problems.

She'd not seen Bates since they'd separated in the crowded parking garage in New York City after abandoning the blue Lincoln. They'd headed in opposite directions—Murdock to Amtrak and Bates to Greyhound—but their destinations had been the same: Washington. Their plan dictated that they never communicate except by face-to-face conversation, a rule to be broken only in emergencies.

The memory of the day in Timber Rivers Junction hung in her head like a hazy nightmare. She handled her daily routine automatically, scarcely hearing or seeing things around her unless they related to the theft. She rediscovered weaknesses and uncertainties in herself that had been buried for years.

Not since her first years working in the Senate had she felt so helpless, so exposed. Back in those days, she knew the sources of the bad moments, the physically nauseating waves of self-doubt. They came from her fat, stupidly fat, acned childhood spent in miserable contrast to that of her brilliant and lean, handsome brother. Things were simple then: Do everything slowly to avoid mistakes and stay out of the way to avoid comparisons.

These easy if miserably simple rules were stripped

away when she took her national college scholarship exams. Her scores were phenomenal. Teachers rushed to get on her bandwagon. Several major universities begged her to come. She got into Swarthmore and her brother didn't.

It took her less than a semester to start using her brain in public, to lose fifty pounds, and to decide that life had some possibilities after all. By the start of her sophomore year, she'd firmed up her body with new-found motions like walking erect and running, and her classmates were telling her that she was beautiful. By the end of that year, with the last pimple gone forever, she was.

From that moment, until her crash to reality in the Senate, she felt like a free person. Grades, respect for her intellect and wit, and a succession of fawning men tumbled before her with little effort on her part. She went on for a master's degree in government regulation of business and accepted a job from the company with the highest bid.

It didn't work out. Despite her immediate grasp of the work offered, she went nowhere. In subtle, can't-put-your-finger-on-it ways, she was a pariah. Having enough self-confidence to put the blame on her environment, she jumped quickly out of industry and into public service—to the staff of Senator Harry Hammer.

At first, the change was like night and day. While the hours were long and the work often tedious and unrewarding, everyone else seemed to be in the same boat. She was excited that the Senator took a personal interest in her work. He took her to meetings, used her memos, and printed most of what she wrote in the *Congressional Record*. He began to spend more and more hours listening to her briefings and working on testimony—often after the regular workday. Flattered and exhilarated, she easily allowed one of the sessions to become a romp on the private senatorial couch.

Weeks later, she discovered she'd been fucked. Or, to

119

state it more crudely, as Burt Strong fondly did, she'd been "JFK'd." The Senator had planned her seduction perfectly, pacing it according to hallowed Senate ritual. She had followed in the footsteps of at least a dozen prior legislative assistants. Other staff members had even helped set things up.

She was crushed. Her self-loathing took her back to childhood. She was still fat, still ugly, a worthless human being. But she made the turn-around discovery that a few years of success freed her to see: *She could hate.* The fat, the fading into the background, the self-deprecation had been nothing more than turning in on herself. She had been unwilling to believe that she'd hated her brother for being first and best, that she'd hated her parents for loving him, so she'd hated herself. Now that she knew herself, she felt not disgusted, but free.

The external changes were small. She plunged back into her work, which was well below her talents, and produced top-quality trivia. At the same time, she dedicated herself to the complete, permanent seduction of Senator Harry Hammer.

There was competition for a time between Murdock and Strong, but with the death of Hammer's wife and the abrupt collapse of his second shot at the presidency, Murdock made her move. Burt Strong soon found himself shunted onto the staff of the Senate Energy Committee and Murdock became Hammer's administrative assistant. A chesty typist, the last of Hammer's casual bedpartners on the staff, found herself working for a dashing young congressman from California, for whom she could take after-hours dictation to her heart's content. The old order had fallen. The new order belonged to Murdock.

Murdock looked for ways to use her newly consolidated power. Drafting legislation, tinkering with agency budgets, and causing federal bureaucrats to shit in their pants periodically were all great fun for a while. She realized, however, that her efforts made very little real difference. The System clanked on, absorbing Murdock's assaults, but showing no signs of ever changing. She learned in a short time what some congressional aides never learn: you're only as strong as your boss.

So Murdock set about rebuilding Harry Hammer from the ground up. Hammer had been one of the nation's most powerful people, and she had worshipped him for it; she was determined that he would be powerful again. Through a regimen of ego-building adulation and forced confrontation with decisions, Murdock slowly turned his brooding over defeat into *planning* for the future, his near-complete withdrawal from the public eye into an energetic resurgence.

She watched her total control over him slip away, but she never resented its loss. At last they were equals, enjoying the intimate give-and-take of a partnership.

She listened enthralled as he talked of his trust in the American people, his distaste for the current crop of leaders, and his ideas for a better future. Because of her superb tactical sense, he said, she would be the key ingredient in the implementation of his long-range strategies.

There was only one problem, and she didn't dare bring it up until she was certain that Hammer was fully back on his feet: He had as much chance for a presidential nomination as Alf Landon. When she finally mentioned it, his answer astonished her: Hammer's plans for leadership required no nomination.

Shortly thereafter, Murdock came across Yoshi Nakamura's letter to the senator. In it, Nakamura asked for "help for atomic bomb victims," "curtailment of the nuclear industry," and "an end to weapons proliferation." The final request was for "help in finding a job that will let me work on these problems."

Murdock, who skimmed and signed much of the senator's outgoing mail, was about to scrawl her "Harry Hammer" on a response drafted by a legislative aide.

She halted, however, when she noticed that Nakamura's return address was a mental hospital. This in itself was not so unusual, but she happened to notice that Nakamura was a doctor of nuclear physics, not of medicine. Murdock was fascinated. Then inspired.

The office of Harold J. Hammer took a personal interest in Yoshi Nakamura. Murdock wrote to Yoshi, then visited her. The two women understood each other's past problems and sympathized with each other's future hopes. Yoshi happened to mention that a fellow patient, Duncan Rossiter, was a friend worth having, depending on one's goals. He was rich. He was a natural leader for the right kind of enterprise, and he was capable. Of anything. But he required cultivating and extremely careful handling.

The tentative outlines of a group had formed.

Murdock's thoughts broke off sharply as she realized that the taxi driver was looking at her bemusedly and repeating the amount of fare. She paid and quickly reviewed what she needed to tell Bates as she waited for a momentary letup in the downpour.

Things were under control. Nobody had any idea that she was involved in the theft. The confidential briefings and conversations had yielded much that would interest her friends in Maine. Aside from these details, the conversation would be brief and they could quickly arrange for their next meeting in a similarly obscure suburban restaurant. Bates would then wait a few minutes before going to a pay phone for a call to a Maine phone booth.

Murdock spotted a break in the gray sheets of rain and dashed for the café entrance.

During the next half hour, Liz Hammer watched the restaurant from a parking place across the street. Then Murdock emerged, as did three men. Since two of the men came out together and went immediately into the toy store across the street, Liz was fairly certain that the third was Murdock's contact. She memorized his features as best she could through the tapering drizzle and watched him drive off. After following for a few blocks, she lost him at a stoplight.

Kaznik was a very disturbed man when he returned to Washington from Connecticut.

One of his concerns was data. Nearly every branch of the federal investigative apparatus hummed along to his tune, and information flooded into the CIA complex in Langley from field investigations, computer searches, and analysts. That was the problem—too much data. He wallowed in facts about obscure criminals, dissenters, radicals, and perverts of every shade. The *special* facts that every investigator craves, however, eluded him.

His one hard lead was the connection between Wesley Rice and Kelly Gilliam. One was dead and the other had temporarily slipped his surveillance with the flair of a Keystone Cop.

Gilliam definitely looked shady, Kaznik thought. An innocent man who discovers that he's being followed would be righteously indignant, report the tail to someone in authority, and insist that he be left alone. An innocent man close to the center of raw congressional power would be outraged and would flex his well-connected muscles. Gilliam had not reacted like an innocent man. He'd slipped his tail with the subtlety of a rhino. He'd reported nothing to anyone. Why?

Gilliam's maneuver had been successful because of its amateurishness, Kaznik reflected. That sometimes happens. It would not happen again. Quantity would be brought to bear in keeping track of Gilliam. His next stupid move would be witnessed by at least five highly trained people. Even now Gilliam was the subject of a private TV documentary, more intimate than "An American Family" could ever have been during prime time. *Total* surveillance.

Kaznik literally itched to question Gilliam and get fast answers any way necessary. Distasteful procedures had never stood between Kaznik and the answers he needed to stop terrorists. But he could not risk triggering a hasty reaction by one of Gilliam's co-conspirators until he had a better grip on the case.

The moment his briefing with the President had ended, Kaznik's built-in clock had started ticking, marking the passing hours, the pile-up of wasted minutes during which the missing plutonium might be scattered up and down the eastern seaboard. He'd flown to Connecticut the previous day to examine the newly discovered school bus in the parking lot of Emerson Junior High School. School district officials had looked everywhere for their stolen bus except in the teachers' parking lot. That was reasonable. Kaznik noted the placement of the bus, the roads around it, its proximity to the ANC plant. He and his subordinates sifted through the strange contents of the bus. He wanted to see the primary leads and evidence himself.

What Kaznik saw unnerved him. The glassy-eyed "children," windows intentionally obscured by muddy water spots, obviously good timing—all pointed to imagination, discipline, and hard work by the attackers. Before leaving the bus, Kaznik read the report on radiation readings taken inside the bus. He borrowed a small alpha-ray detector and made his own check, just to be sure. Nothing. Not even "harmless amounts" or "statistically insignificant" radiation. *Nothing.* Someone had known exactly what to do and had done it perfectly. The attackers had transferred eighty kilos of powdered plutonium dioxide from heavy casks to other containers under conditions of high stress without spilling a hundredth of a gram. Someone this careful probably would not accidentally release plutonium into the atmosphere. Kaznik was not relieved. The implied trade-off was no bargain. He made a mental note to find out precisely how atomic bombs are made.

His next step was the ANC complex near Timber Rivers Junction where he personally inspected the demolished convoy vehicles. While poking through neatly piled rubble that had been carefully scraped or torn from the various vehicles, he listened to a briefing by a federal investigator on the scene. Microscopic bits of wire and casing allowed educated guesses about the type of explosives and detonators used in penetrating the Kenworth's trailer, the man said. Military C-4 was the likely candidate.

The artillery used by the attackers, however, remained a complete mystery. Kaznik approached the Kenworth, which looked like a prize exhibit in a bomb museum. He ran his hand over the jagged hole in the left side of the cab and reached inside to feel the charred upholstery.

"RPG-7," said Kaznik under his breath.

"Excuse me, sir," said the fed. "What do you need? An RBT what?"

"I need a phone," replied Kaznik. The dusty gray rays around the rim of the hole in the cab were unmistakable. He'd seen the effects of RPG's too often in Vietnam, Laos, and Cambodia. His most recent encounter with the weapons had been outside an airport in Belgium. A Black September terrorist had tried to escape his attention while carrying a bass violin case containing two RPGs.

Kaznik was led to the ANC lab director's secure telephone line. Billingsly picked up his telephone in Langley after a single ring.

"It's an RPG-7, Nate," Kaznik began without pleasantries.

"Okay, Joel, I'll look for any and all CHICOMM weapons on the Continent," replied Billingsly, "but I don't think it will do much good. They show up everywhere, practically."

"Concentrate on likely channels into the States. There are probably some good prospects in the Company's files. I'll be home tomorrow and you can let me know what you've got on your other stuff."

Saturday was another day. Kaznik was glad he had to work through the dismal, rainy weekend.

Curt Quillico, his FBI liaison, entered the cramped office with a smile that promised something positive. "We have a computer match with the fingerprints from the cartridge case. The guy's name is John Bates, age thirty-one. He's an Okie who turned up in California long enough to show on California's print files."

"Rap sheet?" asked Kaznik.

"We're still filling in the history. I figured you'd want to know the minute the match was made. I'll give you what I've got. Bates was born in rural Oklahoma, near Shawnee, and stayed there until he graduated from high school. Then he took off for L.A. and worked odd jobs, which we're still trying to run down. About six years ago, he got a crew job with the local CBS television station and worked up to a pretty good studio technician's job. Apparently learned his stuff OJT."

"And?"

Quillico's face twitched oddly as he worked his muscles to repress a smile. "He's a *flasher*, Mr. Kaznik."

"It's Joel, not Mr. Kaznik. A what?"

"A flasher. According to the police records, Bates was running commercials between some early-afternoon soap operas. Tens of thousands of housewives watching. Suddenly Bates's shlong shows up for twenty seconds on the tube. Since no videotape was running, the police couldn't get a . . . uh, a . . . definite match, but Bates confessed. I can tell you more after we get the records from the looney bin."

"So what's the punch line?"

"Bates walked away from the mental hospital and was never seen again, as far as we know. That was almost two years ago."

"And that's all we've got?"

"That's all we've got for now, Mr. . . . I mean, Joel."

"I want him found, Curt, today. Not apprehended, just *found*. You can't use wanted posters or the state and locals' channels, obviously. You've got to find him yourself. It's a fine chance to show your stuff."

"Right," said Quillico. "I'm already looking."

Quillico left and Kaznik reflected on his new suspect. Bates definitely was not a bomb builder, Kaznik reasoned. He had no college, according to the records, and probably didn't know physics from influenza. Bates certainly must be incapable of digesting the knowledge on how to handle plutonium dioxide. While he might be involved in the theft, just like Gilliam, there had to be others. Bates was an oddball, a wild card. Kaznik didn't like wild cards. He much preferred clear, unveiled facts he could depend on. Bates's "resumé" contained nothing indicating that he was dangerous or even cunning.

Kaznik's security intercom buzzed.

"Someone to see you, Mr. Kaznik," said the voice in the wall. "He's got a Nuclear Regulatory Commission 'Q-Unlimited Access' clearance and he's cleared 'Cosmic' by Defense. Name's Theodore Rippling, Department of Energy. Can you see him?"

Kaznik thought for a moment. "Did he say why?"

"No, sir."

"Well, okay, send him in."

Kaznik extended his hand to Rippling, a tall and thoughtful-looking man in his mid-fifties. Rippling had the slightly disheveled appearance that Kaznik had often seen in scientists.

"Come in, Dr. Rippling."

"Ted," said Rippling before Kaznik could ask if people called him Theodore. Kaznik was pleased. Most high-ranking bureaucratic-type scientists preferred the formal "Doctor" as if they could fix knees.

"I'm Joel. Sit down and have some coffee."

"I run DOE's nuclear energy shop, Joel, and I get to

hear a lot of things. I've heard something I'm certain you'd be interested in."

"I'm all ears."

"I got a call yesterday from an old friend who works for the NRC. Name's Goldman."

"I'll bet his first name is Ralph," said Kaznik. "He's the safeguards inspector who okayed a convoy with a double load of Pu O_2 out of Timber Rivers Junction, right?"

"Right. He's broken up over it, if that makes any difference."

"I wish it did. Go on, Ted."

"Ralph has been disturbed over a lot of little things the last few years—the looseness of security, the attitude the industry has slipped into, even the attitude he lets himself slip into. He's been especially antsy since experimental breeder reactors have come on line and the amount of plutonium in civilian hands has increased so drastically. He thinks the whole game is insane. He thinks the NRC is insane. Ralph doesn't trust a single NRC decision any more. That's why he called me."

"I can't say I blame him. What's he got?"

Rippling paused, drew a long breath, and spoke quickly. "Ralph learned from a couple of his buddies that the NRC has authorized more shipments of special nuclear material. He was almost panicked when he called. I don't think he's all back together yet. He normally wouldn't be passing information outside his agency, even to a friend."

"It must be good information, Ted, or you wouldn't have taken it outside *your* agency, either," said Kaznik.

Rippling's voice lowered reflexively. "It checks out. Several nuclear companies are scared to death that the Timber Rivers thing will mean an end to shipments of high-grade fuel. To make things worse, the breeder reactors haven't yet come close to ending shortages in the supply of enriched uranium. The utilities have gotten into the act because they're starting to feel a pinch. The lobbying is getting furious, Joel. The industry wants to get back to business as usual and has apparently found some sympathetic ears in the NRC."

"So what else is new?"

"Most of the pressure is coming from the South. American Nuclear has a contract to deliver a hefty load of enriched uranium to a reactor in Mississippi. The shipment is due next week from ANC's Dallas plant. The NRC has decided to let them roll."

Kaznik swore silently. "What's with the NRC, Ted? Shouldn't it be obvious that American Nuclear's got massive security problems?"

"That's just it. American Nuclear does *not* have security problems that are any worse than any *other* company's. The safeguards have been beefed up dramatically in the last two years. Ralph told me that the Timber Rivers plutonium would have been stolen even if no corners had been cut in the safeguards inspection and procedures. For Christ's sake, the attackers stole eighty kilos that were locked in a rolling safe, guarded by nine armed men. What bothers me is that the NRC has decided to authorize a shipment of enriched uranium when it's clear that even the most stringent safeguards can be hacked to pieces if the thieves are determined and well enough equipped. Besides, if I had some plutonium dioxide and I wanted to build a bomb with an even bigger bang, I'd try to get some enriched uranium."

"Can you stick around, Ted?" Kaznik asked in a controlled voice while punching buttons on his black house phone. "I'd like a quick course in bomb building."

"Sure."

Kaznik was already speaking into the receiver. "Henry, get me some Nuclear Regulatory Commission stationery within an hour. I also need a form book of letters, memos, and press statements—the kind used by the commissioners and their top staff. Work out a computer transposition code that'll let me write NRC trash with no fuss, no muss." He listened for a moment and grunted something. Rippling thought he heard "security suitcase."

Kaznik replaced the black receiver with one hand and reached for a green phone with the other.

"Is this Chairman Osgood of the Nuclear Regulatory Commission? Good. Sorry to bother you at home on the weekend, Commissioner. This is Kaznik. I need twenty minutes of your time. I'll be in your downtown office in three hours. You may wish to have some of your top policy people on hand. Don't worry about letting me in. The guards know me."

Kaznik replaced the receiver without waiting for an answer and swung around to confront an amazed Rippling. "Down to serious business," said Kaznik. "Suppose I have eighty kilos of plutonium dioxide, skilled help, lots of time and money. What could you do for me?"

Rippling cleared his throat and asked if he could smoke. Kaznik nodded.

"First of all," Rippling began, "if you had me around, you'd have no trouble building a bomb. I used to design bombs for the government at Los Alamos. A few of my creations even made it into the bomb museum." Rippling exhaled a cloud of smoke.

"Bomb museum? Is there really such a thing?"

"There is. Open to the public, too. That's one of many reasons you don't need someone in my salary class to build a decent bomb. I once lectured some students on the physics of fission bombs. An Atomic Energy Commission agent planted in the audience later accused me of spilling classified data and succeeded in creating a minor flap. But Christ, my whole lecture was built around a college physics textbook. I added a few details from the *Encyclopedia Americana!* It was all from the public domain. With a college-level knowledge of nuclear physics and a tinker's mind, *you* could build an atomic bomb *without* my help. Your one problem might be coming up with a workable shape for the chemical charge needed to set the thing off."

"But how about handling plutonium and making it do what I want it to? Isn't that tricky?"

"Oh, it's tricky, no doubt about it. But, for under ninety dollars you could buy a good guide to plutonium technology. You'd probably want both volumes of the *Plutonium Handbook*. For the actual processing, though, you'd need the *Reactor Handbook*. That's in four volumes. I've referred to it many times myself. Probably costs one-fifty by now."

"You mentioned chemical explosives. I happen to know a great deal about chemical explosives. But what if I didn't?"

"There's enough in print, Joel, to enable you to come up with a lousy, inefficient atom bomb—one, say, that would fizzle and only knock down the Empire State Building and kill maybe fifty to a hundred thousand people."

Kaznik was delighted to have found someone in the nuclear establishment who was on his wavelength: a professional whose common sense superseded the company line.

"So atomic bomb *theory* is available," said Kaznik. "So what? I might have eighty kilos of plutonium dioxide, but without an expensive fabrication plant and high-powered metallurgists and chemists, I might as well have horseshit. I could raise hell if I spread the powder around or emptied it into the municipal water supply, but I'd have no bomb!"

Rippling smiled and tamped out his cigarette in an empty styrofoam cup. "You sound like Clayton Mercado, but just for the record, I *could* make you a pretty good incendiary bomb from horseshit if I had the right equipment and chemicals. Plutonium dioxide is much, much better. I could use it as it is—in powdered form—and make a whopper bomb. That's assuming I had a

131

well-shaped chemical charge. Or I could steal some uranium dioxide like the kind ANC will ship next week from Dallas, mix it in, and make a city-buster, a downright strategic weapon. If I really knew what I was doing, I'd reduce the dioxide to metallic plutonium and build a nice, big bomb like the one that leveled Nagasaki."

"I thought the metallurgy for reducing $Pu\ O_2$ was impossible outside a big expensive lab."

"Some experts, like Mercado, think that because you can't do things their way, you can't do them at all. Mercado thinks in terms of military weapons that must be light, highly efficient, and above all, predictable. That's the kind of weapons he and I used to build. A terrorist doesn't need a bomb that will fit on the tiny tip of an air-to-ground missile, Joel. But on to your question: Without a big lab and sophisticated equipment, you'd probably want to handle the plutonium in small batches—maybe a few hundred grams at a time— to help guard against accidentally assembling critical mass. You could possibly work up to a pound or even a kilogram. Depending on the size of the core that you wanted to end up with, you'd face many repetitions of a rather tedious and potentially dangerous process. But, believe me, you could do it."

"Okay, it's possible, and I'm ready to start. What materials and equipment do I need and how do I use them?"

Rippling folded his hands on the desk and spoke as though he were a building contractor bidding on a job or Julia Child explaining a casserole. "You'd need a clean laboratory with hard-surfaced counters, workspace for two people, and some tools. The biggest item would be an induction furnace. Next, you'd need the common array of crucibles, transfer equipment, radiation detectors, and a glove box. You could build your own glove box out of aluminum, plexiglass, or wood by cutting two holes in one side and attaching a pair of flexible plastic gloves to the holes. The only requirement is that it be airtight when there's plutonium inside and that you can handle the stuff from the outside. If you bought the lab equipment and the various chemicals retail, you'd spend maybe ten thousand dollars. Ready to start work?"

"Ready," said Kaznik.

"Seal a few hundred grams of plutonium dioxide into the glove box with your various chemicals in separate containers. Do your mixing inside the box while being careful to follow the standard procedure for handling the chemicals as well as the plutonium. Remember that an accidental chemical blast would spread the plutonium all over the premises. Don't screw up because some of these chemicals are corrosive as well as volatile, and you don't want any leaks. Bake the mixture in the induction furnace and come out with a little lump of light-gray plutonium metal that you can hold in your hand. It might feel a little warm—even after it's cooled—since it's constantly emitting alpha particles. Put it away in a nice dry place. Repeat. Weigh, transfer, mix, bake."

"How long would it take me to do eighty kilos of oxide?"

"A month and a half."

"What if I pushed it fast and reckless?"

"You wouldn't want to do that."

"What if I did?"

"Maybe a week. I wouldn't want to be near the lab."

"Now that I've got the metal, what do I do with it?"

"You make a bomb. Let's start from the middle of the bomb and work outward. That's the easiest way to explain it and probably the only way to build it.

"Remember, a nuclear device—a bomb—goes off because enough fissionable material comes together to trap subatomic particles that would normally decay away. In this case, we're talking about neutrons. If you get the neutrons bouncing around real well within the mass of the fissionable material, they start to strike the nuclei of atoms, which in turn give off other neutrons. You have a chain reaction. The closer you pack the fissionable material, the less is required to set the reaction off.

"Most bomb material needs a 'pressure spike' in the middle to make sure that the neutrons are mixing it up right. A plutonium dioxide core would need a pressure spike unless your design is absolutely perfect. Plutonium metal, however, is denser and you can do without."

"That's why I just spent a month reducing the oxide to metal, right?"

"Partly. You also did it because you want a higher yield from a lighter, more predictable bomb. But now you've got bigger risks as well. All that extra density and all those extra neutrons bumping around mean you must avoid lumping too much plutonium together or you become part of a fireball."

"So the center of my bomb is plutonium, packed closely, but not too closely."

"Right. You might end up with a core of metal not much bigger than a softball. Then you cover it with a reflector. This is a coating to keep the neutrons in when you squeeze the ball together. A steel shell with a layer of wax inside would do the job, but beryllium would be best."

"Now I've got beryllium on my shopping list."

"Yes. It's a toxic metal, semihard to get, but it's also the best damned neutron reflector in the world. You'd have to be extremely careful while you're putting the beryllium around the plutonium. If your size and purity calculations are wrong, you trigger a reaction by turning back a few too many neutrons. It wouldn't be a big yield, probably, but it would be enough to do you in and a few of your neighbors to boot."

"Okay, I've been careful. I've got a plutonium ball in a beryllium shell. What's next?"

"The most important part—the chemical explosive. TNT would do, but let's assume you don't have to scrape by. A high energy plastic explosive would be optimal."

"Like C-4?"

"Like C-4, or something similar. You could learn how to handle it and mold it by visiting any mining school library. Practical experience, however, would save some time."

"I like saving time. Our bandits know about C-4, so we can assume they won't be in any libraries. They've got access to CHICOM rocket-propelled grenades that use something very much like C-4. That means they won't have any trouble getting the chemical explosive. For all we know, they may have cases and cases of C-4."

"Any modern grenade explosive would work just fine, Joel. C-4, for example, can be molded just like kids' modeling clay. It's so stable you don't even have to be gentle. Molding is important, too, because the shape of the charge determines *how* it compresses the plutonium when it's detonated and can make the difference between a fizzle and a beauty."

Rippling became momentarily enthusiastic as he explained the ins and outs of the chemical charge. "You can mold the charge right over the beryllium ball, but you'd better have a detector handy to monitor radiation. The C-4 itself is a partial neutron reflector and will turn some neutrons back into the core. You know what that means. If your detector says the core is on its way to critical mass, you'd better start dismantling that son of a bitch in a hurry. You'd be back to the drawing board.

"Molding the charge is tricky because you don't just want to compress the plutonium when you detonate, you want to *hit* it, too. That means you've got to have a uniform chemical blast. It also means that all segments of the chemical charge must detonate at precisely the *same* time. Your detonator has to be good quality and you've got to have a good way of measuring the symmetry of the explosive shell."

"Tell me more about the detonator."

"You could make one yourself, but good ones are easy to buy. The very best comes from Sweden. Nobel got the Swedes into the explosives business early. Most mining companies buy Swedish detonators. Once you've obtained yours, all you need is some sort of casing and something to set off the detonator. You could use a timer or a radio-activated switch if you needed remote control."

"Anything else?" asked Kaznik.

"That's all," said Rippling. "You've got your bomb."

Kaznik sat for a few moments. "Ted," he said evenly, "I have this feeling that someone out there is building an atomic bomb."

Rippling's eyes widened, but he said nothing.

Kaznik continued. "I'll want more details from you when we have some time. Get yourself a beeper so I can yank you out of bed any time I think of a question. Before you go, I need one more thing. If you were looking for bomb builders, where would you get your leads?"

Rippling looked thoughtful. "Well, I would assume—just to cover the odds—that they would buy some beryllium if they wanted it, rather than risk stealing it. Second, they might try for a Swedish detonator. That would be tough to track down, but there's a slim chance that a manufacturer might have a record of sale to someone outside the mining business and the scientific community. You might also be able to find out who got himself an induction furnace for no good reason."

"Anything else?"

"No. Aside from those items, everything they'd need is common as dirt. Once they got their equipment and materials in place, no one would guess what they were doing as long as the door of the lab stayed locked. Once the bomb was finished, they could lug it around in a truck and no one would notice." Rippling's eyes seemed to cloud. "One more thing, Joel. They could get two *very* good bombs out of that batch of plutonium —three if they're sure of what they're doing. I hope you find them soon." He stood to leave and then turned back to Kaznik. "Good luck on your little visit to the NRC this afternoon. Remember that material you thought you may as well have instead of plutonium dioxide to build a bomb?"

"Yeah. Horseshit."

"There's a critical mass of that material at the NRC."

Once Rippling was out the door, Kaznik was on the telephone. He ordered his various liaison officers to start priority searches for purchasers of beryllium, induction furnaces, detonation devices (with emphasis on Sweden), and—as an afterthought—glove boxes. A CIA shop technician entered his office as Kaznik contemplated the logistics of a nationwide computer scan of invoices marking the sale of ordinary lab equipment. Several other men bearing armloads of various items followed the technician.

"Hi, Henry. Gentlemen," Kaznik said. "Show me your wares."

Henry, a small, balding man in his early sixties, peered through his bifocals at the pile of material he'd just placed on Kaznik's desk. "I have here, Honorable Sir, nothing but the finest bond stationery worthy of any bureaucrat. Note the Nuclear Regulatory Commission letterhead. It can't be distinguished from the real thing because it *is* the real thing."

"Henry," said Kaznik, "did you steal this stuff? Shame."

"We had some left over from an earlier operation. Here are the form books you wanted. You probably won't need them because the computer transposition code should make you sound just like Old Man Atom."

"I only want to sound like Osgood."

Kaznik took a loose-leaf binder from the pile. After a few minutes of study, he started dictating into a microphone that Henry had plugged into a jack in the wall. A technician in a nearby room typed his words directly into a computer terminal. A man sitting across from Kaznik took notes in shorthand as a backup.

Henry selected a type style and fed various kinds of paper into a printer next to the terminal. Before an hour had passed, Kaznik finished proofreading the final sheet of an "official communication" from the Nuclear Regulatory Commission. He thanked the crew and stuffed the papers into a hard folder, which he put into an empty oversized suitcase. Kaznik said good-bye and left the room.

He drove alone past the handful of cars parked illegally near the main gate of the Langley CIA complex. The cars contained reporters from the various networks and wire services who waited patiently for some piece of news on the Timber Rivers theft to materialize. Most recognized Kaznik on sight. The Langley security people periodically chased the reporters away only to discover that they invariably returned in the hope of catching a word with Kaznik or one of his liaisons. Several attempted to follow him as he departed the complex. Such attempts were futile. Kaznik could not be followed if he chose not to be.

He strolled into Commissioner Osgood's plush office suite three hours to the minute after their short telephone conversation. The door to Osgood's personal office was ajar and Kaznik could hear low voices on the other side. He walked past the empty receptionist's desk into a room perhaps eight times as large as his own office. The room smelled of expensive leather and furniture polish. Gleaming chrome framed a huge sofa and armchairs.

Lionel Osgood rose from his seat and offered his hand. "Come in, Mr. Kaznik. We decided to have an impromptu meeting since you . . . uh . . . summoned us here today. We were discussing the findings of our reactor safety review team. You'll remember Stan Perchale?"

Kaznik waded across the deep carpet to shake Osgood's hand. "Thank you for making time for me."

"I understand from Stan that you're hardly a man to be put off," said Osgood.

They crossed the room to an elegant conference table where Osgood introduced Paul DeSmit and Chester McGafferty of the NRC. Clayton Mercado of the Department of Energy was also present. Kaznik noticed that Stanley Perchale seemed nervous and fidgety; it was probably because of the sour note on which their first meeting ended, Kaznik thought to himself. He placed his large, heavy-looking suitcase next to an obviously comfortable chair and sat down.

"I'm sorry to disturb you gentlemen on a weekend, so I'll keep my promise and take only twenty minutes. After all, I do have an investigation to run."

"I'm sure we all appreciate that," said Osgood.

"I want to know *who's* shipping special nuclear material, *how much* they ship, *when* they ship it, and *where.*"

Osgood waited a moment for all eyes to turn to him and nodded to his underling, DeSmit.

"Actually, Mr. Kaznik," said DeSmit, "nothing is now being shipped. We naturally suspended shipments of SNM when the Timber Rivers incident occurred. We took this action on our own initiative so we could review our transportation security regulations. Of course, I'm certain that the commissioners considered your, uh, *request* that we impose a temporary moratorium."

Kaznik smiled warmly, putting DeSmit and his bureaucratic clones at ease. "Have you completed your review?"

"Yes," answered DeSmit.

"And the result?" asked Kaznik, still smiling, though not as warmly.

139

"It's been decided that an NRC inspector must be present at the shipping point from the moment of notification that a shipment will be made to the actual time of departure. Every single aspect of any proposed transfer will be scrutinized. That inspector will have authority to call off the shipment if anything—no matter how slight—isn't exactly right. In addition, strong shielding on the transport and escort vehicles will be required. Two more escort cars and four more armed personnel will accompany each shipment. We certainly don't want a rehash of the Timber Rivers incident."

"I take it, then, that you're lifting your suspension," said Kaznik.

Osgood missed the edge in Kaznik's voice. "Yes," he said. "But shipments will be allowed only after special application on the grounds of emergency need."

"Like the 'emergency need' alleged by American Nuclear Corporation for enriched uranium shipping to a light-water reactor in a major Southern utility grid?"

"That's correct," said McGafferty quickly, incurring a deadly scowl from Osgood.

Kaznik spoke reflectively. "So you're giving ANC another bite of the apple? I wonder how they got to you."

The chairman of the Nuclear Regulatory Commission and his minions flushed in perfect unison. At length, Osgood responded with barely suppressed anger. "Though the Commission has no need to justify its actions to *you*, Mr. Kaznik, I'll be happy to explain them since such knowledge might somehow be useful to you. Adequate safeguards are now in place to the extent that we can authorize limited shipments on an emergency basis. If that reactor doesn't get fuel from American Nuclear, hundreds of factories throughout the South will be short of electricity. Tens of thousands of families will face curtailed supplies. People will be laid off, Mr. Kaznik. People in government—like you and me—sometimes lose sight of the millions of others out there whose lives stand to be affected dramatically by our whims."

"Mr. Osgood, eighty kilos of plutonium are missing, and right now someone might be building a bomb with it. I'd rather have a few towns short of electricity than one leveled by an atomic blast."

Clayton Mercado broke in. "The shipment in question, Mr. Kaznik, is uranium dioxide—UO_2. It's not enriched to weapons grade. Even if a hijacker could master the incredible engineering difficulties of building an atomic bomb, the laws of physics would stop him short if he used UO_2 from this shipment."

Before Mercado had finished speaking, Kaznik was ready to hate him. Faceless bureaucrats were one thing. Scientists who toyed with the truth were another. He hoisted his bulky suitcase onto the table, pushed back his chair, and stood. "Then your decision is final?"

"I'm afraid so, Mr. Kaznik," said Osgood, as though the challenge to his authority had been decisively blunted. "We have our procedures here and they work well. As Dr. Mercado has explained, there is no real danger in allowing this particular shipment."

Kaznik spread his hands on the top of the suitcase and leaned slightly forward. "I promised that I would take only twenty minutes of your precious time. That means I have only three minutes left—just about enough to deal with Dr. Mercado's theory on uranium dioxide."

He spun the dial of a combination lock beneath the handle of the suitcase. "I don't have a scholarly paper in here, Doctor. I have some real, live UO_2 that one of our agents recovered after a little mixup in your nuclear materials inventories a short time ago. Happened in Tennessee, remember? The NRC's investigators never really straightened it out, I might add. The Company decided to keep it a while since nobody seemed too upset that it was missing."

"Mr. Kaznik," said Osgood with all the menace he could muster, "you have exceeded any possible mandate by retaining nuclear material. Besides, what does a lump of uranium dioxide prove?" His question betrayed his uncertainty.

"It doesn't prove anything by itself," said Kaznik, "but when you melt it together with plutonium dioxide —that's Pu O_2, Dr. Mercado—it takes on at least some *theoretical* interest. Doesn't it, Professor?"

Mercado's eyes wandered nervously to the surface of the conference table. "Such a mixture makes a bomb theoretically easier, Mr. Kaznik, but the engineering problems remain. Did you acquire the plutonium through the same illegal means you used to get the uranium dioxide?"

Kaznik's manner became almost friendly. "As a matter of fact, Professor, we did. Remember when you ran the Nuclear Institute at Tech before coming to DOE? You had a certain graduate student there whose name I won't mention. He tipped off the FBI that a small experimental quantity of plutonium was missing—not only missing, but unreported. The Company merely kept it after getting it back. The FBI certainly didn't want it."

Mercado paled. To no one in particular, Kaznik said, "You know, I only met one man in my life who deserved to be called 'Professor' and he played piano in a filthy little jazz place in New Orleans."

Fabric squeaked on leather as someone squirmed. Kaznik opened the suitcase a crack and continued. "Our technicians don't know a great deal about nuclear metallurgy, but they muddled through. They could have done a better job if they hadn't been pushed for time. We didn't have any beryllium for a reflector, so we had to use a spherical metal tank to put the core in. One of the guys coated the inside with paraffin. After all, this thing is just for demonstration purposes so we needn't worry too much about yield."

McGafferty jumped to his feet. "You have a *bomb* in there?"

Kaznik blithely ignored McGafferty and continued while the others sat rigidly. "Our technicians were much more at home with the chemical explosives. They dismantled a caseful of army hand grenades and molded the plastic charges around the storage tank. The idea was to shape a lens-focusing charge around the device, but I told them to just slop it on and make it look round."

As he raised the lid of the suitcase, Kaznik said, "Here. Let me show you how we rigged the detonator."

The others pushed back from the table, knuckles white against the dark wood. They bolted from their seats as Kaznik's hand came over the top of the suitcase lid. Osgood was a stride away from the door when Kaznik shouted, "Freeze!"

Mercado whirled in midstep. "Kaznik! You're in over your head! Do you want to destroy this building and contaminate entire city blocks? Get that thing out of here! The President is only a few blocks away. Take it somewhere and dismantle it carefully."

Kaznik's hand came into full view. In it was the hardcover folder containing "official communications" from the NRC. He placed it on the conference table. "Today's briefing, gentlemen, told me two very important things. Thing number one: The people who stole the plutonium can build an atomic bomb if they have the expertise—no big labs or tons of equipment— regardless of what this asshole says." He nodded to Mercado.

"Thing number two: Additional shipments of SNM and similar material are definitely out, at least until we recover the plutonium. Osgood, this folder contains your ruling that there will be no further shipments unless your ban is lifted by order of the President. It also contains a news release explaining your concern and an appeal to utility planners throughout the nation to brace for a nuclear fuel shortage. You will also find a letter to the American Nuclear Corporation confirming the call you're about to make canceling their proposed shipment of uranium dioxide until further notice. All the supporting documents are there."

Kaznik closed the suitcase and walked toward the door. He approached Osgood and stood for a moment, his eyes riddling his face.

"If you vary those orders, Osgood," warned Kaznik, "you'd better have the President's permission. If you vary the orders *without* the President's permission, I will personally do something horrible to you."

MONDAY, MAY 17

Deputy Sheriff Fritz Steadman loved the graveyard shift, especially on late Sunday nights and early Monday mornings, because the weekend party-goers had by this time retired to their homes to recuperate for the coming work week. Highway 1 between Bath and Newcastle became a deserted winding path through the forest, shrouded occasionally by patches of fog that rolled in from the ocean to gather in gullies and valleys. There were seldom any speeders to catch or accidents to investigate, and Steadman liked the quiet. He sometimes suspected that the radio dispatcher at county headquarters was asleep, so seldom did he receive or monitor any calls during these hours. The shift was so restful, in fact, that he almost hated to see the approach of 5:30 A.M., the time for him to call the dispatcher, check off-shift, and head for his house near Damariscotta.

Steadman turned north on Highway 1 after cruising quietly through Damariscotta's tiny business district where the windows were dark, the doors locked tight, and the lobster boats bobbed peacefully in the slips. The pavement was slightly moist, the result of a hard rain on Sunday that had saturated the entire eastern seaboard, according to weather reports. He immediately encountered an opaque wall of fog that not only slowed him to a crawl, but also set him to fantasizing over this

145

being *Hound of the Baskervilles* country. Steadman, in his younger years, had been an addict of Arthur Conan Doyle until finding out from the *Saturday Evening Post* that Sherlock Holmes had not been a *real* human being. Years had passed before he could recall the literary joys of Doyle without feeling foolish and gullible. Only lately had he even undertaken to reread the mysteries.

Steadman was not the least disturbed over having made no progress at all toward solving the latest crime at Rosenheim's Marina. His lawman's sense of urgency over the burglary had been short-lived since Nattie had ample insurance coverage against theft. Moreover, his investigative routine had been interrupted by the weekend and the graveyard shift. Four A.M. saw Steadman patrolling northward on Highway 1 thinking, not about the marina burglary, but about a particular ship in its harbor.

What troubled him was the fact that not one of the realtors or independent lessors along the coast had rented a vacation cottage to a Mr. Godwin of Corpus Christi, Texas, owner of the magnificent yacht in Rosenheim's Marina; the county's records revealed no deed to any private property registered to Godwin; and no hotels or motels had anyone named Godwin as a guest. It was possible, he knew, that the Godwin party had merely docked their yacht in Chamberlain and had begun a northward coastal journey by car, perhaps to Nova Scotia. But why Chamberlain? There were a number of more likely places both up and down the coast, each with marinas better equipped than Rosenheim's to care for a vessel like the *Golden Girl*. It seemed to Steadman that Chamberlain, tiny lobstering village that it was, must have been specifically selected for one reason or another as *the* place. Something was peculiar about this Mr. Godwin and his friends, yet he'd not mentioned his misgivings to Sheriff McIntyre or to anyone else. What itched was the joint federal-state dispatch of a week ago and its charge to investigate thoroughly *all* unusual activities and occurrences. He wanted badly to scratch the itch, but feared that his revelation of a "mystery" might be followed by a ridiculously logical and innocent solution, that he would emerge as an aging flunky whose imagination had run wild.

The darkness was heavy with salt spray wafting inland from the breakers. Yoshi Nakamura had heard each and every one of them as they crashed throughout the night against the boulders below the house. Though tired and tense from two days of going over the ticklish metallurgical steps of reducing plutonium dioxide to metal—a ritual she insisted be acted out with tedious attention to every detail—there was no sleep for her.

By 4:00 A.M. she became concerned. Today she and Rossiter would start the metallurgical process for real. She would need all her faculties and nerves to handle the highly volatile and corrosive chemicals under intense heat and pressures without letting them explode. Aside from the initial effects of an explosive accident, a likely secondary effect, and one much more deadly, would be the scattering of finely powdered plutonium dioxide into the atmosphere. She was far too taut.

Nakamura wanted badly to meditate. Anxiety, however, prevented meditation as surely as it prevented sleep. She knew that there was only one answer: She must exercise, must bathe every muscle cell in oxygen. Only then would the tension subside enough for her to meditate in preparation for the pressures of the coming day.

Taking care not to awaken Rossiter and Jackson, she stole out of the cottage, dressed in gray sweat pants and a T-shirt. The towering conifers around the clearing seemed to collect darkness, intensify and concentrate it near the ground; Nakamura had to walk gingerly to avoid twisting an ankle on the ruts in the curving, muddy road that led to Highway 1.

She came at last to the highway, turned to her right, and broke into a comfortable, metronomical run. Inhaling the tart air was refreshing and soon she felt the warmth of renewed circulation. She loved to run because it kept her healthy, her muscles hard and lean. Freedom from physical ailment, she'd discovered early in life, allowed her to concentrate on the intuitive side of her being, to become closer to her own spirituality without distraction. Her tiny body could have belonged to a woman in her twenties, and though her face sometimes showed her past, it was hardly the face of a forty-five-year-old woman.

She started to meditate even as she ran. Time seemed to thicken until seconds became hours and minutes were days. Before she'd gone a hundred strides, she encountered a wall of dense fog that closed about her like a dark dream.

"*Ichinichisenshuno omoi,*" she repeated over and over in time to her steps. It was a phrase her uncle had often sighed as they gazed through the barbed wire of the detention camp in the arid hills of Southern California. Interpreted roughly, it meant that each day had become like a thousand years.

It was her devotion to the principles of Zen that had given her the strength to plod dutifully through the "thousands of years" since that day in 1940 when her parents left her on a San Francisco dock in the care of her aging uncle, Tomokiyo. A Western creed or philosophy would have failed her miserably, for it would have demanded that she base her actions on rational decisions, that she submit to the depersonalizing effects of modern society. Zen, on the other hand, allowed her to reject the rational, to act according to her feelings and emotions. It demanded only that she understand those emotions and that she exercise self-control.

Through Zen she was spared the emotional horror of trying to rationalize the imprisonment of a Japanese diplomat's tiny daughter as an "enemy of the Republic."

Her father, Uncle Tomokiyo explained shortly after they'd been imprisoned, had not left them to escape their fate. But as a member of the shizoku, the inheritors of the samurai tradition, he had a responsibility to rejoin his people in his native land, to take *otoka no nichi*—the manly way—on behalf of the Emperor and Japan. It was a matter of keeping face, her uncle said. He himself was old, he said, and had rendered his service countless times on diplomatic missions; he'd even helped train his brother, Yoshi's father, for the same difficult service. Moreover, he had a responsibility to save and protect Yoshi, the sole survivor of the children of the Nakamura household. Her parents and he agreed that fascist Japan was no place for her.

She was a precocious child who followed news of the war with an understanding and feeling that rivaled those of most adults. The head of the detention camp noticed her abilities and resolved to see that she was given the opportunity after the war to develop them. She visited him regularly in his Quonset-hut office to trade observations on global politics and to borrow the books he willingly offered. She often shared with him her anxiety over her parents, wondering where they were, when she would see them again. To the commandant fell the task of telling her on the eve of her freedom that her parents had lost their lives on a sunny August day in Nagasaki to the atomic bomb.

Suddenly the fog was alive with harsh, confusing light and the sound of screeching tires. Nakamura whirled to confront a pair of monstrous eyes barreling down on her from behind. Her meditation had blocked out the sound of the approaching car and the fog had shrouded the headlamps. For a split second, she was riveted to a spot near the middle of the road, frozen by the spectacle of impending death. The fender of the car was close when she lunged sideways, propelling herself in an out-stretched dive toward the shoulder of the road. She felt the surface of the fender brush her tennis shoes before she crunched against the gravel shoulder and skidded on her stomach into the thicket.

The car lurched to a stop where Nakamura had stood, rocking violently on its springs. Fritz Steadman sat for a full five seconds, anchored to the steering wheel by his clenched fists. He wondered if he'd hit the person who had materialized out of nowhere like a ghost in the thick fog. Christ, if only he'd had another second he might have been able to stop! What was that guy doing in the middle of the goddamn road at five in the morning anyway?

He slid across the seat and out through the passenger's door, grabbing his long metal flashlight from its mount on the dash. Its beam swept the gravel of the road shoulder and settled on Nakamura's form. Steadman exhaled in relief to see that she was moving; he knelt beside her, pushing away the bushes that hid her head. Nakamura slowly brought her knees under her and withdrew from the thicket to face the harsh beam of the flashlight. White scratches not yet reddened by swelling lined one cheek, the marks of twigs and branches, while angry red abrasions covered both elbows. Miraculously, she was otherwise unhurt.

"For the love of God, young lady, are you okay?" asked Steadman, his eyes wide with concern. "Here, hold on to me, but just sit. Don't try to stand. That's it, just sit down now. You hurt anywhere?" His eyes widened even more upon discovering that she was Oriental, probably Japanese.

"I—I'm okay, I think," stammered Nakamura. "I . . . wasn't . . . you didn't hit me."

Steadman regarded her scrapes and bruises and asked her to move her limbs; satisfied that she had no broken bones, he told her to sit quietly. He returned to the cruiser, snapped on the police flashers, and parked it at the side of the road.

"Let's get some antiseptic on those scrapes," he said while gently taking hold of her arm. "I've got a first-aid kit in the cruiser."

Nakamura grew suddenly rigid. She'd collected her faculties sufficiently to know that prolonging her contact with this police officer would inevitably lead to questions: What was she doing out at this hour? Where did she live? What was her name? Would she accept a ride home? Nakamura stood up.

"No . . . please . . . I'm all right," she answered. "They aren't bad cuts. See, they—they're hardly bleeding. I'm not hurt at all. Really."

Steadman was beginning to sense that something beyond her close brush with death was disturbing her.

"Look. You were almost killed. It's a damn miracle, young lady, that you're standing here at all. Now, I'm not going to turn you loose till I've bandaged those scrapes and gotten you home safely."

"*Please!*" she protested. "You needn't feel responsible. It was my fault. I—I shouldn't have been out in the middle of the road. Please don't go to any trouble for me."

Steadman regarded her for a moment. Her features flashed on and off in the cruiser's police lights. He saw growing apprehension and fear where there should have been relief and was reminded of the expressions he sometimes saw on kids' faces when they'd been caught shoplifting or driving with open beers in their hands. What's more, this woman fitted Nattie Rosenheim's description of the one who had landed in Chamberlain aboard the mysterious Mr. Godwin's *Golden Girl*. His mind rang with the charge to investigate *all unusual activities*.

"Now listen, young lady. You're in no shape to do any more wandering around the highway, and besides that, I've got a few questions I want to ask you." His hand tightened slightly on her arm, just above the elbow.

Nakamura winced. For an instant, she let her body turn toward the cruiser. Then the motion accelerated as her fists clamped about handfuls of his shirt. Before he could draw his next breath, she'd twisted her body. Steadman felt himself lifting and turning. Suddenly the world was topsy-turvy motion and flashing blue light. He landed with a bone-crunching thud, the coarse asphalt biting the skin on his back. As Steadman struggled to rise, Nakamura put the total force of her hundred-pound body into a kick at his neck. He fell into the roadside thicket.

Steadman couldn't move, but in the flashing blue light it looked to Nakamura as if he was pulling out his gun. She bolted away into the fog.

The eastern sky grew pink as Deputy Sheriff Fritz Steadman forced his uncooperative right hand to depress the push-to-talk button in his parked cruiser. He tried to sound normal and matter-of-fact.

"Yeah, this is Oh-Two, go ahead."

The radio speaker crackled urgently as the dispatcher's voice came through in a metallic twang. "Fritz! Is that you? That *you*, Fritz?"

Steadman tried to ignore the raw pain in his throat and fought dizziness by gripping the steering wheel tightly.

"Roger, Obie, this is me. What do you need?"

The speaker crackled again. "For the love of Mike, Fritz, you haven't checked in for over an hour and I haven't been able to raise you. Where the hell have you been—on the shitter or something? You were supposed to be off-shift half an hour ago."

Steadman drew a painful breath and contemplated the ridicule he'd endure if the guys in the department knew he'd just had his ass stomped by a tiny Japanese woman. While he had no intention of letting the matter lie, he simply could not bring himself to talk about it.

"Fritz, are you there? You sure you're okay, buddy? *Fritz,* what in the hell's going on?"

Steadman depressed the button. "Course I'm here, Obie. What are you getting all excited about? Everything's fine. Everything's just fine."

Hoping desperately that no one had seen him lying for nearly an hour in the road, Steadman started his cruiser and headed for his bed near Damariscotta. He'd call the department tomorrow with a story about having picked up a spring cold or the flu. He needed a day or two to nurse his wounds and plan his next move.

Duncan Rossiter sipped coffee over an empty plate muddied with egg yolk as the hostess of NBC's *Today* show interviewed a celebrated choreographer. Nakamura, her omelet untouched and cold, finished the story of her encounter with the policeman and steered her gaze to the television set, avoiding Rossiter's troubled stare. Leon Jackson leaned against the doorjamb, an M-16 rifle cradled in his arms as he scanned the landscape beyond the porch, listening but saying nothing.

"Then you didn't kill him?" asked Rossiter in a level voice.

"I don't think so. I don't think I . . . *hit* him hard enough."

Rossiter leaned forward slightly, his eyes boring holes through her, his voice low. "Yoshi, you should've killed him. You should've made sure he was dead. Don't you see what this means?"

Nakamura summoned the courage to meet his stare, even though a slight tremble took place deep within her. She knew from her experience with Rossiter in the institution that he was insane, wildly insane. Together they'd endured the scrutiny of doctors, analysts, and each other, and she'd noted that his outbursts always had a reason. She hoped that he felt no purpose for violence now.

"It means that we've got to be doubly careful," she ventured, "in case we're investigated for this thing. I'm sure you can think of a way, Duncan, to keep me hidden if that happens. You're good at these things. You're the reason we've gotten as far as we have. . . ."

Rossiter threw his head back and laughed. "Yoshi, Yoshi, Yoshi." He grew serious, but seemed relaxed and controlled. "You don't have to humor me. You don't really think I'd turn loose on you, do you? After what we've been through together? You guys—you and Leon here, and John and Jeannie—are the only family I've ever had. You don't have to humor me."

For the moment Nakamura chose to be comforted by his words. Rossiter would not, she knew, do anything to complicate or upset the execution of their plan. What troubled her now was the complication *she* had brought down on their heads. It was reasonable to expect that the local police were now searching for a slight Japanese woman who had severely beaten a police officer. They would probably canvass the cottages and homes along the coast and alert residents of the surrounding villages to be on the lookout for such a woman. Even when this stage of her mission was complete, it might be difficult to leave without being seen. Nakamura feared that her little complication might tax even Rossiter's brilliance to the limit.

"We obviously can't decide exactly what to do because we don't know exactly what we're up against," he said. "I'll tell you what, Yoshi. You get things ready for the start of the process while I buzz into Damariscotta to look around. I'll talk to the lady who owns the grocery store to see if she's heard anything. You know how these small towns are; if anything out of the ordinary happens, word travels like wildfire. If the cops are looking for you, they'll probably put your description out to the people around here. In the meantime, keep an ear on the radio. It might tell us all we need to know."

Nakamura nodded her approval as though it were needed.

Jackson turned from the doorway. "Be careful what you say, Dunk. From what I hear, these small-town folks can get awful suspicious of outsiders."

"Don't worry. I'm just going to trade a little small talk with the grocer while I pick up a few odds and ends. Might even visit the lobster market again. Don't forget that we're the community's newest industry and it never hurts for a new industry to develop good community relations." He smiled, obviously pleased with his own humor. "I won't be gone more than two hours," Rossiter added. "When I get back, Yoshi, you and I'll start making some honest to goodness plutonium metal out of that powder."

"I'll be ready," replied Nakamura.

Rossiter had been gone only a minute when the *Today* show's reporter started a newscast. Jackson turned up the volume on the television.

"This morning's lead story: Federal, state, and local police in New Hampshire conducted a predawn raid today on an agricultural commune just east of Wolfeboro, New Hampshire, in an apparent attempt to recover the plutonium missing since last week's bloody attack on a convoy near Timber Rivers Junction, Connecticut. More on that story now from NBC's Patrick Driscoll."

The scene changed to a pan of New England countryside just after dawn. White frame buildings stood out against the early-morning backdrop, and hordes of helmeted police and National Guardsmen mingled between parked squad cars and military jeeps. A line of haggard-looking civilians knelt in the foreground, their hands clasped on their heads, under the watchful eyes of a dozen uniformed riflemen. Other camera shots showed the dirt road leading into what was obviously some kind of farm.

"The Winnipesaukee Commune is named after

nearby Lake Winnipesaukee, one of New Hampshire's prize scenic and recreational treasures. It's a peaceful area, known for the friendliness and hospitality of its people.

"The peace and tranquility were shattered at four A.M. today when nearly three hundred federal, state, and local law-enforcement personnel stormed into the Winnipesaukee Commune to detain its residents and to search every inch of the area. The reason? A series of tips to federal undercover agents alleging that the commune is the center of a plot that last week resulted in that murderous attack on a convoy of plutonium in Connecticut.

"Maybe it's miraculous, maybe it's the result of good planning, or maybe it's just plain lucky that no one was hurt in this morning's raid. Not a single shot was fired. The Winnipesaukee Commune, we're told, has long been the object of suspicion by the FBI and other federal authorities as a haven for underground radicals wanted in connection with crimes ranging from inciting riots to bank robbery and kidnapping.

"The authorities here aren't talking to reporters, apparently because of strict instructions from Washington, except to confirm that they haven't found the plutonium. They won't say what they'll do with the sixty-four residents of the commune who are now being detained at gunpoint, or whether any will be charged in connection with the Timber Rivers theft. Neither will they confirm or deny that someone here at the Winnipesaukee Commune has anything to do with the eighty kilograms of powdered plutonium dioxide that at this moment is still missing. Patrick Driscoll, NBC News, at the Winnipesaukee Commune in eastern New Hampshire."

They watched the remainder of the newscast, hopeful for additional stories on the Timber Rivers investigation, but there were none.

"Looks like the feds got some bad tips," said Jackson with a half smile.

Nakamura switched off the set and replied without looking at him. "It seems so. But New Hampshire isn't that far from here. How do we know they're not surrounding us with hundreds of troops right this minute?" She raised her eyes to the picture window that afforded a sweeping panorama of the Atlantic. It was surprisingly calm. The high tidal fury had long since subsided and lobster boats lazed at a distance of perhaps a quarter-mile, unhurriedly collecting the morning crop from traps marked with brightly colored floats. "I guess that answers my question," she said, nodding toward the vast, nearly empty expanse.

Jackson shook his head slowly. "I don't want to alarm you, Yoshi, but that ocean might as well be a brick wall a hundred miles high and a hundred miles thick. If they come, you can't run to the ocean."

She wondered what they would do if suddenly they were attacked by soldiers and police from every direction. She saw herself wielding an M-16 rifle, firing through doors and windows, remembering the points Jackson had drilled into her and the others over months of training with the weapon. She knew that she could function under such conditions because she'd proved it at Timber Rivers. But then she recalled the spectacle at the Winnipesaukee Commune, the hundreds of attackers who came in the dead of night, and she wondered what chance she, Rossiter, and Jackson would have against such odds. She discovered that she was expressing her concern out loud.

Jackson approached and stood before her, a towering and reassuring giant against the brightness of the picture window. "We'll fight them, Yoshi. We'd have to. I, for one, got something to live for and I'm going to collect it or die trying. I owe those mothers something, but more important, they owe *me*." He paused, his face turned down to confront her worried stare. "How about you?"

The question conjured the horrors she felt fifteen years ago when she found the battered doorway of a tiny, ramshackle hut in the slums of Nagasaki. Gawking in disbelief, she rechecked the address given in the letter from the Japanese government. The letter said that a mistake had been made, that after all these years, the Nagasaki Atomic Victims Relief Organization had discovered that her mother—Nakamura Oichi—had *survived* that August day in 1945. Yoshi Nakamura, a newly graduated Ph.D. in nuclear physics, postponed acceptance of an assistant professorship and liquidated her modest possessions in order to buy passage to Japan. She stood in the doorway with the stink of squalor filling her nostrils, the filth of poverty and hopelessness covering her shoes. Somehow she forced herself into that ugly hole. When at last her eyes adjusted to the trickles of light flowing through holes in the corrugated aluminum roof—holes that admitted water and cold as well—she saw her mother. She lay on a mat on the muddy floor with her face to the door. Her right arm was nothing more than bones covered by filmy, scalelike skin, the flesh having been burned away. Her right leg, though partially obscured by a tattered dressing gown, was clearly in much the same condition, but ended just below the knee. The right side of her face was nonexistent, a gnarled and scorched tangle of misshapen bone and cartilage that gave no inkling of eye, ear, or nose. Her mother's eye widened in a hopeless effort to focus on the image in the door. "You may as well steal what you didn't steal yesterday," she said in wheezing, distorted syllables. "Take yet one thing more —my blood on your knife." She somehow raised her clawlike hand in a short, beckoning gesture. "Come. Don't be afraid of me like all the others. Come. Come. Take my blood on your knife."

Nakamura fought back the tears as she stared at

Jackson's shoes. "How about you, Yoshi?" he asked again.

Struggling to avoid the flood of feeling that once landed her in a mental hospital, she forced a normal smoothness into her voice.

"How about me? What do I have to live for?" She turned away, suddenly mindful of the chores that awaited her in the laboratory. "I'll tell you what I have to live for, but I won't explain it to you. For fifteen years I've lived for *zensho*, and it's all I live for now. *Zensho*."

Jackson stood bewildered as Nakamura strode toward the laboratory.

THURSDAY, MAY 20

Senator Harold J. Hammer pushed a button on his remote control box and the television screen went dead. The ten o'clock news was history.

"Goddamn assholes," he whispered to himself, half laughingly. Then he shouted so that Jean Murdock could hear from the kitchen. "The idiots are still trying to wring confessions out of those poor nuts from the commune. They're all assholes, Jeannie, every one of them. *That's* what we're up against. Assholes."

Murdock looked up from the crab quiche she was preparing. "I know, Harry." She hoped that he would forego another scotch before dinner. He didn't.

Hammer took his drink through the glass doors out to the deck. A night breeze stirred audible ripples on Lake Barcroft and generated a whisper in the surrounding trees. Hammer watched as a pontoon boat floated by; the two young couples on board waved amiably and resumed their conversation.

Hammer didn't wave. Earlier in his life, when this house was new, he would have hailed the young strangers with a gusty hello. He would have felt kinship, hope for the country and hope for its future. But not tonight and perhaps never again. So soft and effete had society become that the only hope lay in *trauma*. America needed a *threat*, a dire ultimatum to stir an inner strength that had begun to atrophy. Hammer hoped that America was still capable of flexing its muscles, of waking up and throwing off . . .

The silence was shattered by deep barking from the fenced yard below. Jean's huge dog warned those on the barge to stay away, and he meant business. Hammer regretted having allowed her to bring the dog here. Though he agreed with her that good security was essential, he felt that this canine monster was a bit much.

"How about some salad, good senator?" offered Murdock, touching his arm. He turned to see salad bowls and colorful placemats on the rustic table.

"I wish you wouldn't call me that," he said. "I've completed my last official act as a U.S. Senator. And stop sneaking up on me."

"Well, whatever you are, you look hungry. Sit down and eat."

Hammer drew a chair up to the table and rolled his flannel shirt sleeves to the elbows. "Too hot to be dressed like this," he said, "at least if you're going to be outside. Why aren't we in with the air conditioning?"

"Because," answered Murdock, "the fresh air will do you good. Besides, there are no moon and stars in the dining room."

Hammer took a few bites of his salad. "What do I smell cooking?"

"Quiche. Crab. Your favorite."

"Shrimp is my favorite."

"If you hadn't fired your housekeeper and cook, Harry, you wouldn't be forced to rely on me to keep you alive. You could have your favorites of everything."

"My cook completed her last official cooking act years ago. The only thing I miss about her is heartburn."

"Will you knock off this 'last official act' crap?" protested Murdock. "You're making everything sound like Armageddon is right around the corner."

"Perhaps it is, my dear. Perhaps this is what our country needs."

Murdock studied his face as he ate. The sparse light softened the sagging jowls and tired pouches under his eyes. The moon cast youthful waves in his silvered hair and his eyes cast twinkles of light that seemed to come from within his head. Never had he looked more regal, more powerful, more fit to lead. This was Harold J. Hammer. This was power. This was once the most recognizable man in America.

Murdock served the quiche as Hammer talked of the books he'd read and the notes he'd made since leaving his office days before. He talked of preparedness, of purges, of the "legitimate uses of power."

Over coffee and dessert, Murdock briefed him on the day's happenings in Congress, and more important, on the progress of the investigation into the Timber Rivers theft. The breeze suddenly became too clammy and they retreated into the living room, closing the massive glass doors and draperies behind them. Hammer nestled into a large chair near a weathered plow blade converted to a pipestand, a souvenir from his native Pennsylvania Dutch country. Murdock lit a cigarette and settled into the thick carpet beside his chair.

"Everybody's screaming for you on the Hill," she said after a long drag of smoke.

"Why don't you fix me a nice scotch on the rocks with a twist, to set off that elegant dinner?"

"The press has been something else. Strong has been insufferable. Gilliam, as always, has been lazy and incompetent."

"Please get me that drink, and please don't talk about our people that way, Jeannie."

Murdock pouted apologetically. "Maybe I shouldn't talk about them that way, but the fact is, Harry, that people are scared and they need you. Everybody, including senators and representatives, the press, even Kaznik, is scared. They need your presence, Harry."

Hammer raised his eyebrows and made his eyes round. "Well, would you listen to little Miss Civic Obligation!

Can this be the same person who only days ago stole I-forgot-how-much plutonium dioxide, killing her fellow humans in the process? I can't believe my ears. Besides, Kaznik is a baboon who deserves to be scared."

"For Christ's sake, Harry, you know what I mean. I'm talking about needing you to help keep the situation under control. Hold some hearings, go through the motions. Show everybody that you're the only one qualified to lead in a crisis."

Hammer chuckled quietly before answering. "You make a compelling case, my love, but not compelling enough. My place is here, studying, making my lists. Let the goddamn press go wild. Let them speculate and spread rumors—while they still can. The time is short, Jeannie."

Murdock jumped when the telephone rang. Though she knew that it could not be answered, she wanted to know who was calling. She rose and went to a switch that activated an external speaker on the telephone recording device.

The telephone rang twice, three times, until a loud click told of a tape recording beginning to turn. From the speaker issued the voice of Hammer's long-gone cook as she read carefully written lines:

"This is Senator Harold J. Hammer's residence. The senator is not now in, but would be pleased to see that your call is returned. At the sound of the tone, please leave your name, telephone number, and—if you wish—the subject of your call."

An electronic tone beeped through the speaker. Hammer and Murdock sat with heads cocked, waiting to hear whether the caller would leave a message. Seconds slipped away before they heard a throat clearing, and then a familiar voice:

"Uh-h-h-h, yeah. Harry, I don't know if you'll ever hear this, but here goes. This is Burt and I need to talk with you soon. Very soon. It's very urgent, Harry. You know where to get me. I wouldn't ask it if it weren't

163

important, you know that. I've been looking all over for you." *Click!*

"H-m-m-m, old Burt again," said Murdock. "I know what he wants to talk about, Harry. The hearings, and maybe an executive session of the Energy Committee. I'll take care of it first thing in the morning."

Hammer held a butane lighter to his pipe. "Don't worry. I'm not going to talk to Burt. Not until it's over. He'd never go along with something like this until it's already *done*. Where's that drink you promised?"

Murdock went to a long bar that could serve either the living room or the deck. With clearly visible resignation, she prepared the scotch.

"You know, Jeannie," said Hammer, "some people are elevated as rulers for all the wrong reasons. Many of them are pretty, and most are glib. They all have good ad men and speechwriters to start with, or the money to buy them. This country has far too many pretty but vacuous leaders."

Murdock nodded in sincere agreement. In her life, she'd suffered amply for lack of prettiness. Having become pretty, she resented its importance.

The senator continued. "I know you hate Burt Strong's guts. Probably has something to do with the way he helped maneuver you into my sack when you were nothing but a punk on the Hill, and I suppose I don't blame you for that. But Burt Strong's my friend, Jeannie. He may not be very pretty, but he's as smart, as hardworking and as loyal a man as I've ever known.

"What I'm saying is this: I'm going to need Burt in the days ahead. But I'm going to need you, too, more than anybody else. Nothing could make me happier, Jeannie, than to see you and Burt bury the hatchet and start working together. Can you do it for me? For the country?"

Murdock doubted that Strong would ever have the guts to join them, but she couldn't resist being moved by Hammer's own emotion, by his forceful way of making a request. She let herself be pulled along.

"Okay, Harry. I'll do that. For you."

"And for the country?"

"And for the country."

They sat for a moment, Hammer nursing his scotch and Murdock smoking quietly. At length she moved close to him and leaned an arm on his knee. "It's a long way to that private office of yours in the Capitol, but it's not far to the bedroom," she whispered. "What do you think?"

Hammer looked down at her and smiled. "I can think of nothing more delightful than taking you directly to the bedroom."

"Then let's go." She giggled girlishly and grabbed his arm, only to find him holding back.

"I'm afraid that I have responsibilities, my love. Important things to think about."

He rose from his chair, kissed her hand, and retired to his paneled den.

FRIDAY, MAY 21

A cockroach skiddaddled across Kelly Gilliam's kitchen table and startled him into splattering milk all over his hand as well as into his bowl of Cap'n Crunch.

"God-*damn*-it!" he thundered, leaping away from his breakfast. The loathsome little creature disappeared somewhere into the growing litter of *Washington Posts* that covered most of his kitchen table. Gilliam could put up with most pests. He wasn't squeamish about mice and he could even tolerate snakes or rats under rigidly controlled conditions like cages. But cockroaches turned his blood to water.

Rummaging for a dishtowel to blot the puddle of milk that now dripped to the floor, he tried to remember what he'd done with his can of Raid Ant and Roach Killer, his "final solution" to the roach problem.

"Okay, you little mother," he told the roach who he was sure must be listening from somewhere beneath the pile of newspapers. "You may be blessed with blinding speed, but you can't escape the gas." He spied the can of poison behind an array of dirty dishes piled on the kitchen counter.

Gilliam stopped his hand before it touched the Raid, his facial muscles relaxing stupidly as the killer's scowl fell away.

The can was not where it should have been.

While Gilliam was what many would call a messy

person, he often defended himself by claiming a method to his messiness. He knew every inch of his cluttered desk in the Capitol, for example, and had trouble locating memos and letters only when one of the secretaries took the liberty of cleaning up. He knew his bachelor's hovel inch by inch. For months he'd known in the back of his mind that the can of Raid lay on the counter in the corner where the refrigerator met the wall. He'd put it there last winter, when the bugs seemed to go away for a while, right next to the wall switch that controlled a long burnt-out counter light. Now the can was more than three inches from where he'd put it, well outside a clean circular spot surrounded by dust.

Someone had moved it.

Gilliam now understood the new, undefined apprehension he'd felt the past week. Little things in his household had been out of place. The can of Raid had been moved slightly away from the switch he never used, piles of clothing awaiting laundry had been disturbed, strewn magazines and letters had been restrewn across shelves, tabletops, and his desk. He'd seen it all, but he'd not *known* it, for the changes had been registered subliminally.

He quickly forgot his determination to asphyxiate the cockroach and turned his mental machinery in a new direction. He envisioned the scene that must have occurred in his absence. Someone had come to poke and paw through his possessions, to take fingerprints maybe, or to snap microfilm pictures of the personal letters from friends and relatives that were now carelessly repiled over the top of his little desk. What else do spies do? he wondered. The answer was not long in dawning: They plant microphones and bugs and taps on telephones and perhaps even miniature cameras.

Since the previous Friday night, Gilliam had somehow clung to the hope that those who had been following him—the man with the hooked nose and the other with cropped blond hair—had given up. After all, he'd made it perfectly obvious that he'd detected the surveillance. While he'd ventured only briefly from his apartment during the weekend, he'd scrutinized every passerby and every car on the street. He was half convinced that neither of his followers were in the vicinity. Gilliam cringed at his naïveté. Sometime during the last week, his apartment had been searched and probably bugged.

He found himself moving stealthily throughout his apartment, trying not to be heard. Oblivious to the fact that he would be late for work if he did not leave soon, he checked lampshades, the stems of his plants and the undersides of their leaves, the turntable housing of his stereo. He ran his hands along the inner walls of his closets, cupboards, and medicine cabinet; he emptied the books from his bookshelves and tore apart the telephone receiver and thermostat. He upended his sofa and leather armchair to examine their undersides and even rooted through packets of encrusted cheese and stale lunchmeat in his refrigerator. He paused amid the clutter of his kitchen, wondering where in the hell he would plant a bug if he were a spy.

Gilliam's eyes focused again on the can of Raid. Why, he wondered, did the intruder touch the can? For a moment he smirked at the possibility of the spook's having encountered a cockroach that needed killing. There was no mistaking that the can had been moved, but why had the nearby dishes not been touched? There was nothing on the Formica-covered counter except dishes, a can of Raid, and a kaput light switch.

The miniature microphone with its tiny radio transmitter almost fell into his hands when he removed the plastic switch cover from the wall. Gilliam's cheeks and ears burned, not so much with his sense of having been violated as with anger. He guessed that the device could not possibly have much range, especially since its signal must travel through plaster and bricks to an outside receiver. On the other hand, a retransmitter could very well be on the roof of the building, broadcasting to a receiver miles away. His fist tightened around the device. Damn the crummy scientific details! Whether they were next door or in Antarctica, they were still listening, and probably watching as well. They'd become more sophisticated, and judging from the absence of the hooked-nose man and his fair-haired friend, more careful.

Gilliam gingerly replaced the microphone behind the wall plate. He hated few things more than bugs, of any kind, but didn't want another infestation of spies breeding another batch.

Gilliam stood for the first time in Harold J. Hammer's filing annex and gawked at the incredible volume of material collected over seventeen years of service. Like most U.S. Senators, Hammer had been assigned a series of featureless rooms—this only one of three—to house the mountains of records and correspondence bearing witness to senatorial action. While the bulk of such material was trivial, it was generally stored for eventual donation to a home-state university or library in memory of a "truly great man."

Rows of metal cabinets marked with mysterious computer codes stretched in front of Gilliam and on both sides. At the end of one row was a door that led to a similar room, and beyond that, he knew, was yet another. A short stepladder rested against one wall, for the uppermost cabinet drawers were beyond even his reach.

Gilliam could not repress a near-hopeless sigh as he pocketed the key, the same key that opened Hammer's main office suite. Somewhere in this mountain of paper, he was certain, there was a clue—however slight or seemingly innocuous—that linked Jean Murdock to the

Timber Rivers theft. He wasn't sure *why* this was so, or even that he would recognize it if by some miracle he could find it.

Gilliam stared at the rows of files, marveling at his ability to concoct outrageous suppositions. He admitted to himself that he had reached the point of grasping at straws. If only he had a nickel for every "maybe" he'd bounced around in his head over the past week; if only he'd not promised Lizzie to hold off going to the FBI to unload his story, revealing to the investigators that they should be on Murdock's tail—not his. For an instant he wished he were hardhearted enough to go back on the promise. The possibility of ruining a respected senator who was once considered presidential material seemed trivial next to the harrowing predicament he himself faced. But he'd promised Lizzie. Though he'd only really known her since Friday, he knew that the one stable feature of his tattered emotional state was the determination to keep that promise.

"What the hell?" he whispered to the empty room.

He pulled open the nearest filing drawer with the conviction that ransacking Hammer's files would at least keep his hands busy. It would be fruitless to go back to the staff office in his present condition.

"Excuse me," said a voice from behind. "Can I help you with something?" The voice belonged to a disturbingly thin young man of not more than twenty-one whose vested wool suit looked far too dignified for the inexperienced eyes and face. There were traces of suspicion in his tone, and his stare suggested a museum curator who'd just caught someone handling a priceless Etruscan urn. Gilliam swore silently, disgusted that he would probably be forced to construct an elaborate lie.

"Yeah, as a matter of fact, maybe you can," he answered. "I'm having a little tr—"

"I'll be glad to help you if you'll follow me across the hall to Senator Hammer's main office," announced the vested suit in a voice that would have been commanding were it ten years older. "This is the Senator's record annex. I'm afraid I can't let you stay in here."

Gilliam was astounded. "Well, there's nothing to worry about," he responded mildly. "You see—"

"There's no way you can have access to these records without Ms. Murdock's clearance. Do you want to come with me, please?" The young man's tone had become unmistakably abrasive.

Gilliam's mouth fell open, but he managed a tentative smile. "Uh, I don't exactly need—"

"I'll explain it one more time, sir. This is the record annex and it's got nothing but files. See? Nothing but filing cabinets. There's nothing of interest to the public in here. It's not a browsing library, so if you'll come with me, maybe you can tell me what you need and I'll—"

"Hey, will you wait a goddamn minute?" barked Gilliam. "Let me explain something to you for a change. First of all, I'm not the public. Second of all, I don't need Ms. Murdock's clearance—or your clearance—or any-damn-body's clearance to be in here." The young man's face paled as Gilliam went on.

"Did it occur to you how I got in here?" Gilliam dug out his key chain and held it high. "See this gold one? Now right offhand, what would you say this is?"

"A key," whispered the vested suit very unauthoritatively. "I see you have a key."

Gilliam was suddenly sorry to have exploded and made a conscious effort to control both his raw nerves and the edge in his voice. "Yes, I do have a key. I have this key because I'm the assistant counsel to the Senate Energy Committee. You know who chairs that Committee?"

"Yes, sir, I'm afraid I do."

"Then you can see why there's no need to call out the National Guard?"

"Yes, sir, I'm afraid I can."

"Good. Now that we're fast friends, my name is

171

Kelly Gilliam. What's yours?" He offered the kid his hand.

"Hudson Merriweather."

"Happy to meet you, Hudson. Now, what do you do around here, anyway?"

Merriweather looked very much relieved and explained to Gilliam that he was a college intern selected from many applicants to spend the summer working in Hammer's office for credit toward his political science degree. Since he'd been on the job for only two weeks, he naturally had not recognized Gilliam. In spite of the kid's odd manner, Gilliam was impressed with his apparent brightness and found himself liking him. Moreover, Merriweather seemed genuinely contrite over his faux pas.

"Mr. Gilliam, I wouldn't hold it against you if you felt like blasting me in the chops after what I just pulled," he said. "I guess I'm still awfully impressed with myself."

"Don't worry about it, Hudson. I'm not what you'd call prone to violence, and besides that, everybody's entitled to feel important every now and then."

"Maybe there really is something I can help you with."

Gilliam hesitated for a moment to consider how much he should divulge to Merriweather. "Yeah, I think there is, now that you mention it," he responded. "Do you by chance know how this filing system works?"

Indeed Merriweather did, for most of his time thus far had been spent learning the computerized filing system—backward and forward. No member of the Senator's personal staff, he'd been told by Jean Murdock, could function without a working knowledge of the system. Merriweather had been yearning for the day when he could put his knowledge to work.

The files, he explained, were ordered numerically by a computer identification code, divided into twenty

172

major subject headings. Under each heading were scores of individual "issue codes" that were assigned to each file. Using these codes, a staff member could instantly pinpoint the status of any case, letter, or project under consideration in the senator's office. By scanning the computer's memory within a given subject category, an operator could determine who had contacted the senator's office on that particular subject, how often such contact had been made, and when the contacts had been made. The field "HISTORY" within each identification entry provided a few descriptive sentences on the person with the identification number.

Gilliam was intrigued.

"Hudson," he asked more conspiratorially than he intended, "do you have an issue code directory I could borrow?"

"Sure. Let's go to the office."

"Hold on a sec." Gilliam had no desire to go to the office and encounter Murdock. "Maybe I should tell you what I have in mind and get your advice first."

To a flattered Merriweather, Gilliam spun the lie. It was his intention, he said, to scan the senator's correspondence relating to various nuclear issues in order to find material for use in committee debates on pending nuclear legislation. He didn't want to use a terminal in Hammer's office complex because he needed to be close to his reference material in his Capitol office. Could the Committee's terminal be used to accomplish such a scan? he wondered.

"Sure," said Merriweather. "All you need is the telephone number to the Senator's account with Digitron, his account number, and the password. I can give you those since you work for the Senator."

Gilliam savored the dawn of hope that his task had possibly been simplified, that he would be spared the tedium of physically wading through the mass of paper in the records annex.

173

"I'll tell you what, Hudson. Can you call me at the Committee staff office and give me those numbers? I'll also need the issue code directory."

"If you have a pencil, I'll give you the numbers right now," said Merriweather triumphantly. "I've memorized them."

Gilliam had characteristically forgotten to bring something to write on, so he recorded the information on the back of his hand with a felt-tip pen. The access password to Hammer's account was the senator's first name—Harry—spelled backward.

"You can take the code directory from this room," offered Merriweather. "We only keep it here so some-one can use it if they get mixed up while poking through the files. That doesn't happen very often and I'm sure nobody'd miss it."

"Outstanding. Hudson, I think you've probably saved my life." Gilliam was handed a folder with several sheets of paper bound inside. He looked up from a quick perusal of the columns of codes typed on the pages. "I've got one last question. If I access your office account from another terminal, do I tie it up so it can't be used from your office?"

"No, not really," replied Merriweather. "Judging from what you need, you'll be using a program package called SCANCOM. Most of the time we use an UPDATE package for putting in new records or changing old ones. SCANCOM and UPDATE can be used at the same time."

"But if I'm on SCANCOM and one of your legislative aides wants to get on, too, he's out of luck. Right?"

"I'm afraid so, Mr. Gilliam. But why don't I just give you a call if I see someone getting ready to go up on SCANCOM? That would probably simplify things, wouldn't it?"

Gilliam couldn't believe it; Hudson Merriweather had turned out to be the best piece of luck he'd had in weeks. "That would be perfect. I promise to sign off

SCANCOM if anyone in your shop needs it. Hey, does anyone ever call you Hud?"

Merriweather looked shocked. "Never," he said.

After a maddening twenty-minute wait for a Committee staffer to wrap up her business on the computer terminal, Gilliam sat down at the machine with its television screen and typewriter keyboard. While following the instructions in the bulky *Digitron Data Management User's Manual,* he tried to visualize the physical features of the vast electrical intelligence he was about to awaken.

The first step was to punch the prescribed number on the terminal telephone and await the constant tone that would connect his eyes and fingers to the computer in distant Virginia. When the tone came after a few rings of a telephone, he planted the receiver into the cradle of the acoustic coupler and the viewscreen came alive:

ACCOUNT NUMBER?

Gilliam consulted the back of his hand and typed the digits.

PASSWORD?

He typed "YRRAH."

WELCOME TO DIGITRON DATA
MANAGEMENT CORPORATION:
OX   21 MAY   10:47AM
PROGRAM?

He selected the appropriate response from the user's manual and now his typed characters appeared below the computer's message on the screen: "SCAN-COMM."

The computer responded with mechanical disrespect from the safety of its artificial cave far away:

175

INVALID ENTRY—TRY AGAIN

After a few moments of rummaging through the user's manual, he discovered that the computer insisted on correct spellings. He muttered a silent blasphemy and retyped "SCANCOM" with only one M, after which the computer responded:

SERVICE?

Gilliam typed "SEARCH."

FIELD?

He typed "HISTORY" because he was primarily interested in the concise summaries of what was known about each recorded entry.

SELECTION?

He answered "YES."

SPECIFY SELECTION REQUIREMENT

Gilliam consulted the issue code directory given him by Hudson and entered the set of numbers under the first heading: "Nuclear Power: Security and Safeguards." Entering that particular code—HO1—would instruct the machine to pull from its incredibly vast memory the ID numbers of those who had contacted Senator Hammer over some aspect of the nuclear security issue. To Gilliam, this looked as good a place as any to start.

After a few more questions and consultations with the manual, Gilliam got his first piece of information. For the next six hours and forty-five minutes, he sat at the console, absorbing two- and three-sentence descriptions of the letters and telegrams that had been sent to Harry Hammer on the subject of nuclear materials safeguards and security. Most of the "histories" told little about the actual writers. They provided tidbits such as how often communications had been received from a given individual and how they had been handled. An occasional history specified that the writer was of special interest to the office—a campaign contributor, perhaps, or a Democratic Party official. A staggering number of letters and telegrams were from executives in the nuclear industry who unvaryingly urged Hammer to reject "hysterical" pleas for more stringent nuclear safeguards. The bulk of the histories Gilliam scanned, however, represented everyday people who had probably become alarmed by newspaper or magazine stories of lax nuclear safeguards.

By the time his aching back and rumbling stomach told him he could sit at the terminal no longer, Gilliam had scanned only 2,400 records, an average of only six per minute. He'd seen nothing that seemed even slightly suspicious, and while he'd jotted the ID numbers of more than twenty individuals whose "histories" indicated an association with the nuclear industry, he seriously doubted that the actual copies of their correspondence would provide any connection with Jean Murdock. To make matters worse, he had no idea how many more entries he must scan before completing just one issue selection. The next entry in the issue directory was HO2—"Nuclear Power: Facilities Licensing"—but there could very well be another 20,000 records to see in HO1.

Burt Strong's gravel-filled voice interrupted the monotonous *bleeps* of the computer terminal.

"Hey, I've been looking for your ass all day, and now I see you've been right here. I hope that whatever the hell you're doing is important, but don't tell me about it because I'm too pooped to even listen." He approached and leaned against the terminal, his face tired and drawn.

"Just scanning a little correspondence," answered Gilliam, hoping that Strong would accept the short answer and pursue the matter no further.

"You're going to be a busy boy for the next couple of days, but it's your own fault since you didn't check in with me today so you could get an earlier start. The Committee's throwing an executive session day after tomorrow, and you know what that means—work for you and me."

Gilliam exhaled a tired sigh. "Wonderful. Looks like we'll be writing memos galore so the Senators can look informed. What's on the agenda, not that I need ask?"

Strong lifted his flask of scotch while the computer warned Gilliam that unless he entered the next command, it would shut itself off to avoid wasting valuable time "on line."

"From the sound of things," said Strong, "our bosses are starting to catch hell over that abortion in New Hampshire—you know, constituents screaming that the raid smacks of a police state, people being arrested and detained without being charged, that sort of thing. Lots of people are getting nervous, Kelly."

Gilliam could understand that. Little was actually known on Capitol Hill about the massive investigation launched by the federal government to recover the stolen plutonium. Involved officials were issuing precious little real information on leads, tactics, and the prospects of solving the case (if there were any!). The newspapers and networks could deliver only unverified scuttlebutt picked up through low-echelon contacts in the agencies, the result being daily news reports full of wild conjecture and rather scary theories. Among the first to feel the effects of public apprehension on any issue were congressmen and senators. The flood of letters, telegrams, and calls had spurred the Committee to take the most drastic action it could think of under the circumstances—holding an executive session.

"What about the boss?" asked Gilliam. "Is he back yet?"

"He hasn't shown up," muttered Strong disgustedly. "Don't look so shocked. Can't you tell from my face?

Everybody tells me I'm cute when I'm worried, and right now I feel so cute I could just shit."

"How can we hold an executive session without Hammer?"

"We'll have to wing it, that's all. Maybe I can get Murdock to get a statement from Harry so we can read it at the meeting."

For the first time during the conversation, Gilliam forgot about his own personal woes. The computer shut itself off, but he didn't notice.

"Burt, don't you think it's time you go to Hammer yourself? You're the staff director of this Committee, for Christ's sake, and this is more your business than Murdock's."

Gilliam waved the flask away when Strong offered it and headed to the nearby coffeemaker instead.

"What about it? The time has come, hasn't it? You said yourself that something weird is going on." He burned his lips on the hot coffee.

"I tried, damn it."

"You tried? When?"

"Last night and today. I called the house at Lake Barcroft. All I got was one of those damn telephone recorders that tells you to leave a message. Well, I left a message—in fact I left five messages—and used the word 'urgent' in every one of them. If you really want to know, I've spent the whole goddamn day calling everybody I know trying to find the son of a bitch. I even called his kid in L.A. You don't think it taxes your creativity to call thirty different people trying to find a U.S. Senator without raising all kinds of wild suspicions? Try it sometime."

"Jesus," said Gilliam, barely audibly. "Hammer's got a housekeeper, doesn't he? You'd think the housekeeper would have been at the house."

"He's got a housekeeper, a cook, and the biggest, ugliest dog I've ever seen. I would have settled for talking to the dog, believe me."

"And Murdock still says he's at home sick with the flu, or something like that?"

"That's what she says, Kelly."

The wall clock emitted a series of sharp buzzes heralding the end of the Senate's afternoon session. Within seconds, members of the steno and clerical staff filed through the office to join the human tide retreating from Capitol Hill after the day's work. Gilliam and Strong suspended their conversation until the last of the staff had departed.

"What are we going to do, Burt?" asked Gilliam after his final gulp of coffee.

"I'll tell you what I'm going to do. I'm going home to break out a bottle of Chivas Royal Salute I've been saving for a special occasion. When my wife leaves for her bridge club meeting, I'm going to start drinking it to see if I can still get soused. Then, tomorrow morning when I wake up in the chair that my wife has left me in, I'm going to swear to start going to AA again, take a shower, feel like a new man, and come in for a nice Saturday full of work. Now, if I were you, I'd go home and get some conventional rest. Your eyes look like a couple of sphincters."

"Eye strain from looking at this viewscreen all day," explained Gilliam.

"You eaten today?"

"Not since breakfast." Actually, Gilliam had left his breakfast untouched in its bowl.

"Well, eat something and get some sleep. You'll need it for the full day you'll have tomorrow. And by the way, don't go wandering off when you come in without checking with me first. I still run this circus, you know." Strong fetched his sports coat and left the staff offices with a steady gait that gave no clue to the volume of scotch he'd probably consumed that day. Gilliam was surprised that Strong, an overindulger in the work ethic, was actually leaving at 5:05, a good two hours ahead of his customary time. For a moment, Gilliam tried to imagine the depth of Strong's anxiety over the disappearance of Harry Hammer, but gave up. Harder yet was understanding the old man's loyalty to the senator, a loyalty that must have been sorely tested since the day Hammer shunted him aside. Somehow Strong's loyalty had survived his tumble from the center of power, the extinction of Hammer's presidential dreams, and his obvious relegation to the status of an outsider.

The jangling telephone jerked Gilliam back to reality.

"Is Mr. Kelly Gilliam in, please?" asked a voice that generated an image of malnutrition in a three-piece suit.

"Speaking. What can I do for you, Hudson Merriweather?"

"Oh, hi, Mr. Gilliam. I didn't recognize your voice. I'm just calling to pass on something I thought you might want to know. I just overheard Ms. Murdock taking a call from a Digitron account representative."

Gilliam cut in, trying to sound unworried. "Hudson, are you someplace where you can't be overheard? I'd hate to get you in trouble with Mur—with Ms. Murdock."

"No problem there," Merriweather assured him. "She's gone out somewhere and I'm alone in the annex. Just about everybody's split."

"Okay, but keep your eyes open. What have you got?"

"Like I said, she was on the phone to Digitron. I only heard one side of the conversation, but I was able to piece it together—know what I mean?"

"I know what you mean. Please don't keep me in suspense, Hudson."

"I won't. Remember when I told you how to access SCANCOM? Well, I forgot to tell you about Digitron's security system."

"Terrific. What about it?"

"Digitron makes a big deal about information security in order to discourage someone from stealing confidential stuff that a client has put into the computer. That's why you have to punch in the account number and the password to gain access."

"I'm with you so far, Hudson."

"Here's the problem, Mr. Gilliam. The senator's office has only two terminals, both of which were in use all day today. One of them was hooked into an UP-DATE program to deal with incoming letters and the other was printing address labels for a mass mailing. Computers can do that, you know."

Gilliam fought against exasperation. "Yeah, computers are amazing. Now, on with your story."

"For sure. Because both of our terminals were on line, the Digitron computer became aware that a third terminal had access to our account and consequently followed its programmed security procedure."

"It started barking?"

"Nope. It told the line technician. When the guy checked, he discovered that someone was accessing SCANCOM on *our* account."

Some innate warning device told Gilliam that he should start feeling sick. "I'm almost afraid to ask what happened then."

Merriweather continued. "The line technician called Ms. Murdock and informed her that there might be an unauthorized access. She asked the guy if he could trace the telephone number of the unauthorized terminal and he did."

"Do you know that for sure?"

"Absolutely. I heard her say your office's phone number back to him, and I called one of your clerks just to confirm it."

"Then you're telling me that Murdock knows that someone from this office has been scanning the senator's files."

"That's right, Mr. Gilliam. Now, I didn't think it was any big deal—if you know what I mean. The sen-

ator's Committee staff is looking at his correspondence
—so what? But then something strange happened."

"How strange?"

"Ms. Murdock got this very worried, very intense look
on her face, like the world was going to end or something. She hung up the phone and went to the steno
annex and hauled out the latest computer ID directory.
You know what that looks like?"

"I have an idea it's probably very big and bulky if
it's got a list of everybody in the files," said Gilliam.
"Is it in alphabetical order or something?"

"Exactly, and it takes up a whole wall cabinet. Digitron replaces it with updated versions occasionally."

"So what did she do with it?"

"She got out a volume with N's in it, copied down an
ID number, and went to the printout terminal—not the
viewscreen, fortunately, but the one that prints out on
paper. She told the guy who was using it to take a break
and sat down at the terminal herself. It was kind of
tough for me to see exactly what was going on, Mr.
Gilliam, so I waited until she was finished, hoping that
she wouldn't bother to dispose of the paper she would
use in her operation. Well, she didn't, and I was able
to get my hands on it when she left. It was very curious."

"How curious?"

"She deleted an entire record—not just one or two
fields under the ID number, but the whole thing. You
want to take a look at it?"

Merriweather met Gilliam at a bench in Capitol
Plaza, where he sat under an apple tree full of noisy
squirrels, and handed him a folded sheet of computer
record paper. A breeze stirred the tree and diluted the
smog from the rush-hour traffic that still raged along
Pennsylvania, Constitution, and Independence avenues.
Gilliam had no trouble reading the sheet of paper.

"As you can see," said Merriweather, "it's not really

an entry—it's a deletion. Ms. Murdock simply erased Digitron's memory of Record Number 378866, Dr. Yoshi Nakamura—I'd guess that's how you'd pronounce it—of Los Angeles, California."

Merriweather pointed further down the page. "See where Digitron asked 'ARE YOU SURE?' and where Ms. Murdock answered 'YES'?" Gilliam nodded intently as his eyes devoured the information on the sheet: RECORD 378866 DELETED.

"And down here," observed Gilliam, pointing to the bottom of the page, "she ran a little test by trying to call up number 378866."

"And Digitron answered 'RECORD 378866 DOES NOT EXIST.' "

"So right now, the only record of this Dr. Nakamura is in your files," said Gilliam.

"And in the ID directory," added Merriweather. "Finding it in either of those two places would mean you'd already have to know Nakamura's name, or have a couple years to kill in just wandering through the files."

"Right. That's what I tried. No way to cross-reference now that the computer has never heard of 378866, eh?"

"That's right, Mr. Gilliam. Of course, if Ms. Murdock were superserious about wiping out all traces of this record, she'd probably tear the appropriate page out of the directory and remove the correspondence file from the records annex."

Gilliam suddenly felt a strong sense of urgency and sat rigidly upright on the bench.

"Hudson," he said, "I've got to ask you for one more favor. I hate to do it, but I've got no choice. It's absolutely crucial that I get all the information I can on this Dr.—what's her name—Nakamura. Can you get me her correspondence file and a copy of the entries under her number in the ID directory?"

Merriweather was alarmed by the hint of desperation

in Gilliam's voice. His face showed confusion over an interesting game suddenly turning into an obviously serious matter. Gilliam rapidly searched his mind for a way to keep Merriweather's help without concocting an elaborate story or taking him completely into confidence. Each of them hesitated, wondering what to say next.

Shooting in the dark, Gilliam said, "You don't trust her either, do you?"

Taken aback by the curveball, Merriweather replied, "It's not that I don't trust her, Mr. Gilliam. I've had no reason to distrust her. I do think it's strange that she'd delete a computer record for no good reason. It's just . . . well . . . I just don't like her!"

"Amen!" said Gilliam, feeling relieved. "You'll be pleased to know that most of the earth's sentient species share your opinion. Why don't you like her, just out of curiosity?"

"Well, the first thing she said to me when I walked into her office was 'You're Merriweather, the new intern? Get me a cup of coffee. Black.' It's been downhill from there. And I'm allergic to cigarette smoke, which she blows straight in my face, even though I've told her about it."

"I guess you might expect that kind of stuff from a senator, but not from his aide, huh?"

"From the Senator? When nobody's around, she talks to him the same way! You wouldn't want to hear some of the things I caught one night when I came in late to call Mom on the free phone."

"You can bet your ass that I would want to hear them, Hudson, but right now I want to get my hands on the Nakamura files even more. Look, you already swiped a computer record from Murdock. Can you do this one more thing for me?"

Merriweather thought for a moment. "Okay, Mr. Gilliam, I'll do what I can."

Forty-five minutes later Merriweather entered the

Committee's Capitol office where Gilliam waited in the company of a silent computer terminal and a fresh pot of coffee.

"Did you get them?" Gilliam asked anxiously.

The young man postponed his answer until he'd studied the carpet under his feet.

"I'm afraid I wouldn't make a very good undercover agent, Mr. Gilliam," he replied at length. "I got my priorities mixed up and went to the ID directory first. I should've gotten the correspondence file first, since it would've been the most important."

"What do you mean 'would've been'?" pressed Gilliam.

"The correspondence file was gone. Numbers 378865 and 378867 were there, but not 378866."

"Then she got there first," hissed Gilliam, half to himself. "Did you get *anything*, Hudson?"

From somewhere in his vest Merriweather withdrew a Xerox copy of a page from the Digitron ID directory. "I hope this is better than nothing," he said, handing the sheet to Gilliam. While he offered a profound apology for failing to accomplish the whole assignment, Gilliam absorbed the information and pondered what to do next, scarcely hearing Merriweather's words.

At 3:22 P.M., Pacific Daylight Time, a telephone rang in the admissions office of the Widener Mental Health Center in Eagle Rock, California. It was 6:22 P.M. in Washington, D.C. At the caller's request, the receptionist buzzed the Director of Admissions, Dr. Simon Blum.

"A Mr. Kelly Gilliam from a U.S. Senate Committee to talk to you on line three, Doctor."

Slumped over his desk in the Capitol, Gilliam waited for Dr. Blum to come on the line and forced his tired eyes to focus on the Xeroxed page concerning correspondence from Dr. Yoshi Nakamura. Various coded symbols deciphered with Merriweather's help told him that Nakamura was not a physician as he'd previously assumed, but a nuclear physicist. She'd written to Hammer initially on America's responsibility to Japanese victims of atomic warfare. Nakamura's later letters had dealt with "Nuclear Power: Social and Environmental Effects." Her "history" was a longer than customary summary referring vaguely to Hammer's efforts toward getting Nakamura appointed to various teaching positions at unnamed universities. Letters had been written by Hammer (though Gilliam was willing to guess that Murdock had been the real author) supporting Nakamura's claim to have been "discriminated against," but the summaries didn't explain how or why the alleged discrimination had occurred. Most striking was the address from which Nakamura's letters had been sent— Widener Mental Health Center, a mental hospital. According to the directory record, Nakamura had not corresponded with Hammer's office in over five years, a fact that heightened Gilliam's suspicion over Murdock's purging the computer's memory of Nakamura immediately after hearing that the files were being scanned.

"Mr. Gilliam, this is Si Blum speaking," said a voice in Eagle Rock.

Gilliam dredged up his "important" voice. "Dr. Blum, I'm acting as congressional liaison to the federal investigation of the Timber Rivers theft," he lied, hoping that his choice of words smacked sufficiently of officialdom. "Are you familiar with the matter?"

"Only from what I see in the papers and on TV."

"Yes, good. Then you understand why we must investigate every possible lead, no matter how tenuous it seems to be."

"I'm aware that it's a very serious thing and that everybody's doing everything they can, if that's what you mean. How can I help you, Mr. Gilliam?"

"It's come to our attention that your institution has or once had a patient named Yoshi Nakamura, a physicist."

"We could very well have had one by that name, but we don't at the present time," replied Blum.

"I see. Would it be too much trouble, Doctor, for you to check on it for me? This is extremely important to the investigation."

Blum put Gilliam on hold and asked his secretary to see whether the center ever had such a patient. Less than a minute passed before he came back on the line.

"Mr. Gilliam, I can confirm that we did have a patient by that name," said Blum, "but she was released five years ago this spring—June first, to be exact."

Gilliam's heart started pounding in anticipation of finally getting somewhere, and he had difficulty maintaining a dispassionately official tone. "I see. Good. That corroborates what we already have. Now, Dr. Blum, I need some specific information on Nakamura herself."

"Sorry."

"Excuse me?"

"I said I'm sorry, Mr. Gilliam. I've given you all I can over the phone."

"I'm afraid I don't understand."

"I'm certain that as a federal official, you can understand that I can't simply recite personal case histories over the phone, Mr. Gilliam. There are laws protecting privacy and confidentiality, but I'm sure you must know that as well. You see, I don't know you from a bale of hay, Mr. Gilliam. Since I haven't seen your credentials, you could be anyone."

Gilliam was thunderstruck. He'd not foreseen this obvious but infuriating obstacle.

"Ah . . . yes, of course, Doctor, I am certainly aware of the statutes you mentioned, and I can appreciate your position. Perhaps you can just tell me where we can reach Dr. Nakamura."

"I can tell you nothing of the sort," responded Blum. "Now if you'll proceed through proper legal channels, I'll be delighted to cooperate fully."

"Yes, of course. Well, then, I'll do just that. Thank you, Doctor."

"My pleasure."

Gilliam resisted slamming the receiver into its cradle and glanced at Merriweather, who sat with his elbows on a typewriter, his head resting wearily on his fists.

"Hudson," said Gilliam, "I need another favor."

The young man looked feebly interested. "Will I ever get to know what all this is about?"

"Yes, you will, my friend, when I can find the time to tell you. Do you have a car?"

"Yes."

"Good. Where's it parked?"

"Around the corner on First."

"Here's what we're going to do. I'm going to call the Dirksen Building guards to tell them to let you into the underground garage. I'll say you're picking up some crates full of files or something like that. You come in and drive down to Level C—that's the third one down —and bear right until you see me beside a red Volvo. Get out, open the trunk as quickly as possible, and I'll get in."

"You've got to be kidding."

"The story's not over yet, Hudson," said Gilliam. "When you put me in the trunk, drive out of the garage and head for a dark alley somewhere off the Hill so you can let me out. I don't want to ride all the way up the Baltimore-Washington Parkway to the airport in the trunk."

"*I'm* taking you to the airport?"

"That's right."

"But why all the way up there? National is much closer."

"Hudson," said Gilliam, hoping with all his might that his new friend could be trusted, "if you haven't guessed by now, someone is watching me. That's why I need your help."

"Do you know who it is?" asked Merriweather eagerly.

"No, not exactly, but I'm fairly certain that they'd see me at either Dulles or National, and I wouldn't be surprised if they've tapped the office phones. I took a calculated risk in calling that mental hospital just now in the interest of saving time."

Merriweather suddenly looked very worried. "Is Ms. Murdock involved somehow?"

"I can't tell you about that yet, Hudson. But I can tell you that if you help me, you'll be doing the right thing. If you be cool, do what I tell you, and keep all this to yourself for the time being, we'll both be all right. Is it a deal?"

"Only if you promise to fill me in."

"I promise, Hudson, I promise."

While Merriweather departed in confusion to bring his car, Gilliam called Liz to say that he'd be away for a couple of days and that her deadline was extended. The conversation was brief and guarded, but Kelly could easily catch the worry in Liz's voice. He hung up reluctantly, wanting to say more, knowing that it would be a mistake.

On his way into the cavernous layers of underground parking, Gilliam wondered what Strong would say when he failed to find him at work the next morning. First Hammer missing and now Gilliam AWOL. Strong would definitely be pissed off.

Oh well, he thought, his mind racing, I'll just have to tell Burt I got the flu and switched my phone off because I needed the rest. Might as well lie about leaving him a message, too. Strong was a good friend but a tough boss. He'd even been afraid to ask Strong for half a day to fly down to Dallas to talk to Rice's widow. She might have had answers to many questions. Too bad that Strong's such a . . . Shit! Dallas! He could fly there tonight and *still* be in L.A. tomorrow morning in time to visit the Widener Center. Dallas is almost on the way. Rice is just as important to this case as Dr. Nakawhatever. And no late flight out of Baltimore would get him to L.A. without pogo-sticking through Atlanta or somewhere. . . .

American Airlines Flight 237 broke through scattered cloud cover at five thousand feet and landed in Dallas at 10:00 P.M. Dallas. Former home of Wesley Rice, the man who had unknowingly put Kelly Gilliam into the chowder pot. Dallas. Present home of Rice's widow.

Gilliam rushed off the plane straight to a phone book, scanned the Rices, and found only one Wesley. He elected not to call the Rice residence. No reason to give the widow a chance to notify the wrong people of his arrival. Better to get her out of bed or even miss her entirely. He jotted the address and sprinted like a television halfback for the rental car desks. Thanks to the map of Dallas that came with the Ford cómpact, he was parking in front of the Rice home minutes before 11 P.M.

Lights burned downstairs and Gilliam could see the entire house and grounds clearly. For pseudo-rococo Spanish modern it wasn't bad. Even the crabgrass, which Texans import under the name "St. Augustine Grass," had a lush, green look in the artificial light.

He squared his shoulders, readied his opening lines, and pressed the doorbell lightly. Booming chimes played Big Ben's theme at what seemed like Big Ben's volume. Conditioned by Washington living, he fully expected the door to open only as far as a safety chain would allow. He was surprised when it suddenly opened wide, framing a short, pleasantly rounded woman in her late forties. She wore a thin dressing gown, slippers, glasses, and a politely expectant smile. After a moment's hesitation, Gilliam realized that he must launch right into his prepared speech.

"Hello, Mrs. Rice?"

"Yes."

"My name is Kelly Gilliam. I'm an investigator for the Senate Energy Committee. I'm sorry to bother you so late in the evening, but I just got to town and I took a chance and drove over to see if you were still up. Do you mind if I come in and we talk for a few minutes?"

Gilliam displayed his Senate I.D. and Mrs. Rice ushered him into a formal living room. There were pale-blue velvet drapes and plush pale-blue upholstery. He glanced around for a seat that wouldn't make him feel like a piece of jewelry in a case and settled lightly into a broad-winged armchair. Mrs. Rice plopped down unceremoniously onto the couch.

"Don't worry about the furniture," she said, laughing at his discomfort. "It's not my taste, so the sooner it wears out, the sooner I can replace it."

"Is it . . . uh, *was* it your husband's taste?" he asked, still feeling uncomfortable.

"No, it was more like our joint decision about what *should* be his taste. I miss Wesley, but this stuff doesn't make me think of him. Only of his associates we had to entertain. Now, how can I help you, Mr. Gilliam? I assume you're here because of Wesley's death."

"I'm afraid so, Mrs. Rice. My Committee is investigating everything that might have some connection, no matter how remote, with thefts of nuclear material. I know it's a longshot, but your husband's death did come right after a big theft."

"You mean the one in Connecticut?"

"Yes. Did the investigators who came around after Mr. Rice's death mention that to you?"

"No, they didn't. The police didn't say anything about it. They naturally wanted to know if Wesley was in any trouble or whether he was depressed. You know, things like that. I heard later that there had been some federal investigators around too, but I'm afraid I wasn't in good enough shape to talk with them at the time. I was under sedation. But, I guess you've read all their reports."

"As a matter of fact, I haven't. Our investigation is entirely separate from theirs." Gilliam left open the question of who they were.

"Well," Mrs. Rice continued, "an FBI man came around a couple of days ago asking whether I had any more information on why my husband would kill himself."

Gilliam noticed that she said "kill himself" without hesitation. Strong lady, he thought to himself.

"He also asked me about his friends and business acquaintances. In fact," she continued calmly, "I specifically remember his asking me if Wesley knew of anybody by the name of Kelly Gilliam."

Gilliam fought to keep his composure, knowing that surprise showed all over his face. "Well," he said with a forced chuckle, "I guess our investigations are more separate than I thought. Investigating the investigators. That's thorough."

"It certainly is, but I'm not at all surprised."

"You're not?" Gilliam asked weakly.

"No, I'm not. All those others never once mentioned that they were investigating a nuclear theft. They were obviously playing it pretty close to the vest. Yet you told me about it right after you walked in the door. Now I know why those goons sit outside, watching my house all the time. They probably think I'm involved in the theft."

"Goons? Outside?"

"Yes."

"But you're not involved in the theft."

"No, I'm not," she answered.

Gilliam smiled, as much to reassure himself as Mrs. Rice. "I know this is a roundabout way to conduct an investigation, but did they ask about anyone else besides me?"

"Oh, the FBI man had quite a list, but I couldn't be of much help to him. I remember the name Bates and somebody called Goldstein or Goldfarb, but nobody on his list rang a bell. And he didn't seem too interested in anyone I mentioned."

"Do you mind if I offer my own list of names?" Gilliam asked.

"No, go right ahead."

"How about Paul Boris?" Gilliam started, dreaming up an imaginary name to head his "list."

"No."

"Jonah Brown?"

"Uh-uh."

"Maybe Jean Murdock?"

She sat up straight, startled. "Yes, that name does mean something, Mr. Gilliam. She was one of Wesley's girl friends. But she works for the Senate, too. Isn't it strange that everyone in Washington is investigating everyone else? Do you suppose she's investigating the FBI?"

"I wouldn't put it past her," Gilliam said more grimly than he intended. Then, to cover his sudden intensity, he asked, "How did you know about her?"

"After the first few years, Wesley never hid any of his girl friends from me. I know about her because he tried to keep her a secret. That seemed strange. So when he disappeared a couple of times for 'business' reasons that didn't ring true, I plugged into the Old Girl Network at the club. I soon knew everything I needed to know. But tell me, Mr. Gilliam, is she involved in the theft?"

"I think so," Gilliam answered simply.

They sized one another up for a moment. He liked her and it was clear that mutual trust was possible. He toyed with the idea of telling his real problem in exchange for more information. Finally, just before the silence became absurd, she spoke. "The FBI agent also

asked me if there was a suicide note. There wasn't one
. . . then."

"But now . . . ?" Gilliam let his voice trail off.

"No note now either."

"But . . . ?"

"I found it yesterday and burned it. Wesley must
have wanted me to find it after I got over the shock of
his death; it was in my locker at the racquet club. I
think he put it there early in the morning, between the
time he left home and his arrival at the office. He was
a major owner of the club, so he had keys to everything.
If you promise to do all you can to keep Wesley's name
clear, Mr. Gilliam, I'll tell you what was in the note.
I can see now how important it might be."

"That's fair. I'll try as hard as I can to keep him out
of it. But"—and here Gilliam took a deep breath—"you
have to do the same thing for me. If anybody asks you
if I've been here, and that includes the FBI, say no. If
I've been seen coming here, you might have to dream
up a name for the nice investigator from the Senate.
Somebody thinks I'm involved in this thing, too."

She studied his face again and smiled. "But you're
not."

"No, I'm not."

"Okay. And I'll say nothing about Jean Murdock?"

"Nothing. If things work out right, I'll tell them all
about her myself. Now, if we're agreed, what was in
the note?"

"I memorized the words and I don't think I'll ever
forget them. Wesley said, 'Jo, I put you through a lot
and you always stood by me, but I can't put you through
what might happen next. I've betrayed you, my company, and maybe even my country. You may find this
hard to believe, but I love you. Good-bye. Wes.'" She
said the words slowly, almost formally, as if she were
reciting a speech in class. "Wesley wrote on the en-
velope that only I was to open the letter, and that I was

to destroy it and tell nobody about it. Now it appears that I've betrayed him, but I doubt that it matters any more. Mr. Gilliam, do you think Wesley was involved with the theft, or maybe even part of it?"

"I don't know, but I don't think so, Mrs. Rice. I suspect that he just gave Murdock the inside information she needed, probably without knowing exactly what he was doing."

"I'd like to think that," she answered, "but it's difficult."

"Not if you know Murdock," Gilliam said bitterly.

"You sound like you know her well."

"Too well and not well enough, but—"

"I'm not asking you for details. It's late and I've run out of useful things to tell you, too." She rose and offered Gilliam her hand, gripping his firmly without letting go. "I'm really glad you came. You gave me the chance to tell someone trustworthy and understanding about the note." She put her arm around his shoulders and took him to the door. They smiled at each other, and she waved from the entryway as he drove off.

Gilliam's thoughts were confused as he headed back to the airport. What had he really gained from his conversation with Mrs. Rice? Certainly not enough to clear himself. The one solid clarification was Rice's relationship with Murdock. He'd established that beyond doubt. He'd also proved to himself that Lizzie was right about Murdock's two-timing Hammer. According to the suicide note, Rice betrayed his wife, his company, and his country. To Gilliam, that could mean only one thing. But how would it sound to a federal investigator? he wondered.

He stiffened when he saw headlights in his rearview mirror. The lights followed him through the residential neighborhood, onto the main highway. He forced himself to relax, to remember that he'd seen no one outside the Rice home. Goddamn paranoia, he thought. Jumpy nerves to boot.

He drove on. The freeway, except for his car and the silent lights in the mirror, was nearly deserted. He glanced at his watch and determined that he had time to kill, time to find out if the car behind him was innocent or guilty.

Gilliam swung into the next exit. The car behind him followed. Blood rushed to his head. He had a wild desire to pull over, rush to the window of the other car, and confess everything, just to end the whole horror show. Instead, he worked his way along side streets to the first on-ramp of the freeway. The other car followed, no longer bothering to maintain a discreet distance. Gilliam realized that he could not now go to the Dallas airport. Suppose the goons followed him to the mental hospital in L.A., discovering the Murdock connection to Nakamura, and acting on it before he had a chance to tell Lizzie? He couldn't let that happen. He must first clear himself and prevent the ruin of a respected senator.

He knew that he must ditch his followers and find another airport for his flight. The odds were fair that the Dallas airport was now crawling with goons waiting for Kelly Gilliam, or at least waiting for someone who was probably Kelly Gilliam. Judging from the way his present follower was tailgating, Gilliam doubted that the guy would fall for a backdoor escape act like the one he pulled in Washington.

So how do you shake a pro who doesn't care if you know he's on to you? he wondered. Duck into a crowded department store, maybe? Sure, if you can find one open in the wee hours. Gilliam even wondered if he should return to Mrs. Rice's house and spend time there until the stores opened. Just as he labeled the idea crummy, his headlights picked up a small figure topped by a large cowboy hat. He slowed, saw an outstretched thumb, and pulled onto the shoulder. The following car likewise slowed and stopped about a hundred feet behind. The hitchhiker climbed in and Gilliam felt the first tentative wisps of an interesting scheme. He gestured back toward the other car and said, "Amazing that you got a choice of rides in the middle of the night. My buddy back there could have picked you up, too."

"Yeah, fuckin' amazing."

Gilliam glanced at his rider. The man was old, maybe even seventy, and his face was sunburned and deeply creased. His breath stank of aromatic snuff. Gilliam decided to launch his scheme before his pursuer had a chance to bring in reinforcements.

"Where you heading?" he asked.

"Fort Worth."

"You live there?"

"Yeah."

"Great!" answered Gilliam with feigned enthusiasm. "That's where I'm going too."

"Yeah. Fuckin' A great."

Undaunted, Gilliam forged on. "I'm just dropping my car so I'll have it next week when I come back. I could let you have it for a few days if you'd drive it in for me. My buddy back there could drive me right home from here."

The man looked at him like he was crazy. "You'd give your car to a fuckin' stranger?"

This was just what Gilliam wanted to hear. Trying not to sound too eager, he slowly answered, "I'll get it back. Just write your address inside your hat there and lend it to me. I know you'll make sure to get it back."

"Fuckin' A straight I would." He actually smiled at Gilliam. Not giving the man a chance to think things through, Gilliam handed him a pen from his jacket. The old man carefully lettered the information on the inside label.

"Thanks a lot, I really appreciate this," Gilliam said, scanning the road for a place to stop. He wanted to get away from The Shadow fast but didn't relish the idea of standing on a deserted highway. In the distance, he could see the lights of a truck stop growing steadily brighter. Gilliam swung the car into the rest area of the truck stop, parking next to a truck that momentarily shielded his car from his follower's sight. He jumped out with a quick "thanks," slammed the door, and jammed the cowboy hat on his head. He then walked toward the rear of the truck as his follower pulled in behind the rented Ford. Gilliam tapped on the startled agent's window. Behind the glass was a bland, fortyish face that could have easily belonged to an accountant. At that moment the old man roared away in the rental car, and Gilliam turned to cast a grateful wave.

"Any chance you're going to Fort Worth?" he shouted to the agent.

"No, there's not, buddy, so shove off!"

Gilliam faked chagrin. The car lurched immediately into gear and shot away, chasing the old man.

Wasting no time, Gilliam headed for the coffee shop, tossing the cowboy hat into some bushes. Once inside, he took a quick shot at the john, bought a couple of doughnuts, and left immediately by the far door.

A tall young trucker wearing a work shirt and blue jeans was about to climb into the cab of his semi. "Where you heading, fella?" Gilliam called out.

"Houston, but I've got company rules against riders." The young man hoisted himself into the seat.

Gilliam fished in his pocket and extracted the last of his money—two crumpled twenties. "Would this help you bend the rules a little for a guy who's desperate to get to Houston by morning?"

"What rules?" retorted the trucker. "Hop in."

Gilliam did just that with a thankful grin.

Later, as the radio played obligatory country music, and as the muted drone of engine and wheels eased his tense body toward sleep, Gilliam planned the rest of his trip. He would buy travelers' checks from a credit card machine in the Houston airport. He would sign the checks with a false name and use them to pay for his plane ticket. With any luck, he would be in L.A. before noon, and nobody would have any inkling of it. His name would appear on no airline ticket record.

He leaned back, thinking about the story he'd have for Liz when he got home. Thoughts of Liz were always comforting, but now he felt a strange, new feeling. Not just for Liz, but also for this incredible new life he was leading. Slipping tails. Sleuthing. Jesus Christ! Was he starting to enjoy this? He drifted off to sleep with his head against the cab's door.

Morning shadow blanketed Highway 1 as Fritz Steadman slowed to examine the turnoff leading into the forest toward the sea. He checked his odometer to confirm the mileage from Chamberlain and did some quick mental subtraction. The remainder coincided with the mileage given by the real estate agent.

There was no mistaking it, Steadman concluded. Here was the ancient mailbox with its flaking yellow paint and the abrupt curve in the road, some twenty yards off the highway.

Steadman braked to a halt and surveyed the opening in the forest, less to confirm that he had found the spot than to ponder what he might find at the end of the rutted road. There would be a neat, small house with picture windows facing the ocean and a rustic stone chimney. There would probably be a white Volkswagen Thing parked nearby if Nattie Rosenheim's recollections were accurate. Somewhere inside the house—presumably asleep at 6:00 A.M.—would be the diminutive woman whose size told nothing of how dangerous she was, a black man about whom Steadman knew nothing, and the wealthy "Mr. Godwin." Steadman hesitated a moment—he didn't know exactly why —absently rubbing his still-tender ribs.

During the "sick leave" after his disastrous encounter with the woman, he called all the local real estate agents. While he didn't expect the agents to remember anything "suspicious," calling them by telephone beat cruising around the area where he was attacked. He was pleasantly surprised when an agent told him of a man named Lawrence Benson who had rented a three-bed-room cottage early the previous winter. The full-year lease had been arranged by long-distance telephone from a number in Washington, D.C., signed by mail, and paid for with an $8,400 money order—*in advance.* This Mr. Benson could not say for certain when the house would be occupied, but three or four people would use it from time to time. Then Mr. Benson had called recently to notify the agency that he and two others would occupy the house for an anticipated two months. The agent also told of frequent midwinter visits by Mr. Benson and his party—three or four people at a time—in spite of treacherous roads and brutal cold. Delighted to have a recreation cottage profitably under lease during the off-season, the agency had asked no questions.

Steadman's roadside hesitancy did not last long. He knew he was onto something big. While he doubted that it would be anything as dramatic as the shootouts of his fantasies, he was confident that he would un-cover something that badly needed uncovering. How else could he explain the attack in the early hours of a foggy morning, or "Mr. Godwin's" use of phony names? "Godwin" and "Benson" had to be the same man with a great deal of money who paid for everything with cash in advance to avoid issuing checks and giving bill-ing addresses.

Not once did it occur to Steadman that he was about to break a rigid rule in police operating procedures—ensure backup help before walking into an unknown situation—or that he could be severely reprimanded for such disregard. Though armed and in uniform, Stead-man was utterly alone. He was home in bed on sick leave, for all the department knew.

Before easing his cruiser onto the ungraveled road, Steadman checked his pistol one more time and loaded the stumpy 12-gauge riot gun mounted over the transmission. Doing these things awakened a gnawing in his stomach, and he proceeded even more slowly than he'd previously planned.

Leon Jackson couldn't understand why he was suddenly awake. Except for the lazy rolling of the surf and an occasional gull cry, the morning was quiet. A peach-colored eastern sky unflawed by clouds offered prospects of a magnificent spring day. But Jackson had *almost* heard something.

The sounds of regular breathing came from each of the bedrooms. Rossiter and Nakamura, he guessed, would resume their laboratory tasks as soon as they awoke. Nakamura's battle with a policeman days before had convinced Rossiter that the metallurgical process should be accelerated dramatically, that what Yoshi had planned to do in a month must be done in half the time. Failure to see or hear any word of the incident in local news coverage had not assuaged Rossiter's fear that the police might be quietly investigating. Sooner or later a squad car might arrive at their door with an inquisitive policeman. The authorities, Rossiter had declared, must be given the least possible time to discover anything unusual in the little house by the ocean.

Jackson had doubled his vigilance while the others intensified their efforts. Working twice as long with half the rest, Nakamura and Rossiter began reducing to metallic form sixty-four grams of deadly plutonium dioxide per batch, instead of the originally anticipated thirty-two grams. This meant handling dangerously explosive and corrosive chemicals in quantities twice as great as they'd planned and practiced for. Jackson had seen the effects of strain in Nakamura's face, for she was a physicist—not a metallurgist—and though her assistant was bright and very well read for a layman, he'd never before set foot in any kind of a laboratory.

For a time, Jackson had watched them as they measured the yellowish powder into precise quantities, taking meticulous care never to expose it to air, wearing surgical masks that became stained with nervous perspiration as they worked through gloved holes in a transparent box. They would then saturate the powder with a vile-looking liquid from a corrosion-resistant bottle until turbid gas filled the sealed beaker. Then came the mixing with other liquids, acids, and powders while the plutonium alternated between liquid and solid states; gasses were siphoned through glass tubing into tightly sealed bottles as the mixture baked in the induction furnace—Nakamura all the while taking readings from gauges and meters, writing things down, and trading nervous glances with Rossiter. At length, a gas-enveloped lump of something was allowed to cool under a glass bell as the gas dissipated into nothingness. What remained was a tiny pebble of grayish-white metal—plutonium, the stuff of atomic bombs—that Nakamura would take from the dish with tweezers to place in—of all things—a cigar box.

Jackson flinched at the sound of Rossiter snorting in his sleep. He remembered a similar feeling from years ago. What had caused it? An accidental splash in a rice paddy where no one should be? The click of a safety switch on a Chinese-made rifle? This wasn't Vietnam or Cambodia; there would be no incoming mortar rounds, no pyramid-shaped grenades hurled out of the dark. In less than a minute, however, he was fully dressed and standing outside on the porch, M-16 loaded and ready, his eyes and ears tuned sharply to the shadows and sounds of the morning.

Steadman cursed himself for the hundredth time since parking the police cruiser and setting out for the house on foot. He'd allowed the door to fall shut with a thud that wasn't really loud, but it stood out metal-lically against the stillness of the woods. He doubted that it could have penetrated the forest to the house ahead, but lamented that years of uneventful service had so dulled his police instincts as to cause stupid mistakes. He silently vowed to use complete caution and to take nothing for granted.

A few steps from the clearing, Steadman leaned against the tough bark of a thick cedar and peered through the brush at the house. His heart began to thump almost audibly as he recognized the angular lines of a Volkswagen Thing that stood twenty or thirty feet from the front door. In the morning half light, it looked gray or beige, but he knew that it must be white, that another small detail of his private mystery had fallen into place.

Though the house was dark and apparently asleep, Steadman heeded his vows of a few minutes earlier and circled the clearing rather than approach the house from its open front side. The going was difficult in the sparse light, but he managed to avoid making little noises by threading his way around the patches of low brush instead of trying to step through them.

When he'd drawn as close to the house as possible without leaving the protective cover of the woods, he glanced at his watch. It was 6:15. By now his wife would be reaching for the stem of the alarm clock, per-haps forgetting for a moment that he was not safely curled next to her. He'd told her about an overnight fishing trip off Monhegan Island to quiet her fears in case his work kept him out too long.

From somewhere in the house came loud rock-and-roll music with a suddenness that startled him. It ended abruptly. A clock radio, thought Steadman, as he ap-proached the outer wall of the house. Clutching the heavy riot gun, Steadman moved toward the window.

Rossiter punched at the clock radio and wished fervently for more sleep, knowing that it was out of the question. The great quantity of coffee he'd consumed while working with Nakamura deep into the previous night bulged painfully in his abdomen. On his way to the bathroom, he opened Nakamura's door and saw her beginning to stir reluctantly out of sleep. And through Nakamura's window, there was the edge of motion as a strange face disappeared outside.

"Yoshi!" screamed Rossiter. "Outside!" He ran to the living room where Jackson usually slept. "Outside!" he screamed again, seeing the empty sofa bed and no sign of Jackson.

Nakamura appeared in the hall, hastily drawing a bathrobe around her. "What is it? What's wrong, Duncan?" Her face was taut with confusion.

"Have you seen Leon?" demanded Rossiter, whirling back into the hall, clad only in white shorts. Nakamura's fearful face answered the question. "Get your rifle, Yoshi!" Chills ran up Nakamura's spine as her mind fluttered through visions of attacking troops and hopeless odds.

"Freeze!" shouted a voice from behind Rossiter. Nakamura's guts tightened at the sight of a uniformed man crouched near the living-room door with an ugly shotgun leveled directly at her.

"You!" shouted Steadman at Rossiter. "On your stomach with your hands on your head. Come on, move!" He waved the shotgun at the floor and Rossiter slowly spread himself on the chilly wood, lacing his fingers at the back of his skull. Nakamura stood like a stone statue at her door.

"Now you, young lady," said Steadman. "Get down next to him. Don't even think about trying anything funny, because this riot gun would just about snap you in two." Nakamura moved stiffly toward Rossiter and took her place beside him. There was no mistaking

Steadman's voice, though his features had been indistinct nights before.

"Where's your friend, the black guy?" asked Steadman as he unceremoniously handcuffed their hands behind their backs. "You may as well tell me so I don't have to hurt him. Come on now, where is he?" Steadman stood back against the wall with the shotgun pointing threateningly at their backs.

Rossiter's voice was surprisingly firm and his native Texas accent was much more pronounced than usual. "Why, he's gone, Officer. He's gone back to Texas."

"Yeah? Did he take that big white boat of yours with him?" asked Steadman, attempting to catch his captives in a lie. He knew that the *Golden Girl* still lay at her mooring in nearby Chamberlain.

"As a matter of fact, he took an airplane," answered Rossiter. "I don't know what this is all about, Officer, but you'd better have a damn good reason because you're going to have some convincing to do if you want to keep that star of yours."

"Don't make this any tougher on yourself than you have to," replied Steadman, walking down the hall, inspecting each of the rooms. He stopped before the closed door of the laboratory, paused for a moment, then kicked it open melodramatically, splintering the latch housing into wooden shards.

"Hey, what have we got going here?" exclaimed Steadman upon seeing the collection of beakers and scientific paraphernalia. "Looks like some kind of laboratory. What are we making? Smack? Acid?" Unable to tell metallurgical gear from electric can openers, he used terms picked up on television cop shows. "You may as well tell me where the stuff is, because I'll find it anyway, Mr. Godwin—or is it 'Mr. Benson' today? Where do you keep it?"

Rossiter answered calmly, "Officer, if you'll take these handcuffs off and let us get dressed, we'll make you some breakfast and tell you everything you want to know. Hell, we'll even show you exactly what we're doing."

"Just tell me where the stuff is."

"Look," insisted Rossiter. "There isn't any *stuff*. We're an industrial research team and we're developing a new kind of plastic. Do you want to see *that?*"

"Then tell me how come you go around using phony names half the time," said Steadman, bending toward Rossiter with squinting eyes, "and why this little lady here damned near broke my head off the other morning. And why are you doing this 'industrial research' way up here in the middle of the woods."

Nakamura, facing away from Steadman with her cheek pressed to the wooden floor, could tell that Rossiter was scouring every nook in his self-educated mind for bits to assemble a believable tale. She'd seen him do it before in the institution and had marveled at his creative ability. She hoped he could do it now.

The story was short. "Officer, have you ever heard of industrial espionage?" Steadman had. "Well," said Rossiter, "we've got a bad case of that in our company. Our competitors have infiltrated us, and none of our industrial secrets are safe. That's why we had to come way up here from our regular labs in Texas. If we'd have worked on this plastic down there, our competitors would have been tipped off and we'd have had no patent. You know what that means, Officer: No money. I have to use other names every now and then, just to throw our competitor's agents off track. I know it sounds a little far-fetched, but the truth often does. There's really nothing mysterious about it, nothing at all. Now will you please let us get up and get dressed? This is just crazy."

So convincingly had Rossiter lied that Steadman's knees grew momentarily weak, along with his resolve. But then he remembered that his encounter with the woman had not been explained and his heart grew stout again.

"Then why in the hell did *she* almost kill me?"

Nakamura saw Rossiter's face go blank and she knew that the ball was in her court.

"I thought you were going to rape me," she whined, meaning to sound like she was near tears.

Steadman was aghast. "You thought a policeman was going to rape you?"

"Yes, yes, I did," she cried. "It's happened before. He was a maniac, and he'd done it to others—six or seven women. You don't know how terrified I've been since it happened. He's never been caught and I can't even see a policeman without being afraid all over again. It doesn't sound rational, I know, but please try to understand. A few mornings ago you took me by the arm and suddenly the old fears came back and I panicked. I didn't mean to hurt you, please believe that."

Rossiter could see that Steadman had started to crack, for the certainty in his face had turned to open-mouthed confusion. As soon as Nakamura finished, Rossiter launched what he suspected might be the *coup de grace*.

"Now that we've answered your questions, let's at least see your warrant."

Steadman almost choked. He didn't have a god-damned warrant! He'd meant to do nothing more than poke around to confirm strange and illegal goings-on in the house, *after* which he planned to call the department to get the warrant. He'd not meant to enter the house, but adrenaline had numbed his common sense when Rossiter suddenly panicked. He'd blundered into an illegitimate roust of innocent people, having no legal cause. His eyes became glassy and his throat dry. He took two faltering steps forward to release his captives. How long, he wondered, would he be suspended from duty?

Fritz Steadman died with the question unanswered. Rossiter and Nakamura heard three sharp pops in rapid succession. Steadman crumbled to the floor like a marionette whose strings had been cut, his spine severed and heart punctured.

Behind a cedar thirty yards from the window, Jackson held his breath, uncertain whether his shots had found their mark and whether there were other police in the house who would return his fire. Minutes passed as he stood, ready to fire again, until Rossiter's yelling brought him in.

They laid Steadman to eternal rest in a mossy piece of ground about two hundred yards from the house, a spot selected for the density of the surrounding brush. Jackson piled branches and weeds over the grave after Rossiter tamped the final spadeful of soil into place, and together they swept the ground with boughs to obliterate the trail of blood from the house.

It was almost ten before they finished covering the police cruiser with brush to prevent its being spotted from the air or stumbled on by a casual hiker. The task of covering the car's tracks through the forest was impossible, for they'd gouged trees, uprooted bushes, and left deep furrows into the timber from the road. Rossiter finally halted the operation, convinced that the time could be better spent.

The lake of blood on the floor required repeated mopping and rinsing by three pairs of hands. The afternoon was well underway by the time they'd each taken turns in the shower. Afterward, Nakamura and Jackson sat silently at the kitchen table while Rossiter brewed a pot of coffee. Though she usually drank tea, Nakamura accepted the steaming cup and was grateful for the warm, clean aroma in place of the stench of blood.

"You're not afraid, are you, Yoshi?" asked Rossiter

209

with surprising gentleness as he took a spot at the table.

"I think I'm beyond that now," she answered, looking up at him with vision slightly clouded by the steam.

"Good," he replied. "I won't worry then. Is it time for the news yet?"

Jackson tore his gaze from the window facing the road to glance at his watch. "Not for a few minutes yet."

Rossiter lit a cigarette and drummed the table with his fingers, his usual prelude to announcing a major decision.

"We're running short of time," he said at last. "Things are getting hot faster than I thought they would."

"How much time you figure we got left?" asked Jackson.

"There's no way to tell for sure. All we know is that the sheriff's department didn't call this guy—what did his ID card say his name was, Yoshi?"

"Steadman," she answered. "His name is Steadman and his radio call number was Oh-Two."

"Yeah, Steadman. We listened to his police radio for more than three hours and didn't hear his numbers even once. My guess is that he was by himself and that he was trying to score a big bust single-handedly."

"And," said Jackson, "he wouldn't have come in here alone if he was doing things on the up-and-up. He'd have brought at least twenty other guys in with him."

"Exactly," agreed Rossiter. "So we can probably say that no one else knew he was here. The only trouble is we can't bank on it."

"So where does that leave us?" asked Nakamura.

Rossiter drew on his cigarette and turned back to Jackson. "You've watched Yoshi and me in the lab, right?"

Jackson nodded.

"I know this isn't up your alley," continued Rossiter, "but do you think you could do what I've been doing?"

Nakamura glanced up, barely believing her ears.

"It's not really that complicated," Rossiter went on. "You just have to keep your mind on your work and not leave anything out. Also you need good nerves, and you've got those. Right, Leon?"

"Now wait just a minute, Duncan," protested Nakamura. "You know it's not that easy. I'm a trained scientist and *I* have trouble with the process because I'm not a metallurgist. Reducing that compound to metal takes more than good nerves."

"You're right on both counts," said Rossiter. "You're a physicist and you should be doing a physicist's job— like building atomic bombs. But Leon here has more than nerves. He's got judgment, ability to concentrate, and he follows directions very well. Just like me. What do you say, Leon?"

Jackson locked his fingers together, then slowly unlocked them. "What do you want me to do, Dunk?" he asked.

Rossiter smiled broadly and clapped a hand on Jackson's shoulder. "You're going to help me with the rest of that powder. And do you know what? We're going to make metal in big enough batches so that Yoshi here can get started with the actual building."

"Duncan, you can't be serious," declared Nakamura. "That process requires a basic knowledge of materials and chemistry. You can't just pick it up from casual reading. Maybe I'm not a metallurgist, but as a scientist, I do have some inkling of what to expect if I see a thermometer or pressure gauge rise suddenly, or if something starts to turn the wrong color. With a little luck, I can do the right thing to prevent an explosion or immediate corrosion—but only because I'm trained, Duncan. You and I together just barely have what it takes to handle sixty-four grams of powder per batch, but you and Leon don't. I'm sorry, but you just don't." She hoped she hadn't been too insulting and was relieved when Rossiter smiled again.

"You've forgotten something, Yoshi," he said. "I've had practical experience. I won't make any mistakes. Besides, Leon has worked with unstable stuff before. Hell, the Army made a first-class explosives expert out of him. Haven't you ever heard his war stories about slapping C-4 explosive on dud mortar rounds, and having to insert those blasting caps like a surgeon working on a tumor? Hell, he can do it, can't you, Leon?"

"Dunk, I don't know," ventured Jackson, his misgivings showing plainly on his face. "Maybe she's right. I don't know my ass from first base when it comes to the things you've been doing in the lab."

"Duncan, maybe you and I can speed things up—do more batches at a time or even increase the measurements," offered Nakamura hopefully. "I can work harder and faster if you can."

"I'm afraid that's out of the question," answered Rossiter. "You're going to be working triple overtime as it is."

Nakamura felt the blood draining from her face. "Just how much do you plan to speed the process up?" she asked.

Rossiter regarded her silently for a few seconds before answering. "We're going to build two bombs and be out of here by Sunday night." Nakamura stifled a gasp as he continued. "Leon and I will process the rest of the powder by tomorrow night, and by that time you should have one of them ready for installing the detonator. You can help us with the reduction process until you've got enough metal to work with. By Sunday afternoon we should be ready to plug in the electronics gear on both bombs. Maybe a few hours' more work and away we go. We won't get much sleep between now and then, but we've all gone without sleep before."

"Duncan," Nakamura said in far less an authoritative tone than she wished, "you'd have to quintuple the compound in every batch. That's about three hundred grams each time. You're going to be doing everything in quantities five times greater than we are now, and even now we're doing batches twice as big as I wanted. I can't tell you how dangerous it is."

Rossiter was becoming impatient. "Then maybe you can tell me how much time we've got, or maybe how that cop became suspicious enough to come barging in here. Think about that for a minute. He didn't just get a wild hair up his ass to bust the nice people living by the sea. He knew about my fake names, damn it. He knew about the *Golden Girl*. That means he's been checking, asking questions, talking to people. When he turns up missing, somebody out there is going to put two and two together."

Jackson leaned forward toward Nakamura. "He's right, Yoshi. We can't take a chance of having to fight it out with the locals. I say we get started now." Then, as an afterthought, Jackson turned to Rossiter and said, "I'm ready, Dunk, but don't you think we should let John and Jean know what we're doing?"

Rossiter, hiding a flash of anger, answered in a controlled voice. "All we're going to do is deliver the goods a little early, Leon. No big deal. By the time John tells Jeannie I wasn't in the phone booth for our regular call, you'll practically be in D.C. yourself." Rossiter forced a softer, more measured tone into his voice. "Besides, *I run this show.*"

They worked as a team of three at the reduction process while the afternoon became evening and evening fell away into chilly night. At 2:15 A.M., Nakamura gathered the small pellets of plutonium and weighed out thirty-one kilograms—half the weight in pure metal that they'd seized eleven days earlier—and prepared a ceramic shell for heating. From the corner of her eye, she watched Jackson and Rossiter as they mechanically followed the steps she'd taught them over the past

213

thirteen grueling hours—the measuring, the precise saturations, the careful monitoring of the temperatures and pressures—and she hoped that they were up to avoiding the score of possible catastrophes. Soon they must be made to stop and rest. Her own vision had become blurry. Lack of rest causes muscles to quiver under even slight burdens. Senses become dull. There was no room for shaking hands and blurry eyes in this business. Yet Rossiter and Jackson continued to work, drinking coffee in great quantities as though it were gasoline and they were engines.

An hour later Nakamura interrupted their operation to present an irregularly shaped mass of light-gray metal on a sturdy rolling tray. So intently had Rossiter and Jackson been working that they'd missed seeing the first step of her "physicist's job," the unifying of separate pellets into a single mass that would become the core of an atomic bomb.

"It's time to rest," announced Nakamura as the others prepared to begin processing yet another 320 grams of yellow powder. Rossiter pulled his hands from the glove box and pointed to the baseball-size lump of metal on the tray.

"The first core?" he asked.

"Not yet," answered Nakamura, "but it will be soon."

Jackson bent down to eye the mass of plutonium.

"Go ahead and touch it," urged Rossiter. "It won't hurt you."

Jackson hesitated and looked to Nakamura, who nodded. He gingerly pressed his fingers against the metallic surface. "It's still warm," he observed.

"It will probably never get much cooler than that," said Nakamura. "It's emitting alpha particles and you're feeling the heat they generate."

"Radioactive, huh?" said Jackson.

"You could say that." Her voice seemed distant, as though her thoughts were light years away.

"It looks so damn ordinary," said Jackson.

"I'm afraid it's anything but that," replied Nakamura. "Why don't you pick it up?"

Jackson wrapped his hands about the lump and suddenly his face contorted. "I'll be— Goddamn, it's *heavy*. How did you . . . ? What's it weigh, anyway?"

"About sixty-eight pounds. It helps to be strong if you're building atom bombs." She went to the window and stared into the blackness.

Jackson could not pull his attention away from the plutonium metal on the tray. "How's it work, Yoshi? What makes it so special?"

Nakamura turned from the window with a hint of a tired smile on her face. "It's no more special than the powder you've been handling. In fact, we could've used the oxide for our bombs by turning it into paste and molding the cores."

"Then why didn't we?"

"Because we'll get much better bombs this way," she answered. "These bombs will be so good that the government will be tempted to think that people like us couldn't have built them."

Jackson saw the smile disappear from her mouth and wondered where her mind was flying as the seconds passed in silence. "Just how good is that?" he asked.

Nakamura glanced hesitantly at Rossiter, whose eyes seemed to convey a warning, then turned back to Jackson.

"If my calculations are right, they'll be the same as the bomb dropped on Nagasaki," she said. "In fact, they'll be better because they're smaller and our configuration is better than Fat Man's."

"Who in the hell is Fat Man?" asked Jackson, forgetting the tremor of misgiving he'd felt a moment earlier.

Fat Man, explained Nakamura, was the name given to the plutonium device detonated over Nagasaki in

1945, as opposed to Little Boy, the uranium bomb that leveled Hiroshima. The latter was fairly compact, slightly over ten feet long and a mere thirty inches in diameter, while Fat Man was a monster, an eleven-foot egg stuffed with bulky explosives shaped to provide an implosive charge around a comparatively small core of plutonium metal. Nakamura's bombs would be much smaller though at least as deadly.

She ran her hand over the clodlike lump on the tray, tasting the subtle alpha heat with the tips of her fingers. "They detonated Fat Man at an altitude of eight hundred fifty feet," she said. "The amount of matter actually converted to energy was only about a gram, far less than the weight of a penny. It was enough to destroy a city."

Jackson was overwhelmed by the revelation, for he'd seen films of atomic explosions and had tried to fathom the forces behind such incredible violence. Being told that one gram of material was the actual culprit defied his sense of proportion. He shook his head and stared blankly at Nakamura.

"Of course," she continued, "our first bomb here will go off over water at ground zero, so it won't be nearly as spectacular as Fat Man. Just a flash, a cloud, a bang, and a column of water. You'd be surprised how little happens a few miles from the blast. With the right wind, you don't even get any fallout, and the noise falls off pretty rapidly to a level you can take."

"I'd be surprised no matter *what* happened," Jackson answered.

"It's time for some sleep," concluded Nakamura. "I recommend the same for both of you. It's too dangerous to do these things if you can't see straight."

Rossiter nodded reluctantly and Yoshi left the lab. He began a safety check of the remaining plastic bag of plutonium dioxide and the sealed acid containers, stoppered flasks, and tins of powdered chemicals. As he worked, his thoughts raced along. Cop or no cop, this thing was going to *happen*. Waiting was too hard, anyway. Maybe that fat slob Steadman had performed a service after all, even though he was just another robot who thought his rules were big enough to hold Duncan Rossiter. He found out who I am, thought Rossiter. All the little robots will find out in a few days. Even Hammer. He thinks I'm up here fucking around with chemicals and bombs for him. Let him have Washington. I don't care if he runs the place or blows it up. I'll have Jean. We'll be far away planning my next one.

As he turned to leave, Jackson caught his arm.

"Dunk, I've got to ask you something," Jackson said in a low voice, "but I don't know just how to say it."

"We've never had any secrets, man. Out with it."

"Maybe you just answered my question. We've never had any secrets, have we?"

"I thought you knew better than that."

Jackson kneaded the back of his aching neck. "I do. Maybe it's just my nerves making me see things, but a while ago, I thought you and Yoshi were holding something back from me. It happened when I asked why we needed such good bombs."

Rossiter's grin was too casual, a bit too quick, but Jackson didn't notice. "You know, man, sometimes I lie awake at night worrying that maybe you're as crazy as I am."

Jackson's face lost its worry but retained the quizzical furrows. "Can you answer one more question for me, Dunk?"

"No sweat, but I hope it's a short one because I'm about ready to keel over."

"Why is Yoshi so worked up over building such good bombs if we're only going to threaten the feds and jack them around a little? I mean, if we're not going to blow up anything but a bunch of salt water, why do you need bombs better than the ones they used on Japan?"

Rossiter had wondered how long it would take Jackson to ask that question, and he'd prepared an answer.

"I thought you knew," he replied. "Hasn't Yoshi ever told you?"

"Hasn't she told me what?"

Rossiter lowered his voice to a confidential whisper that Jackson should have known was slightly too dramatic. "Leon, her old man was killed by the Nagasaki bomb and her mother was—well . . . she was turned into something not quite human. For years, Yoshi thought they'd both been killed until one day she got a letter from Japan saying that her mother was alive. This was like fifteen years after the war."

"Did she ever see her again?"

"Yeah, she saw her again, in some broken-down pig sty in a slum where most of the bomb victims ended up. From what Yoshi told me when we were in the nut house, the atomic victims are avoided and ignored in Japan. People are scared of them or something— know what I mean? The government provides food and a few necessities, but not much more. Anyway, Yoshi goes into her mother's hut and gets totally blown away by what she sees. I won't go into the details, but you can imagine how bad it must have been. Not only does her mother not know her, but she asks Yoshi to kill her."

"Fuck," whispered Jackson, closing his eyes.

"So Yoshi killed her."

Jackson could not reply and stood stunned as Rossiter continued.

"She turned herself in, but being an American citizen and everything, the Japanese government offered to return her to the U.S. for psychiatric care. I guess they were convinced that hers was a special case or something, and that's how Yoshi ended up in Widener Center."

"But how does that explain the kind of bombs she's building?" persisted Jackson.

"Don't you see, man? It's a symbolic thing with her. She's got to build the same kind of bombs that destroyed her family, because she's trying to rebuild history, except with a different ending. I guess when it comes right down to it, she's still sick. You and I, on the other hand, have no choice but to let her do things her own way. It's a cinch we can't build these things by ourselves."

Jackson pondered the mixture of truth and lies he'd just heard and wished he knew more about the human mind, its quirks and flaws. He'd never before doubted Rossiter's word, and in the end, he chose not to now. His inability to judge the feasibility of the story offered no alternative.

"I guess it makes sense," Jackson replied finally. "We've all got our reasons for doing this thing. By the way, do you know any Japanese?"

"Just a few words Yoshi's taught me. Why?"

"A few days ago she said she was living for—let's see. Zensho. Yeah, that's it—*zensho*. You know what it means?"

Rossiter swallowed hard. "No, can't say that I do. Never heard of it. Hey, let's get some sleep."

SATURDAY, MAY 22

Eagle Rock was archetypal California suburbia, a nest of fast-food franchises and filling stations. Gilliam pulled into a Texaco station on crowded Colorado Boulevard and parked the rental car outside the men's room. Once behind the locked door, he shaved and washed.

He felt surprisingly fresh upon emerging into the hazy morning sunshine, though his joints were stiff from the early-morning flight from Houston. He spread an L.A. map on the car seat and rechecked the location of the Widener hospital before joining the rush of traffic headed away from the city.

Widener Mental Health Center—like everything in L.A.—was "twenty minutes" away for a Los Angeleno who knows how to get there. The drive took Gilliam forty-five minutes, but he didn't mind the delay. He used the time to go over his presentation to Dr. Si Blum, to work himself into the part of an important federal official in search of important information. He had to impress Blum enough to get a look at the records of one Yoshi Nakamura, a nuclear physicist with a history of mental disorders.

The Widener Center stretched out amid palm trees and flower gardens at the end of a long, white-graveled driveway. From the parking lot next to a hacienda-style office building, Gilliam could see that the center's fence enclosed perhaps three square blocks and that well-kept bungalows with tile roofs nestled in rows garnished with flowers. Here and there were larger multistoried buildings, presumably cafeterias or laundries.

Gilliam hauled himself out of the car, unkinked his creaking body, and walked purposefully to the administration building. A plump receptionist directed him through several turns in a carpeted corridor to the office of Dr. Simon Blum, Associate Director for Admissions. Gilliam waited in a small anteroom while the receptionist told Blum of his presence. A few moments later, he appeared at the door of his office and waved Gilliam in with a warm smile. The doctor was a stocky man, black-haired and imposing in an expensive suit.

"I'm Si Blum, Mr. Gilliam. Have a seat." He motioned toward a comfortable armchair across from a surprisingly small wooden desk. Books lined the walls. Sliding glass doors admitted sunlight from a small veranda hung with ferns. Gilliam let himself relax.

"I'll confess, Mr. Gilliam, that I'm a little surprised to see you so soon. You must have flown all night."

Gilliam forced a smile and took a cup of coffee from the receptionist. "I'm afraid I had no choice, Doctor."

"I see, I see. Yoshi Nakamura must be very important to your investigation."

"You're absolutely right. We have reason to believe that she might have information that would be helpful. She's a nuclear physicist, you know."

"Yes, I discovered that when I went over her records."

Gilliam was heartened by Blum's friendliness, a contrast to his curtness during the previous evening's telephone conversation. The doctor went on. "I apologize if I was rude on the phone last night, but I hope you can understand my position."

"Of course I can," said Gilliam. "I should have realized before I called that you can't give out confidential information to just anyone who asks for it."

Blum chuckled. "Well, I'm glad you're so understanding. Now, what can I do for you?"

Gilliam's palms started to tingle, but he repressed his excitement. "I suppose I should get to work now that I'm here. May I see Dr. Nakamura's medical records and any other information you might have regarding her acquaintances and present whereabouts?"

"No problem. Naturally, I'll want to have a look at your credentials first."

"Oh, sure," said Gilliam, perhaps a bit too eagerly. He dug for his wallet, silently beseeching the gods that a Senate ID would satisfy Blum. It didn't.

"I found out this much by checking the *Congressional Directory*, Mr. Gilliam," he replied, turning the card over in his hand. "My congressman sends me one every two years. You're a lawyer for a Senate committee, just like the card says. Now what can you show me that says I should give you confidential information on a former patient?"

Gilliam paled and swallowed hard—once, twice. His voice lost its important depth and came out a shade above a whisper. "What would it take, Doctor?"

Blum's eyes grew hard. "A badge, Mr. Gilliam, or a letter of instruction from a judge, or better yet—a warrant."

"Dr. Blum, I've come all the way from Washington. It's absolutely imperative that I—"

"Now look, Mr. Gilliam. I don't know what your game is. The only thing I know is that you're a big-shot Senate staffer with no badge, no authorization, and no good reason as far as I'm concerned to go leafing through my confidential records."

"I can assure you, I've got a very good reason."

"Then you'd better tell it to me so I can call the FBI to corroborate it."

Gilliam's tingling palms went cold. "I don't think there's any reason to do that."

"I didn't think you would. But I'll tell you what I'll

do, Mr. Gilliam." Blum stood and leaned across his desk. "I'm going to let you walk out of here, and I'm not going to call the FBI or the police or anyone else. Because Mother Blum raised no dummies, I'm naturally hesitant to embarrass the assistant of a powerful U.S. Senator unless I absolutely have to. But understand this, Mr. Gilliam. If you persist after those records, I will not only call the FBI and the police, but I'll also call a very influential friend with a major wire service and tell her that one of Harry Hammer's men is nosing around, masquerading as a federal investigator, trying to get his unauthorized digits on very private and confidential records. Now, what do you think of that?"

"Not much," Gilliam replied.

Blum actually rose and shook his hand as he left the office.

Gilliam stopped at a men's room on his way out, as much to contemplate his next move as to unload the coffee fed him by Blum's receptionist. He could come back tonight, break into Blum's office, and conduct his own search and seizure operation in the filing cabinets: one count of burglary, good for maybe six years. He could tell Blum the whole sad story and hope in vain for his co-operation. He could try to bribe one of the staff. He could . . .

"You wouldn't have seventy-five cents, would you?"

Gilliam jumped, nearly burning his hand on the hot-water faucet. He hadn't heard anyone else enter the men's room.

The voice belonged to an old gentleman who looked as if he belonged in the House of Lords. He wore a perfectly tailored dark-green flannel blazer over proper gray vest and trousers. He carried an ivory-handled umbrella in one hand and a black bowler in the other.

"Dreadfully sorry to have startled you, old fellow, but I'm fresh out of silver," said the old gentleman through his white mustache. "Bloody cigarette machine refuses pound notes." He chuckled politely.

Gilliam reached for the towel dispenser, keeping his eyes glued on the old man.

"It wouldn't be a mere gratuity, you understand," said the Englishman. "I would repay you by post."

In his lifetime, Gilliam had encountered a wide variety of panhandlers, but this guy took the cake. Rather than refuse him and be obliged to fend off more pleadings, Gilliam dug into his pockets. Seventy-five cents was a small price for ridding himself of distraction. He desperately needed time to plan.

The old man's bushy brows arched in gratitude as Gilliam forked over three quarters. "Beastly civilized of you, old fellow. Can't tell you how embarrassing this is. I'm Wynslow G. L. H. Brackingham, of the Plymouth Brackinghams." He tucked the umbrella under his arm and thrust forward his hand.

Gilliam shook it and forced a weak smile. "Pleased to meet you. Now if you'll excuse me . . ."

"But you must give me your name and address so that I might send you my check. I couldn't possibly allow this debt to fester into eternity."

Gilliam wrinkled his nose. *Fester into eternity?*

"But of course. Think of it as a service to a crazy old fellow with no wish so fond as to die debtless."

"Look, Mr. Brackingham, I'm really very busy . . . wait a minute." Gilliam stopped short. Could this old man be a patient? An idea formed.

"I say, my dear fellow, you appear on the verge of manic depression," said Brackingham. "I'm schizophrenic myself, but perfectly harmless."

"So you're a patient here?" asked Gilliam.

"Oh, my heavens, yes. Sort of a trustee, as it were, and I daresay a source of revenue for this institution. I have considerable resources, you know. But I happen to agree with my family that I couldn't possibly cope with the outside world. And I find it very pleasant here. So many interesting people. We have all the books we need, films, good food . . ."

224

"Mr. Brackingham, how long have you been here?"

"Nine years in January. Good heavens, that's nearly a bloody decade, isn't it?"

"Mr. Brackingham, can we go somewhere and talk?"

The morning haze burned away as the day wore on. Gilliam sat in a wicker chair on the veranda of the visitors' lounge, sipping coffee and taking notes as Brackingham rambled about his "dear old friend Yoshi."

Between numerous interruptions from strolling patients who wanted to pass the time of day with him, Brackingham confirmed what Gilliam already knew and added many discomforting details.

Yoshi Nakamura had become a mental case after killing her mother, a mangled victim of atomic warfare who begged for death.

"The therapy seemed to help her," said Brackingham, "though it was difficult to tell."

"How so?"

"You see, Kelly, she was a devout follower of Zen, a philosophy that, for all its good points, ignores the rational. And there was the samurai thing."

"Samurai thing?"

"Yes. Somehow she thought of herself as an honor-bound warrior, in spite of the fact that the warrior part of samurai tradition was built exclusively around *men*."

"How did it affect her behavior?"

Brackingham withdrew a cigarette bought with Gilliam's money, tamped it, and inserted it into a holder. "That, my dear fellow, is an interesting question. She went through periods when she was perfectly normal, as you and I—you, at least. But at other times, she was very depressed and talked about losing the chance to fight for her family's honor. On occasion, I would overhear her discussing it with her friend, Duncan."

"Who was Duncan?"

225

"His name is Duncan Rossiter. Dreadful fellow, if you don't mind my saying so. Frightening, in his own sort of way."

Brackingham digressed into what he knew of Rossiter: rich, wily, rumored to have burned his father to death.

Gilliam, almost reluctant to receive an answer, asked, "What exactly did they talk about?"

"It's difficult for me to explain, Kelly, because my recollections are fragmentary. They spent a good deal of time together poring over Yoshi's books in the library. Her shelf was near mine. Physics books, they were. I made it a point to notice. There were other kinds, too, but mostly all scientific. I never fully figured it out."

"Didn't you ever ask her?"

"Good heavens, yes. Her answers depended on her mood. Once when she seemed especially depressed, she told me that she had a dream, that it was her purpose in life. But her dream was just one word."

"One word?"

"Yes. I assume it was Japanese. I heard her use it quite often, actually, especially in her discussions with Duncan."

"And the word was?"

"*Zensho.*"

"*Zensho?*"

"Accent on the last syllable, old boy. Zen*sho.*"

Gilliam jotted the word on his legal pad next to the name Duncan Rossiter.

Brackingham expounded on his detestation of Rossiter, telling how he dominated other patients, usually for the sheer pleasure of exercising control. On the other hand, Rossiter was very careful to convey a totally rehabilitated image to the attendants and medical staff, an accomplishment that served him well.

"I'm convinced that he was never really cured, much less rehabilitated," said Brackingham. "I'd wager that he was as sick when he departed as when he first darkened our doorstep. He simply outsmarted his analysts, if I may say so. It probably did him no harm to have friends in high places."

"Like who, for instance?"

"I never knew her name, but I had the distinct impression that she was a key assistant to someone in a very powerful position in Washington. She would write letters to both of them, Yoshi and Duncan, after which they would retire to one of their conspiratorial discussions. From time to time the woman would even visit Widener."

"Can you describe her?"

"Well, as I recall, she was quite tall, brown-haired, tastefully dressed, carried herself in a remarkably commanding way."

Murdock. Without question.

"Tell me, Kelly, why do you need this material?" asked Brackingham. "Not that I'm complaining, old boy. I'm delighted to have someone new to talk to."

Gilliam resolved not to lie. "All I can tell you is that I must find Yoshi Nakamura. It's very important to me. Someday I'll tell you." He drained his fifth cup of coffee.

"Well, if anyone can appreciate the need for confidentiality, I am he," said Brackingham.

"You've been very kind," said Gilliam, scooting his chair away from the wicker table. "I want you to know that I appreciate it. Sincerely."

"Think nothing of it, old man. But wait. If you do find Yoshi, and God knows I wish I could help you there, would you please convey my regards?"

"Absolutely."

"And tell her one more thing, please. Tell her that Wynslow G. L. H. Brackingham hasn't forgotten about the four dollars and fifty cents he owes her."

"I'll tell her."

Gilliam shook Brackingham's hand. As he stood to leave, his eyes wandered across the veranda, over the rolling lawn, to the rear portico of the administration

building. Standing at the window of his office was Dr.
Simon Blum. Even from that distance, he could see that
Blum was looking straight at him. Gilliam was surprised
that the Associate Director for Admissions was not waiting for him at the visitors' gate.

The traffic was deadly by the time Gilliam hit the
freeway headed south toward Los Angeles International
Airport. His return flight was direct to Baltimore, leaving L.A. at 8:15 P.M., so he was not pressed for time.
He had just under four hours to drop off the rented car,
check in at the ticket counter, call Liz, and do whatever
else one does while waiting for a flight to leave.

Gilliam's stomach growled painfully, and he remembered that he'd not eaten all day. His digestive system
insisted on something to digest, even though his head
told him he wasn't hungry. There was too much to
worry about to think of eating.

Gilliam's stomach growled again, this time threateningly. The message was clear: "Feed me something besides coffee. Soon."

He exited the freeway at Century City, L.A.'s rendi-
tion of the ideal urban future. Here and there loomed
radically designed hotels, apartments, and office buildings, tributes to airy modularism where once sprawled
a dark suburban slum. Gilliam cruised the boulevard
in search of a restaurant to placate his angry gut.

He drifted past establishments offering seafood,
Italian, French, and German cuisines, pancakes, tacos,
and steaks. Nothing sounded good. He just couldn't
focus on food with the troublesome mystery of *zensho*
clouding his head. What the hell. His gut could wait
until he arrived at the airport, where he'd grab a quick
hotdog.

A sign caught his eye just as he started a maneuver
into a lane marked "L.A. International Airport."
Lighted Oriental script framed the name of a Japanese
restaurant:

Shukaido's
Original Japanese Dining

Gilliam darted into the parking lot.

The waiter looked very Japanese but sounded very American. He took Gilliam's order and beckoned one of the cooks to the open grill directly in front of the low table. There was no waiting since the place was nearly empty. The dinner-and-drinks crowd hadn't arrived.

The cook was older, but just as Japanese in appearance. Gilliam was disappointed with the man's obviously native American accent. He'd hoped to find someone who could translate a single Japanese word into English.

The cook performed acrobatics with a wicked-looking cleaver, fresh meat, and vegetables. He sliced wildly, hurling chopped bits of this and that onto the sizzling grill—all within an arm's-length of Gilliam's nervous nose. In a remarkably short time, the chopping, slicing, and hurling came to a halt and the cook stood back to let the concoction brown and sputter. Gilliam exhaled with relief and looked up at the smiling cook.

"That was impressive," said Gilliam. "Did you learn that in the old country?"

"Hell, no." The man laughed. "California's the closest I've ever come to the Orient. I was raised in Lincoln, Nebraska."

"Oh. I don't suppose you know any Japanese."

"Just a few words. My grandparents used to speak it around the house."

Gilliam's eyes wandered to the glowing coals under the grill. "You ever hear of anything called *zensho?*"

The cook rolled his eyes briefly to the ceiling and then shook his head. "Nope. Doesn't ring a bell. What's it mean?"

"I was hoping you could tell me."

"Sorry. Hey, wait a minute. Some of these other guys might know." He turned and called to the waiter who had seated Gilliam. "Hey, Doug. You know what *zensho* means? This gentleman is wondering."

The waiter placed a finger on his jaw. "Yeah," he said, "I think it's made by Yamaha."

"Get serious," said the cook. "Do you think any of the bartenders might know?"

"Give me a minute and I'll check around. What was it again? *Zensho?*"

"Right."

The waiter made the rounds of the other employees as the cook collected his concoction and placed it on Gilliam's plate. After the first few bites, Gilliam found that he was eating ravenously. Occasional sips of sake slowly introduced a feeling of relaxed well-being. Gilliam scarcely noticed when the waiter returned to his table.

"Sir, one of the other waiters speaks pretty good Japanese, and he thinks he knows what *zensho* means."

Gilliam swallowed a strip of succulent beef. "And what's that?" he asked.

"He's pretty sure that it's an ancient health drink made from a mixture of berry juices." The waiter bent close and whispered, "It's supposed to make your schwantz hard for a week."

Gilliam struggled to swallow his food and took a stinging mouthful of sake. "You don't say?"

The waiter nodded and wandered away.

A few moments later, a perplexed Gilliam felt a gentle hand on his shoulder and turned in his chair to confront an aging well-dressed Japanese man. Magnified by thick horn-rimmed glasses, his eyes were both merry and concerned.

"Please forgive me," said the old gentleman with syllables a bit too precise to be native American English. "I could not help but overhear your inquiry." He gestured to the nearby table where he'd sat. "I think the young man has made a very humorous jest with you, or perhaps he himself is the object of another's joke."

"Do you know what *zensho* means?" Gilliam asked.

"Yes, I do. Its meanings are many, depending on how one accents the word. In one form, for example, it could mean a clean sweep of victories, as in baseball. If the Dodgers were to defeat the Yankees in four games, losing none, that would be *zensho*." The old man smiled. "You know how we Japanese love baseball."

Gilliam returned the smile absently, pondering what he'd just heard. Judging from what he knew of Nakamura, he doubted that she was a baseball nut. "But there are other meanings?" he asked.

"Ah, yes, many others. It could mean a military outpost or a sentry. Sailors also use the term to refer to the tall post in the front of a ship—I'm so sorry that the English word escapes me."

"Foremast," offered Gilliam.

"So! You are quicker than I."

Gilliam fell silent again. *Outpost. Sentry. Mast.* Was there some connection with the military?

The old man continued. "In a more philosophical sense, *zensho* means a *judgment*, all-encompassing, akin to your Western tradition of a final judgment by God."

Now they were getting somewhere, Gilliam thought with uneasy excitement. "Could it have something to do with the Zen tradition?"

The old man's forehead wrinkled doubtfully. "I know of no approximation in Zen," he said.

"I'm sorry to take so much of your time," Gilliam apologized, "but I'm trying to understand something about a Japanese friend of mine. She's often used the term, but she won't tell me what it means. The meanings you've given me just don't seem to . . . they don't . . ."

"Please don't apologize. What I have offered falls short, I know. Such things can be very confusing because our respective tongues have so little in common. In Japanese, context and accent mean so much. *Zensho*, for example, can mean the burning of a building until nothing stands. Written another way, it can mean a compendium of laws or an encyclopedia. Still another, a last letter or message written by—"

"Wait," interrupted Gilliam. "Did you say 'burning'?"

"Yes. In modern usage, it refers to a fire, usually within a structure or a row of houses."

Fire, thought Gilliam. *Universal judgment. Last message.* He began to feel sick again.

"And of course," said the old man, "there is an old, a very archaic meaning, but I fear that it's ill-suited to one's thoughts at dinner."

"It's okay, I'm finished now. It's very important to me."

The old gentleman appeared hesitant, but went on. "Very well. It does not lend itself to precise translation, but its connotations are similar to your word 'holocaust' or even the religious words 'apocalypse' and 'Armageddon.' It means *destruction*—total and final destruction by a great, unquenchable fire."

Gilliam paled.

The first hazy light appeared on the eastern horizon. Nakamura, with less than three hours' sleep, stood fully dressed before a Formica-surfaced counter, oblivious to the coming of dawn and the snores of her colleagues.

Her hands worked carefully and quickly with grips and rubber mallets, gas burners and measuring tapes. To one side lay a thick loose-leafed notebook that was the result of her years of planning and study toward the design of an atomic bomb with a metallic plutonium core. In it were her neatly drafted and typed diagrams, her calculations, her notes to herself—all ordered as steps in the fabrication process.

Piled within easy reach were other volumes she'd used in designing her device and the step-by-step plan that she now followed. The National Technical Information Service had furnished publications on critical mass summaries, useful in constructing plutonium core and beryllium cover thickness. The Department of Commerce had sold her a heavy volume chock full of data on nuclear metallurgy, and from the Nuclear Regulatory Commission she'd obtained the *Los Alamos Primer* for its useful hints on suitable configurations for atomic bombs. Commercial publishers put out good plutonium and reactor handbooks and she had them. All were ready for quick reference, along with a score of others, if she wished to confirm the calculations in her loose-leaf notebook. She doubted that she would need them because she'd spent countless hours recalculating her tables of dimensions and quantities. She had faith in her work.

Nakamura was not distracted by the coming of daylight or by Rossiter and Jackson when they rose to work on the remaining plutonium dioxide powder. At length, she stepped back from the counter and savored the satisfaction of creating two perfect hemispheres of plutonium metal, the single mass divided precisely in half for greater ease in handling and better control of radioactivity levels. Ignoring the ache in her shoulders and arms, she cupped her palms over the glossy surfaces and tasted again the heat that radiated from the hearts of the hemispheres. Her dream of *zensho* verged on reality, already half alive in the inklings of unfathomable energy seeping into her pores. She relished it like an expert wine taster sampling the bouquet of a rare vintage.

Breakfast was short and quiet. Rossiter's urgency over time intensified with every cup of coffee and each cigarette he consumed. Jackson looked bedraggled, great bags welling under his eyes. But he resumed his work with surprising energy, possibly the delayed effect of caffeine.

Following the light meal, Nakamura attacked the job of assembling the core of the first bomb. She positioned three microphone stands on the countertop and attached to each of their booms a radiation sensor. She adjusted the booms to bring the sensors within inches of the first hemisphere of plutonium, which now rested on its flat surface atop three wooden blocks. Each sensor cord led to its counter box directly facing Nakamura's work area. She'd used red nail polish to paint a line on each detector dial that corresponded to the level of emissions at plutonium's critical mass. Thus, she was able to tell at a glance whether gamma, alpha, or beta radiation levels were within the safe range. The arrangement also let her work without wasting counter space.

Nakamura took from the closet a box with a label warning of toxic metal, cut its steel bands, and dismantled the styrofoam panels that padded a hemispherical shell. It was made of beryllium, an extremely light, brittle, and poisonous metal. Beryllium is also an excellent shield against neutrons, for its atoms are so closely grouped that beryllium literally "reflects" a sizable percentage of neutrons. More than anything else, beryllium would improve her bombs over early U.S. efforts, which used thick, heavy steel for this purpose.

The counter needles jumped markedly closer to the red lines as Nakamura lowered the beryllium half shell over the plutonium. She wasn't alarmed, for neutrons routinely seeking freedom from the plutonium mass were being bounced back inward. The flat side of the hemisphere was still uncovered so neutrons would escape through it, unhindered by the wooden blocks.

Nakamura confirmed her projected radiation levels with the actual readings on the scopes and was heartened by the accuracy of her calculations. She was just as pleased by the precision craftsmanship demonstrated in the plutonium hemisphere and the beryllium shells. The plutonium metallurgy was to her credit alone, but the reflector shell had been fabricated months earlier with Rossiter's help. The inner surface of the beryllium shell fitted snugly against the plutonium curvature like the skin of an orange. She repeated the steps with the remaining halves of beryllium casing and plutonium core, and once again was pleased by her accuracy.

The union of the two hemispheres was a more adventurous stage of the operation. Wishing for the assistance of Jackson's strong arms, but not wanting to interrupt his work with Rossiter, she edged one on top of the other. While the bottom half was secured flat-side-up in a countertop vise, the heavy top half was unwieldy because Nakamura wore thick gloves to protect herself against beryllium contamination.

Her knuckles twinged painfully as the top half bore down, squeezing them between the hemisphere edges. The counter needles climbed closer to the red lines with each small movement of the top half toward complete encasement of the plutonium.

As the halves approached matching, some of the weight of the top hemisphere began to rest on the bottom, slightly relieving the pressure on her straining hands. At the same time, one of the counter needles shot up for a moment, and Nakamura instinctively pulled back on the top half, knocking one of its support blocks free.

The needle fell as the weight shifted and tipped away, but Nakamura was left trying to support a massive chunk of metal with nowhere to rest it.

Up to this moment, she had dealt with her balancing problem in complete silence as Jackson and Rossiter labored over yet another mixing job, reducing powder into solid metal for the second bomb. Jackson was closer to her, preparing to transfer one of the liquids, when Nakamura suddenly said, "Leon!"

Normally, hearing his name barked out from a few feet away would not have caused Jackson to twitch a muscle. But his tired body and shot nerves responded with a jump. He jerked the flask he was holding against the side of its tray and sent some of its contents sloshing across the counter and onto the floor.

Ignoring his potentially fatal spill, Jackson rushed to

235

Nakamura, saw her problem immediately, and reached in to help support the metal. He stiffened for a second time as Nakamura spat out, "Don't touch it! Just slide that block underneath!"

Jackson hastily complied. Nakamura slumped like a loosened marionette at the simultaneous release of pressure on her aching wrists and the sight of all her counter needles resting safely away from the red lines.

The sight of Jackson's spilled flask seized her. She backed off a step, partly in panic and partly to survey Jackson's hands and clothing for any sign of splashed liquid. Relieved that Jackson was probably uncontaminated, she got her voice under control and said evenly, "Dunk, Leon, don't either of you move."

The two of them froze into standing positions. Nakamura asked, "Is there *any* chance either of you stepped in that stuff?"

Jackson checked his shoes. Rossiter said, "No, Yoshi, I stayed clear of both your areas. Is it bad?"

Nakamura thought a moment and said, "That was the plutonium tetrafluoride, wasn't it, Leon?"

"Yes."

"Flask full when you started?"

"To the line you drew."

"Then there's enough of that stuff around this room to kill all of us a hundred times over."

The three of them looked at one another as Nakamura's mind raced on. "Don't move while I explain this," she warned, "and then only move to do exactly what I tell you. If you're not sure which direction to go or even which foot to move, ask first."

Rossiter remained silent. Jackson was visibly shaken over his mistake. Unmoved in the past by the many times he had faced possible violent death, Jackson was visualizing the slow, retching collapse associated with plutonium poisoning.

"Okay," said Nakamura. "We've got to do this step by step. We're going to strip, bury our clothes, flush out this whole lab, and run the detectors over the place. Then I'll tell you how long we have before one or all of us asks to be shot."

A visitor to the remote seaside cottage would have been pressed to figure out what was happening. Three adults, all naked, placed a large pile of clothing into a plastic bag and took it out into the woods to bury it. They threw buckets of water all over one another and went back into the house. It would have looked like some sort of summer horseplay except for the fact that it was all done slowly and quietly.

Once back inside, the three of them, still naked, hosed down the lab, washing every available trace of liquid on equipment or surface into a drain in the middle of the floor tile. Then they all took showers and dressed.

While the others waited in the living room, Nakamura ran her radiation detectors over herself and every square inch of the lab. Rejoining them briefly to search for stray traces of radioactive material on the two men, Nakamura then went around the house, mechanically sniffing out the deadly plutonium. Only after crossing and recrossing the outside areas where they had splashed off their bodies and buried their clothing did Nakamura return to slump near the others on a couch.

"Well?" asked Rossiter.

"Clean, as far as I can tell," said Nakamura. "The stuff was all in a liquid, so it's unlikely that we breathed any of it in. I can't coax a peep out of the counters even near the clothes' bag."

"Now what?" asked a relieved Jackson.

"We go back to work," Rossiter cut in before Nakamura could speak. "That is, if you're not too tired."

"I'm all right, Dunk," said Jackson. "How 'bout you, Yoshi?"

"I think I needed that break," Nakamura answered, smiling. "A bucketful of cold water in my face didn't hurt, Dunk. I know we don't have much time and have to keep going, but I think we should work a little slower and keep checking one another for fatigue problems. No solo work unless we're feeling completely on top of it."

While Jackson went back to work producing plutonium for the next bomb, Rossiter helped Nakamura put the first one together. This time, the needles crept slowly upward as they eased the halves carefully together. With all pointers remaining well below the red lines, exactly where Nakamura had expected them to rest, she and Rossiter joined the hemispheres.

Once everything was checked out, Rossiter relieved Jackson of his chemical chores so that Jackson could help Nakamura with his specialty: the application of plastic explosive. After the events of the afternoon, working with the explosive was child's play for Jackson, but he worked cautiously and followed Nakamura's instructions completely. The counter needles remained stable throughout the long hours of layering and shaping the wads of material.

Finally, consulting her notes only a few times, Nakamura carefully wired the detonators and completed the outer casing. They finished in midevening and Rossiter, with their help, completed production of metal for the second bomb well before midnight. It took Nakamura less than ten minutes to check out and close down the lab for the night, but Rossiter and Jackson were already asleep when she turned out the light.

SUNDAY, MAY 23

Dawn passed for the first time in days with no signs of activity within the cottage. Rossiter awoke, still disoriented and slightly stiff, as the sun warmed his room. He suspected that it was close to seven.

He rousted the others out of bed, put on the coffee, and presided over a morning meeting while the muffins toasted.

"Yoshi," he began, "How long . . ."

". . . will it be before the second one's ready?" she finished for him. "About five or six more hours, I'd say, now that we've had practice with a real one. Is that good enough?"

"Fine, if we can keep it to that," answered Rossiter. "Who does what?"

Nakamura waved off the coffee pot, grateful that she was finally feeling alert without being chemically dosed. She thought briefly and said, "If Leon helps me again, you could close up shop while we're working and get the boat ready."

"Good," replied Rossiter, picking up a muffin to carry with him out to the *Golden Girl*. Soon, Nakamura and Jackson were in the lab shaping the plutonium halves. This time, they worked quickly and surely, doing in a couple of hours what had taken Nakamura six hours to do the first time. The explosive shaping and detonator placement went smoothly as Rossiter, under Nakamura's direction, locked away chemicals and equipment. Since only two people could work comfortably on the bomb at one time, he resisted his impatience to get moving and humored Nakamura by securing everything. He did not share her desire to make sure that no inquisitive children stumbled upon the radioactive materials but saw no harm in granting her wish. If anyone were strong enough to break the locks, they would be old enough to read the warning labels.

The *Golden Girl* motored into Portland too late for Jackson to arrive at the car rental agency before it closed. Rossiter had provided him with a false but meticulously paid-up credit card and a driver's license to match. Now he would have to wait for morning to use them. They hailed a cab and had the bemused cabbie wait as they loaded a large, heavy package into the trunk for the ride to a motel.

Since all coordination had been taken care of on the boat ride in, farewells were brief. Jackson was to drive slowly, taking rest breaks, making his trip in a full day. He was to make certain that the rented car had the right kind of trunk and good shocks.

Rossiter helped Jackson settle into his room with the package and left for the boat to cast off with Nakamura that night. To avoid annoying Jackson or belaboring the obvious, he waited until the door had closed between them to whisper to himself a phrase that would have seemed normal to anyone overhearing a parting conversation: "Drive carefully, Leon."

Gilliam awoke as a sneeze gathered steam in his nose and chest. Suddenly it was over, and he needed a Kleenex.

"Goddamn gnus," he croaked while padding to the bathroom. Why did they have to put the National Zoo right next to *his* building? Why must he have an allergy to hooved beasts? Why didn't his air conditioner work? Why does nothing ever change?

He blew his nose and rummaged to find some casual clothes. His arms and legs were still stiff from too many hours in airplanes. He'd dozed only fitfully during the red-eye flight from Los Angeles to Baltimore, and his watch told him that he'd had only five hours of actual sleep in the past two days. Now it was nearly 9 A.M. Time to call Lizzie and muster courage for the great revelation to the authorities. Courage. Not his strong suit, he conceded to himself.

A glance into his refrigerator cured whatever appetite he thought he had for a quick breakfast. Green mold crawled over fruit and packages of cheese. The milk was sour. He was afraid to look into a bowl covered with aluminum foil, since he couldn't remember when he'd put it there. The only safe consumable in his refrigerator was a lone bottle of Heineken's, which he withdrew reluctantly. He needed *something*.

Gilliam drank the beer slowly, trying to believe that he was enjoying it. He told himself that beer had nutritional value. Calories to be burned. You bet. Some breakfast.

He felt conspicuous as he left the apartment building, striding into the sunshine and Sunday traffic noise of Connecticut Avenue. He turned northwest, stretching his steps to renew his lagging circulation, past the little liquor store and the bus-stop bench where he'd first seen the derelict.

Traffic, as usual on Sunday mornings, was thick. A long queue of cars wound from the entrance of the zoo onto the avenue. Hawkers along the sidewalks sold balloons, hats, stuffed pandas, and inflatable Boeing 747s. People were everywhere. Young and old, rich and poor, foreign and domestic. . . .

Gilliam knew that trying to spot his followers would be hopeless amid the throng, so he didn't even make the attempt. By now, the "authorities"—whoever they were—would know that he was back. Back from where? Dallas, of course.

He was certain that the agent who followed him from Mrs. Rice's home must have filed a detailed report, and that someone somewhere had deduced that her visitor had been Kelly Gilliam.

Even if that asshole psychiatrist Blum keeps his promise and I'm not traced to California, he thought, everyone who has anything to do with the Timber Rivers theft investigation must have me pegged as being involved.

No matter, thought Gilliam. Within hours, perhaps even sooner, he'd set them onto Jean Murdock, judiciously keeping his promise to Mrs. Rice. The feds already know of Wesley Rice's involvement in the affair, or they would not be following Kelly Gilliam. He would need to say nothing of Rice. The leads to Murdock, though circumstantial, came from a good source—the Nakamura correspondence records in the Senator's computer. Quick checks of the visitors' records at the Widener Mental Health Center would implicate Murdock directly.

He'd tell the agents about Nakamura and Rossiter. He'd tell them about *zensho*. He'd steer their investigation in the right direction and would free himself of suspicion.

At the moment, however, he needed a telephone free of bugs, for he had one additional promise to keep. To Lizzie. She would surely agree that there was now reason enough to contact the feds. Her father, moreover, would certainly be compelled by the evidence against Murdock. Hammer could join Gilliam in calling in the troops against her. That poor son of a bitch, thought Gilliam. Living all these years with a traitorous terrorist right under his nose. How could he have been so blind? At least now he has the chance to be a hero instead of being destroyed.

Gilliam found a phone booth, ducked in, and dialed

Lizzie's number. He wished fervently that he could see her, but was not about to lead his followers to her doorstep. No reason to turn them onto her trail as well as his own.

Lizzie's phone rang. And rang. Again and again. Eight times, ten times.

"Damn!" was all Gilliam could say to himself.

By 10:30 P.M., Gilliam had visited eight telephone booths within a six-block radius of the National Zoo. He'd called Lizzie's home from each telephone booth; he'd called the senator's office and Georgetown Law School. Lizzie Hammer was nowhere to be found.

Gilliam collapsed on his dusty sofa, feeling ill. Until he found Lizzie, he could tell his secrets to no one. But more than that, he worried that something might have happened to her.

MONDAY, MAY 24

Kaznik doggedly began picking up the pieces of the Winnipesaukee Commune raid. It wasn't that he was embarrassed by the massive national coverage given the raid, or that his small hopes for its fruitfulness had been dashed; he hadn't really expected much. What bothered him was the fact that he'd succumbed to desperation, that he'd allowed a potentially hazardous fishing expedition. The raid had underscored his failure to make headway. Yet, he'd do it again. With the same tips and background information, he wouldn't hesitate to order a similar strike force into action. The commune, after all, had been on the federal watchlist for a long time. It was radical as hell, remote, and known to house a number of scientific types.

There had been a pattern of tips, not just an isolated gripe from a right-wing farmer seeking to rid the neighborhood of hippies. One lead mentioned comings and goings at all hours of the night. A totally independent source had seen "strange scientific instruments" in a pickup truck belonging to the commune members. The raid confirmed this allegation by turning up an alpha-wave monitor used in biofeedback experiments and an E-meter used to "talk" to tomatoes. Worst of all, in Kaznik's mind, the raiders hadn't found a single lousy reefer or pep pill to justify the operation to a curious public. Now he must waste valuable time trying to explain it.

Kaznik had spent the previous week poring over a tantalizing pastiche of near-breakthroughs and almost-hot leads. The trace on weapons and explosives had gone nowhere. He had no clue as to how RPG7s had found their way from Asia to the United States, or who might have brought them. The investigations into "hot" Army rifles and black-market explosives were equally unrewarding. The initial flood of promising leads diminished to a trickle, despite the efforts of Kaznik's agents.

Kaznik decided it was time to flush out his brain, to replace the unproductive ideas with new ones. He picked up his phone and summoned the people he trusted most. Within half an hour, Nate Billingsly, Curt Quillico, and Ted Rippling were seated around his cramped office.

"Gentlemen," he said as he poured brown swill into four dirty cups, "in this room we have assembled what I believe is the most potent investigative brainpower in the country. Curt, you've been doing great work on criminal cases for years. Nate, you've done the same on military stuff. And, Ted, I've often thought that a top-notch scientist could make monkeys out of us intelligence types if he switched to our kind of problems. I've got the brainpower and resources at my command to have cracked this case a long time ago. But—" Kaznik hissed, slamming a fist down on the table, "I haven't come up with a fucking thing. This mountain of leads you see piled here might as well be baseball cards. I'm no closer to recovering the missing goods than when I started."

He paused and looked around the table. These men had never before seen his anger bubble over. They sat quietly, sensing that he was on the verge of launching a tirade. But it didn't come.

Kaznik took a sip of his coffee and continued calmly.

"I've never been a fan of bullshit sessions, but it's pretty clear that we need a little luck to mix with our expertise and good intentions. We need to loosen up and regroup. That's why you're here."

"You mean that you want a fresh analysis of all the known facts?" asked Quillico.

"Not exactly," answered Kaznik. "If we try to put together all the facts, we'll be right back in the same old bind. There are just too many of them to work with. Just listing them would take hours and we'd be too bored and worn out from that to do any useful thinking. No, I want to give you certain facts to look at, not all of them. Then I want you to play games, to make the rest of us want to hit you with cream pies for having the gall to make such ridiculous suggestions."

Kaznik pushed back his chair, opened his middle drawer, and pulled out a pint of Jack Daniels.

"To do this right," he said with a trace of a smile, "we need an appropriate work environment and a productive frame of mind. That means you each take one shot of this on my say-so and a couple more if you think they'll help."

The bottle went around as solemnly as a peace pipe. When it reached Rippling, he looked at it dubiously. "I'm afraid that one swig of this will put me to sleep," he said. "I don't drink."

Kaznik nodded, withdrew a pack of Marlboro filters, and tapped it until one cigarette fell out. Its end was twisted closed.

"I've always been prepared since I was a Boy Scout," he said. "The same instructions go for you, Ted. One toke on my orders, any more at your own discretion."

Billingsly's mouth fell open. Quillico looked aghast. But Rippling repressed an insistent burst of laughter long enough to light the joint and pull deeply. When he finally exhaled, Billingsly edged away from the pungent smoke.

"The meeting," said Kaznik sternly, "will now come

to order. I have three categories of information to lay before this committee. One category concerns our leads on purchases of detonating equipment and a metal called beryllium. The second involves one Kelly Gilliam, a congressional staff member. And the third has to do with known facts on John Bates, a flasher who escaped from a looney bin a couple of years ago. I propose we begin with the material purchases."

Billingsly clapped his hands together and replied, "Hear, hear!" He clearly wanted to get into the spirit of things.

Kaznik continued. "The first leads are things you've put me onto, Ted. You mentioned that the world's best detonators are made in Sweden, so I sent some people over there to check out the companies that make them. I started on the assumption that our bomb builders knew what they were doing and had the money to do it right. I told my people to concentrate on companies that made the very best equipment. One of these, an outfit called Elektrokem, turned up a suspect. We asked them to screen their records for new purchasers within the last year who bought only a few detonators, not hundreds. Bulk purchasers would probably be legitimate mining companies or similar operations.

"As it turns out, there was one purchase about six months ago that looked suspicious. Elektrokem recorded a sale of several devices to a Mr. Randolph of Randolph Mining Company, a Texas-based exploration firm. Randolph, or whoever he really is, said he wanted to test a few and would order more if they worked out. He intimated that purchases would run in the hundreds of thousands of dollars a year. Elektrokem's vice-president handled the deal and gave us a general physical description of the man, but he couldn't produce any business cards or letterheads from the Randolph company. The gizmos were paid for with a check from a Swedish bank, but we've since found out that there is no Randolph company in Texas.

"The other lead is even less substantial. When we checked out metallurgical supply houses for suspicious buyers of beryllium metal, we drew a blank. Except for one thing: A small outfit in Denver called Elementals told us about an unexplained inventory shortage of several pounds. We offered to put up a thousand-dollar reward to anyone in their employ for solid information on where the stuff went. One of their stockmen, a black guy named Brooks, came forward after some persuasion with a story about a 'brother' he'd only recently met at a local bar near the company gate. The guy had offered him five thousand dollars for a few pounds of beryllium. Brooks delivered it within a week, the guy paid him in cash and disappeared.

"Well," Kaznik concluded, "that's what you've got to work with. Now, let your imaginations go."

Quillico tried first. "The guy who bought the detonators probably has a lot of money and a lot of balls. That means he probably wasn't kidding when he said he was a Texan. I'd be stretching my imagination, though, to assume that he's connected with the Denver incident."

The men traded glances, groping for the next logical conclusion. Kaznik broke the silence. "Looks like you guys need some more raw material. That's something I have plenty of."

He then laid out the story of Kelly Gilliam's escapades, starting with his call to Rice and ending with Gilliam's sudden reappearance the day before after an unexplained absence. Noting that Quillico's face was too pink for having had only one nip from the booze bottle, Kaznik punched the FBI man lightly on the shoulder and said, "Since I've already ripped you a new asshole for letting Gilliam get away so damn many times, Curt, I'll consider the matter closed. As long as it doesn't happen again."

Quillico relaxed and Kaznik continued. "What really bothers me is that the guy doesn't behave like a terrorist. And there's nothing in his background to suggest conspiracy with terrorists or hijackers, let alone building an atom bomb. But he sure doesn't behave like a goody two-shoes either!"

"Look," said Billingsly, "the way you describe this guy, he's guilty as hell about something. He slips the best tails in the business; he goes around looking for microphones like he knows they're in his apartment, like he expects them to be there. And judging from the reports of our Dallas people yesterday, I'd bet money that it was this guy who popped in on Wesley Rice's widow the night before last. But what really gets me is that he doesn't report any of his harassment to anybody. He's got no complaints. Nothing. He may not be a professional bad guy, but he's connected to this thing somehow."

"What do you suggest, Nate?"

"I suggest that we spirit him away, ask him a lot of questions, and ring his bell if the answers don't check out."

"That's a good idea, Nate," Kaznik said. "It goes against my grain to do anything that might make the conspirators trigger happy, but if nothing breaks in a few days, I think I'll take your advice. Any other ideas?"

Rippling responded. "I don't think we'll do any better than you have, Joel, on any *one* set of facts. I think you ought to load more of your stuff onto us and see if we can put it together differently."

"Good," said Kaznik. "Let me give you the one that bothers me most. Nate and Curt know all about a prime suspect we've managed to identify, so I'll fill you in. We got prints in Connecticut on an Okie by the name of John Bates. He worked in an L.A. television studio for a while, but got shipped off to the looney bin when he displayed his third leg on afternoon TV. We know nothing about him since he took a walk from the mental hospital a couple of years ago.

If I could just figure out why a nut like that is stealing plutonium, I might get a lead on what his fellow hijackers are up to."

"Shit, that's easy," said Rippling. "It takes a nut to want to steal plutonium. The others probably all came out of the same hospital." He laughed at his own joke. No one else laughed.

Kaznik grabbed the phone and then realized the man he wanted, Quillico, was there in the room.

"Curt," he said. "I want twenty—no, make that thirty of your agents ransacking the records room of that hospital this second. I want them to go through the charts of every goddamn patient who was in that hospital while Bates was there. I want them to pull the records of every scientist, every homicidal maniac, everyone with a lot of money, and everyone else who looks interesting. Then they're going to send me photocopies of those records by military jet."

Quillico jumped to the phone. While he was talking urgently, Kaznik turned to the other two.

"Nate and Ted, I want you to go through my notes on this case from cover to cover and let me know if you come up with other ideas. You guys just gave me the first good thing that's happened in days. I'm going down the hall to catch a couple of hours' sleep. Is there anything you need before I crash?"

Billingsly shook his head. Rippling thought for a minute before saying with a straight face, "Yeah, Joel, I could use a couple more tokes."

Jean Murdock sat alone at a table in the back corner of a small luncheonette in Silver Spring. Cigarette butts overflowed her ashtray, several of which lay crushed in her saucer under a cup that held its third refill of coffee.

Where was John Bates? Though she knew that Bates was flaky, she also knew that he obeyed orders and kept to his schedules. This wasn't like him.

She got up from the table and scrounged matches from the fat man behind the counter, ignoring his appreciative glances as well as his pathetic attempts at conversation. "Ain't you gonna have some breakfast?" he asked. "You been here half an hour an' all you do is sit there an' smoke an' drink coffee. That ain't good for you, honey." Murdock sat down with the matches.

Damn that Bates! He'd better have a good excuse or she'd slowly pull off a layer of his skin. Here she sat, killing Monday morning in a crummy café. A whole new week's worth of hell might be breaking loose back at the office.

Murdock knew that her annoyance over Bates's tardiness was only an emotional cover for her real worry: What if something had happened to John? Or worse, what if something had gone wrong in Maine?

She examined the sludge in the bottom of her cup and drained it anyway. While reaching for another cigarette, she saw a dark form appear outside the café entrance, its features obscured by grime and grease on the glass. Murdock held her breath and exhaled only when she saw that it was John Bates walking through the door. She read worry in his freckled face as he surveyed the sparse crowd in the café. After spying her, he crossed directly to her table, not stopping at the counter for a cup of coffee. He dragged a chair out, sat, and said much too loudly, "No call!"

"Nothing?" she asked stupidly, as though she'd get a different answer.

"Nothing."

"Are you sure you called the right phone booth at exactly the right time?"

"Positive."

Murdock's mind spun. A missed call could mean any number of things: There could have been a nuclear accident; Duncan and the others could have been captured; or there could have been a harmless screw-up. While she sorted through the gruesome possibilities,

Bates sat staring at her, chewing his lower lip. Never had Murdock seen him look so nervous.

"Don't worry, John," she said reassuringly, "it's not your fault."

Bates's whole body seemed to loosen and Murdock had a sudden vision of a contrite puppy. "Is that what delayed you?" she asked.

"Yeah. When I got no answer, I waited around for a while, hoping Dunk was just late. After I called a few more times, I was hopin' so hard he'd answer that I almost started hearing him say hello. And he wasn't even there. Know what I mean, Jeannie?"

Murdock nodded. She knew exactly what he meant. "Maybe you had a bad phone booth."

"Well, it worked for other things. Want to know the weather forecast for today? Or how about the Dial-a-Prayer? I know 'em by heart."

For a long moment Murdock considered her options, discovering that she had very few. "I suggest," she said at length, "that you try to place the regular followup call today, right after this meeting. If you can't contact Duncan, try again tomorrow at the same time. That's what we're supposed to do if something keeps us from getting in touch. If there's no contact tomorrow, then we'll start worrying."

"Do you want me to call you if I raise him?"

"No, I'll call you. Just make sure that you stick around your place until you hear from me. I can't take the time to go running around for any more secret meetings. We'll just have to risk talking by phone. Okay?"

"Okay."

The meeting ended.

Lizzie sat in her car, parked a few doors from John Bates's townhouse. Following him from his second meeting with Murdock had been easy. He'd driven straight home from a small café in Silver Spring, stopping only once for a telephone booth call.

That was four hours ago. Since then, Liz learned something of the boring realities of detective work, but nothing of the man in the house. She was strung out from the suspense of waiting, anxiety over her father, and worrying about nuclear theft. To make matters worse, her tailbone ached murderously. Looking on the bright side, she was thankful to have found a parking space shaded from the midday sun. On the dark side was her pressing need for a bathroom.

She decided that more idle waiting was out of the question. Her muscles needed movement, her lungs needed air, her head needed to make something happen. Her questions demanded answers. Not knowing fully what she was up to, she got out of the car and stamped a sleeping foot a few times on the ground. After shaking her wrists to loosen up, she walked briskly down the block away from the man's townhouse.

The safest way to view the place, she reasoned, was to approach from the rear, strolling down the alley as though she were a neighbor taking a shortcut home. The trip took only a few minutes and yielded nothing. She saw a back door hung with unbroken cobwebs, obviously unused in years. There were two large windows with iron bars, customary in Washington, and closed venetian blinds. The trash cans near the rear stoop had several inches of rusty water in their bottoms. The man in the house either generated no garbage or simply kept it.

Liz retraced her steps down the alley around to the front of the block. The brief walk had placated her muscles but had done nothing for her insistent bladder. Not knowing how much longer she could last without a bathroom, she headed down the block toward her car. Then it happened. The door she'd watched for so long opened. The man she'd followed stepped out, closing it behind him. He ambled down the steps, got into his car, and drove off as Liz stood frozen to the sidewalk.

She couldn't believe it. "Jesus fucking Christ!" she spat out, kicking the nearest rung of a wrought-iron fence. He'd made a clean getaway because she'd left her car for five minutes after four hours of patient waiting. There was no justice, no decency.

She walked down the street to her car, banging the heel of her hand against her hip and mumbling further obscenities. Her back hurt, her bladder was ready to rupture, and now her toe throbbed. In a kind of daze, she walked past her car and wandered onto the step of the guilty townhouse. At this point, she didn't much care who saw her. As she stood trying to ignore her hurting body and bleak prospects, a scruffy brown tabby emerged from under a parked car and made moo eyes at her.

"No, you don't love me," Liz said. "I don't love me, and you sure don't know me as well as I do."

The cat, reading exasperation as affection, rubbed against Liz's leg.

She sat wearily down on Bates's steps and absently petted the cat, who, of course, purred. Liz's eyes wandered to the window by the door. The curtain was open and she could see sunlight on the far wall. Summoning a final surge of determination, she scooped up the cat and climbed the three short steps to the front door. She put the cat on the window ledge and stared in while continuing the petting.

All she could see was a couch, a lamp, and the edge of a coffee table. Magazines with prominent bare breasts on the covers were strewn on the furniture and floor. Besides that, nothing. While staring through the window, she absently stopped petting the tabby, who jumped down onto the step to rub against her legs. By now, the purring was in high gear. The cat rubbed alternately against Liz's leg, the edge of the doorpost, and the front door. The door cracked open. Liz slowly relaxed the muscles in the hand which she found clenched around the brass doorknob. She waited two, three, then four centuries, as her pulsing heartbeat returned from her throat back into her chest. Had the man actually left the door unlocked? Had she actually opened it? Liz pushed the door inward. Teeth clenched, she slipped through and pressed it shut behind her. She could hear the cat rubbing and meowing on the other side.

Her broken promise to Gilliam rang in her mind as she contemplated the penalty for unlawful entry. But she'd gotten a break that made four hours of tedium worthwhile, provided she had guts enough to capitalize on it. She took a deep breath, briefly wondering what sort of a criminal would leave his own door unlocked.

There was not much to see downstairs—a few mismatched chairs in the living room and a throw rug that looked like a carpet remnant. The kitchen had a nondescript dinette set and a few glasses and plates. Canned food in the kitchen cabinets. Nothing at all in the hall closet. If this place had a bomb factory, it had to be on the second floor.

Liz went up the steps. One of the upstairs bedrooms was completely empty. No rugs, no furniture. Liz involuntarily tiptoed as she walked out of the room. The floorboards creaked and her breathing seemed to echo off the four walls of the room. The hall bathroom was likewise empty. Liz stood on the landing and looked back into the empty bedroom, the empty bathroom, and down the barren steps. The sounds of the city, no more than thirty or forty feet away, were from another world. "This was easy," she muttered to herself, but the "easy" trailed off to dead silence as she suddenly saw herself lying dead on the floor of one of those empty rooms. What would she do if the guy came back? she wondered. Having no answer, she steadied herself on the railing and turned toward the one uninspected room in the house, the master bedroom.

Here, although not exactly normal, things looked reassuring. Dirty wall-to-wall plush carpet. A dresser standing next to a substantial bed. A mirror hung on one
wall. The room would have been almost homey were
it not for the tits. Magazines with tits. Everywhere. On
the bed, the carpet, the dresser. Everywhere she looked
were *Rogues*, *Playboys*, *Hustlers*, and dozens of sleazy
little numbers with black-and-white covers that didn't
even have names. Liz started to laugh. She couldn't
help herself.

Whoever this guy is, she thought, he certainly must
have a lot of time on his hands . . . or something. This
thought choked her up again, but she quickly recovered her sense of mission. She pawed through the
contents of the dresser and found a few changes of
underwear, socks, and shirts. No papers, no notebooks,
no bombs.

The open closet contained several pairs of pants and
a trenchcoat. Liz dutifully checked pockets. In the
trenchcoat pocket was a thick roll of hundred-dollar
bills with a rubber band around them. She gasped at
the discovery. She estimated that there must be fifty
bills. She stuffed the money back into the trench coat
pocket. What were the chances that this guy had really
not done anything wrong? But what if he had? Could
she slow him down by taking the money? Liz retrieved
the roll of bills and stuffed it in her own hip pocket.
Turning from the closet, she stopped to look under the
bed, lifting the bedspread.

Suddenly she wanted to bolt for the door. All her
muscles were poised to spring up and run down the
steps, but she held on tightly to the bedpost and kept
staring. Under the bed were guns. Large guns and
strange guns. All of them ugly. Liz knew without ever
having seen guns like these that they could blow many
large holes in strong objects. She rose weakly from the
bedside, her mind reeling. Time to go. Time to put
miles between herself and the guns, the tits, and any-

thing else horrible she hadn't yet found. She made it to the stairs before her bladder wrenched in a painful spasm. The bathroom. Everything must wait for a quick trip to the bathroom. No ifs, ands, or buts. She raced back through the bedroom into the bathroom where the balloon in her stomach slowly subsided as she sat, pants around her ankles. She tried not to count the seconds. As she reached reflexively to flush, she heard the front door push open.

No, she said silently to herself. No . . . please, no. Footsteps hit the stairs. She started out of the door of the bathroom and stopped cold. The stairs were the only exit. Hiding in the bathroom would never work. What then? The window? On the second floor? Forget it. Her rusty karate, maybe? Not likely.

Footsteps reached the top of the stairs and turned toward the master bedroom. Liz looked frantically around the bathroom and realized there were no razors, no knives, no bottles to be broken off. Suddenly she remembered the damn skin magazines. She closed the door, and flushed the toilet. Liz shouted, "Be out in a second, honey!"

Bates hesitated before pulling out a small-bore pistol from his pocket and jerking open the bathroom door. Liz stepped out smiling, with her T-shirt and bra in one hand. Her smile vanished as she saw the gun. His mouth fell open as he surveyed her naked top. Realizing from his expression that he wouldn't shoot her immediately, Liz started talking as fast as she could.

"Hey, Ronnie didn't tell me that this was going to be some kinky job! I mean, with some dude pulling a gun on me. I mean, if you want to change your order, you can just call Ronnie up and tell him you don't want me. You don't have to wave that thing around and scare the hell out of me. Look, I'm sorry if this is the way you like to make it, but it's just not my scene. I'll be seeing ya, fella." As Liz frantically extemporized, she gathered that the man only half understood her words, that he was rooted to the floor. Capitalizing on his astonishment, she marched by him and down the stairs. Reaching the landing, she glanced backward to see him standing dumbly at the top, his gun lowered. Liz flounced her breasts once for effect. "You can tell Ronnie I'm not workin' for him any more," she spat out. With that she walked through the front door, slamming it behind her. Then she ran, struggling with her T-shirt.

Liz drove across downtown Washington in less than ten minutes, running traffic lights and eyeing the rearview mirror. By the time she reached the Northwest section, her panic had subsided. Nobody had followed. Her thoughts turned to what to do next as her heartbeat slowed to normal. There was no reason to return to the law school since her one summer class had already ended its daily meeting. She had, moreover, cut all the previous week's classes and the thought of encountering her professor and classmates repelled her. How could she possibly explain her absence?

The idea of visiting her father's office on Capitol Hill was equally distasteful. Could she handle Jean Murdock if she were there? Or her father? Liz was certain that her own behavior would be noticeably strange after this afternoon's activities.

Her empty apartment held no appeal. She needed to be with somebody, preferably Kelly.

She parked next to a small Chinese restaurant with a phone booth visible inside the front glass doors. Once inside, the smell of frying Oriental food momentarily nauseated her. Repressing the nausea, she plugged fifteen cents into the phone and hastily dialed his apartment, carefully composing what she would say. Kelly's telephone, after all, could very well be bugged. After the sixth or seventh ring, she realized that she was wasting her time. Kelly wasn't home. She dialed his Congressional number and was told by a committee staffer that he'd not been in that day.

Liz replaced the phone in the cradle and stood in the foyer of the little restaurant. By now, the aroma of frying food was no longer nauseating, and she remembered that she'd tackled her day of detective work on a hasty piece of toast and a cup of coffee—ten hours ago. Having nothing better to do for the moment, she waved to the hostess and followed her to a small table in the rear. Within forty-five minutes, Liz had eaten a bowl of soup, two egg rolls, and a full order of Governor's shrimp.

On her way out, she stopped again at the phone booth to try Kelly's number, once more without success. But by this time, she was able to face returning alone to her apartment, though she was not yet sure whether she was prepared to spend the whole night alone. Concluding that she should be in a place that Kelly was likely to call, she headed for home.

Waiting was not pleasant, especially in an apartment that was too dark and too quiet. Liz closed every blind, pulled every drape, and turned on every light. She combated the silence with her television set and a rerun of *Star Trek*. Captain Kirk, Spock, and Bones failed to distract her, however, from the memory of that moment in the townhouse when she fully expected to die. She would focus hard on the problem of Scotty's runaway anti-matter warp drive, only to drift back to that instant when her hand was on the bathroom doorknob and footsteps were on the stairs. She jumped slightly when she actually imagined the sounds of a door pushing open followed by heavy footfalls, and felt foolish upon discovering that it was only the sound of her own blood beating in her temples and a large Chinese meal doing garbly things in her stomach. She shrieked when she heard the telephone ring.

Hearing Kelly's voice was the therapy she needed,

259

and she lost no time in asking him to come over immediately. Though he sensed her anxiety, he pressed for no explanation of the urgency, assuring her instead that he would be there in minutes.

Liz settled back on the couch to wait, grateful that *Star Trek* had not ended.

Gilliam's knock on the door came during a commercial. Liz cautiously asked who it was before opening. A stage whisper responded from the other side, "Eet eez I, Natasha! Ze Tzar's Horsemen are on my heels! Let me in at once!"

Liz drew back the deadbolt and admitted a worried-looking Gilliam who nonetheless wore a forced grin. He gave her a hug and she hugged him back.

"It's about time you surfaced," said Gilliam. "I spent the whole damn weekend trying to track you down."

"I was just about to say the same thing. You're not exactly easy to find yourself."

"Hey, wait a minute," protested Gilliam. "It's not as easy for me to show as it is for you. You don't have a squad of federal thugs all over you like a dirty shirt. You should've seen what I had to do to lose them today. I'm actually getting good at this."

"I don't think I'm up to hearing about it," said Lizzie. "But just so you'll know, I had a delightful weekend following Jean Murdock all over the map. That's why you couldn't find me. Now. How was your trip 'out of town' for which you so mysteriously extended my deadline?"

Gilliam grew suddenly serious. "That's why I was so anxious to find you." He then told her about his meeting with Mrs. Rice and about the suicide note in the tennis locker. Liz enjoyed his account of escaping pursuit in Dallas, but was horrified by his findings in Los Angeles. She shuddered when he told her of *zensho*.

"In other words," she summarized, nearly whispering, "you think that Jean Murdock recruited this maniac

Rossiter through this—this Nakamura, and that they've been planning this incredible *zensho* for years?"

"I'm afraid so," said Gilliam. He let himself flop into an easy chair. "Now tell me what *you've* found, if anything."

Gilliam's story had renewed Lizzie's fright over her own detective work and her face showed it clearly. But she calmly related how Murdock had met twice with a nondescript freckle-faced man, how she'd followed the man to his house and waited for hours outside, only to lose him after a stroll down the alley. She told of mustering her courage for a peek in the window.

"Wow!" said Gilliam. "There must have been something pretty heavy inside that window for me to rate such a fine hug."

"No," said Lizzie.

"But you were really scared when you called me," Kelly replied. "Did he come back while you were looking in the window?"

"Not exactly," said Liz, her eyes avoiding his.

"You broke in," ventured Gilliam in a flat voice.

"The door was open, Kelly. I couldn't believe it. I didn't really think about it very much. It was just . . . all of a sudden . . . without even thinking . . . I was *inside*."

"You were inside," Gilliam repeated, his voice neither studied nor controlled. He suddenly had a vision, not of Lizzie lying dead in an unknown house, but of himself, standing in a phone booth, dialing Lizzie's number, then dialing it again, again, and again. He felt a sour taste between his stomach and throat, and reflexively grabbed Lizzie's hand and held it tightly, while she blurted out the rest of the story in big chunks. Gilliam listened intently as she matter-of-factly told of the empty house, the skin magazines, the arsenal under the bed, her own bare-breasted escape. As she finished the story, she noticed that Gilliam's eyes were fixed on her T-shirt. "Well," she said, as Gilliam flushed, "at least there's a chance he never got a good look at my face."

He stared at her in silent amazement, envying her presence of mind, her courage, feeling a missing piece of his life slip into place. He wanted to fold her in his arms.

In the back of his mind, he knew that she had not really had a choice in turning to him. He'd been handy, the only logical choice. But suddenly, they were huddled together on the couch, bodies pressed close. Liz's shoulders shook and her eyes filled with tears. Slowly, as if she had to let go of her nerves and muscles one by one, she wept. Gilliam held her tightly and pondered the horrible tension she must have felt the past few days. He thought about her following Murdock, patiently sitting outside that pervert's townhouse, searching it, and finding what might have been a brutal death. It must feel good, he thought, to cry. He fought the hot tightness in his own throat as he contemplated the tension he'd felt since the previous week. But Liz was soft, Liz was warm, and he needed her as she needed him. Crying seemed right, and they held each other for many minutes.

They kissed with a thrust and immediacy that surprised them both. Liz pressed her head into the hollow of Gilliam's shoulder, feeling his breathing and heartbeat subside. She finally broke the silence.

"Kelly, what should we do?"

The question hung in the air. "Well," he said at length. "You're a law student and I'm a lawyer. Between the two of us, we should be able to sort out the facts and come up with some decent ideas."

Her eyes begged for help. She'd done enough thinking for one day and was more than willing to let him do it for her. Gilliam started again.

"We've got to face the fact that all we've done so far is screw up. I've been acting strangely enough to convince the guys who're following me that I deserve to be followed. You could've gotten yourself killed in that house. I say we've been lucky, nothing more. Somebody is probably still after me, and if Murdock hears about your visit and makes a connection with you, some really dangerous people could be after you. I don't think either of us can trust our luck any more."

"You think we should go to the police now?"

"Yes, I do," he said. "It's no longer a question of protecting your father's reputation. There's your life, my life, and the lives of those who might be facing contact with radioactive material. I keep thinking about those guns under the bed."

"You're probably right," said Liz. "It's funny how I can balance off the missing plutonium in my mind against my dad's career, but the guns somehow seem a lot more frightening and important. Kelly, I don't want to go to the police without giving my dad a chance to join us. I mean, it's past the point where we can avoid dragging him into it, but I want to give him the chance to come out of it with something intact. Can't we talk to him first and *then* blow the whistle?"

Gilliam thought about it. Recent terrors notwithstanding, it was really quite unlikely that anyone would attack them in Liz's apartment. Even if Murdock got a good description of Liz and her car from the man in the house, she might not make the connection immediately. For that matter, the man might not see Murdock for a while to tell her about it. The only immediate threat was the missing plutonium.

Gilliam and Liz discussed the problem and agreed that their consciences could not withstand responsibility for mass murder. But what could a few hours' delay possibly matter?

"What the hell," said Gilliam. "If you can face going out that door after dark, I guess I can, too. Let's drive out to your father's place before I call the FBI."

"Kelly," said Liz, "it's after eleven, and I don't want

to be out on the streets. Besides, Murdock is probably
. . . uh . . . out there with him."

"Wait till morning?" asked Gilliam.

"Wait till morning."

A lump caught in Gilliam's throat. "Then what do you think we should do now?" he stammered.

Liz put her hands on his temples and kissed him on the mouth. "I think," she said firmly, "that we should go to bed."

The sound of Murdock's arrival filtered into the back yard and awakened her huge dog. His barking reverberated through the trees, causing even Murdock to flinch with each step from the driveway to the front door. She was thankful for the fence between the front yard and the rear, even though the animal would probably still recognize her in the dark.

It was after eleven o'clock and Murdock was exhausted. Throughout the day she'd fended off reporters, congressmen, senators, and constituents, all wanting information on the Timber Rivers theft and the whereabouts of Harry Hammer. There was even a combined antinuclear/civil liberties protest march that ended on the Capitol steps.

She'd handled a thousand routine office chores. She'd been nagged by inklings of worry over last week's strange occurrence with the computer. Why should someone in the Energy Committee office search the Hammer correspondence files without permission?

Today's meeting with John Bates, however, troubled her more than anything else. Why had Bates heard nothing from Maine? What could have gone wrong?

Just as she was inserting the key into the lock, the front door jerked open suddenly. The senator stood before her, framed in backlight from the living room. He was dressed in his most formal business suit with starched linen shirt, club tie, and vest. His scowling expression was the one he used for important committee meetings and business on the Senate floor. Flickering in his eyes was anticipation of action and conflict, a flicker Murdock had not seen in years. He looked ready to strike down political enemies by the score. At eleven o'clock at night.

"Where in the hell have you been?" he demanded.

His strong tone astounded her. "Where do you think I've been? I've been in the office taking care of business all day. Is it okay if I come in?"

Hammer stepped briskly aside.

The living room was meticulous, as though the housekeeper had gone on a cleaning binge: furniture dusted and sparkling; no coffee cups or plates with half-eaten sandwiches; magazines and newspapers neatly placed in racks. But there was no housekeeper, Murdock remembered, not since Hammer had fired her weeks ago. Until now, the house had shown the effects of the woman's absence.

"Did *you* do all this?" asked Murdock, setting her briefcase on the newly vacuumed carpet.

"Do you expect the next leader of the free world to live in a pig sty? Get your coat off. We have business to discuss."

Murdock hung her coat up while Hammer poured himself a scotch. When she returned to the living room, he was standing with a notebook in his hand, waiting impatiently.

"You met with Bates today," he said crisply. "I want a full report on the progress in Maine and your assessment of the operation."

Something in Hammer's eyes made Murdock uneasy, but she gave no evidence of her unease as she answered. "Harry, something's come up and I'm not exactly sure what it means. I met with Bates this morning, but he had nothing to report. When he called the phone booth in Maine for a status report, nobody was there to answer."

"And Bates received no call from Rossiter at any time?"

"That's right."

Hammer drained half his scotch. "If anything were wrong, Rossiter would have called Bates in Washington. If anything catastrophic had happened, you would have heard about it through our nuclear industry or intelligence contacts. You've heard nothing, right?"

"That's right."

"Ergo, we have nothing to fear at the moment. From the authorities, that is."

That Hammer was way ahead of her surprised Murdock. "What are you thinking, Harry?" she asked.

He headed back to the bar to freshen his drink, talking as he went. "I'm thinking about Rossiter. He's insane—totally, irretrievably, homicidally insane. Moreover, he's uneducated. I'll grant that he's intelligent and well read, but he thinks he knows a great deal more than he actually does. He thinks he's in command of this operation; he thinks that he controls you, that I'm a doddering old fool with megalomanic fantasies. You and I have found considerable utility in these misconceptions, Jeannie, but we must be prepared for the next logical development."

"And that is?"

"That Duncan Rossiter will take it upon himself to alter the plan without consulting anybody, if in his judgment it's warranted."

Murdock had reached precisely the same conclusion during her meeting with Bates.

"You and I," Hammer continued, "have little choice but to trust Rossiter at this point. After all, we know that he can make good decisions and that he's totally committed to his mission. We must be prepared, however, to put a stop to him at the very moment his self-importance starts to get out of hand."

"What does that mean?"

Hammer leveled his gaze at her and smiled. "It means

that we must be ready to kill him at a moment's notice."
He belted down the rest of his drink and reached for
the scotch bottle.

Murdock felt suddenly chilled. This in itself surprised her. Why should any suggestion under the sun,
no matter how monstrous, chill her? Much less the suggestion of killing someone? Hadn't she killed already?
Wouldn't she kill again?

"Harry," she began, "didn't we agree that Rossiter
might be helpful after we take over? I mean, even before we brought him into the operation we knew that
we'd need someone like him to help run things. We'll
need—"

"I've accounted for all our needs!" Hammer shot
back. He gestured sharply to a stack of notebooks near
an armchair across the room, and began talking loudly,
rapidly. "See those? What do you think I've written
down in there, Jeannie? I'll tell you. I've written a detailed plan of action for my first sixty days in office,
including every contingency, every possible thing that
could go wrong. Once my authority is initially established, I'll arrest the President, the Joint Chiefs, the
leadership of both Houses of Congress, and—do you
know what I'll do then, Jeannie?—I'll put them in the
White House! Close to me! Locked in rooms, of course,
but close enough to prevent some maniac from storm-
ing the White House, close enough to ensure that
they'd be vaporized if we touched off the goddamn
bomb."

"Harry, I don't doubt that you've—"

"And do you know what else? I've written nearly
fifteen pages of things to do just to ensure that the
federal government can't evacuate Washington, leaving us here high and dry with our bomb." Hammer
strode quickly to the notebooks, withdrew one, and
held it high. "This one! Right here: key military agencies in the Pentagon. I'll promote new officers out of
the ranks to run them, replacing those old bastards

267

who've fucked things up so badly all these years. New faces, Jean! People promoted by me, loyal only to me."

"Harry, please—"

"Silence!" He was close to raving now, gesticulating wildly, waving notebooks in the air. "And this one is an economic plan of action, a way to keep the stock exchanges open and the market viable. No economic crisis, Jeannie! Think of it! Continued prosperity under a unified and cohesive federal policy. And look at these. Housing programs, new welfare reforms, new tax reforms. All immediately attainable without a clumsy and self-serving Congress to—"

"*Harry!*" Murdock's own volume shocked her.

Hammer stood motionless, his mouth open. Then he dropped the notebooks and walked stiffly across the room until he stood over her. "Jeannie," he said softly, "I want Rossiter dead. Soon. You may want to keep him around for a while, but *I* don't. I want him dead. I never want him to have you again. Hear me? Never again."

She could see that he was shaking, that his body was a chemical battleground between alcohol and adrenaline.

The jangling telephone cut the silence. Two rings, three. Then the click. She threw the speaker switch and caught the end of the instructions. The beeping tone told the caller to leave his message.

Murdock was galvanized by the next drawling voice. "This is John Bates callin' Jean Murdock. I gotta talk to her soon as possible. She can get me at . . ."

Murdock flew to the telephone and cut the recording switch. Hammer stood wide-eyed as she snatched up the receiver and shouted into it. "John, this is Jean. What is it? What've you got?"

She stood for several minutes, nodding her head vigorously, uttering "m-m-hum's" and "I see's." As suddenly as it began, the conversation was over. Murdock turned from the telephone and approached

Hammer, who looked dazed and deflated. The alcohol was winning.

"Harry," said Murdock, "the bomb is in Washington." The message seemed not to register, but she continued. "Leon Jackson brought it in tonight, to Bates's house. Duncan accelerated the fabrication schedule in Maine. They had to kill a policeman, Harry, but Bates says everything is okay."

"Wha-a?" responded Hammer, his eyes glazing. "Bomb? In Washington?" His stare wandered stupidly. "I think I'll stay downstairs from now on."

Murdock closed her eyes rather than see his face. "It will be over soon, Harry. Very soon."

TUESDAY, MAY 25

The early-morning change of the guard proceeded smoothly for the U.S. Capitol Police. Nearly two hundred policemen were deployed around the complex at their normal stations. The red phone in the central command office in the Russell Senate Office Building was quiet. Radio and TV monitors showed nothing unusual. Patrol cars, bicycles, and dogs began their regular beats. Radio guards on the roofs of buildings reported their areas "secure."

The bomb squad was present and awake, if not particularly alert, in its Senate office. There was little reason to be alert. Of the thousand bomb threats the unit had received since its inception, not a single one had been confirmed. The two actual explosions in the Capitol had happened without forewarning. The one in 1971 resulted in considerable damage to a new ladies' washroom, but not much else. That bomb had been smuggled into the Capitol in a woman's handbag, an easy thing to do since the Capitol police at that time had strict orders to keep their hands off women's handbags. They were to search briefcases, attachés and all else, but not women's handbags.

The handbag rule told much of the congressionally controlled police force, an operation whose superficial omnipresence masked near impotence. Through its sheer numbers, it managed to discourage the casual thief, mugger, or rowdy, but the protection it offered against serious crime was farcical. Fewer than 10 percent of its policemen had prior law enforcement experience. Most were retired Marines or patronage appointments demanded by powerful congressmen. Training was brief. Performance standards for police work, weapons use, and physical fitness were nonexistent.

On this day, Capitol Hill's security would be breached. The two men in the utility truck a block from the Capitol's west front could have walked through the front door with their equipment, but they were accustomed to avoiding risks. They emerged from the truck and placed two orange conical markers next to a manhole. Then, with practiced ease, they removed the cover, and one of them climbed into the hole. He wore plain repairman's clothing and a cap. The other, a black man similarly attired, pushed a large roll of wire to the hole from the truck. The two then lowered the heavy roll into the hole in the ground. The black man reemerged, hopped back into the truck, and drove away. Nobody noticed.

A few minutes later, after parking the truck several blocks away, the black man entered yet another manhole and made his way underground to rejoin his companion. The two set out for the Capitol, the roll of wire slung between their shoulders.

Visitors are often overwhelmed by the maze of corridors below the street level of the Capitol complex. They would be astonished, however, by the labyrinth below that. Capitol Hill is honeycombed with pedestrian tunnels, steam tunnels, and utility tunnels. Most have multiple access points in various out-of-the-way corners of the Capitol. The Architect of the Capitol's office contains detailed plans that give the location of everything on the Hill, but few have occasion to look at them closely. Most of the intricate maze has outlived its usefulness.

The architect's files are open, of course, to qualified

congressional staff, so Jean Murdock had had little
trouble familiarizing herself with the subterranean
routes. During her long visits to the architect's research
and information office, she chatted knowledgeably with
the staff about the Capitol's history. With them, she
discussed the art and the architecture while she memorized minute details of the physical plant, from the
statue on its dome down to the foundations. The architect's staff was delighted to find someone interested in
their stories about sealed stairways, hidden passages,
and dormant dumbwaiters used by long-forgotten but
once powerful committee chairmen. Murdock was
"fascinated" by these historical details.

Bates's previous trips to the Capitol had confirmed
the accuracy and thoroughness of Murdock's research.
Dressed as a workman and armed with influential names
to drop if stopped and questioned, he'd conducted his
reconnaissance with a casual sense of purpose.

The Capitol building covers sixteen acres and has
more than five hundred rooms connected by miles of
corridors. Bates and Jackson carried their heavy load
unnoticed into the west basement, an area with in-
numerable nooks, crannies, and crawl spaces suitable
for hiding a large container. After several minutes, they
halted for a cigarette in a corridor housing workshops,
boiler rooms, and other service areas for the giant
Capitol building. One floor above them, toward the
center of the building, were the offices of the Architect
of the Capitol. A stairway wound from there to the top
of the massive Capitol dome, totally enclosed and 365
steps long. After tamping out their cigarettes and nodding amicably to passersby, Bates and Jackson reshoul-
dered their 150-pound baby and set out on their journey
to the top of the dome.

They hauled the roll of wire to the nearest elevator.
There was no sense in starting this weight-lifting task
any earlier than they had to. After a short ride to the

next higher level, they emerged from the elevator, nodded pleasantly to a Capitol policeman sitting at a nearby desk, and turned into a passageway leading to the entrance of the dome staircase. Casually skirting the eye of a closed-circuit television camera by swinging into a suite of rooms and exiting from another door beyond the camera, they reached the entrance. Jackson skillfully unlocked the door. They started their climb, hidden in the interior of the dome's structure, and were breathing hard by the twentieth step. They rested briefly each twenty steps or so thereafter. Months of conditioning paid off, however, and the men were remarkably fresh after the thirty-minute climb.

The Capitol dome is a massive skeleton of iron ribbing supporting the ornamental inner and outer faces. The iron alone weighs nine million pounds. Viewing the dome from bottom to top, a visitor sees a circular row of pillars topped by an observation deck, a row of high windows above that, and yet another observation deck. More windows ascend to a high closed dome, another deck, and finally to a row of pedestals supporting a massive statue two hundred feet from the ground.

From the inside, standing on the beautiful tile floors of the Capitol's second-floor rotunda, a visitor looks up to inner balconies that correspond to the outer ones. At the top of the dome is a false ceiling about 180 feet above the rotunda, displaying an impressive fresco that cramps the neck muscles of seven or eight million Capitol visitors a year.

The staircase petered out at the summit of the dome. Bates and Jackson emerged into the columned cylinder that supported the dome's statue, still twenty feet above them. Jackson opened a hidden panel in the roll of wire and produced some handtools and a collapsible hoist with a pulley and thin nylon rope. He quickly shimmied up one of the dome struts and began attach-

273

ing the hoist to an arched cross-member of the dome. Directly above him was the base of the statue. Within ten minutes, he and Bates were ready to heave the roll of wire through an aperture in the ceiling, into a cramped workspace below the statue.

Capitol workmen seldom, if ever, entered this tiny area, since its original purpose involved raising and attaching the statue to the dome. These days, exterior maintenance of the dome and the lightning rods around the statue was a matter of erecting scaffolding and lifts from the outside observation decks. The "Statue of Freedom," a lovely lady of the nineteenth century, wearing sword, shield, and eagle feathers, was cast in bronze and required no cleaning, so visits to the top of the dome were extremely rare.

Jackson positioned the false roll of wire containing an atomic bomb directly beneath the Statue of Freedom, and flipped the switches that armed the device. He extended a tiny, unobtrusive wire from the underside of the roll to the outer edge of the workspace, and attached to it a small but powerful radio receiver, a device that at any moment could receive a signal to change the course of world history. This final link would allow anyone who knew a certain series of numbers to set the bomb off from anywhere in the country.

The idea was simplicity itself. The bomb could be set off with a touch-tone telephone. No satellites, no lasers. Just a few new gadgets. The proper number would ring a phone in an obscure room of a Senate office. Nobody would hear it, however, because the phone was not on the Capitol switchboard. It was a direct line paid for out of a separate office account allotted to Senator Harry Hammer. Connected to it was a common automatic answering device, a radio-activated switch, and a small transmitter. There was no bell. Anyone in a position to check the phone would simply conclude that it was a telephonic link to a computer—nothing unusual on Capitol Hill.

A recorded message would inform an accidental caller that he had reached the law offices of Scott and Rovig, but that Messrs. Scott and Rovig were not in. The caller would be invited to leave a recorded message of up to twenty seconds at the sound of the beep. Since the firm of Scott and Rovig did not exist, the caller would probably hang up, but even if he left a message, nothing would happen.

If, however, a caller tapped out a short code word beginning with the letter Z, a circuit would close and a message would speed through the transmitter in a direct beam to the top of the Capitol dome. An atomic bomb would explode.

Neither man in the dome knew the code that could at any moment turn them into bits and flecks of atoms. Neither had reason to know it. Their part of the mission was, for all intents and purposes, complete. A few things, however, remained to be done. They lowered themselves to the spiral staircase and began their descent. They were prepared, as they had been all along, to be challenged, but no one gave them a second glance as they retraced their steps through the public areas of the Capitol. They walked casually among scores of workmen, tourists, and legislative employees. Unlike most of those on Capitol Hill, however, Jackson and Bates had already put in a hard day's work. So they stopped at a Senate carry-out for some traditional congressional bean soup.

Gilliam opened his eyes to sunlight diffused by closed bedroom curtains. He lay on his side, wrapped tightly around Liz, knees behind knees. He smiled at this minor miracle. Something good had happened in his life. For the first time in weeks, he'd awakened free from the lingering fears of dreams—a minor miracle in itself. No images of army colonels, derelicts, or lobbyists armed with knives, chasing him around Georgetown.

275

No Murdock, half clad, clutching handfuls of eerie green powder, waiting to blow it into his face.

Liz stretched, rolled over, and hugged him hard. After a lingering good-morning kiss that tasted like warmed-over Chinese food, she drew back the blankets and climbed out of bed.

Gilliam let himself be led to the shower, reluctantly conceding that yesterday's world had not gone away. Liz pretended not to hear as she readied the water. They washed each other slowly, recapturing the delicious mood of the past night. For a few moments, reality went down the drain with the soapy water. They emerged from the shower smiling, then laughing, then snapping each other with wet towels. Liz retreated to the bedroom in mock panic from the "Mad Gooser" who was hot on her naked heels. She fought him off long enough to pull on her panties, but then paused. Gilliam stood in a ludicrously obscene pose, ogling her breasts. "I pity that poor guy in the house," he said. "It's a wonder that he didn't have a cardiac arrest."

Liz cracked up, but a sudden thought cut her laughter short. Her eyes opened wide as she reached for her jeans. Gilliam watched her rummage through pockets and nearly gasped when she produced a thick roll of money—*lots* of money.

"Kelly," she said in a low, tentative voice. "There's something I forgot to tell you. I'm a felon. A rich felon. I found this in the guy's closet, and I didn't know what to do, so I took it. Do you s'pose it was stolen?"

Gilliam exhaled explosively. "It is now. Do you realize that you've committed grand larceny?"

"I'm trying not to think about it."

"Well, think about it. And start hoping that guy is really evil in the eyes of the law or you can forget about ever being admitted to the D.C. bar."

"This doesn't change our plans, does it?" she asked.

Gilliam thought for a moment and put his arms

around her bare waist. "No," he said, "it doesn't. But I suggest that you hand that bankroll over to the FBI when we see them."

Liz nodded eagerly.

They slapped together a quick breakfast, stopped for one last long kiss at the front door, and headed out to the parking lot. As they approached Liz's Datsun, Gilliam steered her toward his old Volvo.

"Let's take mine if it starts," said Gilliam. After the customary chokes and wheezes, the Volvo started, and Gilliam headed toward Route 50 and the senator's lakeside home. As they drove west out of the city, it dawned on Gilliam that even though he'd worked for Hammer a considerable time, he'd never visited the senator's home. He had to ask directions from Liz.

On the Virginia side of the Potomac, amid shopping centers and high-rises, he asked, "Are you sure there's a Lake Barcroft out here?"

"You think I don't know where I used to live? Of course there's a Lake Barcroft out here. It used to be Alexandria's water reservoir. But the city outgrew it and some developers converted the shore into a ritzy little community. Take a left at the next light and you'll be able to see it in a few minutes."

Gilliam followed her orders and was surprised when the commercial strip gave way to quiet woods, bucolic estates, and placid lakeshore. Within minutes they came to a parking lot with a big "KEEP OUT" sign, fronting a beach with brilliant white sand. Liz pointed and said, "Pull in. I want to get my head together before we go any further." Gilliam parked the car and got out. Liz followed him toward the water.

He could see why people would want to live here. There were ducks, gulls, and beautiful green water. The traffic sounds of Route 7, a busy highway less than a mile away, were a muted whisper in the background, less noticeable than the wind in the trees. An occasional glint of sun reflected off windows around the lake, but most of the houses were hidden by a thick growth of trees.

Gilliam knelt and ran his fingers through the sand. The fear of the preceding days had returned in full force. He felt it weighing down on him and saw it in Liz's eyes. He made one more stab at retrieving their light mood of the night before.

"How in the hell did this beach get here?" he asked. "This is an ocean-type beach where there ain't no ocean."

"Oh," Liz replied innocently, "the Civic Association brought in two marble museums and rubbed them together." Her heart wasn't in it. Gilliam listened without hearing her short explanation about annual truckloads of sand brought in from somewhere. "If you look directly across the lake," said Liz, "you can see Dad's place. It's the one where they cut down the trees to make room for the beach."

"You mean that place that looks like the Kennedy Center?" he asked.

"Well," replied Liz, "maybe the architect did get a little carried away."

They stared across the water at the Hammer house, allowing reality to seep back in. For the first time since they left Lizzie's apartment, neither could think of something to say. Finally, she turned away from the water and said the inevitable.

"I guess we have to decide what we're going to do when we get there."

Gilliam nodded. "What do you think we should do?"

"I think we should tell Dad everything, Kelly. We've got to let him know about your being followed, about what you found out in Dallas and L.A., the things that I found in that house, Murdock . . . everything. It won't be easy to break him free of her, I'm afraid."

"You're right," he replied. "I came to the same conclusion a while ago. But it still worries the hell out of me. If he's really completely dependent on that woman, for whatever reason, he might just tell her everything we've told him the minute he sees her. I suppose we'll have to watch his reactions to see if he's with us."

"And if he's not?" asked Liz. "How can we tell if he's with us?"

"He'd come to the same conclusions we have. He'd suggest going to the cops."

"What if he takes Jean's side? That could happen, I suppose."

"Then you watch him like a hawk—sit on him, if necessary—while I pay a call to the FBI. The main thing is to keep him away from Murdock. There's no telling what kind of plague she could call down if she finds out what we're up to. Those guns you found prove that we're dealing with dangerous folks."

"But what if Murdock's there, too?" asked Liz.

"That's a chance we'll have to take. What would you do?"

"I think we'd just have to tell her that we came out for a quick swim, and then hang around for a while to see if she leaves without Dad. From what you and Burt tell me, she spends more time at work than he does, so the odds are she might leave us alone with him."

"Okay," said Gilliam. "I don't really like leaving it to chance, but I can't think of anything to do either, so let's give it a try. Oh yeah, one thing. Don't try to bait the woman for information. She's better at these games than we are, and I wouldn't bet on who would learn what from whom. It's more important that we keep what we know to ourselves. Deal?"

"Deal."

They walked back to the car and drove around the inlet to the Senator's house, arriving too soon to suit Gilliam. The house was oriented toward the lake, with floor-to-ceiling glass in every room on both levels. The single car in the driveway looked like Murdock's, much to Liz's chagrin. They proceeded up the steps, and Liz rang the front doorbell. She whispered to Gilliam, "Dad changed the locks a few months ago, and I was too embarrassed to ask him for a key. He probably changed them because I had one."

After a second ring, the door opened. Jean Murdock looked at and through them.

"Yes?" she said in a controlled voice with a slight edge to it.

Liz searched desperately for an opening line. Though it was perfectly reasonable for her to show up at her father's house, a simple phrase like "I want to see my father" seemed to have a second and third meaning that issued a challenge. Liz felt herself turning red and knew that Gilliam was not about to open his mouth. Murdock didn't blink.

Liz grabbed Gilliam's hand and blurted, "Kelly and I are here to tell my dad something important, Jean." She turned toward him, forcing a huge, adoring smile, and it was his turn to turn red.

"That's wonderful news," said Murdock in a tone decidedly unwonderful. "I'm sure your father will be thrilled when he hears it. Unfortunately, he's not here now, so it'll have to wait."

This was the one possibility they'd not considered. What was Murdock doing there alone, and where was the senator? More to the point, what should they do next?

"Where did he go?" asked Gilliam matter-of-factly.

"He went off to work early this morning," said Murdock. "You could probably catch him at the office if you left right now."

Liz detected a sense of urgency in Murdock's voice. The woman clearly wanted them out of there, and this reinforced Liz's determination to stay. "Well, I guess the news can hold a few more hours," Liz replied. "Kelly and I thought we might stick around for a quick swim as long as we're here at the lake."

Murdock appeared unruffled, but Liz couldn't resist one more dig. "You don't mind, do you?"

Ignoring the ironic turn in Liz's voice, Murdock replied cordially, "Of course not. I was just about to leave for the office myself, so make yourself at home. And," she added as an afterthought, "make sure the front door is locked when you leave." With that, she walked past them out the front door. A moment later she was driving away.

Liz and Gilliam looked at each other dumbly. "She didn't seem too interested in what I've been doing lately, did she?" observed Liz in a puzzled voice.

"And she sure as hell wanted to get out of here as fast as possible. Wasn't at all worried that we'd stay. Maybe we should get back to Washington and talk to your father."

"No," said Liz. "Let's stay here a while so she doesn't get suspicious. Besides, I'd like to look around the house."

"Haven't you had enough looking around houses lately?" asked Gilliam dryly. Liz ignored him, eager to get inside.

They walked through the house, checking each room carefully, but finding nothing out of the ordinary. As Gilliam walked into the main bedroom, he glanced through the window and whistled in surprise.

"That's the biggest fucking dog I've seen in my life," he said, nodding into the back yard. "He's got a mouth like a steamshovel. Did you grow up with that monster and romp around the garden with him?"

"No, I've never seen him before," Liz replied, as surprised as Gilliam. "He looks like a cross between a mastiff, a wolf, and a St. Bernard."

"Perfect dog for Murdock—it's probably hers."

The dog seemed docile enough, so they turned to survey the rest of the room.

"The bed, Kelly!" shouted Liz. "Dad didn't sleep here last night!"

"How do you know that?" Gilliam asked, seeing that one side of the bed had been slept in. "Maybe Murdock didn't stay last night. She might have gotten here this morning."

"No way," Liz said. "I know that my father didn't sleep in this bed. Mom used to call him the world's biggest blanket thief. He'd roll all over the bed, pushing her around in his sleep and have the blankets all wadded up by morning. Jean lied to us, Kelly. She must've done something to Dad!"

"Hey, calm down. He could have slept in another room."

Liz grew distraught. "Look, I know my father. He's an incurable creature of habit. He's slept in that bed since he and my mother were married. I know it's not much to go on, but when I saw this bed, I knew somehow that something has gone terribly wrong with Dad. I can't explain it, Kelly, but I know it. We've got to go to the police now!"

Gilliam grabbed her shoulders firmly. "Lizzie, think for a minute. What's going to happen if we run to the cops, shouting 'Kidnap!' and your dad picks up the phone and answers when they call? If something's happened, it's happened. Let's check to see if he's at work and try to talk to him there. It's nearly afternoon now. We should be able to find him if he's at the Capitol. I think we've got to wait until dinnertime before we conclude that he's missing. I think we should talk to Burt and let him in on all of this. Maybe he can keep us from making a really big mistake."

"Okay," whispered Liz. "But if we can't find Dad by tonight, we go to the FBI. Deal?"

"Deal."

They kissed once and then again in the cool shadows of the quiet house. Arm in arm they went out the front door, carefully locking it as Murdock had instructed them. They climbed into the old Volvo and headed toward Washington. A plain beige Chevrolet pulled out of a parking spot around the corner and followed them.

Kaznik waded through piles of clinical summaries flown in from California, sifting through broken-down lives and bizarre incidents for those few mental patients who might have had close connections with John Bates. Among the two dozen most promising records, only three stuck out with little need for leaps of intuition. One, an explosives nut and arsonist, was still tucked safely away in the hospital. The other two instantly struck Kaznik as sure-money bets.

Yoshi Nakamura's folder looked like a resumé prepared for an interview with a terrorist company. After clearing away the long clinical notes on "schizophrenia" and "depression," Kaznik focused on Nakamura's background in nuclear physics, her obsession with Japanese religion and tradition, and the repeated references to *"zensho."* Most incriminating was the incident that triggered her admission to the hospital: *She granted her mother's death wish.* Kaznik grimaced with anticipation. All that was missing from Nakamura's potential for mass violence were the focus and drive provided by either a strong, directed person or by a group with a single-minded purpose.

Kaznik was alarmed by references in Nakamura's file to correspondence with Senator Hammer's office. At first, he concluded that this forged a strong link between Gilliam and the hijackers, but references to Nakamura's letters ended well before Gilliam joined the Energy

283

Committee staff. Moreover, Nakamura had written to the President and several other Congressional offices on the same matters. In a strange way, the letterwriting seemed to indicate a certain harmlessness, perhaps even a concern for public welfare. Kaznik nonetheless thought that Nakamura was a likely suspect.

The other likely hijacker was one Duncan Rossiter. As Kaznik scanned Rossiter's history (from the ultimate in spoiled brats, to hardened convict, to fully repentent looney), he built a mental picture of Nakamura's "other half." He could easily see Rossiter and Nakamura building a bomb and intending to use it. All they needed was a couple of extra hands, which Kaznik was willing to bet were attached to Bates's fingerprints, and they were off and running.

Every other page of Rossiter's early record contained references to his lack of remorse and violent instability. It was not the least unreasonable that someone with his material resources and intelligence could have disciplined himself, finally, to play the doctors' game well enough to get out, clear his money, and go underground. References in his file to correspondence with a Leon Jackson led Kaznik to an immediate guess that Jackson had a weapons background.

He sent for Jackson's prison file, adding that he wanted Jackson questioned if still available. Knowing instinctively that Jackson and the others had surely vanished, Kaznik ordered detailed descriptions circulated for an East Coast search. He had every backup agent pulled and put into the field to coordinate a massive search, but he had the feeling that none of the three would turn up without some other break in the case.

A few hours later, Quillico brought in a report from Maine that the bomb lab might have been found. When a Deputy Sheriff Steadman failed to come home on his day off, his wife was at first unworried, but when his friends came back from their fishing trip without him, the lie marked his first weird behavior in decades of married life. She called the sheriff, who was similarly alarmed by Steadman's absence. He put out the immediate word that Steadman was missing and possibly in serious trouble.

Though the limited search for Steadman produced nothing, alarming news travels fast in small communities. Soon the realtor who put Steadman onto the "Benson rental" came forward and described the deputy's melodramatic interest in the property. Searchers discovered the car and the lab about the same time; bloodhounds found Steadman two hours later. The local sheriff had called the feds immediately.

Once Kaznik got a general idea of what was in the lab, he had Quillico call the agents in Maine for a detailed inventory. As Quillico described the items one by one, Kaznik relayed them by phone to Ted Rippling. Rippling, at first elated by the find, became more and more agitated as the list droned on. He broke in before Kaznik got halfway through.

"Jesus Christ, Joel, they've got an induction furnace and all the right chemicals to make metallic plutonium. From the liquids they left behind, it's a good bet that they did it, too. Check on the exact amount of what's there, especially the plutonium tetrafluoride residues. They've probably converted the whole mess into bombs."

Kaznik slammed the phone down on Rippling, intending to issue an immediate pickup order on Kelly Gilliam, his only known link to the terrorists. Then he remembered that he still had no good idea of how long they had been away from the lab, much less where they'd gone. Picking up Gilliam without knowing more could trigger a bomb or two. He told Quillico to find out, any way possible, *how* the terrorists had departed the rustic little cabin and what they looked like.

Quillico had already ordered more men into the area to do just that, but noting Kaznik's unusual agitation, he ordered in more.

Rossiter idled the *Golden Girl*'s engines and dropped anchor southwest of Kent's Point in the Chesapeake Bay. As Nakamura helped him ready the dull gray life raft, she wished that she were back in the wide expanses of the lower bay, where the miles of open water made it seem as if she were still on the ocean. No people, no animals, nobody to be hurt. But they had passed Tangier Island and its fisherfolk hours ago and since then they'd never been more than a few miles from shore.

A spot off Kent's Point was the farthest they could get from civilization and still be certain that the blast would be visible near Washington. Nakamura hoped that her calculations and Rossiter's knowledge of geography would be enough to ensure that all but a handful of people would be outside the bomb's killing radius.

Rossiter gave directions softly as they heaved the raft over the side. He then climbed into the raft to secure an anchor. Once convinced of the raft's soundness and stability, he motioned for Nakamura to hand down packages from the yacht so he could place them inside the raft under a fitted tarp. Nakamura lowered the last package gently on a sling supported by two pulleys. It was very heavy and demanded easy handling.

After carefully arranging the equipment in the raft according to Nakamura's tersely worded specifications, Rossiter traded places with her and watched as she made adjustments and connections. Finally satisfied, she secured the waterproof cover around the edges of the raft, saving the last few fastenings until she'd ascended a few steps on the *Golden Girl*'s transom ladder. Rossiter helped her aboard. They restarted the engines and cast off, leaving behind a gray lump that soon merged with the blue-gray swells around it.

A half mile due west by sightings and instruments, Rossiter briefly halted the *Golden Girl* to drop an anchored crab-pot marker. Its hollowed interior held a transmitter that would broadcast a brief signal every fifteen minutes. He had no desire to ever return to the spot, but he wanted to make sure he could do so if necessary.

Then Rossiter opened the throttle all the way and headed northwest for the inlet where Bates had left a car earlier in the week. Nakamura meditated quietly with her legs folded under her and arms crossed on her chest. This was her way of telling Rossiter that she had no desire to talk. Intent at the helm and lost in his own thoughts, Rossiter hardly noticed.

Liz was waiting when Strong and Gilliam returned to their office from the Energy Committee's executive session. As Strong headed to the desk to pour himself a tall drink even by his standards, Gilliam whispered to Liz, "Your dad never showed. Senator Browning had to chair the meeting."

"Did you get a chance to talk to Burt?" she whispered back.

"No, and I'm not even sure he knows we're, uh, *together.*"

"Was Murdock there?"

"Of course she was."

As Strong crossed the room, Liz self-consciously removed her arm from Gilliam's waist.

Strong raised his glass in salute as he surveyed the couple. "Is there finally something good to drink to around here?" he asked.

"Yes and no," replied Gilliam, glancing at Liz.

"Actually, it's Jean who brought us together. It's the *way* she did it that we want to talk to you about."

Strong replied with his first smile of the day. "After that meeting, I wanted to wrap my knobby old hands around that expensive scarf on her throat. I hope you're not trying to tell me she's wonderful?"

"No," said Liz, "we're trying to tell you that she might be involved with the Timber Rivers theft, and we want your advice about going to the police."

Strong sat down very carefully. After a pull on his drink and a long silence, he said, "Murdock's a bitch. She watched Harry fall apart after he blew his presidential bid and then she chewed up some of the pieces. But hijacking? *Murder?* If we blow the whistle on her and you're wrong, it's Harry who's finished, not her. What have you got?"

Gilliam explained how he and Liz met while trying to burglarize Murdock's office, how they both suspected a connection with Wesley Rice and the American Nuclear Corporation. He revealed all their separate suspicions of Murdock, of blackmail, lies and connections with the Timber Rivers theft. He told how it all started and where it had gone—to buggings, tailings, mad chases through Georgetown and Dallas, and a trip to a mental hospital.

Then Lizzie took over. "We're not exactly the world's best detectives, Burt, but I did follow Jean to a couple of meetings she had with a guy. I trailed him home the second time and found an incredible pile of weird military weapons under his bed."

Strong was incredulous. After thinking for a minute, he said, "If you're right about Murdock, you could have been killed. If you're wrong, you're going to wish you were. How did you get so deeply into this without going to the cops long ago?"

"For the same reason we're asking you for advice before blowing it open," Gilliam replied. "We don't really believe what's happening and aren't sure we want to believe it. And we can't sort out who is going to be hurt, who to go to, or how to do it."

"Kelly, tell me more about your being followed," said Strong. "Give me the details."

"Okay, you remember that cab ride we took back from the NRC two weeks ago and the lobbyist who bummed a ride with us?"

"Yeah, I guess so."

"He was the same guy who wore an army brass uniform and sat at the bar the next day when we had lunch at the Monocle. In between, he was a bum on the bus stop across from my apartment. My car's followed all the time and I found a bug behind my kitchen light switch."

"Small wonder about that in your place," Strong replied. "But I prefer to believe your whole story rather than admit to myself that my favorite woman and my best employee have both flipped out."

"Burt," Liz said, "we wanted to lay the whole thing out for Dad, but we haven't been able to find him. I'm afraid that Murdock may have already done something to him. He wasn't home when we went out there earlier today, and I'm sure he hasn't slept there for a while. I think we have to do something now, and we just want you with us."

"You know," said Strong wearily, "from the moment Murdock got him by the balls after his White House try fizzled, I was worried about what she was doing to him. He had some pretty heavy bouts of depression after that, and I don't think I've ever seen him in such bad shape. Not even when he was outdrinking me. But I was afraid that it was my own mind telling a jealous old man that nothing short of evil incarnate could take away his oldest and best friend. Maybe I should have fought back instead of sulking."

Strong seemed lost in memories, and Liz was just

about to speak when he suddenly sat up straight and started talking rapidly. "You're right, dammit, I'm afraid you're right. Kelly, wasn't Murdock much too interested in finding out what the investigators knew about the hijackers' whereabouts? About any leads that they had? Hell, I was interested, too. That's what we were there for. But I was interested in their conclusion and predictions, not about the details of their search and where they planned to look next. We've got to nail her now. Let's go."

"Okay," said Kelly, "but don't you think I should go to the FBI alone? I'm the one who's been followed. And if my story turns out to be a total bust, maybe I can just get myself quietly fired and keep everyone else out of it. What do you think?"

"On the outside chance that we've all read this thing totally wrong, it can't hurt for you to go alone," Strong said. "Besides, you know the whole story and can tell it faster than three of us could. FBI Liaison is across the street. Why don't you get over there and we'll wait here in case you need us?"

Kelly gave them a weak smile and headed for the door.

The pieces came together suddenly for Kaznik. His agents in Maine had received from Nattie Rosenheim a complete description of "Mr. Godwin," his two friends, and the *Golden Girl*. Kaznik checked out the boat's registration, but he knew that there was no "Mr. Godwin," just as he knew that there was no "Benson" attached to the cottage rental. He wasted no time on these. Rossiter clearly was traveling somewhere with Jackson and Nakamura. The trio had at least one atom bomb.

Kaznik ordered the Coast Guard to mobilize an exhaustive search of the entire Atlantic coast and to alert all commercial facilities and coastal police departments.

All such orders went out in code because Kaznik feared that Rossiter might be monitoring them. Rossiter, after all, had spared no expense thus far, and it was conceivable that he could be listening in on a sophisticated radio.

As Kaznik debated his next move, Quillico rushed into the room, looking as worried as Kaznik himself felt.

"Good news?" asked Kaznik dryly.

"Joel, every reporter in Maine is crawling around Chamberlain and Damariscotta. A few are even trying to talk their way through our cordon around the bomb lab."

"Real good news, Curt. How the hell did it get out so fast? I thought we had a lid on it."

Quillico answered, obviously distressed. "One of the local cops—I think it was a dispatcher—leaked the story to a friend before we could clamp down. I think—"

Kaznik cut in. "How much do they know?"

"I think the whole story is out, Joel," Quillico replied, unable to look Kaznik in the eye. "One of my own press contacts expects a TV network news story sometime soon, probably tonight. The story will link Steadman's murder directly to the discovery of a nuclear bomb factory."

Kaznik cringed, then replied sharply, "He's wrong, Curt."

"Wrong?"

"Dead wrong! There's *no way* that network news is going to broadcast the status of our investigation to the whole goddamn world. Those maniacs on the boat would hear it, and God only knows what they might do. And we have no way to stop them because we don't even know where they are. Get moving and shut that story down. I don't care who you have to threaten or what threats you have to carry out, but shut it down."

As Quillico reached for the telephone, Kaznik added,

"And after you get that lid squarely back in place, start shutting down the local reporters. Curt, do anything necessary, and I mean *anything*. I'll take the shit for it."

While Quillico frantically dialed, two other telephones rang simultaneously. One, taken by Billingsly, was news from Fort Leavenworth that Leon Jackson had extensive experience not only in weapons, but also in demolitions. The other call was a report from federal agents in California. The Widener Mental Health Center staff had revealed that Kelly Gilliam had recently been there seeking information on Yoshi Nakamura, the nuclear physicist, possibly to keep it out of federal hands.

Kaznik decided that now was the time to move. He needed to know immediately the destination of the *Golden Girl*. He needed to know how many people were aboard and what they planned to do upon reaching their destination. Kelly Gilliam was Kaznik's only hope, the only human being in the whole insane world who might be able to supply answers or at least steer him in the right direction. Kaznik grabbed Billingsly and headed out the door, determined to lay his hands on Gilliam immediately.

ZENSHO!

Nakamura disentangled her arms and legs from the lotus position and stretched as Rossiter eased the boat through tangles of water weeds to a decaying but still serviceable slip. He tied up directly to an end post, ignoring an old dinghy on the other side of the boat that would have allowed enough slack line to avoid being stranded by receding tide. He had owned the expensive boat for a long time and she'd served him well. But he would never again board her.

He headed up the overgrown, pebbled road from the dock without looking back. He walked toward an old farmhouse used only as a weekend base by local duck hunters. He'd put a stop to such use when he rented the property.

Bates had left him an innocuous-looking blue Chevy with a clean registration that matched the name on his new driver's license. He studied the papers briefly, knowing that he could be "John Barker" as easily as "Benson" or any of the others. The keys were under the back mat, just as Bates had said they would be. There were a couple of *Playboys* on the front seat, which Rossiter had not ordered.

Nakamura reached the car as he climbed in behind the wheel. She ignored his impatient gestures to the passenger door and stood next to his window, staring

back at the dock. Restraining his impatience to get rolling, he quietly asked, "Yoshi, is everything okay?"

Her answer was immediate and totally unexpected.
"Duncan, I'm not sure the timer's hooked up right."

Rossiter blanched. "You've got to be kidding! You
checked everything over twice from beginning to end.
I watched you from the boat."

"I know that," she replied softly, "but I've been
going over and over the steps in my mind and I'm not
sure I hooked both wires to the contacts."

Rossiter was incredulous. "You just don't make mistakes like that, Yoshi. You never have before and you
were perfectly careful back there on the raft."

"I think I did it right, Dunk. I'm almost positive it's
wired properly. Maybe I'm just now getting nervous.
You're right, everything checked out while I was actually doing it."

"Good," said Rossiter harshly. "Get in."

Nakamura knew how explosive Rossiter could be
when crossed. She took a slow breath, held it in for a
moment, and went on. "We've put a lot into this,
Dunk. I'm almost positive that it's hooked up right.
But shouldn't I go back and make sure?"

"We can't do that, Yoshi. It's starting to get dark
and there's no guarantee that we can find the raft once
we reach the marker. And if we do, there's no guarantee
that we can get back to the car in time to get everything
done in Washington. Think. Think hard, Yoshi. Are
the wires right?"

Nakamura ignored the question. She had already answered it as well as she intended to. "You're right," she
said. "I don't think you should go back. You're needed
in Washington now. It's my problem; I'll fix it myself."

Surprised as he was by the response, he was more
taken aback by her tone. It was pleading, almost child-
like.

"Yoshi," he answered, "you can't run the boat and
the navigation equipment without help."

Nakamura's answer came back almost too quickly. "I did it for hours while you were asleep. I can do it now if I go back before it gets much darker."

"You don't *want* me to go back with you, do you?" he asked.

"Dunk, you have to get on to Washington. Everything falls apart if you don't. You don't need me there, and I don't need you on the boat. Even if I can't find the raft tonight, I can anchor and fix things up tomorrow with plenty of time to get away."

Rossiter seemed to ignore her words and to respond to only the tone of voice. "Okay, Yoshi, I think we understand each other. We both know what we want. Just make sure that it goes off at the right time. Not before, not after."

Nakamura nodded gratefully and retraced the path to the boat. She started the engines and cast off. Rossiter stood for a moment next to the car, watching her ease the *Golden Girl* into the bay, plotting her direction and course on a mental map. She turned once from the helm and cast him a wave that seemed a bit too self-assured. Then she disappeared around the headland's edge.

The evening was thick and humid. Liz watched Gilliam from the window in the Capitol as he walked to the corner and waited for the light to change. He moved much faster than usual. She wondered whether his speedy pace reflected relief over "coming clean" with the authorities, or whether he needed the momentum to counteract his misgivings.

As the light turned yellow, two men passed under the window at a fast trot and caught Gilliam a few steps into the intersection. Liz stared in silent amazement as they flanked him, each seizing a forearm. They wheeled him around and said something to him. He offered no resistance as they marched him silently back along the street, directly under her perch.

"Burt, come over here fast," Liz yelled across the room to Strong, who was refilling his glass.

Strong rushed over and looked out, open-mouthed, as the two middle-aged men, one black and one white, led an ashen-faced but silent Gilliam up the street.

"My God, Kelly's being kidnapped!" Liz blurted. "We've got to do something."

Strong pointed to the phone across the room. "Call the Capitol Police," he said.

"Oh, come on," she protested. "By the time they figure out what we're talking about and get out there, Kelly will be in Russia."

"You're right, let's get moving," Strong said with sudden conviction, steadying himself on the edge of a desk. "We can get out there before they disappear. We'll yell for the cops when we're outside."

They bolted for the door, turned a corner in the corridor, and headed out the nearest exit. They nearly missed the Capitol policeman sitting behind a desk next to the entrance.

Strong stopped himself before passing through the revolving door and shot back, pointing, "We just saw a mugging on the street over there. Call up every squad car in the area!"

The startled cop reached for his phone as Strong rushed to catch up with Liz, who had already reached the corner. He narrowly avoided slamming into her as she stopped, staring down the next block. The two men pushed Kelly into a parked car and pulled out to make an illegal U-turn.

"My car's on the street today," Strong said, breaking into a run after the vanishing car. Liz snapped out of her leaden stance and followed him a few cars down to his old Plymouth. They jumped in and Strong executed the same lightning U-turn and gunned the motor. Thanking a God he usually didn't believe in that his car didn't stall, he ran a red light to keep from losing Gilliam and his captors.

Breathing heavily, and suddenly sober as a judge, he asked Liz without turning his head, "Now what, Boss?"

"Keep after them. Do you think we'll do better by following or do you think we should lean on the horn, drive crazy, and try to attract some cops?" she asked back.

"Don't know," he answered. "Let's keep after them until they give us a chance to hail a police car. I'm not sure what they're driving. It's sort of gray and I can't come close to making out the plates."

They followed the sedan through town, running a few lights in the process. The car swung west on Constitution. The only cops in sight were either on foot or on horseback. "Great," muttered Liz as they turned onto the access ramp for the bridge to Virginia. The setting sun temporarily slowed them, but they didn't lose sight of the other car. Soon after crossing at a fast, but not unusual speed, the gray sedan left the main road and pulled up to one of the tall, nondescript apartment houses on a hill just off Route 50.

Strong shrugged helplessly as the three men got out of the car and walked into the building, again in lockstep, shoulder to shoulder. Liz pointed out a place next to a hydrant near the building and Strong took it. By the time they got a good look into the lobby through the glass doors, the three men were gone. Liz ran into the building in time to see the pointer on one of the elevators stop at eleven. Another elevator sat empty, its doors open wide. After Strong caught up, Liz grabbed his arm, pulled him into the open elevator, and punched eleven.

The ride was long and silent. Liz didn't let go of Strong's arm until the doors slid open. They stepped out onto drab, thread-bare carpeting. Strong grimaced. All around, stretching in both directions down long corridors, were featureless doors.

Summoning up courage to face both danger and futility, Liz whispered, "You go that way and I'll take the other side around. Listen a couple seconds at each door. If we don't cross in back, I'll meet you here in five minutes."

"Okay," said Strong. "But if you're not here in five minutes, I'm leaving to call the cops. You do the same. Promise?"

"Okay," Liz replied. She moved off to the left, pausing briefly before each door. The apartments seemed well soundproofed, much to Liz's chagrin. Muffled voices and music filtered through several doors, but she heard nothing promising. Strong met her at the exact midpoint in the rear corridor. He had a plan.

"You get down to another floor, Lizzie, and convince someone to let you in. Call the FBI, not the cops. Let them know who you are, get them moving, and stay down there."

"Close, but not perfect," she replied. "You're going, not me. You can convince them faster than I can and nobody is going to notice a stray girl in the hall. And come back up instead of manning the phone. We're going to need two people if they decide to take off while we're waiting."

Strong didn't move, thinking it over.

"Look, Burt," Liz said with a try at a smile, "your hearing's been shot for years. Let me do the wall-leaning."

Strong realized that she was right on each point. He gave her a light squeeze on the arm and strode back to the elevator. Before turning the corner, he held up nine fingers. Liz nodded her understanding and moved closer to the nearest door. The hall was suddenly quiet and empty.

Nakamura calmed down as soon as the *Golden Girl* cleared the final outcroppings of the bay's western shore. The last rays of sun made the entire expanse of water glow. The boat's steady rumble was soporific as she steered through the gentle swells.

She ignored all instruments but the compass and radio receiver that gave her direct readouts of the crab buoy's direction. Three minor course corrections brought her to the marker shortly after sunset. By this time, the whole world was a wash of grays. Low clouds on the horizon blended with the muted waves to create a blurred expanse of flowing lava, softly glowing on the surface, opaquely gray below. Nakamura scanned the bay, knowing that the raft would be difficult to pick out, camouflaged as it was in this obsidian world.

She set out eastward, estimating the half mile and then beginning a slow zig-zag search pattern. Twenty minutes into her search, Nakamura spotted the raft a few yards away. She quieted the engines, dropped anchor, and settled down in the cabin for the night, undressing and pulling a blanket over herself. Knowing what she must do but having no desire to enter the raft before dawn, she fell to sleep uneasily, resting on the undulating flow of water.

Later—she had no idea how much later—she awoke to a bright light playing across the boat. Shadows jumped starkly about the cabin. She sat up, disoriented but alert. Her first thought was the lighthouse on nearby Kent's Point, but the idea evaporated with the sound of a large boat's engines drawing close. She groped for *Golden Girl*'s starter, knowing that she had only a few moments to draw the boat away from the raft.

The big boat drew much too close, and she soon realized that she could not get away from the raft before it closed in. She looked up. It was big—*huge*—probably a Coast Guard cutter, and it was definitely interested in the *Golden Girl*. Fortunately, the raft was on the *Golden Girl*'s dark side. She waited for the light to fall astern for a brief moment, darted up to the deck, and dove over the side, hitting the water cleanly.

A few quick strokes brought her to the raft. She fought the fasteners on the covering and hauled herself in, shuddering with the cold. An electronically amplified voice boomed across the water, ordering all persons on board the smaller boat to show themselves on deck. She groped under the covering, cursing her inability to see what she was doing.

She located the timer, but not before the cutter had come about to cast a steady, blinding light across her face. She knelt, naked, with diamonds of water droplets pouring off her shoulders and breasts. The armed man on the cutter's deck saw her close her eyes and press two wires together.

Kelly looked around the plain efficiency apartment and waited for his captors to speak. The furniture looked rented, which it was, and the place had the smell of a recent cleaning by a janitorial service. There was no sign of recent use. The pictures on the wall were contemporary, meant to be soothing, like those in any Holiday Inn.

Kelly waited quietly on the couch. The white man pulled a chair close to him, identified himself as a federal security officer and warned that if he opened his mouth without permission, he would be knocked unconscious. Up to that point, Gilliam had displayed a composure that had surprised himself more than anyone.

"Mr. Gilliam," the man began in a calm, conversational tone, "in the next two minutes, you are going to tell me exactly where the *Golden Girl* is now, where it is heading, and what Duncan Rossiter plans to do with the bomb he has on board. You may start talking."

Gilliam was completely taken aback. How could his stalkers, finally out in the open, know everything about Rossiter and not know about Murdock's involvement? Suddenly fearful that he'd better start saying *something* as his questioner rose slightly out of his seat, Gilliam blurted out, "You mean the one who was in the California hospital with Nakamura?"

Now it was Kaznik's turn to be taken aback. Gilliam's answer was certainly on point, but hardly what he expected to hear. This guy was either very good or very bad. Gilliam took advantage of the pause and of the puzzlement on the man's face to risk a question.

"Look," he said, "if you really are some kind of federal security officers, why am I sitting here in an apartment building instead of your headquarters?"

"Son," Kaznik replied, "at the risk of sounding obvious, you're here to do some long-overdue answering, not questioning. And you're probably not going to like the reason anyway. Headquarters was both inconvenient to reach and embarrassing for the methods I will use to get answers out of you if you don't start making me very happy *now*."

Gilliam drew back into the corner of the couch like a sandcrab burrowing away from an approaching gull. He knew that he'd looked guilty as hell for a long time and that he would have to tell his whole story quickly and convincingly to avoid unspecified pain.

"I don't know about any golden girl," he said. "This whole thing started when I returned a phone call by mistake to a man named Wesley Rice. It was meant for—" Kelly suddenly stopped, realizing that he still had no real proof that his captors were from the CIA, FBI, or whatever. What if he gave them Murdock's name and they just killed him on the spot? He sat mute, paralyzed, afraid to continue or to push the man for identification.

Suddenly, he realized that Kaznik was leaning forward and staring intently, not at him, but at the window behind his couch. The color drained from the man's face, which now almost matched the pallor Gilliam felt.

"Nate," he said, using his companion's name for the first time, "I think something big just went off out there."

Billingsly looked confused. "What do you mean?"

Kaznik replied while pulling out some sort of communications device and fiddling with it impatiently, "I thought I just saw a big nuke go off over the horizon. If that's what it was, all we'd see first is a flash. Something like heat lightning. But this flash lasted a couple of seconds and it had some shape to it. If I'm right, we may see something else when the column of gas gets a few miles up. Maybe not. No noise for a while, depending on the range."

"Are you serious, Joel?" pressed Billingsly. "You really think you saw a nuclear flash?"

Kaznik finally got his communicator working. Gilliam sat amazed as the small, wafer-thin box spat out without any verbal prodding "Quillico at base, over."

"Curt, this is Joel," Kaznik said. "Get me an instant report on a possible atomic detonation somewhere between the Beltway and the ocean."

All three men sat, not moving, while the box went silent. No radio crackle, no background noise. Not even a hum to inform its holder that it was on. A minute later, the box spoke again, breaking a total silence in the room. "A nuclear bomb just went off in the Chesapeake Bay, Joel. What do you want me to do?" Kaznik closed his eyes and spoke automatically, almost as if he'd expected this situation to occur.

"Send a squad that way right now, and make certain that they've got radiation protection gear. Arm them to the teeth, and tell them to scope out everything thoroughly, by land, sea, and air. Tell the President I recommend that he get out now to Hardsite L. And send a helicopter from the Pentagon to Building 311 to bring me home right now. Out."

Kaznik turned to Billingsly, ignoring Gilliam completely. "Nate, we lost a round. Thank God the device probably went off on the boat by mistake, but we can't be sure of that. And we can't be sure that there's not another one somewhere else. That's why you're going to give Gilliam a full ampul of this stuff to make sure he's not conning us."

He tossed a small vinyl case to Billingsly and turned to Gilliam.

"Mr. Gilliam, I'm inclined to believe you, but I don't have time to consider your rights or your health in view of what just happened. So I'm not going to waste time."

With that, Kaznik stepped across to a cringing Gilliam and pressed a spot on his neck. Gilliam slumped unconscious.

"That should keep him out for the time you need to give him the shot, Nate. I can't wait around to hold him. Know how to do a vein shot?" he asked, suddenly worried.

"It's been a while, but I've done them," Billingsly replied. "I'll call his story in as soon as I can."

"Thanks," Kaznik said as he opened the door to the hall. "I know you don't like this either."

He stepped out and strode quickly for the elevator, passing a startled Burt Strong, who had just gotten off. Strong tried hard not to stare as he watched Kaznik get in. Once the doors closed on the grim-looking man, Strong turned his attention to the sound of an apartment door that had just closed behind Kaznik and nearly failed to notice that the indicator over the elevator pointed up to the top floor, not down to the lobby. This meant he might come right back.

Strong hurried down the corridor to find Liz. He saw her in the middle of the next hall, ear pressed solidly against a door, leaning on the side support and off balance. She heard him coming and straightened up guiltily, lurching for an instant before seeing that it was he. Before either could say a word, the muffled beating of an approaching helicopter drew near. Both listened for a few seconds without speaking as the *whup-whup* sound built up to a roar and moved off in the distance. Strong, who by now understood, just pointed upward and said, "The white one just left from the roof. Find anything?"

Liz shook her head mutely, too surprised to reply right away. She let out her long-held breath and said, "Not a thing unless you count the heavy screwing going on a couple of doors back. I only made it a third of the way around here while you were gone because it took me a couple of minutes to figure out that nobody was being tortured in there."

Both of them smiled weakly. Strong finally motioned back down the corridor and said, "I called the FBI and gave them a news capsule, but didn't wait to see how they reacted. Just told them to get their asses over here. And I think I know where they've got Kelly, but what can we do about it? Shouldn't we just wait by the elevator for the fuzz?"

"No way, Burt," Liz replied. "I want to know where they have him. And I want to do something about it if he's in real trouble. Point out where you think he is and listen for the elevator or people in the halls."

Strong shrugged helplessly and led Liz up the hallway, trying to softstep to match her catlike walk. He pointed out the first apartment and took up a watchful stance behind Liz as she leaned against a door, straining to pick up sound through the thick wood.

Inside the apartment directly across the hall, Gilliam came to, his eyes swimming and temples pounding. His legs were tied together with his own belt and one arm was somehow strapped to a chair arm with another belt. "Nate" stood over him, staring at a filled syringe in his hand. He had been unable to work up a vein properly in Gilliam's arm and had just about decided to question him without chemical help. But Gilliam didn't know that. He was mortally afraid of needles. As the man bent forward to lay the instrument down on a nearby coffee table, Gilliam screamed.

The sound shot through to the hall outside like the last wail of a wounded animal dragged down by wolves. Liz shot upright from her post across the hall, and before Strong could stop her, pounded on the apartment door. Billingsly, not suspecting that someone connected with Gilliam could be outside the door, surmised that either a passerby had heard a scream and was moved to intervene or that Kaznik had detailed someone from the chopper to help him.

He pulled his gun from its shoulder harness and warned Gilliam in a whisper not to move. Otherwise he would be shot instantly. Then Billingsly strode to the door and shouted, "Who's there?"

Liz, having no plan in mind, shouted back the literal truth. "I heard a scream from in there. Is anything the matter?"

"No," answered Billingsly. "It must have been the radio you heard."

Liz paused a moment, trying to think of a way to increase Gilliam's chances of survival without drastically reducing hers and Burt's. She drew a blank. "Let me in or I'll call the cops," Liz said as Strong looked on in dismay. Then she turned and whispered to Burt, "Run! Make some noise!"

Strong looked startled, but obediently broke into a run as Liz shooed him away.

Billingsly, realizing that he had to stop the woman belonging to the voice and spirit Gilliam away or face long delays explaining things to the Arlington police, opened the door and leaned out to shout. Liz stepped forward and kneed with all her strength into his groin.

He reeled back a step and Liz saw the gun. She stepped forward again, delivered another knee thrust to the staggering man, and kicked away the gun. As he slumped to the floor, she grabbed it before he could regain his footing. Billingsly, thinking that she must be a very foolhardy good Samaritan, stayed down as Gilliam looked on in amazement.

"Burt!" she yelled as Strong looked back down the empty corridor, agonizing over whether to go back or to get the police. "Get back here and give me a hand with Kelly."

Strong rushed in to see Gilliam taking off his arm lashing. He went over to help with the footband and showed Gilliam, who was still groggy, that it came from his own waist.

Liz kept the gun pointed at Billingsly, holding it with two hands, not knowing whether the safety was on or off or whether she would pull the trigger if Billingsly attacked. When nobody else spoke, Liz said, "Burt, get Kelly out of here." Then she took a step closer to the man on the floor and said, "I could knock you out now, but I don't want to risk getting near you. If you're somebody legit, you'll just call your boss and say you blew it. If you open the door after we're gone, I'll shoot. And I'm going to wait outside until they're safe."

Strong and Gilliam went into the hall and Liz backed out after them. She took off her shoes so that only two sets of footsteps would be heard from inside. They reached the elevator without incident. On the ride down, Kelly told them about the bomb detonation and the horror he'd seen in the faces of his captors. Liz and Strong listened silently and wide-eyed.

Strong had no desire to wait for the FBI. The news of the bomb strengthened his desire to get them all away. They drove off in his car, Liz still clutching Billingsly's gun. Seconds later, four FBI agents pulled up to the curb and got out of their car. Because they were at ground level, they could not see the top of a mushroom cloud that appeared low on the darkening eastern horizon. Eleven stories above them, however, Billingsly could see it as he attempted to open a comm-line to CIA headquarters while doubled over with abdominal pain.

Rossiter's car, after sitting through several days on the humid Chesapeake shore, would not start. Repeated twists of the ignition key yielded groans and sputters. Impatient to get moving for Washington, Rossiter managed to flood the carburetor, which took nearly an hour to drain. He sat and fumed in the darkness, inpatient to arrive in Washington, but helpless.

Finally, it started. He'd gone only a few miles on back country roads when he saw the flash. Even in his rearview mirror, the intensity was blinding. He stabbed for the brake pedal and jerked the car to the side of the road. By the time he jumped out to stare back toward the bay, the light had faded, but the vapor cloud stood out against the horizon. The cloud slowly dissipated as the airwave hit Rossiter like the backwash from a passing truck.

"Damn you, Yoshi, you couldn't wait," Rossiter spat out. "You got out there in one of those fucking trances and forgot all about the plan, about me, about years of work!"

He punctuated each phrase by slamming a fist on the hood of the car. Intent in his fury, Rossiter felt no pain from the blows that left dents in the metal surface. He missed completely the gentle ground shock that passed underfoot as the last transient reminder of the blast.

Finally, as an aftershock to his own personal explosion, Rossiter realized something that he had assumed all along, but never quite believed.

"It worked," he whispered. "It went off."

He stood silently, anger spent, staring at vague shapes and whirling vapors to the east. Nakamura was there in the sky, less than dust, transformed by her *zensho* into an ether more delicate than stellar clouds. Yoshi was so far beyond hate, beyond thanks, beyond forgiveness, that Rossiter's thoughts spun wildly from her, back to his plan, to the sudden sharp reality of the bomb.

He pulled back from the chaos in the east to the world of things, of cause and effect. A half-spoken thought materialized: "Something must have gone wrong. She tried to fix the timer and screwed up."

Rossiter climbed into the car and continued toward

Washington, convinced that the plan could be salvaged. If Jean knew that the bomb had gone off, she could immediately trigger the threat of another blast. It would be believable. What had been lost by failure to announce the first bomb *before* its detonation could be recovered in the dramatic announcement of a new threat. Rossiter had to get back fast to help.

He knew he was in trouble when he reached the first main road into Washington. Though there were only a few cars flashing by as he waited for a break in traffic, they all headed west. He quickly realized that this sparse traffic probably represented a sizable fraction of all the vehicles in that part of the bay's coast. Washington would be impassable; the traffic jams would set records when news of the bomb got around.

A right turn put Rossiter on an empty eastbound lane leading to a large nearby inlet where a seaplane club kept its aircraft. If he made it quickly, he reasoned, he could catch one of the pilots about to flee the fallout that at this moment might be drifting overhead.

Rossiter turned onto a private drive marked with the club's sign. As he drove between a cluster of cottages and docks, he spotted three planes on the water. The place seemed deserted and incongruously quiet except for the usual bayside hum of insects and water lapping against the dock. Rossiter took stock of the situation: He had three planes and no idea how to jumpstart any one of them, much less how to fly it once he'd started it; the planes' owners had apparently left the area along with the club's employees.

A gleam of light from one of the nearby cottages caught his eye. Pulling his pistol from his belt, Rossiter slipped out of the car, taking pains to prevent the door from slamming. Quickly and quietly he approached cottage number four, tried the door, and found it unlocked. Stepping inside, he saw the source of light—a small lamp on a bedstand. Next to it, on a cot, lay a middle-aged man, clad only in boxer shorts, face down with his arm dangling to the floor. Near the hand lay an empty pint of blended whiskey.

Rossiter approached the man, who was awake but didn't seem to understand what Rossiter was saying. Rossiter finally gave up and threw a glass of water on his face. The man put a hand over his eyes to block the light and rolled over on his side. Rossiter surveyed his find.

"Do you realize that you almost slept through an A-bomb blast?" he asked conversationally of the fleshy lump on the cot.

With that, Rossiter hauled the man to his feet and half carried him out the door to the dock. He pushed him abruptly into the water and watched the display of choking and flailing for signs of physical coordination. The man, after survival instincts did their work, managed to paddle to the dock and extend a hand to Rossiter, who pulled him out.

Before he could ask questions, Rossiter spoke. "Put on some clothes, pick up your keys, and get into your plane. Don't say anything, just move." He leveled the gun at the man's forehead and gestured toward the cottage.

The man mutely did as he was told, shaking both from wetness and fear. Dressed at last, he led Rossiter to the plane docked outside. Rossiter silently congratulated Lady Luck that the man actually owned one of the planes and was not just a watchman or neighborhood drunk looking for an empty bed.

He motioned the man inside the cockpit after allowing him to cast off the tie-lines. The man stared at the gun, still groggy and bewildered.

Rossiter spoke slowly and evenly, taking care with each syllable. "You are going to fly this plane to Washington. You are going to fly north of D.C.'s restricted airspace without drawing attention to yourself. You are going to fly so well that I won't get nervous about your ability to take me exactly where I'm going. Because if I get nervous, I'm going to throw you out and take the plane myself."

The man, not saying a word, turned the motor over and taxied into the middle of the quiet river. The take-off and turn to the northwest were perfect, so Rossiter settled back to plan his arrival.

Burt Strong threaded his way through one-way streets and access roads back toward Route 50 into Washington. Gilliam sat upright in the back seat, eyes still slightly out of focus, but otherwise alert and unhurt. Liz fiddled with the radio dials, trying to find a station with news of the blast. They listened disgustedly to obviously prerecorded "news stories" about a series of particularly brutal muggings in nearby Alexandria and the prospects for Middle East peace talks.

Gilliam, leaning forward to catch the fleeting pieces of audio, asked, "Where are we headed?"

Strong and Liz looked at each other in surprise. Neither answered immediately; Strong had been driving automatically and neither he nor Liz had any precise thoughts about a destination.

"Maybe the FBI building," Strong finally said, half as a question.

Kelly jumped slightly at the thought of anyone connected with federal investigations. Investigations meant interrogations.

Liz continued to twist the radio knob. She began to doubt that an explosion had occurred at all, to doubt that Gilliam had misunderstood his captor's conversation. At that moment, she picked up the urgent voice of a newscaster: ". . . was definitely a nuclear device, but its precise size has yet to be determined. Casualties, though presumed few, have not been estimated at this time. Civil Defense officials have said that the main body of radioactive fallout is drifting down the Chesapeake Bay at high altitudes, but that there is still a possibility that some fallout may reach populated areas. The White House has announced that the President will issue a statement later this evening, but now advises everyone to remain calm. There is no need to leave the Baltimore or Washington areas. We repeat: There is no foreign threat to the United States and no need for evacuation. The Emergency Broadcast System has not been activated. . . . This just handed to me: The Governor of Maryland has declared a state of emergency and has asked the President to declare the Chesapeake a federal disaster area. There are also reports that automobile accidents are numerous throughout the area, especially in the vicinity of Annapolis where the blast was clearly visible. Many roads and highways, say the Maryland State Police, are impassible due to accidents and extremely heavy traffic. All area police advise people to stay off the highways. That's all for now, but stay tuned for further developments."

Unbelievably, the station launched its next regularly scheduled commercial, this one for a processed cheese spread. Liz turned down the volume, but kept the radio on.

As they neared the river on Route 50, they saw that the sky was alive with the flashing lights of many aircraft. The loud rhythmic slapping of helicopter blades filled the air. At the bridge, they encountered cars trying to back away from the access ramp, and Strong was forced to pull sharply to the right to avoid hitting them. The bridge was obviously blocked, but because of the low angle of sight from the ramp, he couldn't see the cause of the blockage.

His only alternative was to exit to the southbound George Washington Parkway, so Strong took it, intending to try the Memorial Bridge further down the Potomac.

Gilliam looked back, craning his neck to see what was blocking the bridge. The inbound and outbound lanes were jammed with headlights pointing in random directions. He realized with a start that some pointed straight up, their beams cutting into the night sky. Nothing moved.

He shifted his eyes to the side window and saw immediately the cause of the massive wreck. The Washington shore was a solid wash of headlights, heading toward Virginia on both the inbound and outbound lanes. Some driver must have seen the Virginia-bound traffic stalled and panicked. Assuming, incorrectly, that nobody would be going into D.C., he must have cut across to the inbound ramp, scores of others following like sheep, thinking only of escape. The head-ons must have been awesome, thought Gilliam.

Liz had an even better view from the front seat. Seeing headlights packed in as far as the Washington Monument, she exclaimed, "Burt, we can't go into the city now! Even if we could, we might never get out."

"Whatever we do," answered Strong, "we should get out of this area. It's damn unsafe." He pulled around a curving ramp onto the exit.

To their left, Arlington National Cemetery stood empty and silent. To their right, cars flew at frightening speed across the Memorial Bridge, shooting northward toward Route 50. As Strong drove toward the traffic circle at the Virginia end of the bridge, Gilliam could see four lanes of high-speed traffic—two wrong-way—converging at the right turn. The scene reminded him of an auto chase from an old silent movie. The similarity ended, however, with the squeal of brakes and the sickening metallic thud of something heavy plowing into something light.

A small sports car spun sideways and careened toward the guardrail. It seemed to suspend for a moment in the glare of many headlights before plunging over the rail toward the Potomac. Cars collided and rebounded into other cars as they tried to avoid the exploding wreckage of the camper that had struck the sports car. Flames shot skyward and Gilliam heard another crash from the chain collision farther back on the bridge.

By the time Strong cleared the circle, the wreck had reduced traffic from the bridge to a one-lane trickle.

"Thank God we weren't a few minutes later," Gilliam said shakily, "or we might have been caught in the circle."

"Suppose we'd been a few minutes earlier," Strong replied. "We might have made it back into the city. We'd have never made it out, I'll guarantee that."

Traffic was still heavy, though not as frantic or deadly as that on the bridges out of Washington. Gilliam's hands ached from gripping the sides of the front seat. Encouraged by the relative orderliness of the traffic flow, he released his hold and leaned back in the seat.

"Hey, I just thought of something," he announced to his friends.

Strong said it for him. "Like where do we go from here? Right?"

"Dad's place at the lake," answered Liz immediately. "When that announcer mentioned fallout, I suddenly remembered that Dad built a humongous fallout shelter under the house back in the fifties. I was just a little kid when Mom finally convinced him to close it off, but I'm sure we could get into it somehow. That's the best place to wait things out. We can call the FBI from there once we decide we really should."

Gilliam was surprised. He was not accustomed to hearing about the young Harry Hammer as a human being with real foolishnesses. "Jesus," he said, "was your father an atomic energy nut back then, too?"

Strong broke the ensuing silence with an observation. "Nah, Kelly, lots of people built them. Harry just had more money than most and a direct inside line to the scare stories put out by the military and anticommies. But you're right in a way. He didn't drift into nuclear safeguard issues just because that's where the committee power was. He was always interested in the whole issue and a little scared by it."

Strong drove along in traffic that became gradually heavier with the influx from feeder roads to Route 50. They passed by a cluster of Arlington police cars parked near the gate of Fort Meyer Army Post. The cops seemed unconcerned about the unending flow of cars running the red light in front of the post, but were clearly more interested in what looked like a military convoy forming up inside the gate. Kelly could see army trucks, jeeps, armored personnel carriers, and hundreds of soldiers swarming about or standing in formations. They wore steel helmets and carried rifles.

"They're probably going to take those poor bastards back into the city," Strong remarked. "I'm glad my army contract ran out about when you were born, Kelly."

"They say the Army's the safest place to be in a nuclear . . ." Gilliam let his voice trail off, not wishing to finish the thought.

Liz didn't hear them. She sat, lost in her thoughts. After a long silence, she said, "We never looked in the shelter, Kelly. Do you think Murdock had him locked up in there?"

Gilliam thought about the prospect of a captive Hammer below the basement and contemplated the possibility of an underground terrorist command post. The FBI was almost comforting by comparison.

"No," he finally said, more in answer to his own unspoken question than to Liz's. "I'm sure we would have noticed *something* if anyone had still been around the place; that is . . ."

"That is," Liz finished, "unless that person is unconscious or . . . worse."

The reunion at Lake Barcroft should have been pleasant. Murdock, Bates, and Jackson had not been together since the day of the attack at Timber Rivers. The plan had functioned more or less as planned throughout the intervening weeks and nothing remained to be done until the arrival of the Chesapeake bomb. But the waiting was taking its toll. They didn't know for sure that the *Golden Girl* had arrived on time or had deposited its cargo safely in the bay. Even though he and Bates had reached Barcroft only a few hours earlier, Jackson was uncomfortable with nothing to do. He was eager to get on with the public announcement and the beginning of the main action. He stalked the periphery of the plush living room, stopping occasionally to look out at the darkness of the lake.

Murdock, both to divert Jackson and to ease her own anxiety, asked, "Leon, what do you want once we take over?"

Jackson stopped pacing, but he didn't sit down. After thinking a moment, he answered. "You know, Jean, for a while after the grab in Connecticut, I started thinking about staying in with you once our work is done. I might still come back if you make it to the top and need some help running things. But I guess I really don't believe you're going to get there. The assholes will do something stupid and you'll probably have to trigger the big one. I want to be out West with my million bucks when it blows."

Murdock weighed Jackson's words. She pondered her years of struggling against an unfair and uncaring system, the abuse she'd endured and the mental anguish of carrying on against hopeless odds. She wondered how her hopes could survive the leveling of Washington, D.C.

She considered Harry Hammer, sitting alone beneath the house in a fallout shelter, safely hidden from the ugliness above. She cared as much for his aspirations as her own, and wished that he were here, forcefully coping with this crisis. But she knew that he would not emerge until it was over.

"The senator," began Murdock in answer to Jackson, "is good at coping with assholes." She tried to smile, but failed. "He knows how they think and how they react to things. You can be sure of one thing, Leon. Harry Hammer will be one step ahead of them, and he won't maneuver them into a corner that cuts our options to blowing them up."

Jackson looked doubtful. "I just saw the senator," he replied, "when I took all the guns down to the bunker. He sure didn't look like he was up to any heavyweight strategizing. In fact, he looked like he's gone off his knob."

Murdock suppressed her anger and kept her voice smooth and calm. "Don't underestimate the senator, Leon. He's been through a great deal, but he's as capable as he's ever been. Like all the rest of us, he has his moments. But he still has his mission. He'll do what he has to, even if it means vaporizing the whole stinking mess."

Jackson looked at her speculatively and said, "You'd *like* to see number two pop, wouldn't you?"

"It's not what I planned for and it's not what I want," she replied, "but I wouldn't cry hard if it had to happen. What about you? Do you want to see it go?"

"Not if the rest of you are too close," he answered with his first grin since arriving. "But it wouldn't tear me up too much either if they bring it down on themselves."

Murdock turned to Bates, who was following the conversation as if it were a tennis match. "How about you, John? What's next for you?"

Bates looked confused for a moment. He had caught the flow of the conversation, but not its details. He realized, however, that some reflection had gone into the others' words and knew that more than his casual opinion was in order. "I don't think past day-to-day, Jeannie," he replied. "I never did do much planning. Life has been good since Dunk, Yoshi, and I got together in the hospital, and I guess I'm not too happy it's finally push-button time."

"Do you want the *second* button pushed?" asked Jackson.

"I don't much care one way or the other," Bates answered. "It sure would be fun to watch from out here, though."

Jackson laughed. "It sure *would* be," he said. "If that happens, you could always come back to California with me and help spend Dunk's money."

Bates brightened. Without stopping to think, he said, "Maybe you could give me some coaching, too, so I don't scare away my next classy whore."

"What do you mean, your 'next classy whore'?" Jackson asked.

Bates looked around at Murdock, feeling no desire to continue the conversation. Jackson, misinterpreting guilt as embarrassment over telling a raunchy and perhaps self-denigrating story in front of a woman, winked and pressed on. "Tell us about *last* time, John."

Murdock, who read most men well at first glance, had no problems at all understanding the discomfort of one she had studied carefully. "Yes, John, please tell us about last time so we can do something about it if necessary," she said.

After looking back and forth at his companions, Bates fumblingly told the entire incident concerning a woman who had appeared barebreasted, like Venus on the halfshell, in his bathroom doorway.

When he finished, Jackson felt relieved. It had been a serious mistake for Bates to conceal something like that from Jean, but the incident itself didn't seem dangerous. Bates mirrored his relief, gratefully, but stiffened again when Murdock asked, "Was she tall, blonde, and maybe looked a little like the senator?"

To Jackson's surprise, Bates nodded yes.

"Elizabeth Hammer," said Murdock. "Our host's daughter. She and Kelly Gilliam from the Energy Committee have been poking around together after Harry. I wouldn't be surprised if Gilliam was the one who got into my computer records before I took Yoshi's name off. Something got one of them onto me and they've been playing detective ever since. Maybe it was just because they couldn't figure out what happened to Harry, but I'll bet it's something more. At least they didn't find anything at your place, John, or they would have called the cops long ago."

"God damn it, Jean," broke in Jackson. "They must have been some kind of worried to bother tracking you to your meetings with John and then break into his place. It just doesn't fit together."

Murdock sat and thought hard. "You're right," she said. "It doesn't fit together. But they haven't blown the whistle yet. If they had, and anybody believed them, the whole National Guard would have invaded this place by now. Leon"—her voice was hard, commanding—"you're just going to have to go out and get them. Tonight. If we wait until tomorrow, they'll run right to the police when they hear our little public announcement. Let's hope that they're spending the night together at one of their places. That'll mean less leg-work for you. The little bitch said something about their being engaged. I hope that wasn't phony, too."

Murdock got up and rooted around in the den for a telephone book. While searching, she shouted into the living room. "You'd better start getting your guns ready. Make sure you take silencers, too."

Jackson walked into the den. "Hey, slow down, Jean. I know my business. Take a few minutes to cool off and think about what I need to know. Like what they look like, for example."

"You're right," Murdock replied. "Give me a little time to get my head together and I'll give you what you need." As she thumbed through the telephone book, she tried to order her thoughts, wishing she could snap in and out of meditation like Nakamura.

Jackson, meanwhile, wandered back into the living room, thinking about this unexpected mission. Knowing there was little he could do until Murdock gave him the information he needed, he looked around for something to occupy his time. Bates slinked out of the room like a whipped puppy, presumably to sulk or simply to make himself scarce for a while. With nothing better to do, Jackson turned on the television.

A few seconds later, he boosted the volume and yelled, "Jeannie, John. Get in here!"

The three watched in disbelief as a network newsman used flat tones to describe the explosion in the Chesapeake. He described the blast (large and atomic). He repeated everything reporters could glean from Washington officials: Don't worry about fallout in D.C.; don't rush out of town; we're working on it, but we can't give you any more details now. He speculated on the cause of the blast: the Timber Rivers theft; an accidentally detonated military bomb; a catastrophe on a nuclear submarine. They had to wait until the newsman had rendered all his noninformation before hearing what they needed to know most: The bomb had gone off less than an hour earlier.

They sat numbly for more than a minute after Jackson savagely pounded the on-off knob. He was floored by Rossiter's probable death. He was devastated by the prospect of wrecked plans, the loss of his promised money, and the thought that Nakamura had probably shared Rossiter's fate. Duncan had been his only real friend. He glanced sympathetically at Murdock. Duncan had been much more than a friend to her, and Jackson sensed her strength ebbing as she sat silently, her face pale. Her first words were totally unexpected.

"Forget the hunting trip, Leon," she said grimly.

"All our work's right here. We have to move fast. If I'm right about little Liza and her boy friend, this place will be crawling with cops. Soon. Let's get our message off, close up tight, and get downstairs."

Jackson, after an initial surge of hatred for Murdock, was grateful that she was tougher under pressure than he'd imagined. His thoughts snapped back to the plan.

"Jeannie," he said, "our message at the studio's no good now. How can we announce that the bay is going to explode when it's already happened?"

"We can't," she answered. "Our canned speech is out, but we can still put it to this city if we write a new one that's convincing."

"But the phone number you gave me just triggers an override at the radio station and broadcasts our tape. What can we do?" he asked.

"We've got a backup system," Murdock explained. "Another number at the same station gives us an override circuit with a blank tape. We have a minute and a half to record and another minute's delay before the computer puts it on the air. It's a real phone answering hookup instead of just a fake one."

"Damn," said Jackson in admiration. "Right now, the only number I want to call is the one hooked up to the Capitol dome relay, but I owe you the chance to make your move before asking you to blow down this whole lousy city. What do you want to say?"

"Help me find a pen and some paper, and I'll write it out for John," she answered calmly. "He's got the best radio voice."

She wrote out the script easily, crossing out only a few words as she went along. When she finished, she turned it over to Bates, who practiced it a few times, adding some small ad libs while she timed it. Finally satisfied, she fished around for the right station on a nearby table radio, led them to the phone, punched out a number, and waited for the identifying message for "Art's Dry Cleaners." At the next tone, she slowly picked out the coded numbers that would activate the second tape and the relay. Another set of beeps told her the recording had begun, so she handed the phone to Bates. He started with a catch in his voice, but the message was slow, clear, and well within the time limit. He handed the phone back and Murdock placed it in the cradle. She turned the radio up loud enough for the music to be clearly audible. They waited, not really doubting that the circuits would work, but apprehensive nonetheless. Finally, there was a pop from the radio and the prerecorded voice of Duncan Rossiter filled the room: "We interrupt this program to bring you a public service announcement."

Jackson and Bates jumped at the ghostly voice. Then, another pop preceded an initially nervous Bates: "The bomb that went off in the Chesapeake Bay this evening was brought to you by the same friendly people who robbed the American Nuclear Corporation truck earlier this month. Fortunately, we had to use only half the plutonium for that bomb. There was enough left over for *another* one, which we've planted somewhere in Washington. It's ready to go when we say so. If you don't want that to happen, be sure that the President goes on national television one hour from now to turn over command of the armed forces to us. *Some* of us will meet him at the White House gate two hours after that broadcast. We'll have additional instructions for him then. In case you don't believe us, the serial number on one of the stolen plutonium casks was RR4722. We will tell you the other numbers at the gate. Otherwise . . . good-bye."

Another pop signaled dead air time, then the music returned.

"Well," said Murdock matter-of-factly, "let's close up tight and move downstairs."

The three went around the house, shutting windows, checking locks, and gathering personal items. Then they trooped to the basement, Murdock explaining how she had a second chance backup message ready with more elaborate proof of their "legitimacy" if their offer were rejected. The next tape was set for broadcast in Kansas City, an easy direct-dial well outside the area the Feds would check for special phone connections into local radio stations. Duncan hadn't wanted their call traced at the last minute.

"Jeannie," Jackson said as they headed down the steps, "I saw you hit that weird star on the phone when you triggered the override. Isn't it hard to remember a code word with a star in it?"

"Easy," Murdock answered. "It was Yoshi's favorite word, *Zensho*."

"But there's no Z on the buttons—" Jackson said.

"And it's a button nobody would push," she answered. "Most people don't even know it makes a sound like the others." Her words carried a hint of smugness she hardly felt. She pictured the star in her mind, but all she could see was the start of a sun-hot blast radiating outward from Yoshi and Duncan.

The basement of the house was furnished lavishly. Murdock led them through a large carpeted room with a pool table and a bar, then into a hallway flanked by bedrooms, a utility room, and a small library. At the end of the hallway was a room used for storage, but it was incongruously paneled in expensive wood.

Murdock rotated a light switch plate to reveal a button embedded in the wall. She pressed it and disengaged a lock, then went to the paneled wall and rolled it aside along hidden tracks. Behind the wall was a stairway leading down.

The three descended the stairs into another short corridor that led to a large subterranean room with soft lighting, carpeting, comfortable furniture, and walls of books. The room had two television sets, a large ham radio, a stereo, and a typewriter. The air was fresh, pumped by a filter and exchange unit from an underground sump far from the house. The backup electrical system was entirely independent, using a large generator housed in the same sump. A door on the far side of the room led to a kitchen, beyond which were bedrooms, a bathroom, and a storage pantry in which Jackson had earlier deposited a cache of guns and ammunition.

Harry Hammer sat in an overstuffed chair, working a crossword puzzle. He had a mellow smile on his face. On a short table next to the chair was a red telephone connected to a buried outside trunk line, which in turn was connected to a switching unit in another part of the neighborhood.

"Is it time yet?" asked Hammer, glancing up at the new arrivals.

"Yes," answered Murdock, "it's time." Hammer's face disturbed her. His expression was totally relaxed, almost sagging, his eyes vacantly serene.

"Harry, have you had a chance to watch any television?" Murdock asked.

"Oh, no," he answered. "Too much violence. There's never anything good on any more."

"Harry," said Murdock, "the bomb in the Chesapeake went off. We just heard about it on TV. Something must have gone wrong for Duncan and Yoshi. We had to go ahead with our radio announcement, Harry, and that means we have to be ready to move fast. It's finally time. The waiting is over."

Hammer smiled up at her. "That's okay, Jeannie. I don't plan to run for reelection anyway. The Republicans are just too strong. Say, could you call Burt and tell him that for me?"

Jackson stepped forward and stared into Hammer's smiling face. "Shit!" he said after a moment. "He's crazy! He hasn't understood a fuckin' thing you've said."

"Stop it, Leon," ordered Murdock. "The Senator's been under a lot of strain and he's just tired."

"Tired, my ass!" shouted Jackson. "He's crazy as a

loon! You expect *this* guy to take over the fuckin' country?"

"Shut up, Leon! Your opinion isn't needed. You were hired to take orders, now take this one. *Shut up!*"

Jackson's rage spilled over. "Yeah, I was hired, all right, by *Dunk*. With Dunk's money. But he's dead, little sister, and there's no leader any more. There's nobody to pay me, honey, you got that? Our only chance is to get what we can from this thing. But we've *got* no chance if we waste our precious time playing games with this slobbering idiot!" He pointed a shaking finger into Hammer's face. "He's not gonna get us anything!"

Bates tried to be soothing. "I think maybe Leon's right, Jeannie. Why don't we just tell the President we want ten million dollars—well, hell, make it a hundred million! We don't need to run the country, do we?"

For an instant, Murdock's head reeled, but she regained control, fighting down incredible anger. She whirled back to the Senator. "Harry! Are you going to stand for this?"

"Oh, you know where I stand," he said. "My position has always been clear. Would one of you mind getting me a Bloody Mary?"

"That does it!" shouted Jackson. "As of this minute, the plan is changed! We're gonna start doing things *my* way now." He strode toward Murdock, who retreated toward Hammer's chair. "Give me the numbers, Jeannie, the ones I need if I decide to blow the lid off Washington."

Murdock screamed at him, "Stay away from me, you bastard!"

"The numbers, Jeannie. Give 'em to me! You ain't in charge any more!" Jackson advanced another step.

"Stop him, John! Don't just stand there, stop him!"

Bates took a tentative step, but then fell back. "Sorry, Jeannie. Better give him the numbers."

Murdock's leg touched the small table near Hammer's chair. She whirled around, jerked open the drawer, and pulled out a short, ugly pistol. Jackson lunged at her, but not before the pistol belched fire, nearly deafening everyone in the room.

Jackson staggered backward, his chest punctured by the bullet. Murdock fired again and Jackson reeled to the floor.

Bates stood horror-stricken, his jaw slack as Murdock swung the pistol at him. The last thing he saw was a blinding flash of light as a chunk of steel-jacketed lead penetrated his skull.

Murdock's ears rang madly from the gunshots, and she could barely hear Harry Hammer's voice. "Oh, no," he said, staring at the blood-spattered walls and carpet. "That's a *heck* of a mess. *I'm* not cleaning it up. I cleaned up last time. I think it's *your* turn to clean up."

Murdock felt very sick. And very much alone.

———

Kaznik had rough estimates of the bomb's size within minutes of his return to headquarters. Because the bomb had gone off over water, no precise displacement or ground-effects data were available. But it was easily big enough to rattle seismographs all over the area. Witnesses provided information on the height of the cloud and gave details, which Kaznik passed on to Rippling and other experts.

The experts, most of whom were employed by the NRC, estimated that the blast was in the five- to twenty-kiloton range. Five kilotons is the explosive power of five thousand tons of TNT. Twenty kilotons leveled Hiroshima.

Rippling had no real quarrel with the figures that the experts offered. He himself thought the bomb might have been well over twenty. But he differed with the NRC, he told Kaznik heatedly, over their bland assurances that the Chesapeake blast must have used *all* the stolen plutonium.

"Joel," he asked the distraught investigator, "who would you give your nuclear material to if you wanted a big blast? Mercado or me?"

"You know damn well who," Kaznik replied.

"I could easily get you two bombs that size out of the plutonium that disappeared at Timber Rivers," he continued. "And so could lots of people."

After a pause, Kaznik asked another critical question. "Is it possible that when one of those two bombs went off, the other one didn't blow . . . maybe just got knocked apart and the pieces sank?"

The answer was immediate and short: "No."

Kaznik thought another minute, made sure that he could reach Rippling again if needed, and hung up. He knew intuitively that another bomb existed somewhere, suspected that it was nearby, and had no way of convincing anyone that he was right. His judgment would surely be questioned now that he had failed to recover the plutonium before the Chesapeake blast annihilated it. Moreover, he was not in charge of Washington area emergency planning. He knew that the President trusted him, but he doubted whether an unsupported hunch would carry much weight against an entire bureaucracy massing to prevent panic rather than to prevent the remote possibility of another blast.

Upon hearing from Billingsly that Gilliam, against all odds, had escaped with the help of a mysterious woman, he merely shook his head and remained unflapped. He issued search orders wearily, but suspected that Gilliam and his friends were only a peripheral part of the picture now.

The news of the threatening broadcast over commercial radio was a shock. Quillico passed on the details to Kaznik from his phone in FBI headquarters. Since the Bureau had already dispatched a crew to the station to determine how the threat was broadcast, all Kaznik could demand was a monitor tape from the station management. He wanted to hear the audio stunt firsthand, for it smacked of John Bates's flashing episode, in a tenuous sort of way. Kaznik wasn't sure what he might gain from hearing it, but he'd solved cases with less to go on.

With nothing immediate left to do, Kaznik analyzed what he had on the threat thus far. Was it *real?* he asked himself. Could it lead him to the bombers in time? Most important, what should he advise the President to do about it . . . if the President even called to ask.

"Curt," he said to Quillico, who was just hanging up one of his phones, "that might have been a prerecorded message. But how in the hell did they trigger it? Unless they knew exactly when the bomb would explode and were damned sure that nothing could go wrong with the timing, they either had to be in the studio or have a way of starting their recording anytime they wanted to."

"Well," said Quillico, "they could have gotten into the studio, or into the transmitting station for that matter, at an earlier time, and planted a phone answering device on a special trunk line. If they had good wiring, they could have merely called in and started it."

"But what if somebody else calls in on that line by mistake?" Kaznik asked. In answer to his own question, he continued, "Sure, they could have set up a fake message that would make the caller hang up, then have a voice trigger to do what they wanted when *they* called."

"Yeah," said Quillico. "I suppose that if they wanted to get fancy, they could trigger their message with another series of tones from the phone at their end. Hell, they wouldn't even have to prerecord, they could—" He stopped.

"They could call in from anywhere in the country," Kaznik finished for him. "And they could use the same fucking method to detonate the second bomb!"

He grabbed for the yellow phone on his desk and

tersely told the startled operator that he wanted the President immediately. A few seconds later, he outlined to the President his analysis of the method used for the bomb threat, his conviction that the message had come from the Chesapeake bombers, and his strong belief that another bomb was set to go off.

"What in God's name do you want me to do, Joel?" asked the President. "Go on TV and invite them down to see me? Most of the advisors I've been able to contact tell me to sit tight and ignore them until you— or somebody—catches them. Even if you're right about what they've got, reacting that way won't do much good. If you're wrong, we can't take back what we've already told the world."

Kaznik answered quickly, fearing that his chance to set in motion the necessary reactions might be slipping away. "I want you to get out *now*, Mr. President. I want you to go to Hardsite L and take everyone you can with you. These maniacs might push the button just because they feel like it."

"I can't do that, Joel. The NRC assures me that even if it *is* the same people doing all this, they don't have any more plutonium. And we have full emergency and security plans going into effect."

Kaznik wanted to continue the argument, to keep the President on the line at the risk of sounding like a blubbering, panicked fool. But he knew his boss's mind was made up. There was but one thing to do: Find the bastards quickly. Very quickly.

"Okay, sir, good-bye," he said hurriedly into the phone, his mind racing. He had to pull out all the stops . . . but were there any left?

By the time Strong and his passengers reached the final underpass before their anticipated turn off Route 50, traffic had slowed to a crawl. Just beyond the underpass, he was forced to stop completely. Cars packed in rapidly behind.

When the traffic failed to resume moving, Gilliam scrambled out of the car and went up the embankment to reconnoiter. There was a big accident about a block ahead, but he couldn't determine how things stacked up beyond the next hill.

The drivers around them behaved strangely, even by Washington standards. Many leaned on their horns. Others cast around for ways out of an obviously block-aded position. At the edges of their vision, Strong and Liz could see headlights crossing the median strip to continue on the wrong side of the highway against sparse traffic. In the midst of the confusion, Strong's old clunker blew its radiator and died.

They sat for a few moments, not bothering to curse. The car's condition seemed irrelevant because prospects for more driving were bleak.

Gilliam, giving in to years of conditioning about cour-teous driving, voiced their shared question. "Should we push this heap over to the side or just let it sit?"

Liz answered quickly. "Let's bail out now."

The three left the car and started hiking up the road, forgetting entirely about the gun Liz had brought along after her encounter with Billingsly. Strong had misgivings both about the pace Liz set and the distance he knew they must cover, but he kept them to himself.

Beyond the accident, traffic was moving again, but it was clear that the slightest tie-up would bring it to another standstill. The congestion was unlikely to let up.

Gilliam, Liz, and Strong crossed side streets, darting between lines of halted cars bearing grim-faced occu-pants who cursed the hopelessness of trying to force their way onto the main road. Most vehicles were jammed with baggage, household possessions, and food-stuffs, leaving little room for people. It was as though the entire population of northern Virginia had packed up to move west.

The wail of sirens filled the air, mostly from the back streets that still afforded police and rescue vehicles some mobility. Here and there, the night glowed with fire, presumably the result of carelessness induced by haste or fear.

Gilliam lost all sense of time as the hike wore on. At length, Liz led them between two tall apartment houses on their left, then toward a Greek Orthodox church that looked like a backlighted mushroom. Gilliam was not in the mood for mushrooms—not in any way, shape or form.

Cars hurtled continually by, their drivers using back roads and streets in search of the path of least resistance to points west. A passing van nearly hit an old woman dressed in black as she tried to cross the street to the mushroom-shaped church; she jumped back to the curb as the van brushed her skirt, causing her to lose her balance. Liz halted and offered help to the woman, who accepted gratefully.

The trio continued on to Route 7, a crossroad that also led west. A bus was overturned and burning at the intersection, blocking several lanes. Other stalled and demolished vehicles forced traffic to detour through the parking lot of a well lit shopping center. Police were everywhere.

Gilliam shook his head. From his vantage point he could easily see that the highway was cut off again just two blocks farther west.

They picked their way carefully across the road amid the wailing of sirens and the unintelligible barking of police bullhorns, through the whirling colored light from the police cruisers. Pedestrians and spectators milled around the rescue squad that worked feverishly near the burning bus. Fire trucks apparently had been unable to respond to this accident.

Gilliam inspected the shopping center as they passed by. The windows in banks and stores were still intact. There had been no looting.

Behind the shopping center, the neighborhood was residential. Several low apartment houses flanked the road. Farther on were still more. Strong and Gilliam were breathing hard as they entered the neighborhood, so Liz slowed her pace and urged them on by announcing that they had only fifteen more minutes of walking ahead of them.

People were everywhere, talking excitedly in small groups, on lawns and sidewalks. Several groups had loud portable radios that boomed competing local news coverage.

Many nearby apartments were dark, their occupants having joined the panicked flow of westbound traffic. A few people were *unpacking* their cars, having returned unsuccessfully from the pandemonium of the highways. Their faces showed both fear and resignation. One grim young couple walked by with packs and sleeping bags on their backs. This was no holiday outing for them.

Gilliam overheard snatches of conversation about looters, Jesus' Second Coming, and the President's expected speech to the nation. He spotted a teen-age boy standing alone with a radio pressed to his ear, walked over, and tapped him on the shoulder. The boy was thirteen or fourteen with flaming orange hair and freckles. Unlike most of the other people standing around, he didn't seem particularly distraught.

"Anything new on that thing?" Gilliam asked, pointing at the radio.

"Nothing new. Nobody seems to know if there's really another bomb."

"Another bomb?" Gilliam felt all the blood drain from his face. "Are you telling me there's another bomb?"

The boy looked at him quizzically and exclaimed, "Wow, where have *you* been? Why do you think the whole world is coming apart? Some guy cut into one of the D.C. radio stations and said there's another atom bomb planted in the city. Said he wants the President to turn the whole country over to him or he'll set it off."

Strong, who had come over in time to hear the end

of the boy's answer, was about to question him further when the radio suddenly said, "Ladies and gentlemen, the President of the United States." Conversation ceased in the surrounding knots of people as volume knobs on radios were turned up high. Over the far away sound of sirens came the President's familiar voice, as though *everywhere*, hollowed somewhat by the small speakers of dozens of radios. The President confirmed that the Chesapeake bomb had been atomic, that the government was now certain of the bomb's origin, and that it had been made from the plutonium stolen weeks before in Connecticut; he stated that the explosion was not the precursor of an enemy attack and was not, in fact, a sophisticated weapon at all. Because federal experts had advised him that all the stolen plutonium must have been used in producing the Chesapeake blast, he personally refuted the anonymous radio claim that there was a second bomb planted somewhere in Washington. Finally, he urged everyone to remain calm. Those fleeing nearby metropolitan centers should return home, for the only real danger lay in public reaction to the threat, not in the threat itself. He closed with FDR's famous line: "We have nothing to fear but fear itself."

The radio stations resumed their individual programs, and the freckle-faced boy moved away to join some friends.

Strong conferred with Liz and Gilliam. Leadership of their newly formed triumvirate fluctuated among them and the mantle seemed to be his for the moment.

"Look," he said. "Do we need any more information or should we get on to the house?"

"Do we *want* to get on to the house at all?" asked Gilliam in reply. "How do we know that's not Murdock's headquarters?"

Liz, her thoughts still on the possibility of her father being at Barcroft, answered quickly. "They could be anywhere, Kelly. If they do have another bomb in Washington, they sure don't want to be this close, shelter or no shelter."

"We could take some cops with us," Gilliam replied.

"No, Kelly," said Strong. "Even if we find any, they're just as likely to run us in first."

Strong started off briskly, feeling far less certitude than his last words seemed to convey. The brief rest had given him a second wind, and the house had an almost magnetic pull over him for the first time. Liz and Kelly caught up and walked with him, past a library and into a section of single-family homes. In this area there were cars in the driveways, lights on, and people huddled inside. The travelers hurried through.

After swinging well north of Washington, Rossiter ordered the shaken pilot to fly the seaplane into northern Virginia, west of the city. Except for occasional terse commands, the ride was silent. Rossiter noted an unusual number of helicopters aloft and military jets winging swiftly overhead.

Once he saw that they were passing east of Dulles International and well clear of its traffic patterns, Rossiter spoke again to the pilot. "Seventeen miles southeast of the Dulles tower and six miles due west of National, there's a Y-shaped lake. I think we're going to pass near it in less than five minutes if I'm reading the ground right. When you see it, you're going to put down at the near end."

The pilot, now sober and attentive though stinking from booze, nodded weakly. Sooner than Rossiter expected, the lights around Lake Barcroft appeared ahead, and the pilot cut back the throttle and eased them down through the trees toward the lake.

They landed easily in a narrow channel and came quickly to a halt. At an abrupt sign from Rossiter, the pilot shut off the engine and waited for further instructions as the small seaplane rocked softly between two wooded shores. Rossiter squinted through the darkness looking for signs of life in the nearby houses, but, strangely, nobody rushed down the banks to see the strange spectacle of a seaplane on Lake Barcroft. Rossiter casually reached behind the pilot, as though groping for something he had placed behind the seat, then slammed his open hand into the back of the pilot's neck. The man snapped forward over the wheel, momentarily stunned. Another blow to the back of the head sent him pitching into the windshield. Rossiter opened the pilot's door, pushed him out, and climbed onto a strut. Seeing no activity on either shore, Rossiter dove into the dark water and swam to the bank.

Because Rossiter was a strong swimmer, he had ordered the pilot to land at the far end of the lake from the senator's house. From here he would swim, undetected and unmolested, to the command post. Soon the authorities would find the plane, but they would have no reason to connect it with the residence of Senator Harry Hammer, or to assume that its presence on the tiny lake signified anything more than a drunken pilot's fatal misfortune. Slowly, powerfully, Rossiter swam, devouring the watery half mile that would end near the dam on the far side of the lake.

As Rossiter swam, Jean Murdock stood in the fallout shelter, still holding the pistol. She stared at Harry Hammer, who sat with his crossword puzzle, oblivious to her and to the bleeding bodies of Jackson and Bates.

The room seemed to close in on her—as if the oppressive atmosphere had no oxygen—and she had trouble breathing. She desperately needed a breath of fresh air and a few minutes to think, alone, so she left Hammer to the deathly quiet of the shelter and headed for the stairs.

She walked up from the basement, scarcely aware that she still clutched the pistol. Alone—totally alone, just the way she had started.

Rossiter and Nakamura were dead because of some unknowable bungling.

Jackson and Bates were dead because they'd turned on her.

Hammer was as good as dead, his brain transformed into mush, useless.

So be it. She would carry on alone. In her head she had the numbers that could unleash hell or bring the mightiest nation on earth to its knees. Murdock had all she needed.

Rossiter crossed the main body of the lake using a breaststroke. He was more tired than he'd anticipated by the time he hauled himself up the swimmers' ladder onto Senator Harry Hammer's dock. His sopping clothes chilled him as he waited for his inner ear to adjust to land. His shoes felt like lead as he crossed to the gate that opened into the back lawn. He groped in the darkness for the latch and let himself in, missing the low growl from the other side. He'd gone two steps when he was struck in the chest by two hundred pounds of startled, hungry, and angry watchdog. Rossiter staggered back into the fence and caught himself to avoid falling as the dog launched itself again, burying its teeth into his thigh. For the first time since early childhood, Rossiter shrieked in terror.

His scream penetrated the glass doors at the rear of the house. Murdock, standing alone in the dark kitchen, could hear throaty growling as the scream died away. She flew instantly to the back door, flipped on the yard lights, and threw back the deadbolt.

Suddenly the night was filled with loud electric clangor. Murdock had forgotten to neutralize the burglar alarm, but she ignored it and darted out the door and down the stairs.

She could hardly believe her eyes. The huge dog was frenzied, savage, like nothing she'd ever seen. There was a man, a familiar figure, trying desperately to fend off claws and fangs.

Murdock screeched at the dog, but it ignored her. The animal lunged at its victim, knocking him again to the ground, and hovered threateningly, a guttural rumbling issuing from its throat.

Rossiter somehow fought down the panic and tried to be perfectly still. From the corner of his eye, he caught sight of Murdock advancing down the grassy slope from the house. His whole leg was aflame with pain, the muscles and tendons ripped savagely, and he could feel the warmth of his own blood flowing away. Nearly choking on the stink of the dog's breath in his face, he suppressed the compulsion to cry out to Murdock, for fear he'd provoke the dog further.

Murdock ventured closer, her pistol ready. Rossiter could stand it no longer. "Jeannie!" he screamed.

The dog stabbed its fangs at his throat, but Rossiter twisted to his side, interjecting his forearm. The jaws clamped shut, ripping the arm from shoulder to elbow.

"*Jeannie!*"

Murdock stifled a gasp. *It's Duncan! How . . . ?* She drew as close as she dared and took careful aim at the roiling animal as it lunged again, opening Rossiter's stomach. The shot cut through the jangling of the burglar alarm, Rossiter's mortal screaming, the vicious snarling of the dog. The bullet struck the dog in the ribs, knocking it twisting and yelping in pain.

Rossiter lay like a rag doll, sprawled grotesquely on the bloody grass. Murdock, standing over him, saw only the geysers of blood spurting from severed arteries and veins. He stirred and looked up at her.

"Jeannie," he rasped. "I'm hurt bad. Get Leon quick. He'll know what to do."

"Leon?"

"*Get* him, Jeannie! He's handled worse than this in Vietnam. Bring him here *now!*"

Murdock hesitated and Rossiter painfully drew his legs under him, then raised himself on his elbow. "What are you waiting for?" he gasped.

She stepped away from him. "I can't get him, Dunk, he's dead."

"*Dead?* How? How can he be dead?"

Murdock's voice was strong and fully controlled. "He turned on me."

Rossiter braved a spasm and struggled to his knees. Cringing, he forced weight on one foot and teetered, half standing, half kneeling. "He turned on you? On *you?*"

"So I killed him, Dunk. He was only interested in money. Your money. He had no commitment to our mission or to me."

"*To you? To you!*"

He suddenly hurled himself at Murdock, but she easily stepped aside, letting him tumble headlong into the grass. She retreated another step and stared down at him as he lay wheezing, hopelessly torn. Despite his injuries, Rossiter's eyes glared killing hatred, and Murdock knew he would come at her again. She raised the pistol toward Rossiter's temple and fired point blank.

Gilliam, Liz, and Strong arrived at the house the moment the alarm went off. Before they reached the front door, the clanging filled the neighborhood. Strong, breathing hard and feeling horribly weak and flushed from the night's adventure, leaned against a tree.

"Jesus," said Gilliam, "we must have tripped a wire or something."

Liz glanced up at the house. "I don't think so. We never had that kind of system. Murdock must have installed it. I can't see any lights from this side, can you? Let's look around for open doors."

The two of them started around the side of the house as Strong regained his breath. Summoning all his strength, he stumbled after them toward the back yard. They stopped for a moment thinking they'd heard a shot, but then went on.

They came to the water's edge, but their view of the

house was blocked by bushes. Running now, Liz and Gilliam turned along the dock for the waterside gate. Strong fought to keep his breath coming in gulps. The alarm obscured what seemed to be yet another shot, and they hesitated again a few steps from the gate.

Murdock saw them first, took two quick strides toward the gate, and shouted, "Don't take another step!"

Gilliam, Liz, and Strong froze in their tracks.

"The first one who moves will be killed."

She came through the open gate. The yard light cast insane shadows across Murdock's face, and Gilliam never doubted her words. Strong's face was chalk-white and awash with sweat. Suddenly, he lurched forward, clutching his chest.

Murdock reacted instantly, not recognizing the symptoms of a heart attack. She fired and Strong doubled up on the ground, shot through the stomach. Liz flew in a blind rage at Murdock, striking her in the shoulder and toppling her backward. The two women landed on the rough boards of the dock as the pistol went flying into a bush.

Gilliam clawed through leafy branches to find the gun, hearing screams and curses behind him. When he found it at last, he turned to help Liz.

He stopped cold. Crouched between him and the dock was the monstrous dog, ready to lunge. Its cavernous mouth was hideously bloodied and its lips were contorted to display huge fangs. Gilliam backed away instinctively as the creature emitted a rumbling growl, inching closer. Blood poured from the bullet wound in its side and its yellowish eyes flashed the savagery of an animal that knows it's dying.

Gilliam steadied the heavy pistol in his hand, fighting uncooperative muscles to prevent its shaking. The dog came forward and Gilliam pulled the trigger.

Nothing happened. The gun was empty.

The animal lunged, forcing Gilliam to the ground by

the sheer force of its weight. Hard, wet teeth pressed against the soft flesh of his neck and he grimaced with fear. He flailed uselessly at the dog's body.

Then the jaws went slack. The two-hundred-pound animal slumped against his chest, pressing the air from Gilliam's lungs.

On the dock, Murdock struggled to her feet and slammed a fist into Liz's face. Liz saw flashing sparks, then went down hard as Murdock kicked her legs from under her. But Liz held on. Murdock struck blow after blow, kicking and gouging, finally pushing Liz over the edge of the dock. Liz barely caught a fistful of Murdock's blouse, and both women crashed into the cold water.

Even as they plummeted into a dark, spinning world, they fought. Buoyancy brought them back to the surface and Murdock managed to wrap her arm around Liz's neck from behind. For the first time, Liz started to panic as Murdock's grip tightened on her throat.

Liz elbowed and kicked, but couldn't shake the stranglehold. She managed to get one small gasp of air that renewed her strength, but it was hardly enough. She felt herself weakening. Her mind suddenly flashed the image of Burt Strong doubling over, shot. Though her lungs burned, Liz managed one final burst of fury.

She reached over her head and grabbed a handful of Murdock's hair. Summoning every ounce of strength, she twisted and rolled to her side, sending them both under water.

Murdock kicked furiously, fighting for the surface, giving up her hold completely. But Liz dragged her down, rolling and twisting, longing to breathe herself, but more determined that Murdock should not.

Murdock was desperate now, like a being possessed, flailing in random gyrations. But Liz held on, fighting both Murdock and buoyancy until the air blew from Murdock's lungs. It rose to the surface in noisy bubbles as Murdock breathed water. Her body shuddered madly, again and again, until it was still.

Liz's pounding heart and temples were like drums. Her oxygen-starved brain slipped close to unconsciousness. Suddenly, she was on the surface, not knowing how she got there, caring only about filling her lungs with great gulps of air.

"Lizzie!" screamed Gilliam from the dock a few feet away. He grabbed her outstretched hand and hoisted her up. She coughed several times, choking, then collapsed from exhaustion in his arms. Suddenly Liz bolted upright. "Burt!" she screamed.

Gilliam followed her to the spot where Strong lay motionless, and together they pressed their ears to his chest. Frantically they applied mouth-to-mouth resuscitation and heart massage until they lay back, exhausted, defeated in their battle for Strong's life.

Liz broke down again, but Gilliam could scarcely hear her sobs above the shrill din of the house alarm. He put his arm around her and waited for her to finally regain control.

Liz looked up at the dark house, blinking back tears. She could just see the dim outline of the open door. Brushing wet, tangled hair from her face, she asked, "Do we go in, Kelly?"

Gilliam, whose first choice would have been to simply slip quietly away and walk back to Montana, considered the alternatives. There was little reason to venture inside the dark house without police protection. If anything interesting were there, it might be too interesting to handle. They could call the FBI from a neighbor's house, couldn't they? The door, on the other hand, was open and there were no signs of life. He took Liz's hand and got up. Together they walked toward the door.

As they reached the steps, a light snapped on in the living room. They froze, hands locked together. The alarm cut off and silence descended abruptly, heavily.

Before they could turn to run, Harry Hammer appeared in the doorway, pipe in hand. He smiled when he saw the two of them and called out, "What a pleasant surprise! Come on in for a drink."

Dazed, and still clinging to each other's hands, they followed him into the silent house.

MONDAY, JUNE 21

Kaznik reluctantly closed up shop on the special investigation six weeks after it had begun. He had no craving for the extraordinary powers he'd been granted and no desire to continue the frantic pace generated over the previous month. His reluctance stemmed from one source: His complete conviction that another bomb had been planted nearby.

When prodded by the special congressional committee, under oath and on national television, he admitted his *near* certainty that all the terrorists had been neutralized. He was, moreover, reasonably certain that all their accomplices had been accounted for.

"Then, where's the problem?" asked an exasperated Senator Browning. "If you are comfortable about having found all the persons concerned, either dead or cleared of any involvement, and the NRC assures us firmly that there's no unaccounted-for plutonium, why are you worried?"

Kaznik had vigorously disputed the NRC's estimates of the missing plutonium. With the help of Rippling and Kelly Gilliam, who had since attached himself to Kaznik as a kind of ally, he tried to convince a skeptical audience that the NRC was dead wrong. Despite the vocal support from a few fringe environmental groups, his words fell on deaf ears.

Browning responded scornfully during the hearing.

"Even if we accept your analysis, Mr. Kaznik, about the supposedly unaccounted for plutonium, why should we worry even if there *is* a bomb somewhere? With nobody to set it off, what harm can it do? This Committee has already indicated that it will support funding for a reasonable search."

In the end, Kaznik gave up. He didn't quit or apply for a transfer out of the potential bomb radius of Washington, D.C. After the beating he had taken, it would have seemed like sour grapes.

It was a clear summer morning, hardly the kind of muggy day that Gilliam and Liz expected to take with them as their final memory of Washington. With no family or close friends available to give Liz away, she and Gilliam had gone to the handiest justice of the peace and gotten married.

They were scheduled to fly to Montana that afternoon, seven hours on Northwest Airlines to one of the most inaccessible "major" airports in the Lower Forty-Eight. Liz had been immediately accepted by the University of Montana Law School for her final year, despite the tardiness of her application. Gilliam was about to start the law practice he had only speculated about a few months earlier. There would be time for a honeymoon—a week of camping and backpacking in the mountains of the Big Sky.

They stopped en route to the airport at a building off DuPont Circle. It looked like any of the expensive apartment buildings that flanked it up and down the street. On the third floor, in a ward room that looked like a "smoker" in the dormitory of an expensive college, Harry Hammer sat placidly. He'd been waiting for them. They had visited only twice before, far fewer times than the many federal investigators who wanted to know whether Hammer was a dupe, an accomplice, or a prisoner of the Timber Rivers plotters.

Hammer greeted them jovially, pumping their hands,

kissing his daughter and motioning them to seats. He smiled at everything they said, seeming to understand, actively interrupting time and again with his own comments. Only, nothing he said made any sense.

Before they left to catch their plane, Hammer managed to convince his daughter that he wanted some dimes. Gilliam was reminded of the panhandling he'd seen in the mental hospital in Los Angeles. Liz, on the other hand, interpreted the request to mean that her father wanted to call someone, probably on a pay phone. The staff, after all, had said that the senator wasn't sufficiently recovered to have a phone in his room. No telling the kind of bills he might run up. He'd have to use the pay phone in the patients' lounge.

Tears welling in her eyes, Liz gave every dime she and Gilliam had to her father. After a good-bye kiss, she took her husband's hand and followed the orderly out the door.